An American Family

An American Family

A Novel of Today

Henry Kitchell Webster

MINT EDITIONS

An American Family: A Novel of Today was first published in 1918.

This edition published by Mint Editions 2021.

ISBN 9781513283524 | E-ISBN 9781513288543

Published by Mint Editions®

 MINT
EDITIONS

minteditionbooks.com

Publishing Director: Jennifer Newens
Design & Production: Rachel Lopez Metzger
Project Manager: Micaela Clark
Typesetting: Westchester Publishing Services

Contents

BOOK I
THE HOUSE

I

When a clock somewhere in the big strange house struck a deliberate three, Jean Gilbert sat up in bed and craned forward for a better look out of the window at the June night. No signs of dawn yet, though there might be if it weren't for a thin old moon high up in the sky. Anyhow, there would surely be daylight in an hour, and she did not believe she would fall asleep sooner than that. If she did not it would be fair to say, wouldn't it (to herself, of course. She did not mean to confide the adventure to any one else), that she had lain awake all night?

It was sultry still. Chicago, it seemed, had gone to sleep at last. It must be half an hour anyway since the last motor had gone howling by in the Drive. She could hear quite plainly the tired little waves collapsing on the beach beyond the slender strip of parkway.

She pulled her two thick braids forward over her shoulders and dropped back on the pillow again. She hoped she wouldn't go to sleep. There were so many wonderful things to think about; memories—fresh warm memories, all less than a week old which she had not half got through the catalogue of.

She had said the other day in answer to Mrs. Corbett's blunt "How old are you, child?" that she was not quite seventeen. And three breaths later she had added scrupulously and with great dignity, "That is, I am more than sixteen and a half." She was—a matter of days.

It had not been an easy admission to make in the circumstances, and indeed Mrs. Corbett had exclaimed, "Heavens! You're a baby." But nothing happened. The maid went on hooking the miraculous bridesmaid's dress, and Anne Corbett, who was going to be the bride, looking at her with half-shut eyes to get the effect, said:

"Nonsense, mother! She's Muriel's height to a hair and the gown might have been made for her."

It would all have remained wonderful enough, to be sure, even if "more than sixteen and a half" had been adjudged fatally too young for this last ineffable honor they proposed for her; just the sober facts, which were—I'll try to be brief with them—these:

Jean's father was Captain Roger Gilbert of the United States Army. He was poor; had nothing to live on but his pay. And he was young— only forty when Jean had her sixteenth birthday. His wife was even younger; only thirty-seven—twenty-one when Jean was born—a fact which proclaims romance upon its face.

Jean's grandmother, old Mrs. Myron Crawford, strong-willed and able-minded, put by her husband's untimely death in unchecked control of a very large estate, had had her own way in nearly everything; certainly with the first three of her children. The girl, Christine, married an English aristocrat and the elder sons lived up to this event. But the last pair, Frank and Ethel,—they were twins—were brought up less rigorously. Frank was allowed his heart's desire, West Point, and it was thus his sister Ethel and young Roger Gilbert met.

They fell in love, it is almost true to say, at sight. It was one of those tolerably rare cases (fortunately rare, a prudent person might be tempted to say, because they always produce an explosion of some sort and not infrequently, a tragedy) of a genuine, unmistakable affinity. They would have married eventually, no doubt, even if the form of the widow Crawford's opposition had been subtle—Machiavellian—serpentine. As it was, a reckless and quite indiscriminate anger simply flung the pair of children together, and they married rather madly, offhand, and had a baby upon a second lieutenant's salary.

So Jean, as if no such institution as indulgent grand-motherhood existed in the world, grew up as best she could, in one army post after another. She went thrice to the Philippines. She spent a miserable year in a Washington boardinghouse. There was a place called, temporarily, home in the Presidio, in Fort Riley, in Brownsville, in other places—more than she could remember.

Her formal education, of course, was perfectly ramshackle and fortuitous. What she had really been brought up on was her father's code—that of an officer and a gentleman. She could ride straight and speak the truth. She could obey orders with a stiff mouth. And when she was afraid, no one knew it.

Nemesis meanwhile had overtaken old Mrs. Crawford. Her two oldest sons were drowned in a yachting accident, one in the attempt to save the life of the other. With one daughter married abroad, the other estranged from her, and her one remaining son in the army, she would be, to all intents and purposes, childless. So the only thing to be done was for Frank to resign his commission, come home, and take his post as titular head of the family. Disaster had shaken her a good deal and softened her a little, and, as she never had really established the habit of tyrannizing over her youngest son, she found it easier to defer to his judgment; especially as it was nearly always good. An example of it, to her notion, was his marriage with the eldest Corbett girl, Constance. This was distinctly his own doing, but she admitted she couldn't have chosen better herself.

The bond between Frank Crawford and his twin sister, Ethel, had never been broken, and his own marriage strengthened rather than weakened it. Constance, who was five years younger than Ethel, had always known her, of course; the Corbetts and the Crawfords both dated back to old West Side Chicago. To Constance, as to her bosom friends Frederica and Harriet Aldrich, Ethel's romantic marriage had been a wonderful event.

The Gilberts were away in the Philippines when Frank and Constance were married, but when they came back, five years later, Constance broached to her husband a plan which she had kept mellowing in the wood for a long time.

"Jean's a dear," she said, "and beautifully brought up. But, Frank, it can't go on like that! It would be wicked to let it. She's just got to the age where things begin to make a difference. And that isn't going to be her life, really. At least it needn't be unless she wants it to. She ought to have the right kind of friends, and she ought to go to a good school for two years anyway."

Frank agreed to all this, but didn't at first see how it was feasible.

"I've talked to Roger about it; come as close as I dared. But they can't afford it and they won't take money. His face looked like a piece of armor-plate when I hinted at it."

"Well, don't hint," said Constance. "Come straight out with it. Let me go and talk with Ethel. Look here! Let's get them to give her to us. Roger's sure to be sent to the border and she'll go with him. But even they can't think of taking the child down there. We won't go into details at all. We'll just say we want her for three or four years to do as we like with." She understood very well the expression she saw go across her husband's face. "It'll be, I suppose," she admitted, "sort of a shock to Mother Crawford when we tell her what we've done. But, Frank, down in her heart that's what she wants. She's hoping for it—something like that. Only, of course, she can't say so."

Frank turned it over meditatively for a while. "How about you?" he asked at last. "With two kids of your own already and another on the way, haven't you got your hands full?"

But Constance was clear that she hadn't. "I'm really selfish about it," she said. "I want her."

After a while Frank finished the subject with a nod. "All right," he said, "go to it. I shan't be surprised if you put it over."

On Jean the news fell, astonishingly, all at once without even a premonitory murmur. Her father said to her one evening, just after retreat, in the crisp serious manner he used for orders:

"Jean, you're to be made a young lady of. You're to be packed and ready to leave for Chicago a week from today. You're going to live for a while with your Uncle Frank Crawford and his wife. They've got plans for you that we've all agreed are good."

So far as getting results went, he understood the girl even better than her mother did. She squared her shoulders and brought her boot-heels together with a click (she was in riding things). "Yes, sir," she said. An old sergeant couldn't have done it better.

He stood before her as rigid as she was, but she saw the tears springing to his eyes before her own came to blind her. He came up close and took her by the shoulders.

"There are a lot of good reasons we talked about when Constance was here," he said. "You *haven't* had an orthodox bringing up, and I suppose you're entitled to it. Within the next ten years there's a good chance that you'll find yourself rich; opportunities open to you that, if we go on like this, you won't understand nor know what to do with. They say you ought to have a look around first. That sounds like good sense, too.

"But my reason—my real reason for letting you go, I haven't told even your mother. I shan't tell it to any one but you. Ethel's getting homesick after all these years. She wouldn't admit it to me under torture, but I know it's true. She'd like to have the door open to her own people again. She'd like to be reconciled to her mother before the old lady dies. And it's through you, by this plan, that the thing can be done. I'm willing to give you up for three or four years for that. Do you see, chicken? Now go find your mother and tell her you're happy about it. We're neither of us allowed to cry where she can see."

She did cry, of course, when she was by herself—experienced some pretty desolate hours. The parents she was leaving comprised an unusually large part of all her world, and what there was besides was to be left behind with them. An emigrant setting out for a rumored America is hardly upon a less foreseen adventure. She had moments of panic when nothing but the life-long habit of military obedience pulled her through—saved her from begging to be let off. To have begged would seem as disgraceful to her as it would to her father.

But, these bad hours aside, there was a joyous thrill about the prospect that was almost as disconcerting as the panic. It didn't seem loyal to be as happy as it made her feel to think of going to "the right kind of school" where she'd make friends with girls of her own age. She hadn't had a girl friend since she was seven years old. And the notion of pretty frocks—plenty of them, and a big house with real servants in it—acting the way they do in books—"Yes, Miss. Thank you, Miss"— and a motor she would be entitled to ride in was thrilling. Would Uncle Frank let her learn to drive it herself?

What gave the adventure the silky unbelievable texture of a fairy-tale from the moment of her arrival in Chicago, almost, was the wedding of Anne Corbett, her Aunt Constance's younger sister. The romance began, it happened, right at the beginning.

Jean's train, which Frank Crawford had engaged to meet, frustrated him by getting very late and then in the last couple of hours making up half an hour or so, with the result that Jean, emerging through the gate and looking in vain for a familiar face, found herself upon her own resources.

She was not at all alarmed and she adopted almost at once the correct explanation of her uncle's failure to be there. There were various things she could do. She could find out at the Information Bureau how to get to Lake Forest, where the Crawfords lived, and go out there all by herself. Only that might give them a bad hour or two wondering what had become of her. Or, she could telephone her Aunt Constance and put herself under orders. But that seemed a rather helpless, bothersome way to act. Her aunt, no doubt, was busy and would probably, Jean suspected, put herself to superfluous trouble about her.

There remained the third alternative of simply waiting in the station for her uncle to turn up. Only how would he find her in a big place like that? The likeliest place to wait for him, she decided, was under the train bulletin, which he would probably consult as soon as he came in for the purpose of finding out how much longer he'd have to wait.

So she lugged her suit-case over to the big blackboard and took her station there. She was quite comfortable both in body and mind. She had learned from her father the military trick of standing still without getting tired, and she wasn't worried a bit. She would give her uncle half an hour. If he had not come by then, she would telephone to Lake Forest. Meantime there were plenty of amusing things to look at.

She was aware, of course, that other people were looking at her. There were men loitering about the place—men of various sorts, who looked at her a good deal. But she was not afraid of their annoying her. People somehow didn't.

Presently her own interest focussed itself upon a man—a big man, a lot taller than her father she was sure, though he stood a full six feet—who came up to consult the train bulletin. There was a sort of general rightness about him that gave her a little thrill of pleasure the moment he came into her field of vision. To her eye, accustomed to a military precision of gait and carriage, there was something pleasurably flexible about the way he moved.

She got a chance to look at his face while he was studying the board. It was a lean, rather narrow, face, just a little like—not the real Indians she had seen so many of, but the sculptured, idealized Indians—bronze Indians in parks. She liked the look in his face, too, when he saw how late his train was, the train he was waiting for some one to come in on; rueful but half amused, as if, after all, it didn't greatly matter. It couldn't be, she decided, his wife or sweetheart he was waiting for.

Just as he turned away he looked at her, his eye simply picking her up as it traversed the space she occupied, and focussing itself on her for an instant, very keenly.

He set himself a long, leisurely patrol of the concourse from one end to the other, and always as he receded from her, she let her gaze follow him. It seemed to her that if anything happened—anything violent or frightful, there in that railway station, that he would be quite certain to be in the thick of it doing tremendous deeds. She made up an idle little romance about him and cast herself for the heroine.

The romance was broken in upon by the realization that a little group of rowdy youths—harmless enough, no doubt, but an affront alike to the eye and the ear, with their jokes, their nudges, their vacuous laughs, their shoves and bumps and remonstrances—had her for an objective; for an audience anyway. They weren't dangerous, of course, but she hoped they wouldn't come any nearer. If they did, she'd have to pick up her bag and move away. And that act in itself would be a form of communication with them.

And then she caught her breath. Because her big man, coming by just then, checked his patrol, turned at right angles, and walked

HENRY KITCHELL WEBSTER

up beside her; not close beside—a couple of paces, maybe, away. He didn't speak to her nor look at her. So far as she could see, he didn't even look at the boys. But the little group faded aimlessly away. He stayed—not rigid like a sentry, nor elaborately casual either, but clearly on guard. If her father's battery of three-inch field-pieces had come galloping up and parked around her, she couldn't have felt more secure.

If only there were some possible way of thanking him! Only, if he'd wanted to be thanked he could easily have given her the opportunity. Of course he wouldn't. He wasn't the sort that would.

Five minutes later she caught a sight of Frank Crawford hurrying toward the board. Could she tell him about it, she wondered? Get him to tell the stranger how much obliged she was? It seemed dreadfully unsatisfactory just to go off and leave him there without any acknowledgment—not even a bow.

To her surprise, it was not upon her, but upon the tall stranger that her uncle's eye alighted.

"Hello, Hugh!" he sang out. "What are you doing down here?"

"I'm collecting another bridesmaid for Anne," Jean heard him say. His voice, she thought, was—well, somehow, just right, like the rest of him. "Half an hour yet to wait."

"I'm meeting my. . ." Frank began. "Why, hello! How in the world did you get here? They said your train was two hours late."

"It made up a little," Jean explained. "I haven't been waiting long."

Her uncle was most awfully sorry. Was she sure she was all right? Hadn't been frightened or anything?

"Not a bit," said Jean.

"Well, come along," her uncle said. "The car is here. We'll drive straight out." Then, "Oh!—this is my niece, Jean Gilbert."

It was one of those one-sided introductions that Frank was addicted to when he felt in a hurry. But the big man swiftly rectified it.

"I'm Hugh Corbett," he told her, and held out a lean hand. "I'll probably see you again before the wedding, but surely then."

It was a friendly, altogether delightful smile he had, a rather—special smile. There was a humorous recognition in it of the something between them—the almost nothing but not quite—which neither of them had said anything to Frank about.

"He's Constance's brother," Frank explained as they walked away; "one of her four brothers. They're all here for the wedding."

Jean rode out to Lake Forest entranced. The dim outlines of the fairy-tale were already beginning to show through. Jean inquired with great propriety about her grandmother and could not be blamed for an inaudible sigh of relief on learning that the old lady was not at home. She was still at Hot Springs—an annual pilgrimage of hers for fortifying her invincible health against all conceivable attack. She would not come anywhere near Lake Michigan until that mercurial climate had settled to its six months of good behavior. She figured, naturally enough, in Jean's fairy-tale as the wicked old witch.

The queen, that is to say her Aunt Constance, was still to be reckoned with. But the first evening—oh, the first five minutes really, settled all that. Constance's smile, like that of her brother Hugh, had something special about it; a humorous friendliness.

"You won't mind," she asked (this was when Jean was going to bed and her aunt had come in, ostensibly to see that she had everything that she wanted); "you won't mind if I—play dolls with you a little? You see my two are both boys and you can't do it with them. I'd like to dress you up. Will you go shopping with me in the morning?"

Thus it was that Constance changed her rôle to that of the fairy godmother. They were, of course, simple, suitable things that Constance bought the next day. But she did a thorough job; provided for all reasonable contingencies. And Jean, to whom any single new garment had always been an important event, who had never dreamed of being new all over, was in Paradise.

She couldn't have believed that the day had not reached its climax in the purchase of a pink dancing frock, almost low in the neck, and with slippers and stockings that matched. But it had not. The real climax was late that afternoon.

"I want to stop in and see mother a few minutes," Constance had said, "before we go home." And Jean caught her breath again when she saw where the car was turning in.

A high iron fence with a monumental gate in it, a wide insolent lawn that reached from one cross-street to the next, and had its own opinion, evidently, of the ornate, close-built mansions on either side that had to get up to the Lake Shore Drive somehow. In the middle of it a house that. . . Well, Gregory Corbett remains one of the few Chicagoans of the great old days who managed to get himself adequately represented in stone. Whoever the architect was (I'm not sure whether it was Richardson or not) he succeeded in building something that stood unmistakably for the old man. The sand-stone of which he built it was Gregory Corbett's color; the great monolithic lintels had something the look of his level craggy brows. The whole thing was self-contained like him, and heavy, and enormously big, and one had the feeling that it would live to be old like him—as old for a house as he was for a man.

To Jean, of course, the fairy-tale took another jump. Here was the palace, the face of it dark against the declining sun. Anything could happen in a place like this.

She followed, breathless, close behind Constance, aware, but afraid to look, that there were a lot of people about, that there was a victrola going somewhere and, she thought, dancing; that a deferential gentleman in a premature dress-suit was conveying a low-toned message to her aunt.

"All right," Constance said. "Come along," and Jean followed her up a very broad and endlessly long flight of stairs, down a hall and to a door where Constance knocked.

It was opened by a maid, but before either she or Constance could speak a barytone voice boomed out from the depths of the room, "Who is it?"

Constance said who she was, and added, "I've got Jean Gilbert with me."

"Bring her along," the voice commanded. "Where have you been? I've been wanting you for hours."

Her aunt's reply, whatever it may have been, was lost on Jean, because by that time she was in the room, and all she could manage for a moment was a panic-stricken attempt not to stare.

A big—oh, a huge!—iron-gray woman sat in a proportionate armchair. Her hair was formally dressed, as if for a ball. She had on a black satin dressing-gown with enormous red and yellow tulips on it. A table with a tea-tray stood beside her chair. She held a cup in one hand and a slice of bread and butter in the other. Crouching before her was a man with a black leather bag on the floor beside him. Her feet and her thick white calves were bare, and he was working away, with a little chisel-shaped knife at one of her toes.

"Kennedy here," she said, indicating him by pointing with the foot, "although I'm his oldest customer, and getting a daughter married off besides, won't leave that precious office of his till after hours. That's why he's here now. I've no doubt there are better men at his business here in town that would, but in matters of corns I'm conservative."

"Mother," Constance said, turning to Jean, "this is. . ."

"I don't need to be told who she is," Mrs. Corbett broke in. She finished her tea in a gulp, set down her cup and held the disengaged hand out to the girl. "Let's look at you, child. You're your mother again—with a difference. Heavens, how have you had time to get as big as that? It seems no time at all since your mother ran off with that lieutenant of hers. Do you want some tea? If you do, tell Briggs and she'll get it up. Sit down somewhere anyway. I want to talk to your aunt."

Thus released, Jean retreated to a window-seat—about the remotest place in sight; out of range, she hoped, of the confidential conversation which was to follow. She knew now who was the queen of the fairy story. She had never understood what they were like before.

In thinking she had withdrawn out of ear-shot, Jean had reckoned without Mrs. Corbett's voice. It boomed straight along without any soft-pedal at all. There was no use trying not to hear.

"I've got to have you down here, Connie, and that's flat. You'll have to come to the house and stay till it's over. Between my father-in-law and my feet, I'm done. I don't blame my feet. They're overworked. I'm too big to trot around, though I could manage it if it weren't for him. But this wedding has stirred him up. He wouldn't believe for a long time, that 'little Anne' was old enough to be married. Everytime we spoke of it, he pretended not to know what we were talking about.

"Now that he's made up his mind to it, he wants to know what's the matter with the boys—why none of them is married. He roars at me till I can't hear myself think; as if it was my fault. Your father simply takes to flight; gets telegrams and things; and the boys are too wary by half. They dodge around like quick-silver. I'm too big to dodge. When I married Robert, it was grandsons his father wanted. Well, he can't deny I did my best for him. Now it's great-grandsons. And he looks to me for them."

"He's got two," said Constance.

"They don't count," her mother assured her bluntly. "They aren't Corbetts. Oh, unreasonable I'll agree! Well, I may be unreasonable myself when I'm eighty-one. But that doesn't make it any easier for me just now. I've got to have you on the spot. You can take him off my hands, or you can chaperon some of these parties and let me get off my feet; that's just as you like."

What Constance said was lower-keyed, and Jean didn't hear it, but the mother's reply made the nature of it evident enough.

"Oh, Frank's a fuss! What if you are going to have a baby! If I hadn't kept going with mine, I'd never have got anywhere, heaven knows."

There was another inaudible fragment contributed by Constance, then Mrs. Corbett said:

"Jean? Oh, bring her along with you. There's room. She's a nice little thing; knows how to stand up, which is more than most girls do now-a-days. She'll be somebody to play with Carter. Has she got any clothes? Not that it matters."

It was getting to seem like a dream, the way the fairy story moved along. No sooner had the fairy godmother provided the ball dress than the queen invited her to come and stay at the palace. It was—well, scary in a way, to have things happen like that. One thing bothered her a little. Who was Carter whom she was to play with?

Driving out to Lake Forest for dinner (because Mrs. Corbett had failed to induce her daughter to abandon Frank without at least an evening's warning. They were to come straight back after breakfast) she asked Constance about him.

"I tried not to hear," she explained, "but somehow I couldn't help it."

Constance laughed. "No. Mother's not a confidential person. Why, Carter's her baby—my youngest brother. He's twenty; has just finished his junior year at Yale. We're all very proud of him," she went on, "because he made end on the All-American last fall and Bones this spring."

"I suppose," she concluded thoughtfully, "that Carter will never be as old again as he is right now. Mother's funny with him because she doesn't see that at all."

Jean was vague about the All-American, and Bones was an unelucidated mystery to her. But her aunt's intention to warn her not to count upon Carter as a playmate was unmistakable. She might easily have been a little alarmed over the prospect of meeting so formidable a person, had it not been for her encounter in the railway station the day before. The big man who had stood guard over her for fifteen minutes, not knowing in the least who she was, and then, finding out, had made himself, with just one look of his smiling eyes, completely her friend—almost an older friend than her uncle was—that man was this terrifying Carter's big brother. With him at hand she need not be afraid of anybody.

The next real step in the fairy story happened three days before the wedding, right when the whirl of luncheons, matinée parties, tea-dances, dinners and so on, was at its swiftest. It had to be a tragedy for somebody else. That's the way things happen in fairy stories.

Muriel Ware, one of the bridesmaids, developed a stye. Of course, it had not been a sudden event for her. There had been a day when she caught up her hand-mirror and looked at that eyelid with suspicion, and told herself positively that it was nothing; another day when she spent her solitary moments rubbing it frantically with a gold ring, studying it in the glass and deciding it was really going away; another day when people began looking at her and asking what was the matter with her eye, to which she had answered that she had almost had a stye, but that it was getting better. There was a day when she flew despairingly to the doctor and demanded surgery—capital surgery, if necessary—anything—absolutely anything, to stop that thing. The resources of modern surgery, the doctor had said, were equal, one might say, to anything except the instantaneous obliteration of all traces of its work. But for that no substitute had yet been discovered for time. There was nothing to be alarmed about. In a week or ten days she would be looking as well as ever. The wedding was three days off.

By the next day the eye was swollen shut and had to be taken official cognizance of. Muriel couldn't go down the church aisle looking like that—a fact she was the first to proclaim. Of course, it might get miraculously better in two days, but was there any real hope of it? No, there was not. Somebody would have to be found who could wear her dress—take her place.

But who? The matter was delicate. Months ago Anne had divided her friends into two categories: those who were asked to be bridesmaids and those who were not. Anne professed herself at her wit's end and rejected the few suggestions made, with vigor, demanding to be told, meanwhile, if no one could think of anybody.

By the time some one said, with the air of making a surprising discovery, "Why wouldn't Jean do?" the child had been holding her breath, one might say, for hours.

She had been watching that stye with the eye of a lynx, since the day Muriel herself had discovered it. She had reproached herself bitterly for not feeling honestly sorry as she saw it grow, saw inevitable Fate closing down upon its victim. Her heart stopped beating entirely, she was sure, when she heard the suggestion made, and didn't go on until Anne said, meditatively, "I believe she could wear the dress." And then it leaped up with a rush that almost suffocated her. It was as good as decided after that. Not even Mrs. Corbett's blunt inquiry about her age did any harm.

The dress was right almost to the last hook, and with her hair up ("You've awfully nice hair," one of the girls said) she should make as satisfactory a bridesmaid as any bride could ask to have.

Well, you are in possession now, I think, of the facts which formed the background of Jean's dream as she lay awake that warm June night, looking out now and then for the gray streak of dawn and hoping not to fall asleep; at least not until it came. A background, I said, but I am not sure but foreground would be a truer word, because the thing to which they all were nothing but a running obbligato, the melody they merely served to harmonize, was, after all, elusive—shy of coming out in the open and getting itself stated.

If ever you have heard a set of variations by Elgar upon a theme which is never played during the whole composition, you will have a clue to the pleasant maze of Jean's reverie that night. Her theme, never stated but perpetually embroidered upon, was that she had fallen in love with Hugh Corbett.

I know of nothing less calculated, or calculable—nothing more reckless in its disregard of facts and reciprocities—nothing, in a word, more mothlike in its evanescent nocturnal charm, than a young girl's love affair.

It had happened, of course, there in the railway station before she found out who he was. And it might have lasted her for weeks, in the failure of another to take its place, even if she hadn't found out at all; just as a peg upon which to hang her filmy night-spun veils of romance.

But with his transformation by Frank's nod into some one she knew and liked, the thing got a novel touch of reality. Every day, after that, the romance accumulated new facts to build on. He really liked her, made occasions for little talks with her; came to the rescue, sometimes, when she was embarrassed, just as he had done there in the station.

Everybody liked her, as a matter of fact, beginning with old Grandfather Corbett and stopping just before you got to Carter (who might not have been the one exception but for a tactless indication on his mother's part that Jean's age made her a suitable companion for him. After that there was no balm for his outraged dignity except in ignoring her as loftily as possible). She was so breathless with wonder about it all, so serious in her acceptance of the responsibilities which Muriel's stye had thrust upon her, her dignity was so delicious, and her unconscious way of coming to attention, heels together, eyes front, when she had to nerve herself to meet a difficult situation, that they all enjoyed her. They alternately teased and petted her, that is, just as one will a nice kitten.

All but Hugh. He won her ineffable gratitude by being different. It was not that he acted differently toward her; not that he treated her like a young lady. He laughed and joked about her as freely as any of them, only when he did it she was always one of the players of the game—not just the ball they played with. He had no special manner for her at all (she presently discovered that he had none for anybody—not even for his grandfather), and the fact made it curiously easy to talk to him; especially to ask him things—and there were no end of them—that she wanted to know.

He told her who people were and how old they were and what they did—a sort of Who's Who to the Corbett clan, invaluable to her and, as he told it, most amusing. He told her stories about his grandfather, who had started out as a wheelwright more than sixty years ago making farm wagons; how he had gone into partnership with his cousin who made plows and then bought him out, and how a family feud that had lasted half a century had resulted. He told of his father's hobby for pictures, especially Corots. (He had bought more of those, Hugh extravagantly opined, than Corot had ever painted.) He told her some of the stock family anecdotes that were always being referred to.

On her first bewildering day at the "palace" he sorted out his brothers for her and his prospective brother-in-law from the ruck of guests, groomsmen and so on. "The darkest one with the thick black hair—over there; he just came in that door—that's Gregory, after grandfather, of course. He's the successful one. He has come right up through the business, has practically taken father's place in it; but what he's really famous for is football. He played guard, back in the days of mass formations, and he still goes back to New Haven in the fall and coaches for a month—takes his vacation that way. And the sandy one over there, flirting with the girl in blue, is Bob—after father. He's the polo player. He lives out at the ranch in Wyoming a good part of the time; thinks he runs it. He's two years younger than I, and Greg two years older. We all come along after Constance. Then, after a while, comes Anne, and Carter last. You know the man Anne's marrying, don't you? Douglas Duncan? They're New York people, a good lot though they're what's called 'smart.' Anne's supposed to have done very well. Well, that's the lot."

A rather terrifying lot, too, she thought at the time; they were all, except Anne and Carter, so prodigiously big, and all, without exception, so confidently sure of themselves. Only, with Hugh around, she wasn't so very much afraid of them.

He was different, somehow, from them all. She felt this much more deeply than she could formulate it. She had commented, with what seemed incredible boldness, upon his omission to tell her, along with the other biographies, what he himself did—and was famous for.

"Oh," he said, "I'm supposed to be a metallurgist. I'm down at Youngstown, mostly, analyzing the steels and other metals they buy for the plant. It's a very routine sort of work. You don't get famous at it."

After that talk, he figured in her romance as a banished prince, out of favor through no fault of his, rather as the result of his own nobility—opposed either by the ignorance of some one who could not understand it, or by the malice of some one who hated it. But he would come into his own some day.

This was all very silly, she knew. She blushed over those romances in the daytime, if she happened to think of them. There wasn't a trace of self-pity about him. He didn't act the least bit disinherited. And all the family seemed fond of him.

But wasn't there, romance aside, a real difference which the clan itself was aware of? Hadn't Jean heard the phrases "That's just like Hugh! Hugh all over! Oh, of course—Hugh!" from every one of them? And had she ever heard anything that Gregory did characterized as just like him?—or Anne, or Carter, or Robert? That proved something, didn't it? Didn't they feel about him just a little as she had felt almost the first moment she saw him, there in the railway station, the latent possibility of his doing extraordinary things, if the sort of circumstances arose that provoked them—things that Gregory or Bob in any circumstances could be counted upon not to do?

She sighed, sat up once more in bed and looked out at the night. She was afraid she was getting a little sleepy. She would think about something very exciting—the dinner dance they had had at the house tonight, in which festivity she, as a prospective bridesmaid, had had a part like a regular grown-up person, Hugh and one of the groomsmen on either hand at dinner, and all her dances taken afterward.

There was just one flaw in the perfection of that party. She had lost a treasure. On the back of her place-card at dinner, Hugh had written out for her, in his fine clear hand, an amusing toast that he had picked up somewhere on his travels. It was very hard to say straight and she, trying to learn it, had asked him to write it down. It was as a souvenir of him that she had really wanted it, of course. It would be her only memorial, and he was going back to Youngstown the night of the wedding. She might not see him again for years. If only she had left it tucked safely inside her dress where she had surreptitiously deposited it as they were leaving the dining-room! But she had fished it out to gloat over it, and then—shame of shames!—forgotten it. Later, of course, she had become aware of her loss and tried vainly to remember where she had left it. She had had no real opportunity for search. But now, at half past three in the morning, it came to her in a flash, exactly where the thing was; tucked half-way down between two of the cushions of the long davenport in the billiard-room. Why couldn't she have remembered before it was too late?

Because it was too late. The army of servants that went to work long before any one else was up in the morning, never missed a scrap. Her treasure would be cleared up and thrown away before she could recover it.

Unless she went now! Why not? She was sure she could do it without disturbing anybody. There was moonlight enough to keep her from running into things, and she'd go very carefully. And in a great solid house like this a little noise wouldn't travel very far.

Trembling a little with the excitement of the venture—she was certainly wide enough awake now—she put on the silk dressing-gown—one of the most superfluously delightful of Constance's purchases, and the bedroom slippers, opened her door and shut it behind her with infinite care, and stole downstairs.

The adventure was rather more scary than she had anticipated. The great rooms she had to traverse on the way to the billiard-room were ghostly in their silent emptiness. Suppose she did knock something down? Suppose there were some special servant, an indoor night-watchman, awake now, going his rounds, likely to come upon her any minute and ask her what she was doing there? What explanation could she possibly give?

She was so thoroughly self-convicted of being a prowling intruder that when she first heard, unmistakably, the footsteps of some one else moving about in the adjoining room, she thought of no alternative explanation to the one she had just been supposing: namely, that it was some one authoritatively on duty. She shrank back against the wall and began, in a rather panicky way, trying to decide between the relative advisability of a flight back to her room and the standing of her ground.

It was a minute or two later that the word burglar said itself very distinctly in her mind. There had been a momentary sheen of reflected light on one of the door-panels, as if an electric torch had been switched on and, as quickly as possible, off again. Somehow, that didn't seem like a watchman. Nor did the silence in there. People on guard kept moving about. The room he was in was the library. Hadn't she heard Anne say something about a safe in the library?

For a moment she went limp; not so much from fear of a possible burglar as from a realization of her dilemma. What could she do?

She could quite safely, no doubt, go back to bed and leave whoever was in the library to his own devices. Even if he proved, next morning, to have been a burglar who had got away with valuable booty, no one would dream of asking her anything about it. This was the counsel of sheer cowardice, of course, and instantly dismissed with an impatient shake of the head. But suppose she went up-stairs and roused somebody—raised an alarm that proved false? That situation would be completely intolerable. The person in the library might well enough be some member of the family doing something entirely within his rights. What would all those big terrible Corbetts think of her—self-confessed little prowler that she would have to be—for breaking into everybody's much needed sleep, as a result of a scare she had got in her meddling?

No, she could not call anybody until she had first made sure that the person in the library was really a burglar. He was doing something in there again. She heard a distinct creak.

Then a feasible plan occurred to her. The room they had put her in was on the second floor. It was not one of the regular guest-rooms, but a make-shift affair, very incompletely cleared out as to closets, bureau-drawers and so on, to make room for her things. In the bottom drawer of a chest in a closet she had found, during her first day's unpacking, an old-fashioned army revolver; had broken it open, automatically, noted that it was loaded, closed the breech again and put it back without thinking much about it, except that the sight of it had given her a momentary pang of homesickness.

Now, however, the recollection of it afforded the solution for her problem. It would be silly, of course, to walk right in upon a burglar, as she was. But armed with a weapon she was fairly skilful in the use of, she could go into that library and make sure whether the person in there was a burglar or not. If he was, she would go and call somebody. She had no notion of trying to capture him herself. The revolver was merely precautionary.

With the maximum of speed consistent with silence, she flew up to her room, armed herself, and then came down again, not frightened at all, and fortified by the confidence that she was doing the right thing.

There was a bright light burning in the library now, which simplified the situation still further. One glance would tell her whether he was some one who had a right to be there or not. The fact that he had turned on the light made it seem a little more likely to her that he was.

She had supposed that the safe was down at the far end of the room, behind an oak door which looked as if it opened into an ordinary cupboard. And it was there, as she stole up to the doorway, that her gaze went first. The cupboard door stood open, but it was a cupboard door. There was no safe behind it. The same glance told her that a window at that end of the room was open, too.

She took one step into the room. A board creaked and a man, in the near corner of the room, sprang up and faced her.

"Stand perfectly still," she said, and brought the revolver around in front of her.

He was a burglar fast enough, although he did not look like those of her dreams. He was thin and shabby. He wore a derby hat, and his mouth was shaded by a drooping, rather scraggy mustache.

His eyes told her that he did not mean to obey her injunction to stand still and she fired the revolver just as he was getting set for a jump.

"Never point a revolver at a man's head," her father had instructed her at once, "unless you are really willing to kill him. It's much better to fire at his feet. That will convince almost anybody that you mean business, and without fatal results."

Jean had obeyed instructions. "If you start to move again," she said very steadily and distinctly, "I'll shoot at your legs."

But she was not obliged to carry out the threat. The one shot she fired had served the double purpose of convincing the burglar that she meant business and—no wonder, for it made a noise like a cannon—of rousing the house.

Carter was the first one down. He had been lying awake, it seemed (the provocative indifference of one of the bridesmaids was responsible for this), and he undoubtedly broke all previous records for speed from the third story of that house to the first. He hadn't stopped for bathrobe or slippers and, arriving barefooted and in pajamas, ready for any dangerous deed that might be demanded of him, he couldn't be blamed for feeling, after the first astonishment, both scandalized and aggrieved that the little playmate his mother had picked out for him had beaten him to it like that. He made handsome amends afterward, to be sure; complimented her pluck the next day, in terms that would have turned any Yale underclassman into an insufferable monument of pride.

To his first rather inarticulate inquiry, she had said simply that it was a burglar. "I had to fire," she explained, "because he wouldn't stand still." And she continued to hold the gun pointed steadily at the man's legs.

Before he could think of anything to do but stare at the litter of burglarious tools about the safe-door, at the man himself, and at the small hole in the floor at his feet, Hugh came in and embittered his brother still further by doing instantly, and without a word, the right thing. He slipped a supporting arm around the girl, and took the revolver away from her with his other hand without deflecting it from the quarry.

"All right?" he asked her. "You did a good job. Now go out to mother. She's on her way down-stairs." Then to Carter, "Go and tell everybody it's all right. Nothing's happened. And tell Greg and Bob to come down here. Keep the rest away if you can."

But these instructions came too late. There were between thirty and forty people in that house and while not many of them had actually heard the shot fired, they were all roused within a minute or two by the collateral noises—slamming of doors, scurry of feet, questions and answers in suppressed but penetrating voices—to an awareness that something in need of investigation had happened. And they came trooping down to investigate.

Jean, beginning to tell her story to Mrs. Corbett (she had on again that astounding dressing-gown of red and yellow tulips) could not complete her recital at all. She was always having to go back to the beginning to answer the feverish question of some new arrival.

It was all chaos for a while, and rendered the more distracting by an insistent ringing of bells, which was found, on investigation, to be the night-watchman in the yard trying vainly at one door after another to get in.

But presently, out of the babble, the crowding up for a look, the panic-stricken disappearance of persons who realized some fundamental lack in their attire, there emerged a sort of common sense of a *contretemps*. It came over Jean when she heard Anne wail:

"Oh, why did they have to catch him? It makes just one more disgusting chance for the newspapers."

With the crystallization of this idea—that here was a situation for tact, reticence, polite ignorance, if necessary the stout assertion that nothing had happened at all—there came a swift dispersal of guests and a peremptory dismissal of servants to their own quarters.

Jean, feeling by now terribly guilty, lingered a while to learn whether her testimony was going to be wanted. But, finding it was not, she presently stole away after the others.

Only, it was characteristic of her that she managed to slip into the billiard-room first and recover her treasured placecard from between the cushions of the settee.

II

Jean, with a child's clairvoyance, had made a discovery about the Corbetts that they were hardly aware of themselves; namely, that Hugh was the different one. Any one intimate with the clan and indiscreet enough to gossip about them, would tell you at once that the black sheep among Robert Corbett's children, was Robert, Junior. He was the one who had got into boyish scrapes; been sent to military school; had needed all the family influence to pull him out of a really bad mess his senior year in college, and, at twenty-five, the year before Anne's wedding, had been put in nominal charge of his father's ranch as, upon the whole, the safest place for him.

But down inside, Robert, Junior, was as orthodox as anybody. In a sense his misdemeanors were accidental. His notion of what desirable conduct was, in any set of circumstances, would have agreed perfectly with Gregory's.

The real black sheep of the family, the genuinely odd one, was Hugh. He saw things, somehow, at a different slant; began at ten years old questioning things the others found unquestionable. The thing that saved him from being a rebel was his sense of humor. His college career is a good illustration of this.

Gregory, two and a half years older, and a senior when Hugh entered as a freshman, was one of the college demigods—already a myth. This was not only because he was "the greatest guard who had ever worn the blue," but because, in all other matters of conduct, he conformed perfectly to the standardized ideal. He did all the things a chap was expected to do, and did them as well as it was permissible to do them. He was solemn when solemnity was appropriate; flippant about the things one was supposed to treat light-heartedly. And all quite honestly and without affectation. Even the extravagant homage and awe which he inspired in underclassmen he took with the precise degree of serious good-humor which the exactness of college etiquette required.

Hugh, coming along behind him, with the same magnificent physique, the coordinations, the same breeding and tradition that ought to have made him the unquestioned heir to his brother's mantle, found it difficult to swim with the current. The thing his brother called "loyalty to Yale"—that cardinal virtue which must be the corner-stone of his edifice, the master passion of his life, he simply could not feel.

When he saw a middle-aged alumnus, red-faced, wet-eyed, voiceless with cheering, at the end of a football game, he experienced the profane impulse to ask him why he felt like that, and if he really did.

In his sophomore year, there was a nice old gentleman who was brought in to address the team just before they went out into the field for one of their big games (these harangues were a specialty of his, it seemed) and the things he said gave Hugh the uneasy, abashed feeling one has over any solemn absurdity. He didn't quite know where to look. Addressed to soldiers on the point of giving their lives to protect their homes against an invading army, it might have been admissible. But he was talking to boys about to play a game. Yet to the others, Hugh could see, the occasion was a sacrament.

Hugh made the team three of his four years and, upon the whole, an athletic record which, had he not been Gregory's younger brother, would have been highly creditable. But, as Gregory's brother, he was a disappointment.

And the same thing was true of other things than athletics. With the score of byways attracting him, he found the middle of the road—the constant doing of the things so relentlessly marked out for him to do, the exclusive association with the sort of men, and the exclusive occupation with the sort of interests, that tradition indicated for him—a rather arid and unprofitable thing.

Sometimes he did take to a byway. Music was one of them. Not the mandolin and glee-club sort of music, but the real thing. He elected two courses under Horatio Parker and worked away at them to the scandal of his right-minded friends. And, toward the end, when he uncovered a real passion for metallurgy, he pursued it, to the neglect of serious athletic and social duties. But he never came out in flat rebellion against the code, and that he did not do so, was due, as I have said, to his possession of a sense of humor—to his ability (it has wrecked many a good man) to make an invisible smile serve him as the substitute for a protest.

In the main he did the conventional thing when the conventional thing was there to do. It was the unprecedented situations that he met in unprecedented ways. Which takes us back to the burglar.

When the first confusion had subsided and guests and servants had gone back to bed, the family settled down, in the billiard-room, to wrestle with the situation. They were not all there. Hugh was still guarding the burglar over in the library across the hall. Constance had made only a momentary appearance and then gone back to bed. Grandfather—luckily, they all agreed—had evidently slept right through the whole row. Because, if he had come down, as he would surely have done had he known that anything was going on, he would have settled what was to be done in one breath; only not necessarily to any one's satisfaction but his own, and certainly not to every one's.

Will you stop just a moment for a look at them at the end of a half-hour's dispute?

Robert Corbett, Senior, stands before the empty fireplace, his elbow on the mantel shelf. He would pass for a big man almost anywhere save at his own hearth; here, with his family around him, his bare six feet of height conveys almost the contrary impression. He looks now, as always, exactly as a man of his age, social position and financial importance, ought to look. He wears a long dressing-gown of a severely neutral brown-gray. He has on socks as well as slippers; and if he did not stop to brush his thick, close-trimmed gray hair before he came down-stairs, then it is because his slumbers had not disarranged it. He wears eye-glasses and mustache. Conventionally he is handsomer than any of his boys, excepting, perhaps, Carter. In a word, his appearance as definitely soothes the eye as his wife's outrages it.

You have already seen her, as Jean did on an earlier occasion, and she looks now much as she did then. She sits very square at one end of the big settee. She is smoking one of Robert, Junior's, cigarettes and grimacing over it because it is not the kind she likes. Robert's cigarettes, it may be noted, have his own monogram on them and cost him thirty dollars a thousand. His mother's are the sort you get twenty of for a dime and the red label on the package has the picture of a ball-player on it.

Gregory is at the other end of the settee in an attitude that duplicates his mother's—arms folded, legs crossed, shoulders back and head bent slightly forward. His jaws are clamped hard on the short stem of a pipe, his lips parted just enough to permit a thin ribbon of smoke to float out and up into his nostrils again whenever he breathes in.

Robert, in giddily striped blue and orange pajamas, half sits upon the rail of the billiard table, one shin in the embrace of both arms, his other foot on the floor, absently watching Carter, who incessantly spins a cue-ball, with varying amounts of English and at different angles, about the cushions.

Anne, looking almost petite from the scale established by the others, outraged, determined, upon the brink of tears, rather indecent in her disregarded dressing-gown, and extravagantly pretty, has flung herself with abandon, into a big armchair. In her, the contest between the sandy sanguine color of the Corbetts and her mother's black and white, has effected the highly felicitous compromise of auburn hair and a milk-white skin. It's a pity that she can't be painted exactly as she sits, though such a portrait would not be one that her decorous husband-to-be would care to hang upon his ancestral walls.

"Well," she said with a self-contradictory emphasis, "I don't care *what* you do." She sprang to her feet and with a flash of tragic dignity, drew her forgotten gown around her and turned upon her father. "Only it really seems, when you think of the perfectly horrid provincial way the papers are acting about my wedding—and it really is mine, I suppose—the silly impertinent things they've said about Douglas and his friends and the vulgar things they've made up about the presents and everything, it really does seem that we might draw the line at a burglar. It's bad enough what the Duncans will think already. But if this comes out, they'll think they're in a mining town. I don't care what you do with him," she summarized with a nod in the direction of the library, "only I won't have anything done that the reporters will find out about."

It was evident that her father was inclined to agree with her. The notion of what the head-lines across the vari-colored pages of the afternoon papers would be like, if the story got out, was as intolerable to his contemplation as it was to hers.

He started to speak but was interrupted by a sepulchral whisper of his wife's. "Wall him up in the cellar. There you are!" And she grinned through a copious exhalation of smoke.

"There's no use trying to do the thing half-way," Robert, Junior, said, ignoring, as the rest of them did, his mother's medieval suggestion. "Invite him to the front door and kick him down the steps. Give his bag of tools to Carter here, for a souvenir, and forget about him. I'm for that, on the whole."

Carter brightened up at that, and stopped playing with his billiard ball long enough to cast his affirmative vote with a nod. Anne, scenting victory, went over appealingly to her father and slid her arm around him.

"You're for it, too, aren't you, dad?" she asked.

"I can't see," he said (this negative way of putting it was characteristic of him), "that we're under any obligation to subject ourselves to any more publicity. It *is* odious; Anne's right about that. And, as Robert says, half-way measures will only make it worse. I don't know but his suggestion is the best we have had."

It was a clear majority for Anne, if one counted heads. But the Corbett family was not a democracy. The two who had not yet spoken, could out-vote the other four.

Gregory said, "We're not criminals. And what you're talking about doing's a crime. The man's an expert housebreaker. We don't know that he hasn't robbed other houses tonight, or that he wouldn't go from here, if we turned him loose, and do another job down the street, before breakfast. And, if he did, it would be our crime almost as much as his. I'm sorry he didn't get away from Jean, even if it had meant his cleaning out the safe. But now that we've got him. . ."

In despair, Anne attempted casuistry. "Why, he isn't a burglar at all," she said. "He didn't *get* anything, did he? I don't believe we've any *right* to keep him."

Gregory grinned and went on. "But, having got him, there's nothing for it but to see it through."

Mrs. Corbett yawned, stretched, and began to get ready to get up. "Oh, it's all a tempest in a teapot," she said. "The papers have always gone on about us and they always will. And if you don't like it, you'd better learn to, as your grandfather says he used to be told about eating with a fork. I do, for a fact. They're amusing little beggars, reporters—as long as you don't read what they say. Anyhow, Gregory's right, unless you want to do as I said—wall him up in one of the chimneys."

Her grim good-humor gave way at sight of her daughter's gesture of despair. "Come, Anne, don't be a little fool. Your Duncans won't die of it."

The next moment, looking not at her daughter, but to the doorway beyond her, she boomed out, "What the devil. . .!" And, as they all followed her gaze, Hugh walked into the room and dropped down on the settee between her and Gregory.

They all, in a variety of phrases, demanded to be told what had become of the burglar.

"Asleep," said Hugh.

"Well," Robert, Junior, observed, tentatively straightening out his bent leg, "that settles the argument. He'll have gone by now. Did he really put it over on you? Or did you wink the other eye?"

"Not a bit of either," said Hugh shortly. "He's really asleep. If you'll keep still a minute, you can hear him snore."

"How did you do it?" Carter wanted to know after an instant of confirmatory silence. "Hit him?"

"The effect of food, I guess," said Hugh. "He was all in."

"Food?" his mother echoed. "What did you feed him for?"

"Why, I felt hungry myself," Hugh explained, "so I flagged Price going by and told him to bring up some sandwiches and beer. I saw the poor devil looking at them like a wolf, so naturally I asked him if he was hungry. He was, all right. He ate all the sandwiches except the one I'd begun on, and I sent Price after more beer. We chinned a while and he went off to sleep."

"He told you the story of his life, I suppose," Gregory put in. "All about how it wasn't his fault and all he needed was a chance—the regular hard-luck tale."

Hugh nodded. "Yes, he told me. Naturally, since I'd asked him. One of the points of the hard-luck tale is that he worked for us—tool-maker; quit about a year ago because his wages were garnisheed."

There was another silence at that. Anne, with a gleam of hope, turned again to her father.

"Why, really," he said, "I'm not sure that these circumstances don't put a new face upon the matter. If the man was desperate—starving— an old employee—and a first offense. . ."

"Oh, come, father," Gregory expostulated. "There's his kit. The fact that he was working on the safe. . ."

"Yes," said Bob, going over to the enemy, "they make hash of that theory."

"He's an expert burglar," Hugh testified. "He takes a sort of pride in it. Says he learned the trade under one of the most expert men in the country—a chap who's doing fourteen years in Auburn now for a bank job." He paused a moment. Then, "Do you care for the rest of the story?" he asked.

The inflection of his voice was casual enough, and on the question he lounged to his feet and reached for one of Robert's cigarettes. But his mother, looking up sharply at him, noticed that he did not light it nor sit down again beside her. He began telling the story stiffly, as if by rote.

"He was sent to the house of correction when he was sixteen. Rightly enough, he admits. He'd been running with a gang who were breaking into freight cars. When he came out, he hadn't any idea but to be a regular criminal. Through one of the friends he had made there, he got acquainted with this expert safe-cracker; worked with him for three or four years. And then they both got caught. He drew a fairly light sentence because he looked like a kid.

"He'd already made up his mind to quit—was doing his last job, he says, when they caught him—on account of a girl he'd fallen in love with. She stuck, and when he came out, she married him. He says he's run straight ever since, till tonight. They've got three children. Got on well—happily anyhow—for several years. And then his wife got sick; the doctors bled them dry, and at last she went to the hospital; was there six months. Had to have a couple of operations. He got an infected hand and couldn't work. Things began happening to the children. He had to go to the loan sharks. . . That finished him, of course.

"It was the stuff in the papers about this wedding that finally got him. And he figured there was a chance for a really big haul with all the jewelry there must be, so he had a shot at it. That's the story."

The timbre in his voice which had caught his mother's ear at the beginning of the recital, had its effect on them all before he finished. Half-way through, Carter had stopped spinning his billiard ball, and at the end he won an instant of clear silence. Anne came over beside him, honestly a little moved by the story, though at the same time, of course, glad to be. She picked up his hand and laid her cheek against it.

"Really, that's shocking!" his father said.

"Oh, it's a good story," Gregory admitted, "if it's true."

"A bit too good to be true, I'd say," Bob put in.

Hugh took his hand away from his sister and straightened a little. "It will be easy to find out if it's true," he said shortly.

"It makes mighty little odds whether it's true or not, according to my way of thinking," his mother said. "This sentimental nonsense makes me sick." One might have hazarded the guess that the purpose of her words was deliberately provocative. "I've a good strong stomach, but it turns over when I hear people whimpering that they'd have been good if they'd had a chance. Nobody who was any good ever turned house-breaker. If that man in there had the gumption to say, 'All right. I'll take my medicine. I'm responsible and nobody else is,' I'd feel like going in and shaking hands with him."

"If he said that, he'd be a liar," said Hugh. "We're responsible if you want it straight."

That drew an exclamation of protest from everybody, except his mother, to whom it was addressed. She leaned back again, crossed her legs the other way, and grinned.

"Of course we are," he went on. "If there was a spark of decent humanity about our place out there, it wouldn't have happened."

"Well, that turns *my* stomach," said Gregory. He got up and marched over to the station at the fireplace his father had abandoned. "I'm an inhuman monster, am I, because a tool-maker's wife gets something the matter with her and has to go to the hospital?"

"I didn't say *you*. I said *we*," Hugh retorted, "meaning the whole organization of the plant. Down at Panama, which is the only place where a big industrial job has ever been done right, they'd have taken his wife to the hospital as soon as she got sick, and the operations and the nursing wouldn't have cost him a cent. But, of course, what I meant was, that in the whole situation, we'd have stepped in somewhere. If we had sick and accident insurance, and a medical inspection at the plant itself, we'd have caught his infected hand. And if we had some sort of an emergency loan fund, we'd have saved him from the sharks. We wouldn't let a valuable piece of machinery out there start a bolt or two and go on and thrash itself to junk before we did anything. That's what we let him do."

"Does anybody know what time it is?" Robert, Junior, wanted to know. He lounged over to the windows and ran up the blinds. It was full day out-of-doors. "If we could get the practical details arranged first," he continued, through a yawn, "then anybody that liked could stay and hear Hugh discuss sociology."

"There's nothing to discuss," said Hugh. "And the practical details are arranged. I fixed it all up with him before he went to sleep. As soon as it gets late enough—seven o'clock or so—I'm going out with him and check up on his story; talk to his wife; talk to the parish priest out there; go over to the plant and see the superintendent. If his story's true, I promised him we'd see him through. He dropped off like a tired kid, when I told him that."

"Just what do you mean by seeing him through?" Gregory wanted to know.

Hugh admitted that he hadn't worked out all the details. He supposed he'd have to go round to police headquarters to find out if he was wanted for anything else, and then to some judge and get him paroled. "Of course, to one of us," he concluded.

Anne's wail, "Then it *will* get into the papers after all," was the prelude to a confusion that there is no use attempting to chronicle. Hugh's plan of action, combining, as it did, all the objections to all the plans that had hitherto been suggested, united the two camps and they all tried to attack him at once.

But it would have taken a more genuine unanimity than they had, to effect anything with Hugh in his present mood. He had taken, as he did sometimes, the bit in his teeth and they came, one after another, to realize this.

"I'll try not to mess up Anne's wedding," he said at last, "at least to the extent of making it illegal. But for the rest of it, I don't give a damn. I've told that chap in there what I'd do, and I'm going to do it. So I don't see that there's anything more to be said. I'll take the whole thing up with grandfather, of course, later in the day."

One by one the others gave him up and drifted back to bed, leaving Hugh to keep a guard—which he felt pretty sure was superfluous—over the prisoner. The last one to go was his father, who plainly had lingered for a word alone with him.

"I must admit," Robert, Senior, said, "that your criticism of our organization there at the plant is, in the main, just. It's a thing I've felt and wanted to see corrected for many years. But I've never been able to induce your grandfather even to consider it seriously. Some day, of course, it will not be so impossible. I'm—I'm really very glad to know that you feel as you do about it." And then, "Get back for Anne's rehearsal at the church, if you can, my boy. And if it's possible to avoid the reporters. . ."

III

Anne Corbett's wedding went off very well. The brilliant cluster of social events, of which it was the nucleus, made their meteoric transit unsullied by any lurid réclame concerning the burglar. There was not a word of that night's adventure in any newspaper; there was hardly any gossip. The thing turned out to have been, as Mrs. Corbett said, a tempest in a teapot.

Little Jean Gilbert was, of course, wholly forgiven. They even made a bit of a heroine of her, and would have gone further with this had not her secret made her reticent about the whole affair. She was asked, to be sure, what she had been doing at the library door at three o'clock in the morning, but her great dignity and her uncontrollable bright blush, in answering that she had been looking for something of hers that she had lost, let her off further inquisition.

She made a highly satisfactory bridesmaid and was carried off, immediately afterward, a little slack and dreamy with happiness and fatigue, by her Aunt Constance to Lake Forest, where she spent the summer learning golf and French, driving the run-about, playing with Constance's babies, getting ready for school in the autumn; doing, in a word, all the things a girl of sixteen and a half can profitably be occupied with. In the process of doing these things she achieved the conquest of old Mrs. Crawford, her grandmother. And she dreamed delightfully, when she did not fall too soundly asleep too soon, about Hugh Corbett.

What she did not dream—what the wildest cast of her net of romance never brought up—was that that nocturnal adventure of hers, her search for the place-card with some of his handwriting on it and the burglar she caught as a result, made a critical change in Hugh's life; constituted a new point of departure for him.

This is primarily Hugh Corbett's story. The capture of the burglar is not the beginning of it, of course. A man's story has no beginning, nor, for that matter, any end either. But looking along the thread for a point where I could pick up this chronicle, that seemed a good place to choose.

For him this teapot tempest turned out to have important results—results totally incommensurate with its own insignificance.

There were as many anomalies in the Corbett domestic establishment as there are in the British Constitution. And the chief of them was

Hannah. Forty years ago, or such a matter, she had gone to work as kitchen-maid for old Gregory and his wife. It would be impossible to say what she was now. Housekeeper she might be called, perhaps, but for certain perfectly incongruous duties to which she still exercised a prescriptive right. She always waited on the table, for instance, when old Gregory came down to breakfast; this was at half past seven in the winter and a quarter past in the summer. Usually his eldest grandson and namesake came down about the same time and breakfasted with him, and sometimes before they had finished, Mrs. Robert, in her red-and-yellow tulips, or an equivalent garment, appeared. But whenever old Gregory left the table, Hannah followed him into the hall, saw that he was suitably garbed for the weather, and abandoned the dining-room to more appropriate attendants. She had more authority over him than any one else. There were some matters in which he obeyed her implicitly. And she always addressed him on terms of entire equality. Had she and Mrs. Robert, her nominal mistress, ever come into collision, they would have tested the longstanding argument between the irresistible force and the impenetrable body. But there had grown up between them a volume of precedents comparable to the Common Law, which warded off this catastrophe.

It was at breakfast, the morning after the burglary, that the old gentleman learned of it from Hannah. He had something on his mind to talk to Gregory about and at the end of ten minutes, his grandson not having appeared, he expressed himself vigorously about the deficiencies of the younger generation in general and his grandsons in particular. When he was young Gregory's age he had done by this hour in the morning what would pass—in these degenerate times—for a day's work. And if he at eighty-one could sit down to breakfast at a quarter past seven he'd like to be told why his grandson couldn't.

Hannah told him. If Gregory went to bed at half past nine, no matter what was going on in the house—no matter if he had a granddaughter getting married—he'd no doubt come down to breakfast as promptly as anybody.

The old gentleman had forgotten all about Anne's wedding for the moment. It had a way of slipping out of his mind. And to cover the slip, which he wouldn't have acknowledged under any compulsion, he grunted skeptically.

Hannah went on. "And if he slept right through after he'd gone to bed, no matter how many burglars broke into the house. . ."

"Burglars!" the old man shouted.

Hannah, who knew quite well that it was by a mere oversight she had not been instructed not to tell the old gentleman about the burglar, confided to him with gusto some of the more melodramatic features of the affair.

The result was that when young Gregory came down, not more than twenty minutes late after all, he stepped into a hornet's nest.

The old gentleman's fury was not quite real. He enjoyed it, indulged it—played it up, just as a young girl will indulge and get a transitory satisfaction from a burst of tears. The fact was that, though it sounds a ridiculous adjective to apply to him, old Grandfather Corbett was growing frivolous. The enormous energy that had driven him for seventy of his years was pretty well spent. All it gave forth now was an occasional flare in place of the unremitting incandescent glow. But his canny Scotch shrewdness was unimpaired, and in default of great objects which asked for a steady driving power he no longer possessed, this shrewdness concerned itself largely with trifles. He was spoilt, of course, by every one—but Hannah. Any old, rich, successful person is bound to be. And in addition to those three qualities, Grandfather Corbett had charm; though there again is an adjective one would not at first think of applying to him. He had never during his active life consciously enjoyed the exercise of power for its own sake. But now that his responsibilities were shifted to other backs, he reveled in it; indulged in caprices like—once more—a popular débutante.

His last portrait, painted by Burton in nineteen ten—just a year before Anne's wedding, that was—shows this very plainly. It is a three-quarters length, seated portrait, and it makes the most, of course, of the huge mass of the body, the thick round shoulders, the great bald dome of a head, and the jutting brows. But the eyes are simply those of a bad little boy and there is a quirk of pure mischief in the corner of the mouth.

Hannah, as I have said, never spoiled him. And when she rebuked him, as she had done this morning, he nearly always passed it on to somebody else. The disposal of the burglar without consulting him gave him more of an excuse than he needed for jumping into Gregory.

A burglar was his own affair. It was upon his personal property that the assault had been made, and it had been a piece of damned presumption to let him sleep through.

Gregory was pretty sleepy, of course; not at all in the mood for a tussle with the old gentleman. So he passed the responsibility along.

"I hadn't anything to do with it," he said. "Hugh caught him. Or rather, young Jean did, and Hugh took him over. And after the line he took when he came in and told us about it, there was nothing to do—for me anyway. Father might have interfered, I suppose, but he didn't."

When the old gentleman wanted to know what the line was that Hugh had taken, Gregory turned uncommunicative—or tried to. "I'd rather Hugh told you himself. He said he was going to."

But the old man wouldn't let him off. "You disagreed with Hugh then," he said. "Tell me what line *you* took."

Gregory, handicapped as he was by the habit of respect and obedience, was no match at all for his grandfather's skill as a cross-examiner, and before they had finished breakfast, the old gentleman was in possession of all the essential facts, including Hugh's attribution of the moral responsibility for the burglar's lapse to their own "inhuman" organization at the plant. Young Gregory even quoted, confessing that it had troubled him a little, Hugh's statement that they wouldn't allow a machine, just because it had started a bolt or two, to thrash itself to junk without interfering.

The old man grunted at this. "But if it *is* junk," he said, "we send it to the junk-pile whether it's started by a bolt or not. We haven't a human junk-pile. Good thing if we had."

Dwellers in an earthquake country require for their reassurance a succession of small shocks. If more than the normal period goes by without one, they begin to wonder. And as the period protracts itself, this uneasiness approaches dread. And with good reason; because the eventual shock is likely to be disastrous.

The Corbett family had much the same attitude toward the old man. Nobody was very much afraid of him except when he was quiet. So the fact that his grandfather fell silent after that last remark of his about the human junk-pile and allowed Hannah to fuss over him without protest as he made his preparations to leave for the office, worried Gregory a good deal.

The Corbett works were out at Riverdale—a suburb ten or a dozen miles west of the city, of which more hereafter. Before the days of the automobile, one got out there by train. There was a period of a quarter of a century, I suppose, during which, on every week-day, with very rare exceptions, old Gregory Corbett might have been seen driving a team of long-tailed trotters to a side-bar buggy down to the Western Depot in time for the seven-twenty-eight train. He was never so regular about coming back, since a day's work never ended for him until it was done. But black Jim used to drive the team down again to meet the six-fifteen.

Of course, he kept no such hours now. But it was still his habit, except in the worst of weather, to drive out with his eldest grandson in the car. His enormous personal mail still went out there (ninety-five percent. of it, of course, was requests for money for charitable purposes, or other) and this, with the aid of a case-hardened spinster secretary, he disposed of. Then he strolled about the plant for a while and was always made happy if he could find some minute thing to make a perfectly terrific row about. The sight of any litter always infuriated him, and he would often pick it up himself and exhibit it, damningly, to some one he could hold responsible for its being there. Humble employees of old standing sometimes accosted him on these rounds with complaints of injustice—a distinctly sporting proposition this, because though he always exploded, it was impossible to forecast whether his victim would be the appellant or the defendant. In a word, that morning round of his was his own version of Haroun Al Raschid. He went back home at noon for the meal he still called dinner—it was dinner, too—and slept for an hour afterward. Then, four days in six, he went out to the plant again and waited for Gregory to come home with him.

On this morning, after the conversation about Hugh's burglar, they drove all the way out to the plant in an almost unbroken silence. Even the ticklish moment caused by another car's cutting across in front of them, failed to evoke the habitual accusation of reckless driving. In the main office, just after their arrival, they encountered a man in the organization whom old Gregory did not like. But his grandson noted that he spoke to him, though absently, with an effort almost at politeness. Really, it was ominous.

Gregory had to come back at eleven o'clock for the church rehearsal of Anne's wedding, and by that time the matter had grown so much more serious that he called Hugh—rid of his burglar, for the time being—aside to talk to him about it.

"I've got you in most horribly wrong with grandfather," he said. "It wouldn't have happened, of course, if I hadn't been grouchy and half asleep. As it was, I spilled the beans." He went on and gave Hugh an account of the conversation at the breakfast table. "It has a rotten look of tale-bearing, I know, and, of course, that's what it comes to. But I didn't mean it that way."

Hugh made light of it, of course. The notion of suspecting Greg of

HENRY KITCHELL WEBSTER

doing an unsportsmanlike thing was positively grotesque. But Gregory hadn't finished his story.

"You're in for it," he insisted. "Just before I came back Bailey told me, confidentially, that grandfather sent for him about ten o'clock and asked him how long it would take him to find somebody to replace you at the Youngstown laboratory; told him to look around for somebody."

Hugh gave his brother an incredulous stare at that; then his face darkened. "All right," he said shortly. "If that's the way he feels about it, it's time he did get somebody else."

"Oh, don't you go off at half-cock just because I did," Gregory urged. "It's all my fault. You can see how he feels. That plant's his. He made it, and a crack like the one you made about it last night got him, of course. Just the way it got me, only more so. But he won't really do anything. After all, father's president of the company and he wouldn't consent to that any more than I would. Only—you spoke of taking it up with him yourself, this afternoon. Grandfather, I mean. Well, don't, if you want my advice. Give him a chance to cool out. Yourself, too, for that matter. Of course, I'm the original idiot, but that's done and can't be helped."

"Oh, I think I'll go to him," Hugh said. "You told him I meant to, didn't you? I'll try not to make him a speech. But don't you worry. It's no fault of yours, whatever happens."

Hugh had got to the point where his sense of humor, his ironic invisible smile, would not serve; to the point where rebellion was the only thing that would. He had reached it cumulatively, of course. There was more behind it than the story of the beaten, hopeless, desperate man he had found in the library last night riveted in his tracks by plucky little Jean's revolver. Three years' life in a steel-mill town was behind it. And behind that, in turn, was the year of travel around the world, the five years' comfortable residence, post and undergraduate, at the University, the expensive school—the best preparatory education that money could buy—and the big house on the Lake Shore Drive.

Behind that, again, and not without their influence for all his personal memory did not reach back to them, were the pioneer hardships of old Grandfather Gregory, who had begun at twenty building wagons for the 'forty-niners to cross the plains in. All that background of vivid contrast lay behind and reflected a lurid light on the lives of those dazed toilers who flocked back and forth twice a day, at the end and the beginning of their twelve-hour shifts, in the street his laboratory windows looked out upon.

The sight of them going by hardly ever failed to give him a momentary feeling of dull discomfort and caused him some hours of deep depression. They worked no harder, he knew, and no longer, than his grandfather must have done in those early days. But what a difference there was in the spiritual significance to themselves of that labor! He wondered that they were so tame—submissive to a lot like that. Their patient acquiescence hurt him. All signs of a broken spirit hurt him. The sight of an old horse meekly dragging a heavy load, was bad enough. But here were men—thousands of them—dragging theirs, with no better a hope.

These were hardly so much ideas of his as they were sensations. He made no attempt to think out a remedy. There was, he supposed, no remedy. Certainly the panaceas—socialism, for instance—were plain impostures. He had gone to a socialist meeting, once, one night in New Haven (an extraordinarily catholic-minded thing for one of his set to do), and one hour of it had been enough for him. Either the speaker was a crafty knave or his simple credulity had been shockingly imposed upon by others who were. He would have had his audience believe that men like Hugh's grandfather were scheming parasites, whose only labor consisted in conspiring subtly, bribing newspapers, corrupting judges, bringing down remote retributions on those few daring souls who opposed their relentless will; which was, the continued and completed— if it were not complete already—enslavement of the working class. Hugh grunted impatiently and got up and walked out. That was all there was to that!

Then there were the unions. His grandfather had always opposed them implacably. His policy had always been to keep a sharp lookout for men of exceptional character and ability among his employees and promote them as fast as he could; and the proportion among the foremen, superintendents and executive officers in his organization, of men who had come up from the bottom, was an eloquent testimonial to the success with which he accomplished it. Certainly *his* men didn't need unions to insure their being fairly treated. Still Hugh was inclined to think unions all right—when they had decent leaders, as they often had not—and in some cases, unhappily, necessary. But he found it hard to believe that "decently" behaved unions would go far to remedy the case of those thousands who streamed by his windows. Very likely there was nothing that would. But it hurt just the same.

It is very easy to go wrong in judging a man by a failure to realize that his thinking and his imagination work, in different fields, on very different levels; that a brilliant mathematician, for example, may talk and think about politics as crudely and dishonestly as if he had no mind at all. Hugh's mind, with its passion for precise data and clean distinctions worked badly in a field where a looser method was called for. The painful throb and blur of the great human problem outside his windows was beyond him. He could not get it into sharp focus. So, when he could, he looked away from it.

What he needed, of course, to break down this inhibition was a concrete case—something that he could look at, not down from his high windows into the street, but squarely, eye to eye. And the meager shivering man he found in the library that night, provided it. The way he'd looked at those sandwiches was the starting point. The man, in sheer exhaustion, had told his story almost as simply as Hugh had retailed it in the billiard-room afterward, without generalities or appeals—nothing about the rich and the poor. Just his facts.

His grandfather hadn't known those facts, of course; nor his father, nor Greg. His grandfather, he knew, would have intervened instantly, if the story of that wife had come to his ear, or the sight of that wounded hand to his eye. Only, among the thousands of employees who came and went, were taken on and laid off, the chance of that intervention had grown too remote. It was horrible to think how remote it was.

The remedies were surely simple enough. They came crowding into his mind before the story was half told. There ought to be men—some sort of humanity inspectors—in the organization, whose business it was to look out for things like that. Wasn't it actually done in other places? Hadn't he seen articles about that sort of thing in the magazines? He felt sure he had. Then there was Panama. He did know about that.

The opposition he had encountered from the assembled family in the billiard-room had simply chilled and hardened his resolution to make good the promise he had given the burglar.

The morning he had spent in verifying the man's story—and he had been able to verify it up to the hilt—had brought him up to the point of incandescence again. It is literally true that he had never had the hideous fact of poverty in his hands before, where he could really look at it—where there was no possibility of looking around it—and the experience staggered him. And, to make it worse, if worse were needed, the social gaieties and futilities of Anne's wedding threw an ironic glare of light upon it.

It was about four o'clock in the afternoon when Hugh went up-stairs to his grandfather's room, in response to Hannah's information that the old gentleman was awake now and would see him. He was probably less incommoded than any of his brothers would have been—even less, perhaps, than his father, for that matter—by the sensation of actual fear. His grandfather had never been quite so formidable to him as he was to the rest of them; but even he felt pretty hollow as he approached the door. His determination to see the thing through without any compromise or equivocation was perfectly inflexible. And, since outright insubordination and defiance were things the old man had hardly encountered from anybody in all Hugh's lifetime, it was hard to imagine the approaching scene as ending in anything short of a complete smash.

Hugh steadied himself with a breath or two before he knocked. He hoped not to rant—not to make, as he had said to Greg, a speech. If he could just leave all the violence to his grandfather, then whatever happened he wouldn't be sorry for. He knocked.

"That you, Hugh?" old Gregory called. "Come in."

Hugh entered, to encounter what was probably the most completely disconcerting experience he had ever had in his life.

The old man lay flat on his back in his great old-fashioned, monumental black-walnut bed, the bandanna handkerchief which had been over his eyes pushed back just enough so that he could see, his hands clasped peacefully across his stomach—an attitude so utterly out of keeping with Hugh's rather exalted mood that it made him, for the moment, feel ridiculous. Then, at the reflection that this no doubt was exactly how his grandfather had meant to make him feel, he stiffened up again.

"Well," old Gregory said with a drawl he used sometimes when he was especially enjoying himself, "they've been telling me about the burglar you caught last night and tucked up to sleep instead of turning over to the police. How about him? Had he been telling you the truth?"

"Yes, sir," Hugh answered shortly. "Part of it."

"So he's one of my victims, eh?" the old man suggested.

Here was a cunningly prepared temptation for a speech, and Hugh nearly fell into it. But he pulled up and said:

"If you like to look at it that way, yes, sir."

"If I like!" his grandfather echoed. "What have my likings to do with it? What do you mean by saying 'if I like'?"

"I mean," said Hugh, "that he's been the victim of the organization out there rather than your personal victim."

"I made the organization, didn't I?"

"I'd always supposed," said Hugh, "that a thing like that grew more or less by itself. You could change it, no doubt, in any respect that you saw fit. That was what I meant by saying it was as you liked."

The old gentleman grunted. Whatever he may have meant by that, he clearly couldn't have expected an answer to it. So Hugh stood silent. Presently old Gregory wanted to know what Hugh had done with the burglar and was informed, briefly, that Judge Harkness had paroled the man to Hugh.

"What are you going to do with him now you've got him? Take him and his family back to Youngstown?"

Hugh admitted he didn't know.

"It's a pretty good idea to know where you're going to bring up before you start," observed the old man with more drawl than ever.

"Desirable," said Hugh, "but not possible always. There's no use trying to decide anything before you've got all the data." He paused, then added: "When I've finished this talk with you, I'll decide what to do with him—and his family, of course."

His grandfather grunted again and the talk lapsed into silence. This time a long one.

Hugh went over to the window and stared blankly out across the lawn. The absence of violence on the old man's part made him almost as nervous as it had made Gregory that morning.

At last, "Where'd you get these notions of yours about loose bolts and junk-piles, medical inspectors and insurance and so on? Been talking with your father about it, eh?"

"I didn't know he had any of those ideas until he spoke to me about it last night," said Hugh. "I don't know where I got mine from. Just out of the situation, I guess."

"It *is* your notion now, though," persisted the old man. "You think we ought to change the organization to provide for cases like that?"

"Yes, sir."

"All right. Do it," said his grandfather, and pulled his bandanna down over his eyes again as if the conversation were ended.

Hugh stared at him stupefied. "You mean," he asked incredulously, "that you want that work done? And that you want *me* to take charge of it? That's a pretty special kind of work, I suppose. I don't know anything about it."

"You could learn, couldn't you?"

"Yes," said Hugh, "I can learn." Irresistibly he added: "If you're serious."

At that the old gentleman snatched the bandanna off his eyes. "Serious!" he shouted. "Why, damn your impudence! Did you ever hear me make a joke about the business?"

"I apologize," said Hugh. "I'm a little bit—paralyzed, that's all."

"Well, don't be paralyzed," growled the old man. "And don't be a damn fool. We'll have a new department—What is it your father calls it?—Welfare? You're head of it. There's a directors' meeting the twentieth of next month. If you're ready to ask for an appropriation by then, I'll see that you get it. Now clear out. I'm going to finish my nap."

He did not go to sleep again after his grandson had left the room, but lay there in bed for a while longer, a curious grim smile on his old mouth, and a gleam, almost of mischief, in his half-shut eyes. It was an expression that flickered across his face more than once during the succeeding days, whenever the subject of Hugh's astonishing victory and its corollaries was referred to in the family circle.

The only person who ever got a clew to the meaning of that expression was Hugh's mother. She talked the matter out with the old man a few days later, when Anne was safely married and out of the way, Hugh gone back to Youngstown to install his successor in the laboratory, and the ordinary routine of life taken up again.

"You haven't gone soft in your old age," she said to her father-in-law. "You can never make me believe that. I'd like to know why you did it."

"Hugh's the best of the lot," old Gregory said. "His older brother's well enough in his way. He's a good worker, but he has to run on rails. Hugh there, can lay his own rails, and I'm not going to have him spoiled the way I spoiled his father. He can have all the rope he wants—try any sort of damned nonsense he wants to try. Get it out of his system. When he finds it doesn't work, he'll he honest enough to acknowledge it. He'll be without a grievance then, anyhow. You'll see. Give him a year."

But Hugh's mother looked pretty thoughtful, and not at all convinced. She applauded the old man's shrewdness—could find no fault at all with his reasoning. But that second son of hers had been, from boyhood, an enigma to her. She could feel none of the grandfather's complacent confidence in those clever calculations of his. Giving Hugh plenty of rope, dashing him against the hard human problem out there at the plant in order to get the nonsense out of his system, struck her as a little like a proposal to throw a stick of dynamite against a wall in order to get the explosiveness out of its system.

Of course, there was no use saying anything like that to her father-in-law.

BOOK II
RIVERDALE

IV

The original Corbett factory was burned up in the Chicago fire, and before it had done smoldering, old Gregory (not old then, though; just getting into his prime) began his preparations for rebuilding out at Riverdale. It was one of the stories he never tired of telling, how he rallied his employees and encamped them in tents upon the twenty-acre tract along the river, which he had purchased while the great conflagration was still raging; how they built wooden shacks to live through the first winter in, and how they began building wagons by hand in a big wooden shed before the first machinery—ordered to replace that destroyed by the fire—arrived. It was a matter of well-founded pride with him that within a year of the disaster, their production was greater than ever it had been before.

Previous to its invasion by the Corbett works, Riverdale had been a sleepy country town which hardly considered itself a suburb of Chicago, although some of its finer houses were owned by men whose financial interests were in the city. The results of Gregory Corbett's activities spread over the town, its indignant elder citizens used to say, like a blight. The original twenty acres soon proved inadequate to the huge expansion of the enterprise. On down the river and up the hillside, it spread and went on spreading. At the end of forty years—in nineteen eleven, that is to say, when our story begins, the area occupied by the works themselves was about a hundred and twenty acres, while miles of bleak, dusty, shadeless streets housed its thousands of operatives and their families.

Hugh, making his first rounds of the place in his new capacity, found it an amazing—a rather terrifying—phenomenon. He had been familiar with it, of course, from boyhood. He, like his brothers, had often been taken out there for a holiday treat. He could remember a day that he had spent the whole of (he couldn't have been more than ten) running one of the great, creaking freight elevators at a glacial speed, answering the calls of the bell—one ring, five rings, three rings—with an almost unbearable sense of responsibility. But he saw it now with a fresh eye.

It would make an interesting study for a historian, he thought—almost for a geologist, with its curious outcroppings; as for instance, that bit of inexplicable old mansard roof with an elaborate stamped iron cornice, shouldering its way into the sky-line between two huge walls of strictly utilitarian brick. Sudden urgencies, now forgotten, had thrown up mushroom-like growths between solider buildings of excellent mill-construction, or had converted buildings to uses wildly inappropriate to their original design.

Hugh made the discovery, although he had been in the room dozens of times before, that his grandfather's office had once been the drawing-room of a fine old house; the elaborate trim still remaining about the doors and windows proclaiming unmistakably the fact that here, encysted in this great industrial body, was what had once been, for those times, an opulent home, caught, surrounded, swallowed up by a tide. There was no tracing its original plan. That big old drawing-room and the dusty little court with a tattered cottonwood tree that its windows looked out upon, was all that was left of it.

There were, of course, great modern shops besides, built of reinforced concrete with saw-tooth roofs. There were great wood-drying kilns whose introduction old Gregory had long held out against, and, in consequence, the newest thing about the plant.

The organization of the business was a rough analogy to the structure of the buildings. There were men in it whose original functions had entirely disappeared and who remained only vestigially like the caudal vertebræ or the vermiform appendix. There were men, on the other hand, whose humble titles had never been changed, though their responsibilities had become enormous. There were old men who had worked in the Chicago factory back before the fire. One of Hugh's discoveries was a grizzled watchman seventy-eight years old, who walked his eighteen miles (three rounds of six miles each) every night in the year, except that on alternate Sundays he walked four rounds and two, respectively, in order to change watches with a not very much younger colleague. Hugh's unsuccessful attempt to retire this worthy on a pension infuriated the man himself no less than it did his grandfather.

The organization was not altogether made up of anomalies like that; naturally, since it worked. Corresponding to the great modern machine-shops and the kilns, were modern, able, aggressive men—men like Bailey, the general production manager, for example, or Howard, head of the purchasing department, whom old Gregory detested.

The plant, so far as its labor went, was what is known as an open shop. For many years—longer than might have been expected—its owner had succeeded in keeping it absolutely non-union. The fact that it was out in the country and, still more, the fact that it employed men of at least a half a hundred different crafts, had made this possible.

It was in nineteen hundred that the policy of nondiscrimination against union men was adopted. That was the year in which Gregory, then seventy years old, reincorporated the business, elected his son Robert president of it—himself retaining the chairmanship of the board of directors—and signified his abdication by going off on his first trip to Europe. The Paris Exposition was his immediate objective, but he went from there on around the world. With every year after his return his grip on the vital processes of the business sensibly slackened. He concerned himself more and more with minutiæ. The new lines of manufacture that were undertaken on the tillage implement side, especially the motor-driven implements and tractors, he paid very little attention to. The old wagon works was, as it had always been really, his chief concern.

He did not, at the time when he so abruptly ordered Hugh to establish a welfare department, at all realize how far out of the main current he was. He still had an enormous acquaintance among the sales force and, on the wagon side, among the operatives. And, anyhow, the business was his, wasn't it? He had made it. Who should know it if he did not? In a word, it was a child of his and he made the mistake about it that parents so often make about their grown-up children. And, as parents so often do, he came in, at the end of his life, for a tragic disillusionment.

The most destructive strike—almost the only serious one—in the history of the Corbett works, broke out about a year after Hugh took charge of the newly-created welfare department. One wishes, looking back upon such a catastrophe, that it were possible really to assess the cost of it; dreams of some superman of science capable of beginning his computation at the point where the mere reckoner of material damages leaves off; a biological physicist he would have to be, who could measure the human energies misdirected, emotional losses in misunderstanding and hatred, lives warped and blighted by it—to the second generation, anyway, if not to the scriptural third and fourth. But his unattainable totals would doubtless be incredible, too.

Our only concern with this great Corbett strike is the effect it had on a mere handful out of the thousands of lives it changed; and of that handful, primarily two, Hugh Corbett and another whose life was, as a result of it, inseparably bound up, for a while, with his—Helena Galicz.

THE THING HAD AN APPARENTLY trivial beginning with the appearance in Bailey's office, one Monday morning, of three girls who announced that they were a committee of the core-makers authorized to demand a decrease in their hours from ten to eight, and an increase in pay of twenty-five percent. If these demands were not granted immediately, the entire force of core-makers would walk out when the noon whistle blew.

These core-makers—they numbered about forty—were, with the exception of a few trimmers over in the upholstery department of the obsolescent buggy factory, the only women operatives in the entire plant.

Core-making is not a skilled trade. If you have ever seen children playing in damp sand, making imaginary cakes and pies with tin molds, you will have a rudimentary idea of it. The core-maker's molds are of brass, exquisitely accurate and satin-smooth to touch. You pack the damp sand (it is dampened with oil and contains some sort of binder like flour) into one of these molds, slide it gently back and forth over a steel-faced table, slice the surplus sand off neatly with a knife, take half the mold away and with the other half push your row of little cylinders or what-not into their rank in the tray, dust your mold with a brush, and repeat the process. When your tray is full you carry it to the oven where your little pies are baked hard. The molders use them for making the hollow parts of castings, which can not be modeled up in green sand.

There is nothing difficult about it; what little knack there is can be quickly learned. There is nothing dangerous about it, either, or unhealthy, or—for that matter—onerous. Any twelve-year-old child would find it fun—for half an hour or so. You get very hot and dirty, of course, especially in summer; for in addition to the roaring cupolas of the foundry itself, and the incandescent iron being slopped around like soup in an untidy kitchen, there are the great core-ovens, their iron doors as near as possible to your tables to save distance in carrying the trays. And if you worked at it the ten hours a day which this little group of girls out at Corbett's rebelled at, and six days a week, and fifty-two weeks a year (if you were lucky enough not to get laid off) you would probably find it intensely monotonous.

The demands which the committee made upon Bailey, like the threat with which they attempted to enforce them, were absurd. The notion of forty unskilled young girls trying these hold-up methods on the Corbetts was almost pitiable. One might have expected the manager to tell them to go ahead and strike, in the confident expectation that three-quarters of them would be back on the job at seven the next morning, ready to go on at the old scale and suffer the disciplinary fine which their half-day's absence during working hours had cost them.

Instead of doing that, Bailey looked thoughtful for a minute or two at the end of the hearing, then told the girls to wait in his outer office and, by telephone, asked for a conference with Robert Corbett, Senior, and his son Gregory.

"I can't see that it's anything to worry about," Gregory said, when he and his father, in that gentleman's office, had heard the manager's report. "What they ask is nonsense, of course. But I don't believe they mean it anyway. They've probably gone crazy with the heat. One of them fainted, very likely, and the rest got hysterical." (It was hot—unseasonably hot for May. Gregory and the manager were both in their shirts with their sleeves rolled up, and Mr. Corbett in silver-gray alpaca.)

"Two of them have fainted," said Bailey, "and it seems there's been a locomotive on the switch-track just outside their windows most of the morning, filling the place with smoke and gas."

Gregory nodded. "That's all there is to it. I don't say it isn't enough. But according to the weather man, it's going to be cooler tomorrow. They'll blow off steam this afternoon, and then come back and be good—till next time, anyway. There's nothing to do about it, unless you want to consider letting them off their fines when they come back."

He arrested, half-way, a move to rise from his chair, while he turned to his father for confirmation. Then, seeing that his father did not mean to confirm his view, at least not unequivocally, he dropped back again with a trace of impatience.

"I don't think," Robert, Senior, said, "that Bailey looks at it quite that way, or he wouldn't have sent for us. Do you?"

"I don't know whether I do or not," the manager confessed. "One of those girls rather stumped me—the one who did the talking. She struck me as being—phony, somehow."

Both his listeners echoed the word; Gregory in sharp concern, his father in interrogation. He didn't know what Bailey meant.

"Why," the manager explained, "she doesn't look nor talk like a regular core-maker. I'm sure she hasn't been here long. I've been in the core-room in the last two weeks and I know she wasn't there then. She's the sort you couldn't miss in four hundred, let alone forty. I don't know," he went on, "she got me going somehow. Talked mighty good English, for one thing, but when she wanted to confab with the other two, she jabbered in some wop language—Russian, maybe—faster than the others. I couldn't get away from the idea that she had something up her sleeve. Not that she had any sleeves on; arms were bare to the shoulders, and mighty pretty. What I mean is she seemed to expect I'd turn them down, and had her next move all doped out. Maybe I'm crazy with the heat, too. But I thought I'd tell you about it."

"If I follow you," said Robert, Senior, "your idea is that she got employment here with us for the express purpose of fomenting trouble? That she's some sort of professional agitator?"

"It struck me that that was possible; yes, sir."

"Assuming that your theory is correct," the president went on, "what course of action would you recommend?"

"I'm not sure that I'm ready to 'recommend' anything. Only, if she is dynamite—and she certainly has the look of it—it might be worth considering giving the girls what they ask for, the shorter hours, anyway, and discharging her."

"Discharge her, anyway, I'd say, on the chance,"—this was Gregory— "and make a point of seeing she leaves town. But giving in to the others strikes me as bad business. It might start a pretty awkward precedent— especially with things in a rush as they are right now. Of course, if they've got a real grievance either as regards hours or pay, we want to consider it. But we don't want 'em to get the notion that the way to get their grievances considered is to hold a gun to our heads."

Bailey turned inquiringly from the son to the father. If he agreed, there was nothing more to be said.

In the main, it appeared, Robert, Senior, agreed with his son. Certainly as far as principle went—that it didn't do to yield under a threat. He shared the manager's misgivings, however, and wanted a point made of abating the nuisance of the switch-engine as far as possible. If the matter could be arranged, it should do its smoking somewhere else than right outside those windows.

"But, as far as this committee goes," summarized Bailey, "I'm to turn them down flat and warn the girl off the place altogether?" He didn't want any ambiguity about his instructions.

"Yes," Robert answered to that, "that seems to be the only thing to do."

Outside the office, the manager detained Gregory a moment. "Want to drop into my office, casual-like, after a minute or two, for a look at her? As a sight alone she's worth it."

Gregory didn't much like to. Any act different in intent from what it appeared on its face to be came hard to him. But he could see that Bailey had not made the suggestion idly. So he walked into the manager's office from the corridor just after the committee of core-makers had been admitted by the other door and stood there with a fairly well assumed air of merely awaiting the manager's leisure to take up a matter of real importance.

"There's nothing doing in the hold-up line today, girls," Bailey was saying. "You run along and strike. This is a good afternoon for it. If you show up tomorrow morning when the gates open, you can all have your jobs back—all but one of you. If you don't, we'll replace you. You want to remember that we're always ready to hear complaints about hours or pay, or working conditions. But we don't like threats and they never get anything from us. That's all."

So far he had been talking to the two girls who had hung back near the door. Now he turned to the third who had walked well into the room and stood near one of the open windows, courting, it appeared, the hot sunlight that was streaming in. It threw her face into the shade, but lighted in her dark hair mysterious, metallic glints of copper. Gregory had not needed the manager's "I have something more to say to *you*," to single her out as the girl he had spoken of up-stairs as "dynamite."

Bailey must be right about her newness in the place. One couldn't have overlooked her anywhere. She was clearly not of American ancestry. She came, he guessed, from somewhere east of the axis of the Adriatic. But there was about her nothing of that squat heaviness which he associated with the Slav race. She had, on the contrary, a resilient look, as of one lightly poised, tensely strung; there was a touch of insolence about the lift of her young head. She was dirty, of course; the foundry alone, on a hot morning, without the assistance of the locomotive outside the window, would have insured that. But it struck Gregory—an utterly unsolicited and distinctly annoying emotion—that he wished she might be washed, her arms, her face, and that extraordinary hair of hers, especially. Wasn't there something almost patrician about her features?

As Bailey rounded upon her with that truculent *"you"* she turned also upon him (she had been intently watching the other girls' faces until then) and her movement had as much calculated hostility about it as his. Gregory fairly felt the shock of their encountered eyes. It was like—to take something as unlike it as possible—two knights splintering lances in the lists. And it was Bailey who was unhorsed; at any rate he had to catch his breath, and the girl spoke first.

"Threats!" she said. "You don't like threats. You've made other people eat them so long it's time you learned the taste."

"Well, I'm not going to threaten you," said the manager. "I'm going to tell you two or three facts and you want to get them straight in your mind, because they're important. First fact: you're discharged. Second fact: we don't allow discharged employees hanging about the place. Third fact: we know all about you and what you're here for, and you'll probably find it more convenient and profitable to leave Riverdale altogether and start your game somewhere where they don't."

"And if I stay?" she asked. "If I decide I like it here?"

"The law's got resources for dealing with dangerous vagrants. I advise you not to try conclusions with it."

The girl laughed and made a contemptuous movement with her hands.

And now it struck Gregory that she was acting—playing out a scene; that if she had written Bailey's speeches for him and rehearsed him in them, he couldn't have served her purpose better. Was he, Gregory, the audience she was playing to, or those two apron-plucking girls by the door? She hadn't looked at him once, save for a glance when he came into the room.

"The same old methods!" she said. "The same old brutal stupidities: hired police, a hired judge, and a hired jail—what you call the Law! You'll never learn. There have been kings like you."

Magnificently she strode across to the door, flung it open and shepherded the girls out. Then, from the doorway, she turned back for a last word.

"Do what you can," she adjured Bailey. "Then see what we can do."

She left Gregory tingling—a fact he was careful to conceal from Bailey when he congratulated the manager on his manner of dealing with the situation. They agreed, with transparent insincerity, that the girls would probably come back to work in the morning and that they had seen the last of the firebrand. Then each went back to his own work. But the memory of the scene kept nagging at Gregory all day. He got what satisfaction he could out of his discovery that the girl had been acting. But the reflection that a genuine passion might well enough garb itself histrionically, pretty well did away with that. He wondered where the devil she came from; who she was; where she had picked up that vocabulary. There was an irritating babu touch about it—the accent of the person who has acquired, somehow, an amount of book-knowledge greater than his cultural level entitles him to. She had negotiated the word "stupidities" quite successfully, save for the hissed *s's,* but she had brought the polysyllable out in the manner of one for whom it was once an achievement. Some of her phrases stuck: "There have been kings like you." Rant, of course, but pretty good rant. Was she really prophesying the guillotine for himself and his father—and poor Bailey?

Half-way through the dictation of a letter to Hugh, late that afternoon (Hugh was away for a couple of weeks studying the welfare system in operation in some of the factories of the Lake Erie district), he broke off short and sank into an abstraction, oblivious for a long while of the expectantly-poised pencil of his stenographer. If Hugh knew that there was a strike on here at the works, he'd come straight back. And wouldn't it, perhaps, be a little better if he didn't come back; at least for three or four days, until they had had time to get rid of that girl? If she could stir up Bailey—prosaic Bailey—and himself—as there was no denying she had done that day—what mightn't she do to Hugh? She was dynamite. Bailey was right about that. And Hugh. . . !

"That's all," he said to the stenographer. "I'll not send that letter."

V

Hugh got his first news of the strike from a Chicago paper he bought Saturday noon, five days later, in Toledo. The story was on the front page and the black-faced, two-column head,

RIOTING AT RIVERDALE—MANY HURT WHEN
DEPUTIES CHARGE STRIKERS—CORBETT
WORKS IN STATE OF SIEGE!

held him staring for a matter of seconds in blank incredulity. It was impossible. There was no strike at the Corbett works. Certainly he ought to know.

However, the detailed account amply confirmed the headlines. It was hard to make anything like a sequence out of it, but the trouble had apparently begun with the molders, who had walked out, Hugh gathered, three days before—on Wednesday, that would have been. Hugh could not find a statement anywhere of what their demands were. Evidently the trouble had spread like a conflagration and had been accompanied, from the first, by serious disorder, which, by Friday morning, had reached the pitch of violence. Of that day's doings, the paper contained a fairly consecutive account. There had been rioting at all the gates in the morning, when the still loyal operatives went in to work. There had been a succession of street fights during the day, arrests and rescues, attempts to tear down or to prevent the nailing up of inflammatory placards, attempts to disperse street-corner meetings; most of which had, it appeared, more or less disastrously failed.

But the incident which furnished the material for the headlines occurred at six o'clock that night, when the plant shut down and the hastily-sworn-in deputies attacked a mob of several hundred men gathered at the Charles Street gate to await the emergence of the workers. In this affair the deputies were roughly handled. One of them was shot and several of them badly beaten. The number of casualties among the strikers was, of course, unknown. This was as far as Hugh's paper went in any detail, though a later bulletin stated that at a late hour preparations were being made to house and feed the loyal operatives in the plant.

Hugh had an engagement to spend Sunday at Dayton, but he

canceled this over the telephone, and took the next train for Chicago, as sore in mind as those beaten deputies must be in body. The feeling he tried hard to dismiss until there should have been a chance for explanations, but which, nevertheless, required dismissing pretty often, was anger against his family—particularly against Gregory—that he had not been summoned home days before; that he should have been left to learn of a thing that came as close home as this, along with the general public, from a newspaper.

He had, to be sure, been out of communication with the office for forty-eight hours, owing to a change of his plans, which it had not seemed necessary to inform them about by wire. But surely Gregory must have seen the thing coming, on Tuesday morning, when he had talked to him over the phone from Detroit. Did they think his judgment of so little account—and in a matter that concerned his own special department of the work, too—as to be merely negligible? Or had his absence been calculated upon as making it easier to adopt a policy they knew he would not approve of?

It was hard to decide which of these alternatives gave him the more ground for indignation. Of course his *amour propre* deserved no consideration anyway, in the face of a crisis like this. If they believed they could steer the ship better without him in the wheel-house, they were perhaps right to try it. Only, such a decision requires to be justified by the event and no one could call this event prosperous. It was inconceivable to Hugh that out of the seeming security of a week ago a conflagration could have spread through the entire works, as apparently this one had done, unless the men engaged in fighting it had been throwing on oil instead of water. Whatever provocation there may have been must have been met with a counter-provocation ten times worse.

He could imagine Greg getting very stiff and Prussian over some unreasonable demand that roused his fighting blood. But what had his father been thinking about to let him go on like that?

In one of the other papers—Hugh had bought all he could find, of course, when he took the train—he had come upon a paragraph about a young woman, giving her name as Helena Galicz, who had been arrested outside the plant upon a charge of disorderly conduct and fined fifty dollars—the maximum under the law. The fine had been paid and the girl was alleged to have stated that her arrest was the result of an attempt made by officers of the company—and in pursuance of a direct threat by them—to run her out of town. She was further alleged to have prophesied a repetition of this attempt at the first opportunity.

The paragraph fairly bristled with the excisions of a discreet city editor—palpably omitted more than it said, and left Hugh angrier than ever. Who could be stupid enough to hope for any but disastrous results from a piece of silly brutality like that? Gregory, of course, couldn't have had anything to do with it! And yet Hugh couldn't manage to feel as sure of this as he pretended to be.

The fact was that between these two brothers a certain antipathy of mind which had existed since boyhood had sharpened and defined itself, since Hugh's return from Youngstown, to the point where it could not always be ignored. These antipathies are the commonest thing in the world in families. They do not prevent their possessors from feeling the highest respect or even the warmest affection for each other; they do not stand in the way of costly sacrifices. They are likely to go unacknowledged for a lifetime. But none the less—all the more, indeed, for this reluctance to define and evaluate them—they cause an immense amount of wear and tear.

The Corbetts were, to be sure, a free-spoken lot. None of them had any trouble in calling much uglier and more indelicate objects than spades by their shortest names. It was the imponderables that bothered them. In the case of Hugh and Gregory the fine particles of grit that so often got in between, when their minds bore upon each other, were too minute to be detected except by the exasperation they produced. Why should they make each other bristle like that the moment they set about talking anything over? They did, even when—as far as a working basis went—they agreed completely.

Gregory was marked, of course, for head of Corbett & Company, Incorporated, as soon as his grandfather died and his father retired. Neither event could be very far—in years—away. He enjoyed the business, the prestige his position in it gave him among the important men of the city. When the time came—and it was not very far away either—when they would be asking him to speak at public dinners and when reporters would be coming to him for interviews on subjects which the news of the day had brought up for discussion, he would like that too, and do it well. On the whole he liked success and in a close case he was disposed to give it the benefit of the doubt. But for all that, Hugh need not put him down for a pompous stupid ass.

Hugh did not, to be sure; but there was, now and then, a glint of something about his manner—an edge in the turn of a phrase, which suggested something a little like that. Gregory was scrupulously anxious, too, not to take advantage of his brother; to see that he came in for his share. He didn't mean to be patronizing about it, of course, but his manifest belief that Hugh could not look out for himself came to about that.

Hugh would have been bored to death by the sort of resonant importance Gregory found enjoyable. He wouldn't have taken the presidency of Corbett & Company except under unavoidable compulsion. The people he liked were the surprising sort and it mattered very little to him, for purposes of ordinary friendly intercourse, what their social status happened to be. He liked to read metallurgical monographs. He liked to spend unregulated hours down at the University laboratory watching some fascinating—though perhaps utterly non-utilitarian—experiment through. But for all that, Gregory needn't think him a visionary idealistic prig. Gregory did not— not more than ten percent. of that.

The job Hugh's grandfather had given him—of "humanizing" the plant—was probably better calculated than any other could have been to accentuate this mental antipathy between the two brothers. It was particularly hard on Hugh, who could not help feeling that Greg regarded all his projects and experiments as so much harmless— harmless, that is, if not too expensive—moonshine; that he was waiting tolerantly for their demonstrated failure to bring matters back to a reasonable basis again.

His job would have been difficult enough without that handicap, as any welfare worker will testify. It is hard enough even now; and a lot has been learned since nineteen hundred and eleven, when Hugh went to work. There wasn't very much recorded experience for him to go on and he made, out there at Riverdale, some of the mistakes, at least, once for all. Reading an article which appeared a year or two ago in one of the sociological magazines—*The Riverdale Experiment: a Retrospect,* is the title of it—one might easily get the idea that the record of Hugh's work during that year was a compendious classic of mistakes, a veritable vade-mecum for the sociologist on how the thing should not be done. But then the cocksureness of sociologists about the present rightness of their methods necessitates, since these methods change from hour to hour, a drastic repudiation of those of yesterday.

Hugh's starting point was Jean's burglar. His idea was to begin at any rate by making it, as nearly as might be, impossible that the disasters which had befallen that man should be repeated.

The remedies he improvised that night in the billiard-room turned out to be a pretty fair forecast of the lines he afterward followed. Disease and injury were the first things to be attacked. He established a dressing station, manned by a doctor and a nurse, where all injuries, down to the most minute, were instantly to be brought, and where all newly-employed persons were to be examined before they were allowed to go to work. He supplemented this almost at once with two out-nurses whose duty it was to look up in their homes all employees who reported sick. And he planned a hospital where not only employees themselves but their families could get medical and surgical attendance free, and pay nothing but their board (this being nominal, and scaled to their wages) if they had to stay there. Men injured in the course of duty would get free board.

Then there were preventive measures—compulsory goggles for grinders and others whose work exposed their eyes to flying particles—safety clamps for handling objects which must be thrust into rapidly-revolving cutting machinery (the toll of fingers and hands taken by a machine like a wood-shaper is appalling), guards for low counter-shafts and belts, safety set-screws in collars, automatic gates for elevators, and so on.

So far he was on fairly safe ground, though even here he met opposition and unexpected difficulties. His out-nurses were regarded—and resented—as spies, and with a certain amount of reason, when you come to think of it. To the workman who has reported sick in order to get an unlicensed holiday, or even to work off the alcoholic effects of an authorized one the day before, the intrusion into his home of an agent of his employer, brisk, skeptical, asking after facts which certainly were no business of hers, was, to put it mildly, annoying. And even when the sickness was genuine, there was likely to be a feeling that it was one's own affair and subject only to such remedial measures as one might, himself, elect.

But Hugh struck his real snag when he attacked the second of his burglar's difficulties. This was, of course, poverty, or—as Hugh, trying to state it a little more accurately, put it—the too-narrow factor of financial safety. They lived comfortably enough, most of these people; were adequately fed and decently housed and clad. The trouble was that they lived so near the edge that any sort of accident—such as a baby, or a period of half-time during the slack season, or a visit from a temporarily-embarrassed relative—brought them at once into the breakers. And a series of happenings like this—as in the case of the burglar—meant shipwreck, ruin, despair.

What they needed, Hugh figured out, was mainly three things all in the line of moving possible disaster a few steps farther away. They needed insurance, they needed some resources of credit, and they needed thrift. It is not necessary to go into details as to his devices for meeting these needs. The sick-insurance fund was provided by a percentage draw-back from the men's wages, which amount was doubled by the corporation. The credit difficulty, which the loan-sharks battened on, was met by the establishment of a banking department, where any employee (with a good record) could borrow, without collateral and at reasonable interest, the small amounts he sometimes needed to tide him over.

There were numerous devices for the encouragement of thrift, but the center of them was the Company Stores, where one could buy, so the slogan went, honest articles at honest prices. The prices were a little better than honest, as a matter of fact, for they represented wholesale cost plus the smallest possible overhead charge for operation and carrying, and no profit whatever. Fuel, food and clothing were what Hugh began with, but he hoped eventually to be able to supply everything anybody could reasonably want, up to and including a common-sense funeral.

He was not long in experiencing the truth of the proverb about the relative difficulty of leading a horse to water and getting him to drink, especially when he does not like the look of the water.

Hugh expected criticism, of course—hoped for it—went out of his way to get it. The details of his plans must be full of mistakes, and the people most likely to be able to point them out to him were the employees themselves. It exasperated him to find, among the older men—the men his grandfather called by their first names—an adamantine Toryism that outdid Gregory's own. They were aristocrats with a truly aristocratic inaccessibility to ideas, and an almost more than aristocratic contempt for the great unassimilated mass of man-power which the suction of the expanding business had drawn in from all over the world.

Going for guidance to samples of this latter class, he found what he was slow to recognize as downright suspicion of the integrity of his motives. It is always bewildering to a candid man to discover that his good faith is questioned, and it was hard for Hugh to realize that these people saw in his benevolent projects a subtle stroke against their liberties; talked of spies and—still more horrible word—"agents."

Of course, it was true that the operation of all his plans necessitated a certain amount of investigation of their beneficiaries, and even supervision of their lives out of working hours. You couldn't pay sick-benefits to a man who was shamming without doing an injury to honest men who did not sham. And you couldn't be expected to loan a man money until you had looked into—and regulated—matters which bore upon the question of his eventual solvency. Why, old Mr. Corbett himself, when he wanted to borrow money—and he had borrowed a lot of it at one time and another—had to submit to the most rigid investigation, and not infrequently to being told what he might or might not do with the money when he got it.

Hugh was rather pleased when he thought of using his grandfather as an example. But it was not serviceable. The people he tried it on looked as if they didn't believe that rich men ever had to borrow money.

It was bad enough to be tolerated, for a fool idealist, as he was tolerated by Greg and the old aristocrats in the plant. But to be suspected of being a subtle scheming liar. . . !

Oh, patience was the main thing the job needed, of course. Confidence was not a plant of the mushroom family, and in as hard lean a soil as this their lives had been planted in, there was no wonder it grew slowly. They'd have to see the thing work for a while to their advantage, before they believed in it.

This hard joyless monotony of their lives came to seem to Hugh as something as much in need of amelioration as anything else. There ought to be some provision for—*fun*. He was in the act of planning, when the strike broke (it was all in the future, of course. His grandfather had, for the present, gone his limit), the erection of a great recreation building which should contain a combined dance-hall and theater, a gymnasium, bowling-alleys, pool-tables, reading-rooms and a soft-drink bar. And there ought to be a park with a bandstand in it.

It had been a blow to him to find, in this last Ohio trip of his, that the great manufacturer who had gone furthest along this line, was feeling bitter about it. It hadn't worked well. His people had seemed actually resentful of his thoroughly benevolent attempts to provide for—and, at the same time sensibly regulate—their recreations.

He had never felt so despondent about this new work of his as on that

Saturday morning in Toledo before he bought the Chicago paper and read about the strike. He had a secret day-dream, as most men have, to seek momentary haven in when the strains and distractions of actuality become too grievous. Hugh's was a metallurgical laboratory of his own; a place where truth was an exactly ascertainable thing—where human greeds and suspicions and exigencies could be stopped at the door. He had never longed for it as he longed for it that morning.

But the sharp emergency of the strike, of violence, of the need for decisive action, stiffened him; cleared his despondency away like a great sweep of wind. He was done with imponderables, thank God!

Hugh's train got in to Chicago just before dinner-time and he went straight out to the house to find his mother dining there alone.

"I thought you'd be coming back," was her greeting, "now that this hullabaloo is in the papers."

"That's the first I heard of it," said Hugh, and wanted to be told where everybody was.

His father, it seemed, was in conference with the governor—no, not in Springfield—the governor had come up to town—over the question of calling out the National Guard.

"Your grandfather doesn't want it done. He and Gregory are out at the plant. I haven't seen 'em for two days. They didn't come home last night at all."

"I'm going out there myself," Hugh said, "as soon as I can get something to eat and find out from you what it's all about."

"The Lord knows what it's all about," said his mother. "At least I hope so. Nobody else does."

"What you know about it will do to go on," he told her. "Only begin at the beginning, please. When *did* it begin?"

It was an odd paradox about Hugh's relation with his mother that while they disagreed violently on nearly all subjects, and while she loudly proclaimed her inability to understand him, she liked him better and got on with him more easily—with less, that is, of those family frictions we have been talking about—than with her eldest son whose side in disagreements she usually took.

"Gregory," she had been heard to say, "insists on respecting me, which is an attitude I can't endure. It's because I'm his mother he does it. Otherwise he wouldn't approve my smoking cheap cigarettes. He drives me wild, bringing me things, standing around like an infernal butler—a bit reproachful about it. Hugh's got none of that nonsense about him at any rate."

Hugh felt, always, perfectly at ease with his mother, even when they were quarreling—or doing what between any other two people would be quarreling—most furiously. It was an unexpected bit of good fortune—this opportunity to sit down and have dinner with her alone, and find out about everything before his encounter with the others.

Her account began with Monday night, when she had seen at dinner that both her husband and her son had something that they were not discussing before old Gregory—who, it happened, had been feeling the heat a bit and had not gone out to Riverdale that day. They told her later about the strike of the core-makers and about the girl Bailey had spoken of as dynamite. "She upset Greg, too," his mother observed, "though, of course, he wouldn't admit it. She must be worth seeing."

"Was that the girl," Hugh wanted to know, "who was arrested and fined and said we'd tried to kidnap her?"

"That was a fat-witted performance," his mother said, answering his question at the same time with a nod. "A job like that wants doing thoroughly if it's to be done at all. These Napoleonic men who come up and give somebody a slap on the wrist! If I'd been seeing to her she wouldn't have needed any more seeing to for a long time."

Hugh scowled. "Do you mean we did do it?" he asked.

"Oh, don't be an innocent lamb!" said his mother. "Of course we didn't do it. Why should we hire a detective agency like Bullen and O'Hara if we had to do dirty jobs like that ourselves? Bullen bungled it, I suppose. I always said that man was a muff, back in the days when he was a police captain."

"We hired it done, then," said Hugh; then headed off his mother's apparent intention to speak with a curt—"Oh, don't stop to poke me up now! Get on and tell me the rest of it."

Mrs. Corbett grinned contentedly and went at her soup with gusto. It was good to have Hugh home again. It is worth noting that she obeyed him.

The core-makers, she said, did not come back to work on Tuesday morning as Gregory had pretended to expect they would. That devil of a girl evidently had them hypnotized. At noon they got the trimmers in the buggy factory to stay out, too. But the real trouble did not begin until Wednesday, when an attempt was made to fill the strikers' places.

Then the molders struck—"and being a hairy horny lot, they started raising hell."

Mrs. Corbett, being Mrs. Corbett, paused appreciatively over this phrase and glanced over at her son. Gregory would have risen to it—and so would her husband—with a shrug, or an uncomfortable smile. But Hugh's scowling abstraction was undisturbed.

"The brimstone and lava began, though, that night," she went on, "when Robert had to tell your grandfather what had happened."

This did not penetrate very deep into Hugh, either. "Yes, he'd take it pretty hard, of course," was all he said.

His mother considered him thoughtfully. Then, "Why, you miserable little whipper-snapper!" she boomed, "what do *you* know about how he'd take it? What do you know about anything—you or Greg, either? Wait till you've lived over a thing for fifty years—put all your brains and your back and your guts into it! Wait till you've lived through years like 'seventy-seven and 'ninety-three, when you didn't know from one day to the next whether you were going to last through or not. Pay-rolls that there wasn't any money to meet and that had to be met, somehow. He always did meet them. Why, there are men out there now, talking this I-Won't-Work hogwash who never earned a cent in their lives that he didn't pay them. And this is the kind of gratitude he gets! And you and the rest, that it's always made comfortable and important, 'supposing he *would* take it hard'!" And then this amazing conclusion. "You ought to get married, Hugh. That'd teach you a few things you ought to know."

Hugh went on eating steadily through what he had on his plate, and it was not until he'd finished that he answered his mother at all. Then it was only to say: "Oh yes, of course. But that line of thinking won't get us anywhere now."

He mused a while, then amplified. "Something's *happened* out there. Those people didn't strike and start in raising hell for nothing. Nor because they're bad, wicked ingrates either. They aren't any wickeder than they've been for the last forty years. And moral attitudinizing over them is no more good than it would be over a delirious man wrecking the furniture. What I'm going to try to find out is what set 'em off; what they think they're trying to do. If I can manage to get at their side of it, I bet I can manage to quiet them down. They've got a side, of course. It must look like *something* to them. They aren't just ramping around for fun."

Then, with a flare of passion in his dark face: "God! Why didn't they give me a chance at it before it got like this? Greg!—Trying to keep me in the dark! He ought to know he's a fool at this kind of business. *Is a fool not to.*"

He thrust back his chair and got up. "I suppose there's a car I can have?" he said.

"Nothing but the limousine," his mother informed him. "Your father's got one and the other's out at Riverdale. Bemis can drive it, though."

"Don't want him," said Hugh. "Drive myself."

"Be easy with your grandfather," was his mother's valedictory. "This picnic's likely to kill him if you boys aren't careful."

VI

It was around eight o'clock when Hugh drove up to the great iron gate at the foot of Charles Street. Here he was peremptorily refused admittance by a man who had most of his jaw on one side of his face and whose clothes were lumpy with concealed weapons. The limousine was responsible for this refusal, or rather, the fact that Hugh was driving it himself, which gave him in the guard's eyes, the abhorred status of a semi-domestic employee.

"Go down to the door marked 'office,' around the corner. If they want this car brought inside they can let me know."

Hugh could have got the gate open, of course, if there had been any point in it. But there was not. So he drove down to the door marked "office" and left the car at the curb. At this door also he was accosted by another of those lumpy, serge-suited, derby-hatted representatives of the half-law recognizable as a private detective as far as one could see him. This was a more authoritative specimen than the other. He inquired out of a drooping corner of his mouth and skeptically, about the nature of Hugh's business.

But one of the old watchmen was on duty here, too, and by addressing him as Mr. Corbett, effected an instant revolution in the gunman's attitude.

Hugh hated this infernal bonhomie even worse than the fellow's truculence. Was the whole place infested, he wondered, with these thugs? He asked the old watchman if he happened to know anything of Gregory's whereabouts, but hardly waited for the answer, which was indeed negligible, before he went on inside.

He found the administrative offices up-stairs all deserted and so walked out at random into the plant. He found here the same atmosphere he had noted about the streets of the town he had driven through on his way to the works—a superficial quiet, with a heaving ground-swell of restlessness underneath. Nothing that he saw was running, though lights were on everywhere, and he kept encountering groups of men—some of them regular employees, but many more—an astonishingly large number—who obviously were not. There was no fusion between the groups of regular workmen—the loyalists among their own people—and the Hessian gangs of mercenaries who had been brought in to break the strike.

The former were moody, silent; fell silent at any rate, when he approached, and showed a marked indisposition to recognize him, though they were mostly men he knew. The others, the strike-breakers, seemed to be trying to pump up a swagger; made a lot of empty noise. A group of half a hundred of them in one of the courts was trying to learn from one of their number a ribald song with which, on selected phrases of particularly pleasing obscenity, they made the walls ring.

It was after half an hour's wandering that he found his grandfather over in a just-completed building designed for a machine-shop, but not yet in service. Its vast, unoccupied area fitted it for just the use old Gregory meant to put it to—that of dormitory and mess-hall. Hundreds of cots were already lined up along its bays. More of them were constantly being brought in. And in the center men were knocking up benches and laying planks on trestles for tables. Down at one end they were installing a kitchen. Old Gregory, apparently on a round of the plant, was here questioning the men in charge and ordering changes made in cases where the existing arrangements failed to satisfy him.

The sight of Hugh seemed to please him. He said, "So you're back, eh," and reaching out a hand grasped his grandson's shoulder with it. Then he went on telling the man he was talking to what he wanted and why.

His appearance and manner, especially in the light of Mrs. Corbett's warning, amazed Hugh. Here was a man, whom the memories of his boyhood hardly reached back to—a man old Gregory had not been for at least a score of years—poised, frictionless, absolutely in command of himself and of every one about him. The violence, the senile wilfulness, which had imposed upon the family a definite method of treating him, all were gone. Just the way he stood there, with an unfinished wagon spoke he had picked up on his rounds solidly grasped in one hand and used to point his orders with, showed the difference.

The impetus of a notion Hugh had brought out to Riverdale with him that the thing to do with his grandfather was to get him to go home to bed and leave him and Gregory to run the show, at least for over Sunday, led him to make the suggestion.

The old man dismissed it with a smile. "I'm all right," he said. "And I'm worth the lot of you at a job like this."

He kept Hugh beside him until matters under his eye were arranged to his satisfaction, and then the two walked on again. The doorway they left the building by happened to command rather a wide view of the works—an impressive view at night, with its perspectives of lighted windows, its blackness of long blank walls, its vastnesses of mass and distance, its huge irregularities of outline. The old man, his arm in Hugh's, stood still for a moment looking at it.

"I've had many a battle for this," he said, "but never one just like this one. I never thought to have. But we're going to see it through, and we're going to win out. They'll find I've got one more fight in me yet."

They walked on again in silence, for Hugh couldn't think of an answer. Presently his grandfather said:

"You were on the wrong tack. You're not to blame. I told you to go ahead; didn't realize that this was just what it was coming to. But if you've learned your lesson from it, it's worth all it costs." He broke off to say "Hello, Charlie!" to a man in working clothes, whom the illumination of an arc-lamp overhead enabled him to recognize.

Hugh recognized him, too. He was a man whose job was the cold-shrinking of steel tires on wagon wheels. He said, "Good evening, Mr. Corbett," hesitated, let them go by, and then came hurrying after them. He spoke with evident perturbation and distress.

"Mr. Corbett," he said, "couldn't you let me off? It's the wife and girl I'm worrying about. I can't find out what's happening to them shut up in here. And the strikers are getting pretty fierce. It's scabs they're calling us. I don't want to make you any more trouble, but. . ."

"But you want the smooth and none of the rough," old Mr. Corbett finished the sentence for him. "You want your wages, but you don't want to fight. I've fed you and kept a roof over your head for twenty-five years and now we're in trouble, you want to go home."

Hugh understood now why men feared his grandfather. There was something really terrible about the cold anger that rang in that voice. He didn't wonder the man cringed.

"There are just two kinds of men, from now on," old Gregory continued. "The men who stood by me and the men who went against me. I'll never forget which is which. I'll see that you get out of the gate if you want to go, but if you do go, by God, you'll never come back.— Well, which is it?"

The man hesitated and in that hesitation old Gregory read his answer. He turned to Hugh.

"Take this yellow dog to the gate," he commanded, "and see that they let him out."

Hugh obeyed the order without protesting to his grandfather and without a word to the man. But coming back from the gate he set out to find—not the elder Gregory, but his young namesake. A talk with this brother of his had become a thing that could not be put off any longer.

He tried Greg's office first and was lucky enough to find him there busy with the telephone. Greg, greeting him with a good-humored wave of the hand and with the divided attention of one waiting for the voice he wants in the receiver, said:

"So you've come back. I suppose you read about our party in the papers."

"Yes," Hugh said, "that's how I heard about it."

"Didn't have time," said Gregory, "to send out a tracer after you. Hell began popping all at once." Then, into the telephone, "Hello! Bullen and O'Hara? . . . Corbett speaking. Are you sending us any more tonight? . . . All right. . . Three truckloads tomorrow, eh? . . . Yes, everything's quiet here in the plant. It's a little early yet for them to be starting anything outside. . . Yes, that's all understood. Good-by."

He hung up the receiver and turned back to Hugh. "It's been hot out here for three days, but I think we've got it pretty well in hand now. Grandfather's a wonder. Have you seen him? He's really enjoying it in a way; years younger than I can remember him. But too much of it wouldn't be good for him and he's had about enough now. I wish you'd take him home. There's nothing more to do out here tonight, though I've got to stick around in case of anything turning up."

"What do you mean by 'having it well in hand'?" Hugh asked. "Do you know what it's all about—what they're striking for—what it was started them off? Have you any plans for settling the thing?"

"We've all the plans we need," Greg answered grimly. "We're going to fight it out on this line till they get a bellyful—and then some more. They started it. Now they can stew in their own juice. Nobody knows what they want, themselves least of all. And as to what it was that started them off. . . !" He broke off with a shrug; then added, "Oh, there's no good going into that now. You don't get anything by crying over spilled milk—even when you've thought for a good while that some of it was going to be spilled."

"Meaning to say," Hugh interpreted, not interrogatively, "that it's my damned 'welfare' nonsense that's at the bottom of the whole thing."

"Why, if you want it straight," said Gregory, "yes."

"You haven't made any attempt, then," Hugh went on, "to find out what it was they wanted? Haven't talked with any of them, I suppose? All you've done is to hook up with a sweet pair of crooks like Bullen and

O'Hara; get them to send you a lot of strike-breakers and rifles, and pull off a little kidnaping for you on the side."

"Keep your temper," said Greg shortly. "They're a perfectly reputable detective agency, in the first place, and in the second, we didn't—as you say—hook up with them when this thing broke. We've had them retained for years, to keep a general eye on things."

"Spies, you mean?" Hugh broke in; "planted all over the place? I never was told we had any system like that. I'd like to know why I was kept in the dark about it."

"I suppose," his brother said, "because it wouldn't occur to anybody that you'd need to be told an elementary thing like that. It offends your—highbrow notions, naturally, but it's a system that's in almost universal practise—and it's been found to work."

Hugh made no immediate reply. Just sat there, his dark face staring down at the desk-blotter, during the little silence that followed Gregory's words. The elder brother glanced over at him and felt a sharp compunction for that sneering word "highbrow." He attempted an apology—a dangerous thing for a man to do when he's been without sleep for forty-eight hours as Gregory had been.

"I didn't mean to start anything," he said. "I shouldn't have taken that tone. Only"—that fatal "only"!—"only you *haven't* been out here, and you *don't* know anything about it, and it *has* been hotter than hell, and when you sit around talking about finding out what they want—*giving* them what they want is what you mean, I suppose—tucking them up and kissing them all good night,—why, it makes me tired. It happens to be a case where rose-water and powder-puff methods won't work. And ours will."

"They won't," said Hugh, lounging to his feet, "They haven't from the start. You say I haven't been here and don't know anything about it. Well, that wasn't my fault. You were glad to have me out of the way, I suspect. But how much did *you* know about it? How much did your damned spies bring you when this thing was cooking up? It must have been cooking a good while. They didn't bring you anything. You've admitted you were taken by surprise. And you've made a hell of a mess of it, though you don't admit that. Talk about 'having it well in hand' and 'fighting it out on this line' as if you were a tin general! *What* have you got in hand? You've got a few hundred thugs inside the plant here, who can't run it, and you've got a few thousand good workmen outside who could but won't. What are you going to do with them? You can't mow them all down with machine-guns. You can't even move them out of town bodily and get others to take their places. You've got to begin running the plant again sometime and, on some sort of terms, you've got to run it with them. The trouble with you is you think you're a sort of medieval baron shut up in his castle. It's time you woke up."

Matters had gone beyond the conversational stage for Gregory. The only relief to his feelings would have been blows. He and Hugh were too old to fight it out, as they had fought out the differences of their boyhood. So all he said was:

"There's no use going on with this."

"You're right about that," said Hugh. "Now I'll tell you what I'm going to do. I'm not in on your plans and I don't want to be. I'm going outside the fence, altogether, to see what I can do. I'll take my rosewater and powder-puff with me. Good night."

Hugh walked out into the street with no definite plan at all, beyond the immediate one of cooling down and getting control of his temper. He realized that he was quite as much to blame for their quarrel as Gregory had been. He reflected that if Gregory had countered upon him with a demand for his own solution of the problem he'd have had him. But as he walked along, paying very little attention to where he was going, the outlines of his plan came to him.

His starting point was the rather far-fetched comparison which the disquieting, unnatural condition of the streets suggested to him. People were moving about in them, but not as when they were pursuing their every-day affairs. There was no laughing, no loud talking. One saw compact little groups moving along as if they were going somewhere. His exaggerated comparison was that it must have been like that in Paris on the eve of St. Bartholomew.

And then suddenly he understood the astonishing ferocity of this strike. It was not a war between organized parties. There was no distinguishing between friend and enemy. Or at least, friends and enemies were all mingled together, living in the same streets. It was the chaos that was exciting everybody; the not knowing whom to count on.

There must be hundreds of men outside—why, thousands of them!—feeling much as poor Charlie felt—not revolutionary a bit, but coerced by the mob idea that it was despicable—treacherous—to work for Corbett. What fed the blaze was the sight of those guarded gates and the knowledge that behind them men went on working for Corbett; profiting at the expense of those who had remained loyal to their kind.

Suppose, then, that we closed down the plant entirely; drew the fires; turned everybody out. "Now," suppose we said, "talk it out among yourselves. Hold meetings. Decide what your grievances are. Send us a committee with a proposition. If we like it we'll open up the works again. If we don't we'll tell you why. In the meantime—for the present, anyway (Hugh smiled over this notion), the Company Stores will go on giving credit. We don't want to starve you into a decision."

Wouldn't that—or something like it—work? Wouldn't the bitterness boil out, the effervescence foam away, the sober majority—the overwhelming majority, Hugh believed—among the men themselves suppress the wild ones better than Greg with his riot guns and his strike-breakers?

The recollection of his grandfather and the last words he had heard him say brought Hugh up short. "There are just two kinds of men, from now on. The men who stood by me and the men who went against me. I'll never forget which is which." A proposition like this of his grandson's would never get beyond his ears. The plant was his; the men were his, loyal or disloyal to him. He had been creating, all these years, an enormous sentimental credit account, in terms of gratitude, against the plant and all concerned in the operation of it; an account that never could be liquidated.

But was it his? Could anything that involved the lives of as many human beings as this really belong—in that personal sense—to anybody? It was the first time Hugh had ever asked himself that question.

He was brought back from this somewhat remote speculation by awakening to the fact that he was drifting along with an irregular stream of people who were going somewhere. It struck him now that now and again the members of some group overtaking him had noted his presence curiously—pointed him out to each other. Well, he'd go along and see what their objective was.

Then the stream thickened suddenly. A crowd debouched out of a cross street and massed back upon the sidewalks, leaving the roadway clear. Down the street were lights and cheering. As the procession itself—if one could call a demonstration so little organized and with so little of rank and file about it by that name—came in sight, Hugh saw that they were carrying transparencies lettered in red and, save for an occasional simple slogan like DOWN WITH WAGE SLAVERY, generally illegible from an attempt to say too much. He saw occasional red flags. There were sporadic attempts to sing *The Marseillaise*. But none of these manifestations impressed Hugh very much. The manifestants were just a trifle shamefaced; self-conscious at any rate. The proceeding had a touch of the doctrinaire about it. They intended to be a mob, but, somehow, they weren't—quite.

In the center of a dense knot of men—fifty of them, perhaps, and evidently picked for their great size and strength—was a girl, her head and shoulders easily visible above theirs in the light of two flaring gasoline torches. She was riding on something and as she went by he made out what it was—an old-fashioned, high-wheeled sulky. Whereupon his memory automatically registered a similar vehicle—could it by any fantastic possibility be the same one?—that once had stood about in a corner of their stable, hallowed by the legend that his grandfather used to drive it, down in the old Washington Park track.

Possibly the evocation of that quaint memory of his had something to do with the ironic detachment with which he looked at the girl. Her position there, with that burly bodyguard around her and the cheers with which she was greeted, made it clear enough not only that she was the girl they had unsuccessfully attempted to kidnap two or three days before, but that she really was one of the exciting causes, if not the chief exciting cause, of the strike. Greg's frantic exasperation over her was not surprising. And yet, how absurd it was to try to train their heavy artillery on a wild young will-o'-wisp like that! She was the torch, no doubt; but what really makes the explosion is the powder.

Hugh's thoughtful smile as she went by, mingled appreciation with pity. She was a thriller, all right. He could see why she excited the crowd. There was a sort of splendor about her, of courage, of high adventure. He rejected the word "devoted" as implying submission to a sense of duty—to some imperative obligation. This girl looked as if she had never submitted to anything. She believed, no doubt—riding along like that—that she was experiencing the sensations of another Joan of Arc. But Hugh felt pretty sure she was mistaken. She had the power simply of radiating herself, and she got an ecstasy out of the act.

He didn't believe that she was very important—to him, unless, somehow, she could be persuaded to help him understand what the deep bitter grievance was—*really* was—that her fires had lighted. If he could once get at that and neutralize it, then the firebrands could go as far as they liked. They'd never succeed in setting off another explosion.

While he stood debating whether to follow the crowd along to the meeting or not, a man who had been standing back in one of the dooryards while the procession went by, came up for a look; then, with an air of surprise and satisfaction, spoke to him.

"Good evening, Mr. Corbett," he said, and on Hugh's acknowledging the salutation, added: "My name's Paddock. I'm with Bullen and O'Hara. You don't need to worry any more about that skirt. We missed her the last time, but tonight we're going to get her sure."

"She looked pretty well guarded to me," said Hugh.

Paddock grunted contemptuously, glanced around, and lowering his voice to the most intimately confidential pitch, he added, "About half that guard of hers is phony. Our own people. Some of the best we've got. There'll be nothing to it. When the meeting's over, we'll run her off as slick as grease."

Hugh asked, "What are you going to do with her when you get her?"

Paddock said this was easy. They would take her in to Chicago and have her locked up in one of the police stations, but not booked. By shuffling her about from one station to another, they'd be able to evade the service of a writ of habeas corpus and hold her almost indefinitely. At least until either the strike had quieted down, or they could find some charge that would give them a legal right to hold her. It was the only way to deal with these bums, Paddock thought.

Hugh asked him where the meeting was to be held and got a few unsolicited details as to the manner in which the kidnaping was to be conducted. Then, with the speculation that he guessed he'd better be getting on, Paddock took his leave, utterly unconscious of the seething volcano whose crater-rim his thick feet had been treading.

Hugh was in a white rage. He had been stoked up to it, one might almost say, scientifically, during the nine hours that had elapsed since he read of the strike down there in Toledo. His mother, his grandfather, the strike-breakers, Gregory, and the girl herself, each had contributed something. This loathsome private detective with his whisky-saturated breath, and his husky whisperings, applied the blow-pipe for the last time.

Hugh let him walk away before he stirred, then set out in the opposite direction, for the office, feeling very light-footed, very confident—completely irresistible. Nothing to question or to hesitate about, nothing to consider, no *pros* and *cons* to weigh:—just a magnificent determination to blow this silly conspiracy to bits.

A white rage like that is likely to turn out expensive. There are no brakes in its simple mechanism, and it often smashes through more than its immediate objective before it stops. But it is thoroughly enjoyable while it lasts.

Hugh noted, with satisfaction, when he turned in at the office door, that the limousine still stood at the curb. He went straight up to Gregory's office, but found no one there. He seated himself comfortably at his brother's desk, looked at his watch, and decided to allow him twenty minutes. If Greg came back in that time, he'd get an oral explanation of what was going to happen. Against the possibility of his not coming, Hugh wrote a note three lines long, as follows:

> Dear Greg
> "I have just stumbled upon another kidnaping project of your imbecile detectives. I am off to break it up. Sorry you aren't here to come along and help.
>
> HUGH
>
> "P. S. Not that I need any."

At the expiration of the twenty minutes he went downstairs again and found, at his post just inside the street door, the authoritative detective, now in his shirt-sleeves, his derby hat over his eyes, his feet on the desk. He took them down, however, and stood up when he saw that Hugh meant to speak to him.

"I want a chauffeur," Hugh said; "one of your men who can drive that car out there for me. I want him put under my orders absolutely. Attend to it as quickly as you can, will you?"

The detective would probably have obeyed Hugh's manner, even if he had not had him identified as a Corbett. With the magic of that name added to his inducements for zeal, he surpassed himself.

It wasn't five minutes before he had just the man Hugh wanted, able to drive that make of car—"through hell," of course. All that was needed was Mr. Corbett's word.

Hugh asked curtly, "Who's in charge of that business after the meeting—Paddock?"

The detective looked a little surprised. He said "Yes, sir," promptly enough, but appeared to feel that he was entitled to some explanation of the question. He got none; and Hugh addressed his orders to the chauffeur through the speaking tube after he had got inside the car and shut the door.

Considering the alternative possibility of a really murderous fight, Paddock may be said to have accomplished his boast that the kidnaping would be run off slick as grease. Two of the girl's loyal guards had to be slugged with brass knuckles, but matters had been so deftly arranged that these were the only two anywhere near her when the job was done. All the others drew their pay from Bullen and O'Hara.

The girl herself was fairly at the door of Hugh's limousine before she suspected the nature of the event. Her realization of something contrary to her calculations was simultaneous, indeed, with Paddock's. For it was in the same instant that a thick hand was clapped over the girl's mouth to cut off a scream and that Paddock, with a gasp at the sight of a different car than the one he had expected at the rendezvous, said, "What the hell. . . ?"

Hugh stepped out of the car to confront the glare of an electric torch. "It's all right, Paddock," he said. "Put her in."

Paddock's wits were completely stalled by this emergency, and he gave no order. But the two men who were holding the girl obeyed Hugh. This was the sort of job that, naturally, they wanted done, one way or another, as quickly as possible; since if they should be caught red-handed in an attempt like this, they could hardly hope to get off with their lives.

Hugh snatched one of them bodily out of the way and sprang in himself through the near door in time to pull the girl away from the other, which she was frantically attempting to open. And he, too, cut off a scream by clapping his hand over her mouth. Then he turned upon Paddock, now sufficiently out of his daze to try to get into the car.

"Don't want you," Hugh said. "You muffed it the other time. I'm running this show myself. Tell the man to drive on."

Paddock dropped sullenly off the running-board, slammed the door and transmitted the order to the chauffeur. He could not have disobeyed any man generating as much human electricity as Hugh, in that fine white rage of his, was generating—let alone a man bearing the name of Corbett. He entertained a painful misgiving, to be sure, that he would get hell for this from his immediate employers, but it was somewhat quieted by the obvious good faith of the struggle the girl was making against her new captor. He stood staring after the car for a moment as it leaped away, then after a sigh in which relief and perplexity were equally blended, he said, with a feeble attempt to recapture his lost authority:

"All right, boys. Scatter."

In the car the girl was fighting like a wildcat. She had her teeth in the hand that was clapped over her mouth, and her chin was wet with the blood from it, when he said:

"Those guards of yours were private detectives trying to kidnap you. You're free now. I took you away from them. Do you understand? This car will take you wherever you want to go. Or you can stop it and get out any minute." Then he released his hold of her all at once.

It was seconds after that before she let go his hand. Then, with a sick limp revulsion, she slumped down in her corner of the seat. Hugh dropped back into his, methodically bound up his mangled fingers in a handkerchief, and presently offered a spare one that he had to the girl.

"Sometime," he said, "—not tonight, of course, unless you happen to feel like it—I'd like to talk the whole business out with you. I'm Hugh Corbett."

VII

In all her life—and it had been a variegated one—Helena Galicz had never known a moment so packed with contradictory emotions as this in which the captor she had been fighting with the utmost fury, released her, told her she was free, and announced his name as that of her arch-enemies, the Corbetts.

Here was a new sort of man—a man who fitted into none of her categories. It was not so much that he, of the enemy's camp, had rescued her from his own mercenaries. That might well enough be a trick. But that a man who could hold her fast like that, keep his hand pressed down over her mouth while her teeth were tearing the flesh of it, should be capable of letting her go without a reprisal either of anger or of lust—of speaking to her, kindly and reassuringly, expressing the wish, subject to her convenience and inclination, to talk things out with her—was only a little short of stupefying. A soft man could not have conquered her. A hard man, having conquered, would have wreaked his victory upon her in one way—or the other. What sort of man was this? Was he human? Yes, he was. Her body had been powerless in his grip, the taste of his blood was still in her mouth. He was an aristocrat. She knew the breed as only long-subjugated races can know it. The voice in which he had dismissed that beast of a detective was the voice of one entitled to command.

She flashed around and stared at him when he told her he was Hugh Corbett, whereupon he added with a short laugh:

"Oh, we're not monsters, really. Though this sort of a thing must make us seem like that. You're perfectly free now to go wherever you like. And I think I can promise that you won't be molested again."

To evidence his good faith, he picked up the speaking-tube and ordered the chauffeur to stop the car.

Instantly the suspicion flamed up in her mind that here was a trick—a plant. She was to be seen by somebody getting out of the Corbetts' limousine in company with young Hugh Corbett. The incident would be elaborated—perverted—industriously spread about, in the endeavor to undermine her influence with the strikers.

It flashed through her mind so quickly—less a logical process of thought than a thing seen complete in a single glance—that she had time to say, "No, I won't get out here, unless you pull me out," before the speed of the car, in response to Hugh's order, had sensibly diminished.

He countermanded the order at once and, in a tone of perplexity that Helena found it difficult to doubt the genuineness of, asked, "What can I do for you then? Where can I take you? If you'll tell me where you live, or where you'll find friends that you can count on. . . ?"

She laughed—not quite inaudibly. Could he possibly be so simple as to think she would permit herself to be turned over to her friends at his hands—to come driving up in a car like that, under his escort, either to the house where she roomed or to the vacant store they used for Strike Headquarters? Did he think she was a fool? Or was he? It angered her that she could not make either of these alternatives stick.

He was waiting, speaking-tube in hand, for her answer. She glanced out the window. It was a dark gloomy part of town. The street was deserted. The point at which he had ordered the car to stop was already half a mile past; the frame-up—if it had been a frame-up—frustrated. She could get out here safely enough. And that would be, probably, the wisest thing to do.

But it was not what she wanted to do. She did not want to leave him just yet. There was the fascination of the mysterious, for one thing. As yet, this ride of hers was an uncompleted adventure. Where would it carry her? What would he try to do with her? There was a strong sensuous pleasure, besides, just in riding along with him like this; in the smooth powerful motion, the relaxation, which the luxurious upholstery of the car invited; in the occasional fortuitous contacts with that fine-limbed, highly organized body of his. There was something dramatically satisfactory, too, in this calm after the passionate, furious struggle with which their ride had begun.

She knew she was playing with fire when she said: "Drive me back into Chicago with you." But then, Helena Galicz had been playing with fire all her life.

It was possible, of course, to give her decision the color of good strategy. And this, with half-contemptuous insincerity, she did. The strikers must already have suspected that she had been kidnaped again, and this suspicion spreading uncontradicted through the night, would inflame them more than her presence could do. And when they learned, upon her reappearance in the morning, that her abductor was one of the Corbetts in person, the flames would rage uncontrollably.

She heard then, down in her depths, the premonitory utterance of a theme which was destined to be the tragic one of her life; a realization of how a stratagem like that would appear to him—would outrage his code of honor. Impatiently she silenced it. Was the warfare against his class, to which she had consecrated her life, to be abandoned, in any phase or moment of it, for the fetish of fair play?

She dropped back slackly in the cushioned seat and stroked her bruised lips with her tongue. They still tasted salt. He was speaking.

"That's very kind of you—to give me a chance like this. I hope you'll talk frankly with me. Frankness is a thing I've found it pretty hard to get."

Her reply was vague, not very intelligible and faintly interrogative. At least he took it that way and began explaining himself: his position in the strike; the reason it came home to him as a personal defeat to all his aims and projects; the ineradicable conviction he had that the solvent for all their difficulties was complete mutual understanding. That was why it was so maddening to see things being done on both sides which darkened the issue instead of clearing it—which sowed distrust and hatred. What he wanted was to learn how it looked to the strikers, what their grievances were. His side didn't mean to be unfair, let alone brutal and tyrannous. They might be blind—very likely were—stupidly blind—to things they might be expected to see. In the course of his welfare work he had often felt that—been made aware of resentments that no amount of brain-racking enabled him to account for. But stupid though they might be, and deplorably though they might have blundered, they were honestly doing the best they could. He was willing to concede that her side were honest, too, and prepared to be reasonable—asking no more than they felt to be their rights. So that if it were possible to get together in a spirit of mutual forbearance and talk things out to the bottom, quite frankly, the whole trouble might be cleared away.

Sometimes the girl put in a word or two, for the purpose of keeping him going. She was not listening at all, beyond an almost automatic identification of the things he was saying as stuff she already knew by heart—the everlasting righteousness of the middle-class point of view—the sense of duty—the wincing away from the logical conclusions of the system they represented—the milk-and-water mitigations they went about proposing in the wake of their car of Juggernaut. It was an attitude that had inspired some of the finest rhapsodies of hatred she had ever written.

Tonight, she heard it calmly, lying back there among the cushions, her arm touching his, his wounded hand—the hand that had clasped her mouth, lying there on his knee before her. The ideas he expressed were nothing to her; meant no more than the croak of bull-frogs in the marsh the road traversed.

But the voice itself thrilled her—finely modulated, inflected in low-relief, it had a bead upon it like champagne. It told her that, calm as he seemed, dull as were the things he was saying, he was excited, too.

Deliberately she let her mind go back to that moment of struggle between them. Her lips burnt again at the memory of it.

The error which all her associates made when they tried to reckon with Helena Galicz, lay in this: they knew—all the radical world in America knew—that she was Anton Galicz's daughter. What they did not know—or, knowing, failed to take account of—was the fact that she was Helena Bogany's daughter also.

Anton Galicz had achieved martyrdom in the Syndicalist cause. His trial for murder—a murder which it was not even contended had been done by his own hands—had been reported by the Associated Press, and radical papers all over the country had rung with it. His conviction and sentence to twenty years' hard labor, had been the occasion for demonstrations and memorials from one coast of the country to the other. He was the sort of man who is foreordained to be a martyr in some cause.

He was an Austrian Pole, a native of the city of Lemburg, of poor but not submerged parents. His frail body, no less than his active mind and his early-developed passion for books, led them to concentrate their hopes on him. Every advantage in the way of education that they could possibly afford, that the utmost stretch of sacrifice could procure, they lavished upon him.

He made what he could of these advantages, but it was not much. For he was a true intellectual—one of those unfortunates whose intelligence can see what it is beyond their energy to reach. Men like that are doomed to live frustrated, disappointed lives. They are usually embittered by a conviction that the world is not treating them as well as they deserve to be treated. It is the stupidity or malice of others, or it is a fundamental defect in the whole structure of civilization that prevents their attaining to the place in the scheme of things to which their talents have entitled them—rather than their own lack of character, energy or imagination.

Up to the time of his emigration to America—which happened in his early twenties, he attributed his failure and the disappointment of his parents' hopes, to the aristocrats. In a democratic country like America, now, merit stood on its own feet and received its merited rewards. In America a man like him would stand a chance. He believed this and proclaimed it for a good while—for two or three years—before he finally arose and came.

America failed him. Its pretended democracy turned out to be a sham. It was the plutocrats here, rather than the aristocrats, who ran things to suit themselves. But the effect was the same.

He was a remarkable polyglot (he could speak and write with equal fluency in half a dozen of the Eastern European languages, and though his English always had an exceedingly foreign sound, he was not long in learning to use it effectively) and he managed to make an exiguous living, sometimes as a reporter on one or another of the foreign-language newspapers, sometimes by acting as an interpreter. Anyhow, he was never quite reduced to unskilled manual labor, though it was a prospect that never seemed very far away.

As far back as Helena could remember, she and her father had always been on the move. Possessions they had never had, beyond the clothes they wore and what oddments would go into a pair of battered old hand-satchels and a tin trunk. A few months was their limit in any one domicile. Jobs, for Anton, were like plums in a bran pudding of joblessness. That they so seldom went actually hungry was due to the fierce practical wisdom of little Helena, who had developed, by the time she was seven, into a domestic autocrat, impounding her father's wages, when he was getting any, and doling them out by pennies when he was not.

Until she was eleven years old she went to school—on her own initiative—whenever she could, and made astonishing progress. She lied to her teachers about her age and was supposed to be thirteen (she looked it, easily) when she finished the secondary grades. All that time they lived in or about New York.

She loved her father dearly, passionately. There was a strain of poetic tenderness in his manner toward her which satisfied all her emotional needs. He made, to an extraordinary degree, a companion of her—as his periods of idleness made it possible for him to do; spent hours reading aloud to her. It was her good fortune that she inherited his genius for languages, since he read indifferently in Russian, English, German and French, as if such things as lingual boundaries did not exist—as if the Tower of Babel had never been built. And he told her wonderful stories. Until she was twelve or so she never realized that she hadn't a mother. Through all those years, though, her love for him was tempered by a feeling not far from contempt—for his idleness, his impracticality, his unsuccess.

But along in her thirteenth year she had an experience akin to a religious conversion. She began listening to the talk between her father and his friends, sometimes in the room they happened to be calling home, sometimes around long narrow tables behind saloons, whither her father had taken her under his arm. It had all been noise, before, the growl of harsh interminable voices, thumps on the table, cigarette and pipe smoke—thick and hard to breathe—the acrid smell of stale beer.

Suddenly, one night, a meaning emerged out of it all. They were talking about war—war on the capitalist class; the rich, that meant; the men of whom you had to beg for jobs and who gave them to you on their own brutal terms; the men who had control of the government and ran it as they pleased and for their own profit; men who lolled back in their soft chairs and grinned as they watched the workers sweat to produce the wealth they grew fat upon.

But it was not to last forever. Some day these sweating workers would awake to their own power. The wheels of industry would all stand still and in that horrifying, breathless pause would be heard the voice of labor—and it would be the voice of mastery. "This is the end," it would say to the fat parasites in their easy chairs. "Your day is over. You and your wage systems and your profits and the mask of hypocrisy you call the State and try to frighten us with and make us worship, are finished all together. You can learn to work as we do or you can starve as you have starved us. This is a new day, and all men are free." And then the workers would take possession of the tools, the factories, the locomotives, the mines—and the new world would be begun.

The day would not be soon, nor would the prophets of it walk an easy path. There would be discouragements, persecutions in the name of that hated lie, the law; the cause would claim its martyrs. But it would triumph at last.

What broke over her simultaneously with the vision itself, was the realization that among the little group of men who expounded it, whose eyes gleamed and whose voices rang with it around that long table, her father was the leader. The others fell silent when he spoke—listened, with awe, while he expounded, or translated pamphlets for them from languages they did not know. It was only when they argued matters of mere practical detail, that they ceased to defer to him. At such times his eyes grew dreamy, his gaze abstracted, and he would reach out with an absent hand and fondle her hair. She conceived suddenly an enormous pride in him. All that she had hitherto felt to be his weaknesses, underwent a transfiguration.

The physiological fact of her adolescence was at the bottom of this, of course. She needed something to dream about—a religion to which she could offer herself as a sacrifice. She found it in this Syndicalist myth of the general strike. She needed a priest in whom she could personify it. She found him in her father.

She soon became aware that his companions were urging him to spread the gospel more widely; to speak at little meetings, and to write articles for some of the radical weekly and monthly papers—dingy, blurred little sheets, enjoying a brief precarious existence. As best she could, she made herself his right hand. She took care of him, encouraged and indulged him; made herself his pupil, read his pamphlets, and brought her difficulties to him for explanation, until he found in her the same stimulus those nightly gatherings around the long table gave him.

All her old ambitions were abandoned—of going to high-school, of getting a good job in an office, of wearing fresh laundered blouses, of marrying, triumphantly, her rich employer, and going to theaters and restaurants in a low-cut gown. All these fancies were discarded like the dolls and toys of infancy. Her one desire now was to accompany and inspire her father and to learn enough from him so that she could, one day, take the red standard from his hand and carry it on.

It was in nineteen hundred and one that Anton and his daughter made their hegira across the continent to the West, where, it appeared, better fields awaited their sowing.

In the East the proletariat was hopelessly wedded to trade-unionism—given over to such abominations as trade-autonomy; to the belief that there was common ground between the employer and the wage-earner, and that the Cause could be advanced by seeking it. Even the Socialists were ceasing to be revolutionaries and were talking political action and compromise. The Knights of Labor, who had had the seed of the True Faith in them, were at their last gasp. But in the mining fields of the great West, where Coeur d'Alene had not been forgotten, another leaven was working.

The journey west was made by stages and required months for its accomplishment. But the goal was reached at last and the new life begun.

For three years Anton Galicz preached his gospel, where and how he could, in large towns and small, in mining camps and agricultural communities. On street corners, in tents, in dingy, tight-packed halls, he proclaimed his easily-comprehended creed. Wherever the industrial barometer was lowest, wherever wisps of smoke through the fissured crust of things betrayed a fire down underneath, there he went and sought to fan and release the flames.

He had organized support, of course. The Syndicalist cause, although it did not go by that name, had strong leaders and considerable funds behind it. But his main support, that he never could have gone on without, was his daughter Helena. Lacking her, he would have been a mere dreamer. And lacking him, she. . . Well, we are coming to that. An amazing fact to remember is that when he went to prison she was still less than seventeen years old. Just the age that little Jean Gilbert was seven years later when she caught her burglar and fell in love with Hugh.

It was in the great Gold Creek strike that Galicz met his fate. He was in the thickest of it from the beginning. Its enormities afforded his doctrines a perfect object lesson, with its bull-pens and stockades, with labor openly taking up the knife and torch, and with the State and the Law showing their naked hands as willing tools of the mine owners. The issue was joined at last.

The dynamiting of a bunk-house, in which a mine boss and a dozen strike-breakers lost their lives was a carefully planned and obviously conspiratorial affair, one of many, but, as it happened, the last. Law and Order had already won their victory and were in the mood, naturally enough, to seek out an expiatory victim. That Galicz should have been seized and charged with the murder, was also natural enough. The actual perpetrators of the deed would probably never be known. Galicz, with his perfectly reckless talk and printed writings, could be held responsible. In this responsibility others shared, to be sure, but he was, for a variety of reasons, conspicuous—chiefly conspicuous in that, among all the leaders, he was almost the only foreigner. So, with due process of law, he was seized and indicted and, after a trial, which offered almost unexampled forensic opportunities to the lawyers on both sides, convicted. His sentence, it was felt, in view of his fragile physique and feeble health, amounted to life imprisonment.

So Anton Galicz became a martyr. He left in Helena a living symbol of his martyrdom. It was as such a symbol that she lived during the eight years which elapsed between her father's going to prison and the outbreak of the Corbett strike. Wherever she appeared in radical circles, she had only to name herself to be recognized as her father's daughter, to receive sympathy and help—to be treated as a personage.

Her benefactors and admirers turned up, too, in strange places sometimes. One of the most important of them was Grace Drummond, a Denver school-teacher, with whom Helena lived for more than two years. She was around forty years old, unmarried, good-looking in a repressed, severely-tailored sort of way—one of that large class among women school-teachers, whose real emotional and intellectual life is entirely an interior thing, dissociated from, and without any adequate means of expression in, their exterior one; presenting to the world a finely-chiseled shell of conventionality which never betrays the fires within. It may be questioned in her case, as no doubt in many others, how long those fires would burn if exposed to the wind of action and of circumstance. Pent up, they seem, to the bearers of them, volcanoes.

It was immediately after the trial that Grace Drummond sought Helena out and carried her off to the tiny apartment where she lived. It was the one act of real self-expression she had ever achieved.

I wish that this too-crowded chronicle afforded space for telling more about her and the life that Helena lived with her. But all that must be summed up in this paragraph. Helena, with that intense eager avidity which characterized her early years, learned an immense lot from the older woman; learned manners, enormously improved her speech, and filled in some of the many gaps in her more formal education, which her father's teaching had left. The friction between the two mounted steadily during the entire period of their association. When they parted, after a furious final quarrel, they hated each other cordially.

Grace Drummond's experience with Helena was prophetic of the experience of many others who were to take up her rôle, or something like it, during the next six years. They got more than they bargained for.

They bargained for Anton Galicz's daughter. And they got, besides, Helena Bogany's. Helena, I think, was sometimes misled about herself in the same way.

As I said, she had never realized, during all her childhood, that she had not a mother. With the other emotions of her adolescence, this sense of the incompleteness of their family came to her, not so much as a deprivation as an opportunity for dreams and wonderings and sentimental thoughts. At last she brought up the subject with her father—one evening when the relation between them was particularly tender, in the hope of making it tenderer still—of getting one more turn out of the emotional screw. But the effect was not what she expected. Her father's face set like marble, and for a minute he pretended not to have heard. Then he said, "Ask me nothing about her. You had no mother. I have been your mother."

But years later, on the last night of his liberty—after the warning of his impending arrest had been brought to him and he had refused to avail himself of it for an attempted flight, he, of his own accord, told her the story of his disastrous love of Helena Bogany—a Hungarian Jewess. She was nineteen years old when Anton first saw her. They were married before a justice—after it had become evident that she was with child, and the marriage had lasted not quite three years. Then she had run away with another man; but she had been unfaithful to him—Anton thought—for a good while before that.

"You are growing into her looks," he told his daughter, with a burning gaze into her face. "You are not yet beautiful like her, though it is possible you will be, one day. Your hair and skin are the color of hers. It may be you will find her blood in you, too. If so, fight it. She was not an upright woman. She was greedy, vain, lustful. She loved finery. She was a milliner by trade, and good at it—made good pay. She pretended to be a radical, but that was a lie. It was only that for a while she was in love with me. When I married her she wished me to leave my philosophy to earn money for her—more money than other women's husbands earned for them—so that she could be better dressed than they. At heart she was a bourgeoise. And the appetites of her body were insatiable. I tell it for a warning to you. They will put me in prison, or to death. But you will be left to avenge me. You are a good daughter, but beware of vanity and of the appetites of the body, lest you become as she."

It was years before Helena consciously and avowedly revised that story in a different light from the one in which her father had told it to her and allowed her thoughts to dwell, in open pity and affection, upon the rapturously beautiful, high-spirited, practically efficient, hot-sexed young thing who had so tragically mismated herself with an abstracted idealist dreamer—who had worked for him for a while, tried to goad him into giving her the satisfactions she needed, stood him as long as she could, and then, under another passionate and perhaps no happier attraction, run off and left him for some one else.

But long before she admitted that view of the story into her formulated thoughts, her blood had been interpreting it for her. Her mind she had inherited, in some of its elements, at least, from her father, and the long intimate association with him had enabled him to stamp his seal upon it. But her body was her mother's, in every nerve fiber, in all its beauty of form, color and texture, in all its swift resiliency and strength and adequacy to every demand that could be made upon it, in all its imperious hungers.

It is fair to say, perhaps, that her father's apostolate and the martyrdom which crowned it, became the high horse upon which Helena Bogany's daughter rode in quest of adventure. This quest served her as the substitute for a genuine ambition. It drove her, from time to time, into furious activities. It stimulated her to write and speak in the radical cause; she did both effectively but neither really well. In speaking, the deficiency didn't matter because her electric personality and her picturesqueness covered it. When one read her articles, however, one realized their thin personal emotionality, and was irritated by her excesses in the use of exclamatory adjectives.

In one way, this sense of riding out upon a high adventure served her better than a more serious ambition would have done. It gave her a certain aloofness from the men her life associated her with; enabled her to set a higher price upon herself than any of her would-be lovers could pay. It was what saved her—this sense of conserving something precious for a worthy event—from a series, during those years, of shabby, and eventually degrading, illicit love affairs. It had saved her; she had experimented, more or less, had gone close to the edge many times, but she had never gone over—and she was immensely proud of the fact.

Such was the woman—the two women in one flesh, one might almost say, Anton Galicz's daughter and Helena Bogany's—who lay back luxuriously against the cushions of Mrs. Robert Corbett's limousine, listening in secret contempt while Hugh told her his plans and his hopes for furthering the welfare of his grandfather's employees, and thrilling at the same time, to the mere sound of his voice, the occasional touches of his arm, and the sight of that hand she had wounded, wrapped in a clean linen handkerchief.

She was roused from her voluptuous reverie—and that is what, in plain terms, it was—by a surprising act of her companion. He broke off a sentence in the middle, sat suddenly erect, squared around toward her, and peered into her face, then reached over and switched on the light.

Thus, for the first time, they were face to face; for a period of two or three seconds, eye to eye. Then the girl, with a gasp, pulled herself erect, shrank back into her corner of the seat, and shifted a lightning glance toward the door—the window.

"I'm sorry if I frightened you," said Hugh, switching off the light again. "I got the idea that you might have fainted, or—fallen asleep. Because you weren't listening. You haven't listened to anything I have said."

She was surprised into admitting that this was true. She had not expected him to become aware of her inattention; a certain thick-skinned complacency going, in her mind, with the sort of ideas he had been expressing; a complacency incapable of harboring the possibility that there could be a wage-worker in the world who wouldn't listen breathless when an employer was telling about the beneficence of his intentions. Once more he had confounded her categories.

"Look here," said Hugh—and now she did listen—"you started this strike. If you're on the level, you started it to remedy some grievance. Here's your chance to tell me what it is. You won't find any one better to tell it to; any one who'll fight harder to bring about a liberal settlement."

She echoed the words "liberal settlement" under her breath, but not quite inaudibly.

"Why not?" he demanded. "Isn't that what you want?"

"No," she said. "It isn't. If I could have my way there would never be a settlement, until the final one."

This time he echoed her phrase, but in blank interrogation. "Final one?"

"Oh, what's the use?" she cried. "We'll get nowhere by talking, you and I. There's no common language between your class and mine. Between us there is nothing but a fight to a finish."

Hugh laughed at her. "That's plain nonsense," he said. "I don't believe you mean it."

"Do you call this strike nonsense? Doesn't it look already as if I meant something? Well, it's only begun. 'Nonsense!'" she fumed. "Is slavery nonsense?"

"Come," he said shortly. "You're not on a platform, and I'm not a public meeting. Have I been talking like a slave-driver?"

With one of her lightning shifts of mood, she laughed. And she did it not scornfully nor rhetorically, but with honest amusement—a fact which astonished him as much as her words themselves. "That's exactly what you have been talking like. Every word you have said." Then she asked, "Have you ever read *Uncle Tom's Cabin?*"

"I don't know," said Hugh. "Perhaps, when I was a little boy. Or else I saw the play. I remember the bloodhounds, but that's about all."

"There was a man in that book," said Helena, "named Simon Legree."

Hugh remembered that. "He's the one that whipped Uncle Tom to death," he corroborated.

"It wasn't because he was a slave-owner that he whipped Uncle Tom to death," said Helena. "It was because he was a bloody-minded monster and a fool besides. If he'd whipped all his slaves to death he wouldn't have been a slave-owner any more. There were other slave-owners with better sense. They were kind to their slaves, never beat them at all, looked after them, kept them happy and contented, fed them well so that they grew big and strong so that they could work harder. It paid. And besides, it was the proper thing to do. That's the kind of slave-holder you are trying to be."

"No, listen!" she commanded, as he drew breath to protest. "You asked for frankness. Well, you shall have it. You've found us workers resenting your welfare schemes and you've wondered why. It's because we'd rather be men than slaves. And you were trying to make slaves of us. Look at your Emergency Loan Fund! That's what you call it, isn't it? . . ."

It was characteristic of Helena that, without listening to him at all, her mind had been automatically recording his phrases all along, and that, now she was aroused, they turned up ready to her hand.

"Well, suppose I am in trouble—need money. I can come to you and borrow it without security, provided I have a good record; provided I have been sober and industrious; provided you have put no black marks against my name. All very philanthropic and helpful. But how does it work? It works like this: that concerning every action of my life I must take your preferences into account. You won't like it if I have radical opinions. I must not be an I. W. W., nor a Socialist, nor even a trades-unionist. If I am, I must keep quiet about it. I must not live with a man unless I am married to him. I must not drink nor gamble. It would be better if I went to church. Above all, I must be contented with my lot—a loyal employee, grateful to you for not taking my job away from me—selling me down the river, that is, the way they did Uncle Tom.

"If you go on as you have begun, an employee of yours will simply be a marionette and all his strings will lead back to your hands. At your whim, he can have unlimited credit at the Company Stores. Or, at your whim, he can have none. And, since those Company Stores have driven all the others out of business, it is at your whim what he shall be allowed to buy. You even talk of deciding for him in what manner he shall be allowed to bury his dead. With his insurance fund in your hands, you send an agent into his home to decide whether he is sick or not—how he shall attempt to cure himself; whether he shall keep his windows open or shut. You have put the authority over his children into the hands of your probation officer.

"And now you talk of providing for his amusement; of taking money that he earned, and that ought to be in his own pocket, and of building a park with it, with your name over the gate, and a bandstand and a pavilion where he may dance with his girl until such time as you think he ought to go home to bed; a reading-room where he may read such books and papers as you pick out for him!

"Maybe your ideas are liberal. I don't know. Maybe you would be willing that we should read and think quite 'progressive' things. Maybe your notions of health and thrift are better than ours. Maybe we would be sleeker and better kept, more moral and healthy and prosperous, if you had your way.

"But the morality and the health and the prosperity would not be ours. They would be yours. Something for you to be proud of and show off to visitors and write articles about in the magazines.

"But we—well, we're so ungrateful and disloyal as to think we'd rather look after our own welfare and live our own morality and enjoy our own prosperity. What we say is that if we got what our labor really earned, we could take care of ourselves without any looking after.

"You will not pay us what we really earn, because if you did, there would be nothing left for you. You will not give up what makes you master of us—what makes life easy and swift and soft, like this"—her gesture indicated the car they were riding in—"until, by force, we take it away from you. We shan't succeed this time. You don't believe we ever will succeed. Well, wait!"

What all along had lent force to her talk was the conversational manner of it—passionless, matter-of-fact, sometimes just faintly amused, and with part of her mind—part of *her* at any rate—obviously somewhere else, as when one, full of his own thoughts, tells an old story to a child. At the end of it she stirred uneasily, as a dreamer will, and dropped back against the cushion, her arm once more in contact with his.

He had not spoken all the while; had not even, after she was fairly started, moved to speak. And he did not speak now.

After a silence, she said musingly, "For the good of the slaves, I wish that all masters were like Simon Legree—cruel and unashamed. The war would come sooner and be sooner over. It is not hatred and violence that darken the issue. It's this hypocritical, cowardly philanthropy. Welfare work!"

Then, instantly, "I don't mean you. You're not a coward and I don't believe you're a hypocrite. I don't know what to make of you exactly."

"I don't know what to make of you," he said. And it sounded as though he spoke through tight-clenched teeth. "What you've been saying to me is surprising enough. I don't know what to think about that. I don't believe you're right, though I am beginning to see where I have been wrong. But what you have said isn't so amazing as what you are—who you are."

"We're from the opposite sides of the earth, you and I," she said. "How should we understand each other? We're talking the same language, but the words mean different things to us. You've traveled I suppose, and so have I. But you have never ridden on a second-class ticket in the smoking-car. The conductor isn't a man you wince from because you're afraid that he'll kick your bundle if it sticks out a little into the aisle. Men in brass buttons are people you expect to touch their hats and take your orders. But I remember them, from childhood, as people who grabbed me by the arm and pushed me about—tyrants who avenged their servility to you on me. To you, of course, the judges and the police are faithful servants anxious for your good opinion, alert and busy seeing that your property isn't damaged, nor your peace disturbed."

"I can see how they look very different from that to you," Hugh said; "—after this experience you've been having with us."

"*This* experience!" She uttered a short grim laugh.

"Oh, I suppose you may have had others as bad," he admitted. "The law's a clumsy, blundering sort of machine, I know. Still the idea of it is to protect you as well as it protects me."

She turned to stare at him, her whole body tense as if with astonishment. "I suppose you really believe that," she said, going slack again with a sigh. "Sometimes I want to laugh. I think, if one could laugh at it as it deserves to be laughed at, he could shake the world down."

Suddenly, in a new voice, that thrilled and horrified him and shook him as never before in his life had he been shaken, she began telling the story of her father's apostolate and his martyrdom. Occasionally the story dipped into her early childhood, but most of it was after they went West. She told of towns where they had been mobbed and beaten by respectable citizens, towns where they had been taken to the railroad station and put forcibly upon a train only to be seized at their enforced destination by waiting police officers and thrown into jail. She told of shifty subterfuges to trick her father into the technical violation of some statute or ordinance, of trumped-up charges and perjured charges against them. She told of cynical violations of even the bare letter of the law, on the part of its officers, when it could not be twisted to serve their purposes.

She showed him some vivid little fragments of the great Gold Creek strike, sharp as cut steel; the night of the raid on their little newspaper; the way her father took the news of the dynamiting of the bunk-house; the pride with which he refused to avail himself of the warning they brought him that he was to be charged with the crime. And last of all she told him about the trial.

All the way through the recital the emotional tension of it had been mounting steadily toward this climax. The note of it, throughout, had been defiant, bitter, as of one who neither looked for nor wished sympathy, but now her voice grew fairly raucous with passion—quivered and flamed with it.

The maddening quality about the trial for Helena, and evidently for her father, had been what she called the hypocrisy of it—the solemn pretense at fair play—the mockery of the presumption of innocence until guilt was proved—the pontifical airs. It was not the foregone conclusion, which sat there leering at them from the beginning, but the mask of an impartial search for truth, which it insisted, to the very end, on leering through, that maddened its victims.

"If they had taken him and killed him with honest, decent violence," she said, "I wouldn't hate them—loathe them, the way I do!"

Anton, it seemed, had wished not to have his case defended at all; had wanted to go into court alone, without a friend or counselor, and let them have their will with him. But he had been overborne by his committee, who had raised a defense fund and had employed a showy criminal lawyer with it. Anton felt himself and his cause besmirched by the tactics, the legal tricks and lies employed in his defense. And when the trial was over, and the verdict, "Murder in the first degree," brought in by the jury, he took advantage of his opportunity before the judge pronounced sentence, to repudiate every plea that had been advanced in his defense, and challenged the judge to inflict the death penalty.

But the grinning mask of fairness and clemency was held up to the end. The judge gave him twenty years—a derisive equivalent to imprisonment for life—a slow living death, instead of a merciful swift one.

Helena had taken her last farewell of her father, there in the court room. He had forbidden her to write to him, or to attempt to see him. She was to consider him dead. His life ended when his freedom did. All she had left of her father was a memory to avenge. His actual death had not occurred until about a year ago.

The story told, the passion it had evoked ebbed out with it. Once more Hugh felt against his shoulder the weight and warmth of her body, could detect the relaxed expirations of slow, deep indrawn breaths. Neither of them said anything for a while. The car was gliding along between the lights of Washington Boulevard. By and by the girl roused herself and looked out the window.

"We must be getting near where I want to go," she said. "Do you know just where we are?"

Hugh was able to identify the next cross street, and told her the name of it. "This chauffeur," he added, "is one of their detectives that I commandeered for the job, so we'd better not let him drive you all the way to where you are going."

She laughed and thanked him for the precaution. She had forgotten that detail herself.

"Better stop here," she said, and Hugh gave the order.

It was a moment after the car stopped before she moved. And in that moment Hugh's heart came up into his throat.

"I don't want to force your confidence," he said unsteadily. "If you want to—disappear from me, as well as from him, why—this is your chance to do it. I'll let you go as I promised."

It was a fact crystal-clear to the perception of Anton Galicz's daughter, that she should take him at his word; that fire, edged-tools, dynamite, would not be more dangerous toys for her to play with than this clean, beautiful young aristocrat.

But it was Helena Bogany's daughter who answered him.

"I don't want to disappear from you," she said. "I'll be glad if you will come with me."

So Hugh dismissed the amazed detective (he and Helena stood on the curb and watched the car out of sight as a precaution against their being followed), then walked with her three or four blocks, to an old-fashioned, rather pleasant-looking brick apartment-building with a whole row of gabled roofs. At one of the numerous entrances Helena stopped.

"A newspaper girl lives here," she said. "I stay with her sometimes. She probably isn't at home, but I know where she keeps the key. Will you come in?"

"I'd rather not tonight," Hugh said. "Not if I can see you some other time. I must talk more with you. We haven't begun. And yet, you've told me so much—taught me so much already, I'm—bewildered, somehow—shaken. I want time to think—get my wits together, before I see you again. But can I find you again, if I let you go now? Shall you be staying here for a while—or coming back?"

"No one ever knows where I am going to be," she said. "But Alice Hayes (she's the girl who lives here) knows as much about me as any one. Her telephone's in the book, so you can call her up."

All that was rather cavalierly said, with an edge of something like derision in the voice. Then, without growing any gentler, the quality of it changed—darkened.

"There's no telling anything about me," she said. "I'm as much surprised at the things I do sometimes, as anybody else. But, tonight. . ."

Suddenly she reached for his wounded hand, raised it gently in both of hers, bent her face over it, and touched the palm with her lips. She retained it just a fleeting instant longer while she said something he could not hear, then bruskly let it go and went in. He did not follow.

VIII

He saw her the next day, though he had no such intention when he left her at Alice Hayes' door. The person who brought this about was, absurdly enough, his brother Gregory.

The clan had gathered in considerable force for that imperishable institution, the one o'clock Sunday dinner. The two Gregorys, leaving all quiet at Riverdale, and Bailey in command, had come back to town about eleven o'clock; Robert, Senior, and his wife, according to almost inviolable custom, had been to church (the Corbetts were Presbyterians); Robert, Junior, had surprised them all by dropping off on his way through from Wyoming to Long Island for some polo. He had read about the strike in the papers just as Hugh had done, canceled his reservation on the Twentieth Century, and come home to offer himself as a volunteer—an orthodox manifestation of the clan-spirit which pleased his grandfather mightily; his father, too, for that matter, and even Greg—though the latter, remembering Hugh's remarks about medieval barons and tin generals, said he didn't know what there was Robert could do. "We aren't sniping strikers from the roofs, you know."

None of them had seen Hugh until he came down-stairs just at dinner-time and took his place at the table. They wanted to know, of course, what was the matter with his hand (he had the two middle fingers bandaged), but on his saying curtly that it was nothing, they forebore, for the time, to press him further. The newcomer from Wyoming occupied the focus of their attention and Hugh was allowed to sit through the dinner in almost unbroken silence.

When old Gregory left the table, however, at the end of the meal, summoning his daughter-in-law to come with him to rub his head so that he could go to sleep—a frequent demand of his—young Greg turned on Hugh with a question that obviously had been awaiting release for a good while.

"What the devil have you done with that girl?" he asked. "Where is she now?"

Robert, Senior, since he did not smoke, had thrust back his chair preparatory to leaving them, and Robert, Junior, slumped down on his backbone, was hooking his mother's chair around so that he could put his feet upon it. Greg's question galvanized them both into attitudes of complete astonishment.

But Hugh, who was drinking his coffee, went on and finished it and set his cup down accurately in his saucer, before he answered.

"I don't know where she is now," he said. "I know where I left her, but I have no idea whether she's still there."

There was a bristling little silence while the other three waited for him to go on. Then, simultaneously, both the Roberts asked:

"What girl?"

Hugh waited a moment to see whether Gregory wished to answer the question, then addressed himself to his father.

"The girl who started the strike," he said. "Bullen and O'Hara have got the idea fixed in their minds that we want her made away with, and they keep trying to kidnap her. I learned about their plans last night, and interfered."

"I should think you did!" said Gregory. "You took an awful chance, but I don't deny it worked. I'd like to know how you did it."

"Did what?" demanded Hugh. "I don't know what you're talking about."

"Why," said Gregory, turning to his father, "the girl has simply disappeared. From the strikers, I mean. They don't know where she is. They're all up in the air about her. She telephoned out to their Strike Headquarters last night—about midnight—told them she was all right, but was going to keep quiet for two or three days. They don't know what to make of that any more than we do. Up to nine o'clock this morning they hadn't heard anything more from her."

Robert, Senior, turned a look of perplexity from one of his eldest sons to the other.

"You are mistaken," he said at last to Hugh, "in thinking we have given any instructions to Bullen and O'Hara that involved foul play. I find it difficult to understand how you can have entertained such an idea for a moment."

"I think you will understand," said Hugh, "when I tell you just what happened." Which he forthwith proceeded to do, relating his conversation with Paddock and the measures he had taken for frustrating the detectives' plans. He made an end of his story at the point where he drove away with the girl.

"I told her she was free to go wherever she liked," he concluded, "and I gave her my personal guarantee that she should not be molested any further. And I'll be glad to know," he added, "whether I shall have to make good that guarantee in person, or whether the firm will take action to make it unnecessary."

His father, who was visibly shocked by the recital, left no doubt under that head. He rang for the butler, and ordered him to get Bullen or O'Hara, in person, on the telephone at once.

"If you have any means of communicating with the young woman," he said to Hugh, "I wish you would inform her that she has been the victim of the excessive zeal of our employees, and convey to her *my* assurance that it will not occur again." He rose with a good deal of dignity and walked away to the telephone.

No one else said anything until he had left the room, but both Hugh's brothers were visibly awaiting the opportunity his absence would give to go into the matter further and more freely.

Bob's line was a rather skeptical amusement. He had great confidence in his own powers with women, and would have backed himself any day to accomplish the feat which, according to his interpretation of the episode, Hugh had accomplished. But that Hugh should even have attempted it, struck him as almost funny.

Hugh was two years older than he, remember, midway between him and Gregory, which meant that during their youth and earliest manhood, he had been a mediator as well; had preached Greg's sermons to Bob and pleaded Bob's causes with Gregory.

Bob, as I have said, was a perfectly conventional black sheep, and his youthful scrapes had been mainly the sort that girls get a man into. When he found himself in beyond the possibility of self-extrication, he usually confided in Hugh and followed his advice far enough to avoid the most immediate and unpleasant consequences. There was nothing reciprocal about this relation, however. Hugh never confided any of his affairs to him; had, apparently, none to confide.

As Bob grew older and began taking his man-of-the-world morality for granted, his attitude toward Hugh, as far as sex-matters were concerned—and these were, it is fair enough to say, the principal interest of his life—became the typical attitude of the conventional libertine toward the man who has remained, so far as he knows, continent—an attitude at once skeptical and contemptuous.

So far as Bob was able to discover, Hugh had never taken the slightest interest either in the outright disreputable and mercenary class of women, or in the semi-respectable and halfway disinterested ones whose more seductive snares lie spread for the feet of college students with ample allowances. Among nice girls—the sort, that is, who could be invited to college dances—Hugh had been popular enough. He danced well and was not in the least shy or self-conscious with them. Only, he was always an unsatisfactory sort of an enigma to them, due to his steering his course, not by the pole-star fact that they were female and he was male, but by some curious orientation of his own. He talked to them just as he would talk to anybody; used the same standards that he applied to everybody in determining whether he liked them or not. He was fond of his elder sister Constance and on comfortable friendly terms with a few of her women friends—notably with the beautiful Frederica Whitney, Rodney Aldrich's sister. And it had been entirely characteristic of him that at Anne's wedding, with a wonderful selection of bridesmaids to intrigue his unattached fancy, he had spent his time making friends in quasi-avuncular fashion, with little Jean Gilbert.

You can understand then, I imagine, well enough how Bob would look at this adventure of his brother's. What the devil had Hugh done to her in those two hours?

Greg was curious about this, too, though it was not the aspect of the affair that interested him most.

"I can't complain," he said. "Because you got away with it. Somehow or other, you accomplished about seven times as much as Paddock would have. Those other strike leaders are simply up in the air, and a little doubt or suspicion in a case like that will go a long way. If she sticks to the line she took last night, the whole damned strike might collapse. But it makes me sweat everytime I think of the chance you took."

"You said that once before," said Hugh. "What I did seemed obvious enough to me. I can't see that I took any such frightful chance."

Bob laughed. But Gregory just stared for a moment in blank exasperation. Then, "You don't!" he exclaimed. "Well, just suppose for a minute you had not got away with it. Suppose any one of a hundred things that could have happened about three times as easily as not. Suppose some one of her crowd had recognized the car and you in it—seen one of our family carrying her off. Suppose the girl, instead of telephoning as she did, that she was all right, had said that you'd tried to carry her off, but that she'd escaped you. Any story she chose to tell would be believed:—that you'd abused her, tried to rape her—anything. And it would have gone from one end of the country to the other. Put a mark on you and the whole family that we couldn't outlive for a generation.

"And what kind of a story could you tell?—Not that it would make any difference, because nobody would believe it.—All you could say would be that we, all the rest of us, I mean, grandfather and father and I, were in a conspiracy to make away with the girl and that you stepped in and tried to break it up. And that would have a likely sound, wouldn't it, since you had the family limousine with a Bullen and O'Hara man driving it!"

He pulled in a long breath and released it with a whoosh! "I can't understand her letting you off like that," he went on. "Look at the advantage she had right there in her hands—the personal advantage, let alone the other. She could have got anything out of us she wanted in the way of blackmail. And it's what you'd expect her to do, on the dope! Because she isn't an honest-to-God working girl at all. Just a professional trouble-maker."

"Well, she's passed up one wonderful chance," said Bob. "Or it looks as if she had. Of course by tomorrow morning we may find she's changed her mind."

"No," said Gregory, "I don't think so. A story like that has got to be told quick. If you don't tell it the minute you're free to tell it, your chance for getting it believed grows pretty thin. No, she's taken her line all right and she won't change it. We're safe enough now.

"But"—here he turned to Hugh—"for the love of heaven, never try to pull anything like that again!"

He saw Hugh looking pretty thoughtful over this, evidently impressed, and gave the talk another turn under the comfortable conviction that, for once, an admonition to his next younger brother had had a good effect.

It was a conviction ludicrously ill-founded. For the aspect of the business that had caught Hugh, was the girl's forbearance—her good sportsmanship, in not making use of the opportunity which Greg had so clearly pointed out.

What with the pain in his injured hand and the excitement incident upon that fine rage of his, he had hardly slept since he left her. In those waking hours, he had had leisure for a lot of what he supposed was cool level-headed thinking.

Hugh was, perhaps, not very exceptional in attributing to himself qualities he did not possess, and in supposing himself deficient in other qualities which he possessed to a marked degree. We all conform pretty much to the superficial characterizations of those persons who see us oftenest. Because, from boyhood, anger had never made Hugh turn purple and sputter the way Gregory did, the family tradition was that he never was angry. And he grew up believing himself to be a rather imperturbable person. Because he never sentimentalized over his conventional affections (his failure to achieve college loyalty or any of the subdivisions of it, is one example of this, and his attitude toward his mother is another) he was supposed to be unemotional. Because of his indifference to acclaimed success, his positive dislike of looking important, he was written down in the family books as impractical—visionary—quixotic—on the way to becoming, unless he was looked out for, a mere disembodied idealist.

This last attitude he did object to; believed he had as much common sense as anybody, and resented the notion that he needed looking after. But for the rest, he adopted the family characterization as a working basis.

If he had been disposed to confide to any one a true account of his emotional states the night before, from the time he arrived at the plant until he left the girl at the door of Alice Hayes' apartment, he would have said that except for about five minutes after Gregory had made that remark about rose-water and powder-puff methods, he had been perfectly cool—a little abnormally cool, if anything. A man might have been forgiven for getting excited over that kidnaping affair. But he, fortunately, had not.

Also, he would have said that his brother Robert's attempt to import a sex-element into his affair with the girl was a sickening calumny. You couldn't blame Bob. He had sex on the brain—had had since he was ten years old. But it was a pity that an otherwise good chap like that, should go so far wrong.

That blazing young anarchist he had rescued from the detectives had given him a glimpse of a point of view that to him was new and most disturbing. He wanted to know more about it—wanted to make sure he understood it. That was why he had spent most of the night thinking how and when he should see her again and what he should say to her when he did. That she had an extraordinarily vivid and stimulating personality was, of course, true. But the fact that she was a woman, was, as far as his interest in her went, wholly fortuitous and unessential. Of course, being a woman, she did things differently from the way a man would have done them. A man, it might be conceded, wouldn't have bitten his hand in the first place, nor have kissed it afterward.

He wished he might have made out what it was she said, almost voicelessly, her face bent over that hand, in the moment of their parting. He wondered if it would be possible for him to ask her, when next they met. It was a breathless notion.

He had considered trying to see her again that day, but during the morning he had decided against it. Evidently, from what she had said last night, there was a literature of syndicalism, and he must try to find and read some of it, in order not to be too great an ignoramus, before he talked to her again. He'd go down to the Crerar Library the first chance he got and see if he could find anything. Then, it was possible that Rodney Aldrich might know something about it. His information was sometimes found to have proliferated out into strange and uncharted territories. But he was, somewhat surprisingly, getting married within a week or two, to a young girl student in the University, and might he hard to find.

It may be questioned whether these prudential resolutions would have held in any case, but the talk around the family dinner-table put an end to them. His father had given him, explicitly, a message to the girl. And, in the light of what Gregory had said, it became important to deliver it at once. Her decision, as reported by Gregory's spy, to remain away from Riverdale for two or three days, might easily enough have been dictated by the belief that her reappearance there would be the signal for another assault, another attempt by the detectives—the more determined for having been twice foiled—to put her permanently out of the way. And, in view of her really fine sportsmanship in reassuring her friends, at the first possible moment, of her safety, it was a simple matter of fair play to tell her that her fears were groundless.

She received him, by appointment, at five o'clock that afternoon. Alice Hayes, with whom he had talked over the telephone, was not at home—rather factitiously not at home, it struck him somehow—though perhaps that notion sprang from the stiff discomfort, shared with him, obviously enough, by Helena, for the first half-hour or so of his visit. It seemed flatly incredible that this young woman and the girl who had struggled with him in the car last night and told him her story, and kissed his hand, could be the same person. She was unbecomingly dressed in a badly-fitting frock that looked as if it didn't belong to her (It did, as a matter of fact, belong to Alice Hayes. Her own things had been badly damaged in the struggle of the night before) and her manners and her speech fitted her no better than the clothes—were full of little conventional observances and school-mistresslike pedantries—things that Grace Drummond had taught her to do, and, more importantly, to avoid doing.

Hugh, sitting in the supposedly easy chair, which she had hospitably insisted that he take, the glare from a brick wall across the court shining horizontally through the low window into his eyes, felt heavily let down. His own speech, he was aware, had become as pedantic and inadequate as hers.

He had acknowledged to himself in advance of their meeting no special expectations regarding it. But he found himself now in a state of exasperated disappointment.

He had begun by conveying his father's message to her—a thing that went naturally into rather set terms, by way of making its assurances more binding. She received it, somehow or other, blankly. He hadn't wanted gratitude, of course, but what he had counted on to break the ice and put him on comfortable terms with her seemed actually to produce the opposite effect.

Then followed, as I have said, the interval of politeness: Alice Hayes and what a good friend she was of Helena's; and how sorry Hugh was not to meet her; and the inviolable engagement that had prevented her being there to meet him. All perfectly sterile and hopeless.

Hugh, at last, determined to get somewhere, began asking her questions about syndicalism. Where the movement started; who its leaders were; wherein they differed from socialists—from anarchists, and so on.

She answered all these questions, some of them at length, and Hugh began getting what he had honestly believed was the thing he had come out here for—information about a new system of ideas—the elucidation of a point of view that was new to him.

But getting all this still failed to satisfy him. What was it he had wanted then? Even now he was not willing to answer that question in so many words. But it was plain even to him that he wanted something more than an abstract and decidedly doctrinaire and curiously half-hearted exposition of a new social philosophy. Where was the fire—the thrill—the electric emanation that had given life to everything she had said to him last night? It came to the pass at last where she had to break off a sentence in the middle in order to bite down an irresistible yawn.

"I am boring you to death!" he said then, and it happened that a genuine emotion of angry disappointment sounded out clear upon the words, instead of the merely polite regret they might have expressed.

He was startled at the sound of his own voice. But this was nothing to the effect it had upon the girl. It roused her, that glint of naked human emotion, as the crack of a branch under the hunter's foot rouses a wild animal. Her eyes came to life again—her face—her body, though the attitude of it in the chair hardly changed perceptibly.

Becoming aware of the difference in her, he let the conventional phrase of apology for his outbreak, that was upon his tongue, die there. There was a moment of taut-stretched silence. Then, with an impatient fling of her body that turned her face away from him, she said:

"Oh, it's all false! This situation between you and me. False! And I hate false things! I believe you hate them, too. We aren't meant to sit and talk. That's what I said last night. We're meant to fight. That's all that a person in your class and a person in mine can do."

"That's nonsense!" he said sharply. "You did say it last night, and then you went ahead and proved that it wasn't so by talking to me, wonderfully, for an hour. The falseness isn't in our trying to talk to each other. It's in pretending that there is any reason why we can't."

Now that the ice was broken, he warmed to the subject eagerly. "That's a mighty superficial view to take of it, it seems to me," he went on, "talking as if we were two pawns of opposite colors on a chess-board; as if the essential facts were that I was nothing but a wooden symbol of my class and you a symbol of yours. We're both human beings before we're anything else, and after we've been everything else. You're Helena. . ." He broke off there with a smile and the explanation, "I have seen your name in the newspapers, but I don't know how to pronounce it."

"Galeece," she told him, with a smile of her own. "And I have always called my first name Heleena."

"Well," he went on, "and I am Hugh Corbett. We have seen life from opposite sides almost, as you say. But that only makes it more interesting and important, in a way, that we should try to understand each other."

"We never could do it," she said in a tone of profound, dispassionate conviction. "No matter how hard we tried. We haven't enough common ground to begin on."

"But we have," he contradicted her. "That's another thing you proved last night—proved it up to the hilt."

"How?" she wanted to know. Her inflection of the word was skeptical, but she turned away from him uneasily, and he thought he saw a heightened color in her face.

"It isn't the opinions people happen to have, that count in a case like that," he said, "any more than it's how much money they happen to have. What makes a common ground between people is their instincts—the sort of things they find they have to do in a difficult situation, whether it's to their advantage or not. And when you telephoned last night, out to your headquarters, to tell them that you were safe and they needn't be alarmed about you—did that instead of taking the advantage that I had put right in your hands—of the chance to make them think you had been kidnaped again. . . Well, you did the sort of thing I hope I'd have done in the same case. It was a piece of fine sportsmanship, that's what it was."

With another of her sudden movements the girl turned farther away from him, so that he could not see her face at all. The expression in it was morose, ironic, contemptuous—but the contempt was not all for Hugh. Her involuntary smile was over the fact that his interpretation of the thing she had done could be so nearly right and yet so utterly wrong.

She had wanted him, passionately, last night, not to leave her. Her whispered invitation, over his wounded hand—an invitation he had either not heard or else misunderstood—had been an explicit confession of this. She had left him to fling herself down on the divan where she was half-reclining now, in a tempest of thwarted desire for him. All that her father represented to her in her life she, for the moment, hated—sterile ideals, hardships, self-denials. These revulsions had come over her before, but never so strongly. She was sick of the strike and every one involved in it—sick of their wrongs and remedies. She wanted to be clear of them for a while, to be let alone so that her thoughts and memories and imaginings could wander where they would. And to bring that result about she had gone, impatiently, to the telephone and told them at headquarters not to bother about her. She was all right and would turn up again when she was ready.

She had been at war with herself about it all night and all today; had been carrying on in her own soul the same sort of bitter recriminatory quarrel that had used to rage between her father and her mother. Her father was defeated but he could not be silenced. It was he who spoke now, when, after a long silence, she answered Hugh.

"It was not good sportsmanship," she said. "It was disloyalty."

Thereupon it broke over Hugh, staggeringly, that he had been guilty of disloyalty to his camp in giving it away to Helena that they had a spy in her headquarters, as, by admitting a knowledge of her telephone message last night, he had done. Confound Greg and his damned detectives! He got up, reluctantly, to go.

She did not rise; on the contrary, leaned back a little farther upon the divan where she sat, in order to look up at him more comfortably.

"The strike does make it awkward, I know," he admitted. "The—the friendship I want between us would be misunderstood, I suppose, by both sides. Because, just now, we are at war, as you said. But the strike can be settled. I am just as confident of that as I was yesterday. Settled in a way that will leave good feeling on both sides. Meanwhile, you will find that we'll fight fair. My father (he's president of the company) is as scrupulously honorable a man as any I know. The things that have happened to you out there have been the result of a misunderstanding. You can be perfectly sure that when you go back to Riverdale you won't be molested. That's what I came out to tell you today. I won't embarrass you with the—the personal side of it, until the strike's over. But when it is over, I am going to make friends with you."

Still she did not rise—did not for a considerable count of seconds, even speak, although the cadence of leave-taking had been unmistakable in his last words.

At last she said, gazing up thoughtfully into his face, "If you were clever—oh, supremely, wickedly clever—more clever than the cleverest man I have ever known—I don't think you are, but if you were—you'd do exactly as you have done this afternoon, and as you did last night."

"I'd like to believe you were," she went on, her face darkening with her voice, as she spoke. "I've been trying to make myself believe it ever since you came." She stirred restlessly, and relaxed a little deeper into the cushions of the divan. "But I can't," she acknowledged with an ironic flash of a smile. "I don't suppose you can see, even now, why it is that I wish it."

The look of complete mystification in his face answered for him.

"You think," she went on, "that you've been making it easier for me to go on fighting against you and your people, with you promises that I shall not be molested. You don't see that you are taking all the fight out of me."

An echo came to his ears as he stared down at her; Gregory's "You've accomplished about seven times as much as Paddock could have. What the devil did you do to her?" He turned abruptly away and strode over to the window.

"I've lived on the hatred of people like you ever since I was twelve years old," he heard her saying. "It was you that made us poor and wretched. It was you that persecuted my father—buried him alive, at last. It's your brutality to me and to people of my kind that has kept me going. I've gloried in it; taken a joy out of it. The only joy I've had has been in hating you and defying you—letting you see that there were some of us you couldn't make cringe to you."

There was the old thrill in this for Hugh—just as he had felt it last night when she told him her father's story. But the next thing he heard reached deeper into him than that.

It was a jerky little sigh. "I guess I'm wearing out," she said slackly. "We revolutionaries go that way. I've seen it happen to others—seen them turning cautious and respectable. I used to think they'd been bought off. Today I've been understanding them. They were spent—burned out. I'm wondering if that has begun to happen to me. I tried last night to make myself believe that you had just been playing me a trick, and that I saw through it and despised you for it. I couldn't. I couldn't help feeling glad that you'd taken me away from those beasts, and sorry that I'd hurt your hand. I couldn't help loving that big, soft, swift car, and the feeling that went along with it, that you were—protecting me; that nothing bad could happen to me while you were there. I despised myself for feeling that—but it didn't do any good."

"It's horrible that any one should have had to live a life in which hate was the only decent emotion there was for him to feel. And especially a person like you. I suppose, though, that nobody but a person like you could have done it. Anybody not unconquerable would have given in. How it makes me feel is like a man who has been cheating at cards without knowing it—cards that were stacked in his favor long before the game began."

There was the ring of undisguised passion in his voice and it thrilled every nerve-fiber in her body. It was no mere abstract sense of social injustice, she knew, that made him cry out like that, but a much older and more primitive thing. He wanted her just as she wanted him.

She rose rather slowly and came across the room to him, halted close in front of him, within reach of his hands, and bending back her head, looked up into his face. Even so, she was able to see the irrepressible gesture his hands made toward her before they dropped to his sides again.

"Good-by," she said. "Oh, no!—Not just for this afternoon! For today it doesn't matter. I'm not sending you home. I mean—good-by for good. You must see it. All our talk today has only made it plainer, that that's the only thing for us to do. You know it's impossible—that thing you call friendship—for us. We should only destroy each other, you and I."

He did not answer, and the silence drew itself out tighter and tighter, like a bow-string in the notch of an arrow.

Whose daughter was she in that moment? She could not herself have told. She believed the truth of everything she had said. And yet, she had come close—close so that all the magic of her physical loveliness could sway his senses. Her own were under a spell, too. She might calculate, but she was not cold. What would she do if that steely resistance of his broke down—if he said "Destruction, then!" and crushed her in a close embrace? Would she obey her father or her mother? Struggle, or rapturously yield? She did not know.

But the crisis passed. The arrow was not despatched. With a sudden slackening of muscles, she turned away.

"I have never met any one like you before," she said, "and it's not likely I ever shall again. It will be—just as well for me if I don't. But I'm glad I did meet you and—and I'm sorry I hurt your hand."

He could not remember afterward what incoherencies of protest against her decision, and determination to resist it, he had stammered out at that. He did remember her, "Oh, please go! Go now!" which had terminated the scene.

But the thing that had paralyzed all his motor faculties, had been that mad, horrifying impulse, as unexpected as the leap from ambush of a wild beast, to seize her in his arms, as she stood there so close before him, and smother those last words of hers in kisses.

The thought pursued him all the way home. It was ice and fire. He shuddered and he burned at the touch of it.

IX

Hugh came down to breakfast on Monday morning with the intention of going out to Riverdale, as usual, with the others. But the family took one look at him and collectively imposed a veto. When a big healthy man like that is sick, his appearance becomes absolutely calamitous. His eyes were dry with fever, and the generally disastrous effect was heightened by an unsuccessful attempt he had made to shave one-handed.

None but his mother gave any particular attention to his bandaged fingers, and she forbore until after the rest had gone. Then, without a word, she reached over, laid hold of his left wrist and pushed back the sleeve.

Already angry red streaks were visible clear to the elbow and the whole hand was swollen.

"What did that young devil of a girl do to you?" she demanded. "Bite?"

"Of course she bit. I had my hand over her mouth so she couldn't scream. I don't believe it's going to amount to anything."

Hugh spoke with evident relief. He had expected to be questioned and had wondered, uncomfortably, whether he wouldn't lie out of it. It had seemed so intolerably ludicrous an admission to make, that a girl had bitten him. Having his mother take his secret by storm like that, was a load off his fevered mind.

She wanted to know now if he had shown it to a doctor, and on being informed that old Hannah was the only surgical authority that had been appealed to in the case, she berated him, in her best manner, for a fool, for a minute or two, ordered him back to bed, and went straight to the telephone.

Hugh obeyed her meekly, for he was sick enough by that time to be glad to have it on an official basis. The doctor who came within an hour found him with a temperature of a hundred and three degrees and a viciously infected wound. Hugh was in bed with it for a fortnight and there were two weeks more of helpless convalescence after that.

That month was an important experience for him. He had never been sick before since childhood, nor disabled in any way. There had never been anything to prevent the prompt translation of his ideas into some sort of action. Now, just at the moment of his life where activity seemed most necessary to him, he was forced into the rôle of a mere passive observer. He was intensely observant from the first, even when his fever projected and distorted the facts he observed into grotesque and monstrous shapes.

The family attitude toward him—dictated by the doctor, who had proscribed excitement—was encouraging—jovial—at times facetious. "Hello, old man! You're looking immense this morning. Can't keep *this* up much longer." That was the note of it. And his nurse read him baseball stories out of *The Saturday Evening Post.* No one would talk about the progress of the strike with him, beyond saying, in reply to his questions, that it was quieting down nicely. There was nothing about that to worry about.

And yet, somehow, he knew about it all the while—knew that it was being fought out in the good old orthodox way; that hunger and hopelessness were being relied upon just as they had been relied on, for the last hundred years, "to bring fools to their senses." That all the time-hallowed tactics of a thousand strikes were being employed to give verisimilitude to the pretense that production was, substantially, on a normal basis again and the strike "practically" broken.

During unnumbered hours, as he lay there, he occupied himself with solutions of his own. Fantastic solutions, of course, when his fever was high, as he recognized when it cooled. But even about the ideas that came to him after the fever had gone away he could feel no confidence—not enough anyhow to nerve him to the task of breaking through the taboo the family had established and forcing a discussion.

But, after all, the strike, though it was the largest object in the landscape his inner eye surveyed, was a long way off and there was a lot of foreground in between. There was nothing important about this foreground; it was merely the daily life and ways of his family, the organization of the household, habitual things, services taken for granted—the family gesture and the family idiom. Except in unusual circumstances or to an abnormal mood, all this is as invisible as air.

Hugh's mood was abnormal. Something had happened that sensitized his perception to all these things. He saw them as if he were some one to whom they were all quite new—as one who took nothing for granted. He saw them somewhat as Helena Galicz would have seen them, or, at any rate, a girl like his notion of Helena Galicz.

A good, wholesome, old-fashioned Americanism was the family tradition of the Corbetts. They never went in for smartness or anglomania. Bob's devotion to polo, for example, was looked at a little askance—was felt to run near the boundary line of the permissible, and came in for a good deal of only half good-natured derision; whereas Gregory's and young Carter's fame at football were matters of unmixed family pride. Harriet Aldrich's marriage to an Italian count, and Christine Crawford's to an English younger son who might quite possibly come into an earldom, were felt to be regrettable experiments. It was fortunate that neither Constance nor Anne had tried to pull off anything like that. All of them, with the exception of Robert, Senior, whose rather pathetic longing to be a landed gentleman was steadily ignored by the rest, were convinced that they were, and took a pride in being, genuinely democratic. Even Hugh, who questioned most things, had never questioned this until now.

But he saw now, or thought he did (he was hypersensitive, no doubt, by way of compensation for his former blindness), how thin a pretense that form of democracy was. They *were* a privileged lot, just as Helena had said. They took it for granted that society should be organized in their favor. They expected to be well served; they wanted the best of everything as a matter of course, and they didn't expect to be put to any trouble to get it.

He heard that arrogant expectation speaking in about half the things they said; saw it swaggering in the hundred unconscious things they did during a day. Why, their very democracy was a form of swagger! It exasperated Hugh, in the light of that new point of view he'd got from Helena the night of the kidnaping—of what she'd said of slave-owners who were not like Simon Legree—good-humored slave-owners who liked to do the decent thing.

He had another source of annoyance against his family, too. But it was one he would not look at quite so squarely. Not once, since his mother's blunt, "What did that devil of a girl do? Bite?" had any member of the family—not even his incorrigible old grandfather— made the slightest reference to the cause of his injury. For anything any of them said to him during their cheery little daily visits, he might have been suffering from some obscure nervous lesion. Of course a concerted silence like that speaks loud. They had held councils over him and it had been decided to take a line—diplomacy was at work. Helena Galicz was being elaborately dismissed from the universe.

But one day he had a letter from her. He had been worrying over

HENRY KITCHELL WEBSTER

what she would think of his disappearance from her life—in the face of his vehement refusal to withdraw from it—but it had not occurred to him that it would be possible to explain it to her. In his imagination, she had dematerialized into that chaotic void from which she had momentarily appeared to him.

So the mere fact that here in his hand was a letter that her hand had written and that the date line at the head of it showed her still to be living in the little flat where he had visited her that Sunday afternoon— the surmise that it would be possible for him to talk to her today— possibly this moment, over the telephone—was tremendous enough. And as for the contents of the letter. . . !

He was in his mother's sitting-room, clad in a bathrobe and packed round with pillows in an easy chair, when a maid, bringing in his mother's mail, handed one of the many letters to him.

"Here," Mrs. Robert said, "let me open that for you."

It was a natural offer to make, for with one hand a mere sling-supported mass of wet bandages and drainage tubes, the slitting of an envelope and the extrication of a letter from it is a complex and laborious matter.

Hugh's sharp disinclination to let his mother do him this small service took him by surprise. He hesitated, palpably, before he put the letter into Mrs. Corbett's outstretched hand. She took it, however, as if she had noticed nothing of the sort, ripped it open and handed it back, and instantly plunged into her own mail.

For half an hour she remained, to all appearance, completely absorbed in it, but in the whole of that time she never missed a move of her son's nor a nuance of his expression. She marked the tremor of his hand as he took the letter from hers; the checked movement to put it, unread, into his pocket, the lapse of minutes before he began to read and the sudden cessation of reading at the end of a line or two. She saw in the set of his muscles the half-translated impulse to get up and walk out of the room and the relaxed abandonment of it. She saw the swift flight of his eye in search of the meaning of a page and then the slow, word by word drinking of it in after the first suspense was satisfied. But it was not until the letter had lain for five minutes safely in Hugh's pocket that she looked up at him.

"Well," she asked then; "what has she got to say? Sorry she bit?"

"Oh, yes, it's from her," Hugh said. "And it's mostly about that. It has worried her, though I don't see why it should."

He was surprised as well as pleased at the sound of his voice—the casual, conversational tone and inflection of it. He had not been sure, when he started, whether any voice would come at all, because the unmistakable, undisguised implications of that letter had bewildered and thrilled and frightened him so that he could not tell which emotion was which.

"Now that they tell me you are safe," she had written, "I have the heart to write to you. I think of you as hating me the way I would hate any one who had done that to me, but then I remember how different you are in ways like that from any one I have ever met and I wonder if perhaps you have—in that mysterious way of yours which I can not understand— gone on thinking of me without any hate at all.

"I do not ask you to forgive me, forgiveness being one of those Christian hypocrisies I hate. Yet there were two days when I found myself wishing I were a Christian—or anything else that could pray or burn a candle for your recovery. That was when there was talk that they might have to amputate the hand. I saw you in my dreams—like that. You see I have expiated—a little.

"It was nearly a week before I heard of your sickness at all. Since then, through Alice, who has a friend who was able to ask, I have had news every day. Often I have walked past that great frowning house of yours. You are incredible enough without that.

"I have nothing to do with the strike any more. I have been out once or twice to Riverdale, but I have no heart in it, and they, I think, have lost confidence in me. Well, they are right to do that. I have gone to work translating a Russian novel for one of the Yiddish papers in New York, and I am offered a job of book-reviewing for a German paper here in Chicago, so you see I am busy enough. For the time, I shall live here with Alice who has a spare room for me through the summer.

"Even if you hate me, will you write a line, just to say you have received this letter and keep me from wondering? And if you do not, will you come to see me again? Or telephone and say where I can come to you?

"I did wrong to send you away. It was wise and prudent to do it; but some things, it says in your New Testament, are hidden from the wise and prudent.

Your 'friend'—if you want her,

HELENA GALICZ

One solid advantage that large rough persons enjoy is that they are never suspected of being tactful. "She knows you've been sick, does she?" said Hugh's mother. "How do you suppose she found out about it?"

This was the one thing in the letter that Hugh could talk about. He explained at length and at random who Alice Hayes was and what sort of newspaper work she did, and he went on to speculate with what he felt to be just the right shade of casual interest as to what her source of authentic information about the Corbett family was. And this led him to a genuine digression. "It was real inside dope, all right," he said. "She knew more about it than I did. No one had told *me* that there was talk of amputation."

But he added in the next breath, "I'm sorry she heard about that. ('She,' in this sentence, was not Alice Hayes.) It wasn't her fault, of course, but it gave her a beastly three or four days."

There is no use drawing a herring across the trail if you give the chase a view of the fox at the same time.

"I suppose so," his mother said, and stopped there, though there were wonderful words on her tongue. There sat this son of hers, the one she loved best of all of them, innocent of all concern as to what her own feelings must have been during those two or three dreadful days, worrying over the putative sufferings of the gutter-snipe who had made all the trouble.

Even the tone of her voice must have satisfied him of her sympathy for the jam broke and the logs came down with a rush. He had been thinking about the girl for weeks and never spoken of her to a soul. His mother got it all. The look of her as she rode along to address the meeting, and the way she had looked at other times. The story of her life as she had told it to him in the car. The strange and troubling novelty of her ideas. The amazing education she had managed to get for herself; her linguistic accomplishments. "She makes me feel like an ignorant young schoolboy—though she's five years younger than I."

The almost unbearably exasperating thing about it all to Mrs. Corbett was that Hugh evidently believed that he was exhibiting a completely impersonal detachment, amusing his mother with a character sketch of the sort of person her own orbit didn't bring her into contact with. The wire edge of emotion in his voice and the tension revealed by his gestures were grotesquely set off by the carefully casual phrases of tea-table chatter. And it was not a pose he had taken deliberately, either. He believed—or half-believed it.

Why—why were they made like that? All the best of them, anyhow. What purpose of a benignant Creator was served by letting this sex thing strike from ambush? Why could not a nice clean boy like this be given a fair chance?

She stood it as long as she could. Then she ended a thoughtful silence he had fallen into by saying briskly:

"Hugh, will you run away with me?"

He started, as she had expected him to, and flushed dark red. "Run away?" he repeated blankly.

"For the summer," she explained. "I don't care where; Norway if you like. Just the two of us."

He laughed uneasily. "That's a wild idea," he said.

"I don't see anything wild about it," she argued. "You're out of a job. Your grandfather has shut down on the welfare work. You're sick of the family and I'm feeling a bit that way myself. It's a thing that takes us all once in a while. . ."

But under his keen dark stare she felt the plausible geniality dying out of her voice, and at that point the sentence itself died.

"Is there any special reason why you want me to go?" he asked.

"You can't stare me out of countenance," said his mother. "There is a reason, and you know it."

"I know what it is," he retorted, "but it's not what I'd call a reason. Because I saw fit to prevent a dirty outrage like that kidnaping, you think I am in danger of making a fool of myself about the girl—disgracing the family name and so on. The family name would have been nicely spattered, I tell you, if I hadn't prevented it. But the correct thing to do is to carry me off to Europe to get over it. I wouldn't have put a notion like that past Greg to think up, or Bob. But I didn't expect it of you."

She sat still and let him fume.

"Oh, it makes me tired!" he burst out again. "I tell you I've got hold of something new. I've just begun to wake up. That welfare work of mine was all wrong. Or at least, the way I went at it was. I don't wonder it made them wild. There are things I never knew existed, that I want to find out about. Helena Galicz (the name bothered him, but he managed to get it out) can tell me some of them, and I'm going to make her do it. But this notion that just because I don't keep my mind hermetically sealed like a can of tomatoes that would spoil if the air got at it, just because I am willing to look around and see what's happening, and treat people like human beings, whether they happen to belong to 'our set' or not—the notion that because of that I am dangerous; in need of a guardian—carried off to Norway. . . Good lord, mother! That's Greg at his worst; or Bob. But you ought to know better. I'm not in the habit of running after women, am I?"

"You're a good boy, Hugh," she said, and her tone held him silent until she was ready to go on. "But any man in the world can make a mess of his life over a woman. If he's in the habit of it, as you say, he's in a way safer. Take Bob, if you like. I've worried about him a lot. But he'll come out all right—or pretty well, anyhow, in the end. When he marries it will be the right sort of girl. . ."

He snatched that phrase from her angrily. "Some society fluff!" he commented.

"Oh, likely enough," his mother agreed. "But in things that matter she'll be—our kind of person. And he'll probably be faithful to her— pretty faithful, anyway, and they'll manage it. And some day, I suppose, Greg will get his widow."

(This is a chapter in the Corbett annals to which I have not referred. Greg had fallen in love at twenty-five, permanently, invincibly, with a girl who presently had decided that she preferred another man—a painter. But within three months of the marriage the painter had died suddenly and Greg cautiously renewed his suit. She liked him, came to him for advice and so on and eventually, as was apparent to everybody but Greg, was going to make up her mind to marry him. His conduct was conceded to be admirable, but the family found it dull.)

"She's a sentimental little fool," Mrs. Corbett went on, "but that will be just what Greg likes. So he's all right. But you. . . I'm frightened about you, Hugh. That's the truth."

"Well, you needn't be frightened about this girl," he told her. "Heavens! I've only seen her twice."

He threw off the rug that lay across his knees and moved to get up. "I'm going to telephone," he explained, in answer to his mother's look of interrogation.

"Do it right here," she said, with a glance at the instrument on her desk.

She saw the blood come up into his face again, as he hesitated, casting about for an excuse. Then, with sudden pity, and over a lump in her throat, she added, "I'm going out. I'd no idea we'd been talking away so long."

He called after her as she retreated toward her bedroom, "We'll think about that Norway trip, mother. Maybe we'll take it after all."

But that project, as it happened, did not come up again.

Mrs. Corbett shut her door behind her and did not appear again that morning. One disadvantage that a big, rough woman like that labors under is that she never gets anything by crying for it; a fact that no one knew better than this one.

X

M rs. Corbett was right in one of her predictions, at any rate. The strike did kill old Gregory. To put the thing in a different, and perhaps truer, fashion, it enabled him to live all the life he had left in the space of a few close-packed, intensely vivid weeks, whereas at the placid jogging pace he had declined into before the strike began, he might have eked it out for two or three years. Perhaps, after all, it did him a service. There is no doubt he enjoyed that last fight— the reawakening of forgotten faculties—the resumption of the old authority.

To the new school men in the organization—men like Howard and Bailey—he was a revelation. For years they had been regarding him as an amiable old nuisance, smiling over his contrarieties when they could, swearing when they must, and wondering in their heart of hearts how the enterprise had ever managed to grow to the enormous thing it was under his hands. Now they gazed at him with undisguised awe. The decisions of his mind were like the miraculous ax-strokes of a skilled woodsman, swift, heavy, trenchant, and of an accuracy they found uncanny. They understood now why Corbett & Company had grown to the thing it was.

They saw him, to tell the truth, at a little better than his best. This new attitude of theirs—of all indeed who worked behind him, for the old-timers who remembered were glowing with pride in him—was oxygen to his old lungs. He glowed with it.

It is probably fair to say that those last active weeks of his were the best of his life. Of course he had to pay the price. The new heady wine was too much for the old bottle.

Riding home from work in the car with him one late June afternoon, young Gregory noticed that the old man was getting drowsy, his speech thickening, and, looking at him, saw that his face was flushed. By the time they got him home, he had to be almost carried up to bed; and when the doctor arrived an hour later, his diagnosis was hardly needed, the apoplectic nature of the seizure was so plainly apparent.

Old Gregory did not die for more than a month. But he never recovered full consciousness again, nor articulate speech; though sometimes they thought he recognized one of them momentarily. Two nurses took possession of him. His life was over.

And yet he could not be mourned as dead. The fiction of his possible recovery, or partial recovery, must be kept up. Such a situation is nerve-wearing at the best. And in this case of the Corbetts, it was complicated, first by the strike, and second by Hugh. And both these complications they felt they owed to Helena Galicz.

On the subject of the strike Hugh had one long and thoroughly futile scene with his father. It took place in old Gregory's office out at the plant, Hugh having formally asked for an appointment and security against interruptions. He spent a good many hours preparing for it, too; marshalling his arguments.

What he wanted to convince his father of was that the sort of victory their present methods were intended to accomplish would be disastrous even if they attained it. The backbone of contention was the refusal on the part of the officers of the company to deal with any organization, or in any way to recognize the existence of any organization among the operatives.

Hugh was for abandoning this line altogether. He would treat with the organization, such as it was. Indeed, he would go further and refuse to treat with anything but an organization. He would facilitate organization in every possible way—not only as a means of settling the strike, but after the strike was settled. He believed that eventually most of his own discarded welfare activities could be turned over to the administration of the men themselves. He even worked out the scheme in considerable detail.

Of course in his talk with his father he never got as far as that. For Hugh's mere approach to the subject looked to Robert, Senior's, horrified eyes like rampant anarchy. Really, I believe Hugh would have come nearer succeeding with his grandfather.

It would be unfair to characterize Robert Corbett as a mere bundle of negations. He had real abilities. His judgment in many matters was better than his father's; his thinking was of a closer, finer grain. Given a decent chance, he might have made a solid if not a brilliant name for himself.

But he had no such luck. He was cursed with a thin skin, and from childhood he had always winced at the things his father did and said and thought. The old Gregory that you have seen, mellowed by age and success, was a very different person from the one his son remembered. Back in his forties the founder of the Corbetts had been a harsh, unlovely character; his domestic outlook as narrow as his business outlook had been broad—his manner uncouth, loud-voiced, his humor ferociously heavy-handed. It had taken genuine courage and determination on Robert's part to win a college education. Gregory characterized college boys broadly, as a pack of damn fools—empty-headed dudes, and so on.

Granted a boy with any stuff in him at all this sort of thing was bound to produce a reaction. And it did in Robert's case. He grew up with the passionate desire to be everything that his father was not—deliberately perfected his speech and manners; discovered and indulged a fondness for good books, and, eventually, for good pictures. In a word, whatsoever things were lovely and of good report. The good report was essential.

(Why, do you ask, did he marry the wife that he did? Well, to begin with, that barytone voice which had awed and fascinated little Jean Gilbert the first time she had heard it speak, was, when the owner of it was twenty, a ravishing, creamy contralto, and the owner of it as splendidly beautiful a creature as a man might find in a lifetime. She was well-bred, too—an old Philadelphia stock that had been growing in the fertile soil of wealth and leisure since before the Revolution. Her rather outrageous ways were really a revolt against the finicky niceness of her family, just as Robert's mannerliness was a revolt against his father's violence. And then, there was a genuine want in him for her free-moving strength and her outspoken courage.)

The least real thing about Robert was his liberalism—the most purely negative thing. But, since it had never been put to the test of action, he had believed in it for thirty years. Things fell out perversely for him, it may be admitted. His father's sudden assumption of authority at the outbreak of the strike put him in an awkward, uncomfortable situation, and the old gentleman's instantaneous removal in the midst of it, left him in a worse one—several degrees worse, as a matter of fact, than if the strike had killed his father outright. He had been dreaming for years of the things he would do when the power came into his hands—handsome, philanthropic things that would be acclaimed with grateful joy by the operatives themselves, and perhaps editorialized by the newspapers—of the inauguration of a recognizable new era of good feeling to the confounding of agitators and such.

It was exasperating, therefore, to have it work out like this and to find himself put in the position by the one of his own sons from whom he had expected complete sympathy and agreement, of a hard-fisted tory reactionary. If the men would repent, abandon their misguided ways and come back to work, they would find no one readier to take a liberal attitude than he. But to talk of concessions now was preposterous. Such talk, besides, came with particularly bad grace from Hugh, since it was his ill-considered experiments that had caused the trouble.

The scene went as badly as possible from the first. Hugh was never quite at ease with his father; always became, by contagion, ceremonious and elaborate and, in the exasperation of finding himself so, incapable of saying the things he wanted to say.

By the end of an hour they were deadlocked in a state of cold anger. Hugh had, by polite implication, been accused of having caused his grandfather's fatal seizure, of having discredited the family name, and, at last, of wilfully blinding himself to all considerations of reason and propriety in a regrettable infatuation over a woman of a type which his father was unwilling even to attempt to characterize.

At this point, Hugh, who had been on his feet, abruptly seated himself at the desk opposite his father, pulled up a writing-pad, dipped pen in ink, wrote out a formal resignation from Corbett & Company, addressed to his father as president, and left the room.

The break need have gone no further. There is nothing inevitable about these lives of ours, unless one is willing to believe that the minute events and coincidences of them were all written down in imperishable books before the world began. A dozen circumstances that might, apparently, have happened fully as easily as those that did, would have altered matters materially for Hugh.

One of these is the trivial coincidence that he was with Helena on the afternoon they brought his grandfather home, apparently dying. It was at Alice Hayes' flat that they reached him on the telephone and summoned him home. There was a touch of drama about that that impressed them all, including Hugh himself. It was one of those facts that fly to their marks like arrows. It gave to old Gregory's seizure the look of a heavenly expression of disapproval of his grandson's wilful misbehavior. It was the sort of thing people lower their voices to speak about. The fact that, against all reason, Hugh experienced a touch of this feeling himself, made him the more sensitive to, and resentful of, its effect on the others.

That resentment was heavily responsible for the quarrel with his father. On top of that quarrel, his mother made what was, I am inclined to think, a blunder. Hugh came home from it in one of those still rages of his, determined on packing a trunk and getting out of the house, for a while, at any rate. She resisted this determination with every weapon she had—and these were many and formidable. She understood him better than any one else and did not at all underrate the pressure of the emotion his quiet manner concealed. She spent half an hour deliberately goading and taunting him, and eventually managed to provoke the explosion she wanted.

There was none of the ordinary maternal and filial inhibitions between this pair. Hugh could talk to her as he could talk to no one else, and after he had turned loose and told her, in terms which I shall not venture to report, exactly how he felt about all the members of his family—severally and collectively—herself, his father, his brothers, and his sister Anne—who had heard dire rumors of what was in the wind, and had been silly enough to presume upon her status as a married woman and write him a chiding letter—after he had got through all that, he felt, in spite of himself, better.

Whereupon his mother turned good-humored and sensible; pointed out that it wouldn't do for him to go out of town with his grandfather's life hanging by a hair, as it was. The old gentleman was fond of him and in the event of a return of consciousness, which the doctors agreed was probable—possible anyhow—would certainly want to see him. And for Hugh to leave the house without leaving town, would in the present circumstances, be sure to create scandal. Besides, and lastly, Hugh wasn't well yet. His hand was still in bandages—a conspicuous sort of injury. Why, he couldn't eat in a restaurant without summoning a waiter to cut up his food for him. And he was to forget his nonsense and be reasonable. She'd do what she could to see that the others were.

Sensible as her reasoning was, I think it unfortunate that she prevailed over him. The family atmosphere of disapproval was poison to Hugh, and at home there was nothing else for him to breathe. If he could have got out of it altogether, as he wanted to do; if the injury to his hand had not precluded his seeking out and getting a job as metallurgist, if—oh, any one of a dozen ifs, easily conceivable but not worth enumerating, might have turned the balance.

Because, as regarded Helena, Hugh did not really know his own mind. He had, for years, been vaguely expecting that some time or other the transfiguring experience of falling in love would happen to him. Exactly what it would be like he had never taken the trouble to speculate. You knew the real thing when it struck you, at any rate; that seemed to be the almost universal experience. He knew that it excited and gratified physical desires, and gave them a moral justification which, outside its sphere, they lacked; transmuted their base metal, somehow, into fine gold. But all that was secondary to a mysterious primary other thing, a joyous, confident meeting of souls, the thrill of a million tiny points of contact all around their two perimeters.

If Hugh had felt like that about Helena—recognizably anything at all like that—the disapprobation of the family would have given him very little concern. He knew their bark was worse than their bite. He had complete confidence in the fundamental good sense of all of them, as well as in the permanency of their affection for him. If what he did proved, in the event, to have been well and wisely done, they would eventually see the wisdom of it and be glad. The only thing they would not forgive him for would be spoiling his life by an act of wilful folly.

Can a man be truly in love when he is capable of questioning the wisdom of it? Hugh was constantly barking his shins over that question during those days.

The girl had taken possession of his thoughts as no other person or interest, however absorbing, had ever had possession of them before. He did not dream about her while he slept, nor while he was in her presence. But all the rest of the time, it is fair to say, he did. For what he supposed to be his thoughts about her had the enormous quality of dreams—like drawings without scale or perspective. He had endless imaginary conversations with her which did not in the least resemble anything they ever said when they talked together. The minutiæ of her life took on grave importance. It was intolerable to him not to know hour by hour where she was—what she was doing. A day that passed without any form of communication with her seemed endless.

And yet, he could not disguise the fact that the comparatively few hours he was able to spend in her society were troubled—unhappy. She was an enigma to him that he made no progress toward solving. He experienced, in talk with her, sudden revulsions, incredulities, as disconcerting as air pockets are to an aviator; they gave him, literally, the sensation of vertigo. He never fell quite to the ground; always, before that final, fatal smash, she swept him aloft again.

The sheer woman of her, roused, excited—half intoxicated him. The texture of her skin, the contours of her wonderful body, the color and warmth of her, the moments of arrested motion, tense and almost as terrifying as those of a panther, and the wonderful relaxations, luxurious—intolerable, almost,—which these subsided into—all thrilled and tormented him.

It horrified him to find himself desiring her, as there was no blinking the fact he did, in that base animal fashion, while what he had always believed to be his higher emotions were still perplexed and contradictory. The fact that he was capable sometimes of suspecting that she deliberately tempted him, roused him to a passionate denunciation of his own unworthiness. With equal wrath, he repudiated the notion which sometimes flamed up in his mind, that the same fiery animal passion which burned in his veins, burnt also in hers. He had always entertained, quite simply and without speculation, the conviction that no nice girl—no decent woman—ever felt like that. Were the impulsive caresses, then, that she half offered him and hesitatingly withdrew, mere symbols of affection? He tried hard to believe that.

He would walk the streets for hours after he left her, literally limp with exhaustion and in a state of mind that it is no exaggeration to call torment. Was he in love with her? Was the beautiful, confident, perfect thing he had always imagined the phrase to mean, a mere pink-and-white confection of the romancer? Was it merely a silly caste distinction that held him back? And was he, in his soul, a snob? Or was he what Bob would think him, if he knew the facts, a plain damned fool for making all this fuss instead of simply going ahead, seeing how much he could get, and taking it? Was Helena in love with him? Would she be heart-broken, or simply relieved of an expiation his crippled hand had saddled her with, if he left her now, as she so often urged him to do? What did those sullen, bitter moods of hers, that he so often found her in, or provoked her into, mean?

The way of the transgressor is hard, no doubt. Bob (I feel compunctions about overworking this essentially decent sort of chap as a horrible example in this connection; but he comes naturally to hand) had had his bad days, and even weeks. He had sworn many a fervent "never again!" But the sum of all Bob's remorseful sufferings over all his escapades, from his first boyish one to his latest man-of-the-world affair, would not weigh down the beam against what Hugh went through in that one month.

It is to be noted also, though the paradox is beyond my powers to explain, that his sense of rectitude was not a support to him. Some imp within him used it merely as a target for shooting arrows of contemptuous interrogation into. Was there something queer about him? Did he lack something of being a regular normal man?

A crisis came in the affair at last one afternoon up in Alice Hayes' sitting-room.

Hugh hated that room. It wasn't big enough for him. When he stood up in it, his head felt the oppression of the ceiling, and when he sat down in it, his legs stuck out too far and got in the way of all and sundry who wanted to move about in it. Night and day it was badly lighted, and he was always peering, trying to see more than he could. There was a cramped little fumed-oak desk in the corner of it, where he frequently found Helena writing. He used to try to persuade her to go out into the near-by park with him, but seldom with success. She usually pleaded that she was not dressed for the street, and this was plausible.

The facts were that she had no good-looking street clothes. What she had, extinguished her—made her look dowdy and second-rate. She was at her rapturous loveliest in a suggestion of undress—a kimono— any old rag of a thing, it didn't matter—and bedroom slippers; her hair a wilderness. Besides, she hated exercise and out-of-doors generally.

On this particular afternoon, Hugh found Alice at home, although, as usual, on the point of departure. She was a pleasant, demure, slim little thing absurdly young-looking when one considered what she did and what an appalling lot she knew. Hugh liked her; found her infinitely easier to talk to than Helena, and was often curiously distraught in his mind as to whether he was glad when he found her there, or sorry. And today, though he fiercely wanted Helena alone— he knew he did; there couldn't be any doubt about that—yet he found himself prolonging Alice's stay, postponing her departure, with a sort of desperate ingenuity.

When she did go finally, Helena broke the stiff silence that followed her departure by asking Hugh why he had not gone with her. "She's the one you really like," she added morosely. "She's much more your sort than I am."

Hugh snapped at her for that, which was, a moderately penetrating observer might have guessed, exactly what she wanted him to do. And for five minutes they quarreled. Hugh hated himself for this—for the things he found himself saying. He didn't want to say them or think them. He realized that he was incapable of following either his judgment or his inclination. It was like driving a car in a deeply-rutted road. You slid down, somehow, into those grooves and couldn't get out.

Then, with one of her lightning changes of mood, she repented, came over to him humbly and said she was sorry; picked up his wounded hand, noted with a little cry of joy the lighter bandages, and pressed her lips down softly on the newly-exposed palm.

He buried the other hand in her hair. He was trembling all over. All the power of resistance he had, all the inhibitions of chivalry and respect for womankind—all that he classified broadly under the term decency, was barely strong enough to hold him down to that merely brotherly caress.

The crisis passed. She took her lips away and his right hand, that had been in her hair, fell at his side again. She made a gesture of impatience and seated herself on the divan.

"I'm not fit for human society today," she said, and told him why. She'd just finished a short story. She'd been writing ever since he left her yesterday; all night, or most of the night, and today, until a half-hour before he came.

"A story?" he said. "That's new, isn't it?"

But it seemed she had tried it before. It was a thing she was passionately eager to do. She hated the drudgery of translating and book-reviewing—all the stupefying, stodgy things that the necessity of getting a living condemned her to. And then, none of the foreign-language papers that she had access to paid more than pittances. Fiction in English, if she could make it go, would be a way out.

Hugh asked if he might hear the story, and she read it to him.

There were two of Hugh who listened. 'Way down inside, and barely audible, was the incorruptible critic, who writhed at the crudity—at the lack of temper—at the lumps of undigested syndicalist propaganda—at the transparent naiveté of the fictional devices the story employed to make itself a story. But all the rest of him was a furious partisan busy shouting the critic down; calling the crudities strength, the lack of temper, passion, and trying to set up a comparison between its harsh formless dissonances and those of the newer Russian music, which he was just learning to admire. Gradually, though, he stopped listening altogether; just looked, as her preoccupation with the manuscript enabled him to do, and drank down the sound of her voice.

She thanked him rather wistfully, when the reading was finished, for the kind things he managed to say about the story, and this note—one he had never heard before in her voice, nor seen in her dark eyes—set him harder at the task of convincing her that she had done well. In his own ears, the things he said sounded false and flat. But she seemed rather pathetically pleased with them.

"However," she said thoughtfully, "it won't do any good. No editor of a popular magazine will think about it like that. I don't suppose they even read things that come in from people they have never heard of."

Hugh, as it happened, shared this wide-spread delusion with her. "I know a chap that writes," he said after a moment of cogitation—"not fiction; special articles, but he knows all the editors and stands well with them. Barry Lake, his name is. He's a great friend of Rodney Aldrich's. Give me the manuscript and I'll get him to read it. If he likes it, he can pass it on to somebody—tell us whom to send it to, anyhow, and write a letter so that he'll read it."

He had to say this rather more resolutely than he wanted to, because the words were uttered over the protest of the critic in him, who by now was fairly clamorous, assuring him that Barry Lake wouldn't like it a bit better than he did; and that he would look an ass, going to a man he knew no better than Lake on such an errand.

But the moment he had said the words, the critic was forgotten. Because Helena began quietly to cry. The tears just welled up into her eyes until presently they spilled over and her efforts to check them seemed only to make them come the faster. In all the wide range of emotional states Hugh had seen her in, she had never been near tears. She seemed no less amazed over them now than Hugh himself.

"I don't know w-why I'm crying," she said desperately, when the fact was beyond concealing. "It's too silly."

"It's the writing all night, I suppose," said Hugh, in a voice as ragged as hers. She had thrown herself down on the divan, her face in the cushions. He seated himself gingerly on the extreme edge of it and, with an awkward hand, touched her shoulder—her hair, and finally took one of her hands in his good one. She abandoned it to him, passively, but she seemed to find some comfort in the contact. Her sobs quieted and presently ceased and at last she looked up at him.

"You haven't any room," she said. "You're sitting on nothing," and moved so that he'd be more comfortable.

"It wasn't the writing," she began at last. "It's easy for me to write, and it never hurts me to go without sleep. The thing that just demoralized me was your—kindness. It's new to me, and, somehow, it hurts. I didn't believe in it at first. I've spent hours trying to figure out what things meant. And then I came to see at last that they didn't mean anything, except just—that you were kind. And this last thing got me, somehow."

Hugh wanted to know what she meant by "this last thing." His offer to show her story to Barry Lake? There was nothing much to that, that he could see.

"There was," she contradicted. "You hated the story and you hated the thought of showing it to your friend. You felt it would make you look foolish in his eyes. But you were going to go ahead and do it just the same."

The clairvoyant truth of this analysis of his feelings was too much for Hugh to deny convincingly. He tried, but quickly shifted the issue.

"Anyhow, there's nothing extraordinary about it. Most people are kindly disposed, I've found."

"I haven't," she said.

And when he exclaimed incredulously at that she went vehemently on.

"It's true. I've never found kindness. People have been in love with me," she said, "—men and women. And they have made sacrifices for me. Grace Drummond did. But she wanted them paid back. She kept an account, put her grievances away, just the way she put her savings in the bank, to draw interest. And it's been the same with all the rest."

"But you—you don't keep any account at all. I have never made you anything but trouble from the first when I began by hurting your hand, and you"—she smiled as she said this, and the tears flushed up into her eyes again—"you gave me a nice clean handkerchief to wipe the blood away with. It's been like that ever since. You haven't let me pay anything back. You haven't—*wanted* anything."

"That," he said hoarsely, "—that's not true."

She turned a sudden plunging look into his eyes, and raised her head slowly from the pillow so that her face came nearer his.

There was a breathless little silence. Then, without any voice at all, he said, "Helena!" and she understood that it had come at last.

She drew in a long rapturous sigh, as her white arm slipped around his neck. Her head dropped back on the pillow, and his followed it.

XI

Constance Crawford was having dinner alone with her father that night at the Corbett house. It was the week of the Republican convention—the famous steam-roller convention which renominated Taft—and most of the family were down at the Coliseum. The flickering existence of the not quite dead old man up-stairs had materially subdued their interest in politics, but not suppressed it altogether. They were divided as usual: Gregory, Bob, and Carter (about to enjoy his first vote) were all determined adherents of "Yale's greatest son." Their mother was a fire-breathing Rooseveltian. She was engaged, at the moment when Constance and her father sat down to dinner, in shouting "Robber!" at Mr. Elihu Root, magnificently oblivious of the consternation she was causing the other occupants of the Republican committeeman's box, in which she had rashly been invited to sit.

Her husband was not attending the convention, being equally disgusted with the tactics of both wings of the party. He was opposed to toryism. No man was more progressive, in the true sense of the word, than he. But he did not countenance Mr. Roosevelt's methods—did not see, in fact, how a gentleman could.

Constance herself had spent the afternoon at the convention with her husband and Jean, but had had enough of it by dinner-time and gone home to keep her father company. Also, she hoped for a visit with Hugh.

She was fonder of Hugh than of any of her other brothers, and had never lost the maternal attitude which four years' seniority had given her in their childhood. And being one of those open-eyed young women, whom marriage does not stupefy (and to those whom it does not affect in this way, it is the beginning of wisdom), she had more of an inkling into her brother's perplexities than any of the rest of them except his mother.

It was Constance's belief that he was being shockingly mismanaged at home. She was quite at one with them in wishing Hugh well quit of the girl. The notion that he might marry her was simply appalling and hardly less so (more so, of course, she tried as a respectable upholder of morality to believe) was the thought that he might already have struck up an illicit relation with her. But the surest way, she felt, of hounding him into one or the other of these quagmires, was by adopting the precise course to which the family as a whole had committed itself. A little decent, friendly sympathy, she felt, might pull him through.

She flushed with hot impatience over the tone with which her father answered the butler's inquiry whether Mr. Hugh was dining at home tonight. Mr. Corbett was glacially ignorant of his son's whereabouts. He might come in later, but dinner was not to be held back for him. So Hugh's vacant place confronted them reproachfully through the whole meal.

She tried once, by means of a cautious question about him, to make an opening for speaking her mind—or a piece of it, anyhow—upon the subject, but her father put a lid upon the project and clamped it down. Hugh's present conduct was not a matter which he was willing to discuss with any one, least of all, with his daughter.

But he was incapable, she saw, of really thinking about anything else. They made talk about old Gregory's condition, vied with each other in small insincerities to the effect that he was really getting better, chatted about Constance's children, the phenomenal growth of the baby, and so on, and at last her father launched a half-hearted explication of his political views.

At nine o'clock Constance pleaded the immediate necessity of beginning her long drive out to Lake Forest and said good night to him. "I want to see Hannah before I go," she added as she left him.

She found the old woman up in the housekeeper's room, and asked, without pretext, for information about Hugh.

Old Hannah was very tight-lipped and tried to convey, without asserting the fact, the impression that she knew nothing whatever about him. Under pressure, however, she admitted that he had come in half an hour before and gone to his room, having declined dinner or even a tray.

"I wouldn't have told you that, if it wa'n't that he looked sick. But don't you go bothering him," she admonished Constance. "I reckon he's had enough of that lately to last him quite a spell."

She did not knock at his door; merely said, "It's Constance. May I come in?" as she was in the act of opening it. She heard some sort of muffled reply, that was not at any rate a peremptory order to get out, so after a momentary hesitation, she stepped inside and shut the door behind her. Then, since her knees went wobbly all of a sudden, she leaned back against it and hung on to the door-knob for support.

A hand-bag and a suit-case stood open in the middle of his bed, amid a litter of clothes and toilet things, and Hugh, with his back to her, collarless and in his shirt was clumsily trying to pack them. She could only suppose, of course, that the fatal blow had fallen. He was making his preparations to run off with that girl.

"Going away?" she managed to ask, and he answered curtly, but still in that oddly muffled tone, "Yes."

That was all between them for quite a little while. She cast about desperately for something reasonable to say, but could not find a word. Presently, though, he turned around—there was something on the table between them that he wanted in his packing—and she saw his face. At the sight of it, she fairly cried out. It was pale, haggard—absolutely the face of a man in torment.

He said savagely in answer to her cry, "Shut up!" But this was a mere reflex thrown back by his overstrung nerves. Then he laboriously pulled himself together. "Sorry, Connie," he said, "only I can't stand a fire-alarm tonight. If you will just go away and let me alone. . ."

Her eyes filled up and she said over a break in her voice, "Oh, you poor dear boy!"

At that he turned away and dropped into a chair. And she, coming around behind him, bent down over his head and pressed her hands against his face.

"If it was making you happy," she said after a while, "I wouldn't care. But, Hugh, dear, if it makes you feel like this. . . Is it too late now to stop? Do you have to go away with her? Oh, not tonight, anyway!"

"I'm not going away with her," he said. "I don't know where I'm going. I'm just going to get out of—this."

Constance was fortunate in having escaped the family irritability. There were few jerks or starts about the things she did. The chief of her charms, indeed, was a lovely legato of thought and movement. She was not a wit nor a beauty—she was a fine, wholesome, good-looking young woman, inclined to freckle—but her social success was indisputable. It was recognized that she had accomplished an extraordinary feat in having managed to live on terms of unbroken amity with her mother-in-law; for old Mrs. Crawford, who had been in her day both a beauty and a wit, was, to put it bluntly, a tartar, and when Constance had married her only remaining son, there had been a lively expectation of squalls. But the simple fact was you couldn't quarrel with Constance.

That beautiful poise of hers stood her in good stead now as, bending over her tormented brother, she learned the unhoped-for and electrifying fact that something serious, perhaps conclusive, had happened to his affair with "that girl." In his state of acute hyperesthesia, the faintest manifestation of surprise, let alone exultation, would have taken him like a blow. But the soothing movement of his sister's hands over his face remained just what it had been before he spoke.

After a little while, unhurriedly, she left him and went over to the bed.

"I'll finish packing for you," she said. "It must be hard to do with only one good hand."

She felt all the time like a burglar breaking into a house. She had a plan—no less than to steal her brother away and carry him home with her. But she knew that if she alarmed him by a single false move, stumbled over any of his inflamed sensibilities, the plan would come to naught.

"Frank's going away, too," she said presently, in the absent-minded meaningless way possible only to persons who are busy with something else at the same time. "It breaks his heart to leave the convention. He's down there now. But the *Lusitania* gets in on Friday with Mother Crawford on it—she's been visiting Christine, you know—and he has to be there. He'll have to go up with her to Bar Harbor, too, I suppose. And the two boys are out at the farm with Mademoiselle, so that leaves me only the baby, and Jean."

She finished packing, he putting on a soft collar and a coat meanwhile, without another word. Then, "I guess that's everything you'll want—for a week or so," she told him.

"Much obliged, Connie," he said, and from his tone she guessed he was thanking her for what she had not done rather than for what she had. She was safe so far. But did she dare risk the sudden irrelevance of the invitation she wanted to give him?

"I must be going on," she said. "I'm driving out home tonight."

"I wish you lived here," he told her, and thus gave her the cue she had been praying for.

"Come and live with me for a while. That'll be much easier than going anywhere else. And we won't bother you, Jean and I."

There was a long silence. Constance held her breath.

"She hasn't caught any more burglars, I suppose," he said at last. "She must be quite a young lady by now."

"She never will be," his sister answered confidently. "She's a darling. Wait till you see her."

With that she picked up the lighter of his two bags and started to the door with it deliberately misreading his gesture of protest. "Oh, I can manage this easily. Come along."

He took up the other bag and followed.

Constance fell asleep that night under the comforting conviction that she had done well. It might be premature to say that Hugh was already saved from the clutches of his beautiful anarchist, but at all events the tide had turned that way.

They had talked very little in the car and not at all to the point. She could only guess at the nature of the thunderbolt which had fallen on him that afternoon; some disillusioning, sickening revelation, most likely, of Helena's real character and her designs upon him. But Constance had been aware that with every mile of the ride he had been collecting himself; that the terrible tension that had racked him was relaxed, and that her own presence comforted him. By the time she got him home he was sufficiently his natural self to pass her husband's inspection—the only thing she had dreaded. But Frank, as it turned out, was not there.

Jean came into the hall when she heard them. She flushed brightly at the sight of Hugh, and there was no mistaking the pleasure that kindled in her eyes. But she was, it appeared, struck speechless, so that Constance, with a laugh, asked what had become of her voice. Then, with that little squaring of the shoulders which he had not forgotten, she recovered it.

"I had meant to ask Aunt Constance," she said, "whether I should call you Uncle Hugh. But I didn't, and. . ."

It brought a lump into Constance's throat to see how the haggard look left his face at the sight of the girl and the sound of her fresh young voice. Sweet, clean, unspoiled, she did not even suggest by contrast that other one who had been tormenting him. He almost laughed when he said that if she tried to call him uncle he would tell her she'd grown, and forced her, by a direct question, into calling him Hugh. There was a sort of contented gravity about her smile when she did it, and it lingered as she turned to her aunt and explained her genuine uncle's absence. He had stayed in town for a very exciting political conference at the Congress Hotel—it might last all night, he said, and had sent her home in the care of that *pretty* Mrs. Williamson.

Everything was coming out, Constance felt, exactly right; even Frank's absence helped. With him there, they wouldn't have raided the pantry for crackers and milk, in the Arcadian way they did, nor parted for the night on quite the same note.

A week of that would do the business, she believed. She'd get her mother on the phone tomorrow and arrange for the establishment of an absolute quarantine; no mail to be forwarded, no messages, nothing. The girl probably wouldn't let him go any easier than she could help, but she simply shouldn't be allowed to get at him.

It was a good plan, founded on a close guess at the nature of Hugh's trouble. He was suffering, when she found him, from a spiritual shock, just as she supposed. But in guessing about the revelation which caused the shock she went wrong.

Hugh would have supported, I believe, the sort of discovery Constance had in mind much better than the one he made. Had Helena said, out of the depths of shame and grief, "I'm not fit to marry you. I'm not—good!" If she had forced the fact upon him with a detailed confession; a story of the early violation of her innocence— even a draggled recital of subsequent affairs—and concluded it by telling him that she knew what true love meant now and with that knowledge realized that she was not worthy of it—if she had told him that, she would have dealt him a blow, indeed, but one that his spiritual forces were, unconsciously, braced to bear. His emotional reactions would have been comprehensible to himself; indignation—pity. He had already dug the channel for that flood, though he did not know it.

But what Helena had said—boasted, indeed—had been the contrary thing. And in her fiercely exultant whisper, "You're the first!" he had experienced a stab of inexplicable horror. In the light of it he read, as in a lightning flash, her intention of giving herself to him, utterly, then and there. He saw the sudden liberation of the beast, which, since adolescence it had been his pride to conquer and control; the defacement, under the imputation of mere cowardly caution—of all his ideals regarding women, chivalrous respect, delicacy.

The action that all this translated itself into, had been a violent wrenching away from her embrace, that left them staring at each other: he, bewildered, crimson, utterly inarticulate; she, darkly incredulous, with anger smoldering in her eyes. To his miserable attempts to explain the thing that had happened to him, she got no clue at all, until his stammering out of something about "marriage" enlightened her.

At that, however, the smoldering spark in her eyes leaped into a flame.

"Marriage!" she cried. "Did you think I was going to marry you?—Would marry anybody?" It was the beginning of a torrent.

Hugh had never seen any human being in an unbridled transport of anger before. It was simply, of course, her frustrated passion for him finding another vent for itself. Her words were molten incandescent metal that clung and seared wherever they struck. The burden of them was the contemptible, cowardly hypocrisy and the equally cowardly tyranny of marriage. True love was degraded by all association with it. It was an infamous slavery, which a base greed for possessions had imposed upon the world. And this was what Hugh had dared suggest to her!

She fascinated while she horrified him. He was not able to terminate the scene by the simple expedient of going away and leaving her. He had no volitional activities left. But at last, her fury having exhausted itself, she curtly ordered him to go. And he, blankly, and without a word, obeyed.

How much later it was when he encountered old Hannah in the up-stairs corridor in his father's house, or where he had been in the meantime, he did not know. His soul, during that time, had been on the rack.

Any form of mental anguish escapes, I believe, the ultimate intolerable turn of the screw, if only the emotion be appropriate to the circumstances which have produced it. No matter how terrible may be the lacerations of grief one suffers from the loss, for example, of wife or child, there is a measure of comfort and support in the sense that his grief is something he is recognizably entitled to—something that will instantly be understood by all acquainted with the fact upon which it is based. Even the criminal, I believe, out of the depths of remorse, derives a certain support from the sense that remorse is what he ought to feel.

Hugh, under however staggering a revelation of the unworthiness of the woman he loved, would have felt that support. The shock of discovering to be vile what he had believed, without misgiving, to be pure and beautiful, would, of course, have bewildered and stunned him. But his grief would at least have been the normal thing—explicable, anyhow, to himself, and, probably, to a good friend like Constance. And even if, on that horrible afternoon, his part and Helena's had been reversed; if he, carried by passion beyond all decent bounds, had met an outraged fury of resistance, his guilty shame would have been the normal thing to feel.

He was shamed now. But, inexplicably, by his own decency and self-restraint; by the fact that he had not acted according to the conventional masculine ideal. Something in him, older than his conscience, and deeper down, had been outraged and was making war upon him.

There is no such thing as thinking one's way out of a situation like that. It is immitigable. Ring down the curtain on it, if you can, and get away—out of the theater altogether. Take to the woods.

I can not imagine anything that would have done this service for Hugh better than the scheme Constance had effected, of taking him home with her and turning him loose to play with young Jean Gilbert. But for the interposition, once more, of what you may call, according to your metaphysical preferences, Providence or blind chance, I think it would have worked.

Constance shooed them away next morning after breakfast, and, it being a fine bright day, with just a nip of the east in the air, they went down to the beach and presently found themselves occupied in building an impregnable medieval castle in the sand, with moat, barbican and keep, all complete—an enterprise which made it easier to talk by removing the necessity for thinking up things to talk about.

It was a delicious morning for Hugh. It did not, of course, obliterate the memory of yesterday afternoon. Sometimes the very intensity of the contrast it presented to that other scene brought the other back with the terrible stabbing twinge of a wound, so that he turned pale and the sweat beaded out on his forehead.

But the contrast also gave it something of the monstrous unreality of a nightmare that he was waking from. Both worlds could not be real; Helena's lurid one and this that Jean had taken him into. Out here, in the frank blaze of sunshine, his eyes resting with an indescribable sense of comfort on this girl, who frankly loved it, this girl so sound, so exquisitely clean—this girl whose transparent child's affection for him was just beginning to wear the reticent grace of womanhood, the nightmare receded.

He found a deep satisfaction in the neat simplicity of her dress, in the tidiness of her hair, in the way in which—without stiffness and utterly without prudery—she managed not to sprawl. Such facts might seem superficial, but they were not. They were true indicia of the girl herself. There was nothing "nice" about her, in the opprobrious sense of the word. It was true, as Constance had said, that she would never be a young lady. That fine resilient rectitude of hers was no more the product of cautious restraints—mean little prudential fears—than the straightness of her strong young back was the product of confining whalebone and laces.

He had seen her only rarely since Anne's wedding—two or three times last summer, after his final return from Youngstown and before she went away to school, and once during the Christmas holidays. Since the beginning of this summer's vacation, she had been spending a month with her father and mother down at San Antonio, and had only just returned. The odd, unclassifiable relation they had started off with during Anne's wedding festivities, had remained a mild sort of family joke. Her genuine uncertainty as to whether she should address him as uncle, or call him by his first name, illustrates the nature of it. They were not related at all by blood, and yet both belonged to the same family; and he was just as much younger than her mother as he was older than she. So there was no conventional label to attach to the affection Hugh felt for her, and no need for trying to find one. The family jocularities on the subject would have annoyed him only if he had seen them resulting in any self-consciousness on the girl's part.

It had occurred to him last night, remembering the bright blush with which she had greeted his unexpected appearance with Constance, to wonder whether she had heard any talk about his affair with Helena. It wasn't inconceivable that Frank might have blurted out something in her presence. The whole lot of them had been talking about it, of course.

Down on the beach this morning, he forgot that fear. Work on the castle became desultory and finally ceased altogether as the girl's talk drifted out of the shallows of lazily amusing description of her school life into deeper channels. She had her perplexities, had Jean—not trivial, either. That month she had been spending with her father and mother had focused them.

"I hated to come away," she said; "back to all this. Oh, I love Aunt Constance—and Uncle Frank—" This addition was a dutiful afterthought—"but I don't think I love grandmother—at all. She's awfully nice to me—that is, she's always giving me things and—and showing me things she says I'm to have when she dies; but she makes me feel as if she was doing it to—buy me away from mother. And as if I was letting her. It's rather—horrid."

Her color came up a little and her eyes searched his face. "You don't mind my telling you about it, do you? You see, there's no one else I *can* tell. Because if father and mother knew how I felt, they wouldn't let me come back. But I know father wants me to see it through because he thinks it will make mother happier and be good for me, and mother wants me to because she thinks it will keep him from worrying over not being able to give me all these"—she stopped to smile good-humoredly over the word—"advantages, himself. And then, of course, it would seem so beastly ungrateful to Aunt Constance."

"It's nice, isn't it," she added, "to have things to do that there isn't any doubt about—clear, straight things that don't tangle up? It's funny, though. This has got clearer just from talking to you about it, though you haven't given me a word of advice. You couldn't, of course. It's one of the things that's up to me. But it's been sort of—comforting, the way you listened."

A fantastic impulse came upon Hugh—it must be fantastic, of course, only somehow he couldn't make it feel that way—to confide his trouble to her; the whole of it—every scrap and rag of it. He felt that it would be an entirely possible thing to do; as easy as with any one else in the world it would be flagrantly impossible. She'd have no advice to give him, of course. But just as she would sit there gravely listening, the horror of the thing would, he believed, blow away.

It was a crazy notion, of course; so obviously impossible as to require no active effort for its repression. But just the momentary entertainment of it left him with a comforting little glow in his heart—a glow that remained after they had set to again and finished their castle and come back to the house for lunch.

They had made their plans for tennis that afternoon. But it was just as they were leaving the lunch-table that the telephone message came in from the big house on the Drive that old Gregory Corbett was dying at last. Hugh and Constance must come home at once.

XII

The old gentleman was dead before they reached the house, but this fact had no importance, since he had gone out without the momentary—anyhow—recovery of his faculties which they had, unconsciously, been looking for.

Logically considered, his death was a matter of infinitely small significance. At one moment he was discernibly alive, and the next moment he was not. The real bereavement of the family dated back to his fatal seizure weeks before. His place in the world's activities had already closed up as the face of the waters closes upon a sunken ship; so far, that is, as human relations went. And yet, so great is the superstructure of financial and social interests and dependencies which a very rich old man like that carries on his back—a superstructure which remains intact so long as the merest fading spark of life persists in him— that the hardly perceptible fact of its extinction, with the collapse of the superstructure which it entails, becomes momentous.

Life in the great house had gone on, for weeks, much as usual despite old Gregory's disappearance from its régime. The others, family and servants, had, in unequal degrees, missed him, grieved for him; Hannah, perhaps, more deeply than any of the rest of them, but not far behind her Mrs. Corbett.

In the thirty-odd years since her marriage to Robert, she had become much more than a daughter-in-law to old Gregory. The daily routine of those years—especially the last of them—had woven him strongly into the fabric of her life. There were dozens of small services he had been in the way of relying upon her for, so that his habits and his wants had been a larger factor in the organization and disposal of her days than her husband's had been. There was a genuine congeniality, besides, between their tastes and ways and notions. The abrupt snatching away of all that left a void in her that really ached; the more because she was not by temper a sentimental woman.

All the others, of course, had felt twinges of that same ache; poignant, trivial realizations of one aspect or another of the great change, yet these moments had not altered the tissue of their lives materially.

But with the last expiration of breath in that old wrecked body, up- stairs, all accustomed activities of the household stopped, or crept about apologetically; and mysterious new activities wore an air of solemn importance. Voices were hushed, footfalls silenced; the air turned heavy, dark, flower-scented. The mail swelled to unrecognizable proportions, and there was a muffled fusillade of telegrams. And, presently, outlying contingents of the family began arriving, until, big as the house was, its capacities were taxed for their entertainment as they had not been since Anne's wedding.

Anne herself was one of the first of these arrivals, attired in the precise density of mourning appropriate to the occasion and, also in the appropriate degree, visibly stricken with grief. Equally decorous, and hardly less genuine, was the solemnity of a flock of cousins—descendants of the original plow-maker who had quarreled with old Gregory half a century before.

Anne was too late to participate in the family council which decided about the funeral, but she put up a spirited protest against the decision she found adopted. It was *too* tiresome of them to go on clinging to those provincial, middle-western ways just because grandfather had got into the rut of them half a century ago. A house funeral, with the undertaker's men handing little folding chairs about over people's heads and a quartette up on the stairs singing hymns! What if grandfather *had* expressed his dislike (with great vigor and not quite quotably, now that he was dead) of the flummery of church funerals! Other people's feelings, Anne felt, might be considered a *little*. Who knew but grandfather himself might be feeling differently about it—now! It hardly needs saying that Anne's plea, for all the support it got, unostentatiously, from some of the others, effected no change in the plans. The denial of it, however, gave her grief a touch of martyrdom which became her very well.

Constance, the first chance she got alone with her mother, had confided to her what she knew, and added what she guessed, about the fortunate misfortune which had befallen Hugh's love affair. Constance had gone on to say what she thought about the very great importance of treating her brother tenderly—of the avoidance of all nagging references.

Mrs. Corbett's mind approved of this plan well enough, but the state of her emotions was unruly. She was not in a tender mood with Hugh, when she passed Constance's news on to her husband and Gregory—through whom it percolated in the course of a few hours to the others—and Hugh found himself being treated like a providentially returned prodigal. It is hard to express that attitude in words, without burlesquing it, but the sense of it was the intense appropriateness of Hugh's repentance in the face of the disaster his folly had wrought. It was well that he had learned his lesson, even though too late. The effect of this was to reduce Hugh to a state of frenzied exasperation.

All passions, of course, are egotistical. The quality of any strong emotion is to enhance the importance of the possessor of it. One watches irritably from the midst of some interior crisis of his own, the rest of the world going on about its affairs. Hugh, in the crisis of what was incomparably the most violent emotional storm that ever had beset him, would have found the smug, ceremonial grief of those funeral days difficult at best to take his decorous part in. This collective family attitude toward himself was almost intolerable.

He did tolerate it—saw it through—kept his face and his tongue, but at the sacrifice of all feeling of solidarity with the rest of them. He brooded as he watched and listened, like an exile. The man that had once been himself seemed almost as much a stranger to him as his brothers and sisters. He began to see, or believed he began to see, how he himself had looked to Helena. Some of the molten phrases she had used on that last afternoon about the smug hypocrisies of respectability, recurred to him with a look of truth. What a lot of—barnyard fowls they all must look—including himself, ostracised from them though he was by his calamitous attempt to fly—in the eyes of that wheeling hawk up yonder.

On the morning of the funeral, amid the heaps of condolatory messages which the mail brought in, he found a letter from her. He carried it away to his room and locked himself in before he opened it.

It was a well-taken precaution, because at sight of the very first word of its closely written pages, he literally turned giddy and dropped into a chair. That first word was "Dearest." It had been his unformulated conviction, you see, that she despised him; that he must have been, in her eyes, since that horrible moment when he had torn himself from her embrace, a fool—a ludicrously contemptible fool.

That one caressing word set his heart beating to a new rhythm. It was a matter of minutes before he read any more.

"I shall mail this in the station," she wrote, "just before I take the train—so that when you get it, I shall be really gone. It is the only thing to do. I have always known that, only for a little while I have tried to be blind. We love each other—I have loved you since that first night of all when I hurt your hand, and that is what I have gone on doing ever since, loving you and torturing you. Yesterday must be the last time. I must go away now, while the thought of how you must be loathing and despising me gives me courage.

"If this letter is in your hands, it means that my courage has not failed; that I have given you up and gone away out of your life forever. But since I have gone and the most beautiful thing in my life is just a dream to remember, I am letting myself write this letter that will try to make you understand—so that when I think about you I can pretend, at least, to hope that you are remembering me without disgust and loathing.

"I do not believe that a person of your cold race can understand what love means to a person of mine—of my mother's. Love has been my religion—the only religion I have had. Like the old prophet, Elijah, I built an altar and laid a sacrifice on it and waited for the fire to come down from Heaven. I would have nothing to do with the prophets of Baal—you do remember the story, don't you?—who have wanted to kindle that fire for themselves. There have been more of them than I can count. No man has ever come near me until you, who would not have lighted that fire if he could.

"And then you came—and the fire from Heaven—the thing I had been praying for.

"It was nothing doubtful, nothing to question or weigh advantages about. I was fiercely impatient of your restraints. I wanted to give myself *freely*—not to drive a bargain. And I gloried in having something of worth to give—in having for my god an undesecrated altar.

"I don't suppose the girls you have always known would boast to a lover of a thing like that. Maybe there are no prophets of Baal about their altars—or maybe the true fire never comes down from Heaven. I don't know.

"It was hours after you had gone, before I could understand what had brought that look into your face, and when I did, I *burnt* with shame.

"Before that I was blindly angry. I know truer than what I said to you in my wrath, about marriage. The things you have been brought up from childhood to believe, run away with you sometimes, your more lately acquired wisdom tugging helplessly at the reins. At another time I could have talked with you sanely enough about it, argued the difference out, compromised it somehow. But the introduction of it at that moment. . .

"I can not write about it. The shame burns me again. Only—I am *not* vile and what I meant was not. I thought I could explain with just this cold white sheet of paper here before me. But even so, I find I can not.

"You need not try to explain to me. As well as I ever could, I understand already. It is that quality of yours which I have never found a name for, though I have tried many. Kindness, asceticism, inhumanness (is there such a word?)—none of them fits. You are not passionless—that I know—but something—the very force of the passion itself, seems to raise a barrier of steel and ice to confine it. Perhaps chivalry, back in the great days of it, was like that.

"But it is not in me—nor anything that answers to it. . .

"Oh, it would be hopeless, my dear! I was right that first afternoon when I tried to send you away; when I said we should only destroy each other. If it could be a swift destruction—glorious—I could embrace it and 'count the world well lost.' But it would not be like that. As a lost lover, I shall be able to dream about you, and part of the dream will be that sometimes you dream tenderly of me. So I am right to go away. Do not try to find me. Oh, my dearest, good-by! I adore you.

Helena

Upon Hugh, the effect of this letter was simply that of a rising tide on a ship which has grounded itself on a sand-bar. It supported him, relieved the racking strain and stress—leveled him up, and finally, floated him free and made his own will the master of his courses. The tormenting paralysis of indecision which had hung upon him for the past month, was gone. He knew now that Helena loved him. The dark enigma of her bitter moods was solved. And what an ignorant, uncomprehending fool he had been. And in his ignorance, how hideously had he misunderstood her—not once; a score of times. That last scene with her had only been the logical climax of a dozen others.

She had been right in saying he did not know what love was. Now he was beginning to understand it. It was one thing, not two. Soul and body, by a mysterious chemistry, united to make its flame. To her, frank, fearless, free, lighted with her "fire from Heaven," what a contemptible clod he must have seemed.

Only she was not contemptuous. Love had inspired her with a divine comprehension which made even forgiveness unnecessary. She had understood him, somehow, better than he had understood himself.

An hour after he had finished reading the letter, he folded it decisively and put it in his pocket; stood up, stretched his arms, and drew in a long steady breath in the luxury of knowing at last exactly what he was going to do.

He would find Helena—perhaps Alice Hayes would help him there, but if she would not, it didn't matter—he would find her anyway. When he found her, he would, if possible, marry her. His inclination, the dictates of common sense, consideration for his family, all pointed out that course as preferable. He thought she would probably agree to that. Her letter had as good as said so. But if she did not—well, that wouldn't matter either. The first thing to do was to talk with Alice Hayes.

He looked at his watch. It was only eleven o'clock and the service was not till two. If he could find Alice, there would be time to accomplish something now. He walked straight down-town to the office of the newspaper she worked for, at a gait that was as different from his ploddings about the street during the past month as if it belonged to another man. He was going somewhere now, and he went with a swing. His appearance in the local-room, where he was recognized by one or two of the early-bird reporters (here was a worm for them, if they only knew it!), roused a certain amount of curiosity. But to this he was quite oblivious.

Alice Hayes had not come in yet, but in the act of going away, he found her, just arrived, at the mail box.

"Where can I talk with you?" he asked. "Five minutes is all I need."

She led him out into the corridor.

"Can you tell me where Helena has gone?" he asked.

She shook her head.

"Do you mind telling me," Hugh went swiftly on, "whether you really don't know, or whether you are under instructions from her not to tell me? It won't make any difference in what I am going to do, which the answer is."

"I really don't know," Alice said. "Not where she is now. And she didn't tell me a word. Just packed and went. That was day before yesterday." She hesitated and looked up to Hugh's thoughtful face. "I do happen to know though," she added, "that she checked her trunk to New York."

His face lighted instantly. "All right," he said. "That's enough to go on. It was awfully good of you to tell me." He held out his hand for hers. "I'm going to find her and make her marry me. Wish me luck!"

She said she did, in a tone which he, in his preoccupation, saw nothing strange about, and he went away as swiftly as he had come; to the bank first to draw some money, and then home again—all on foot. His perplexities were over.

But he had left Alice in a perfect quagmire of them—a story on her hands—a wonder of a story; a story with which she could beat the other papers in the city by twenty-four hours. And she could earn eternal gratitude—eternal that is, as anything on a newspaper—by just going up to the city editor's desk and telling him the tip she'd got. The story was sure to break sometime, too, with a really tremendous bang.

We have no room, though, for Alice's perplexities. It must suffice to chronicle the fact that when she went to the editorial desk a few minutes later, she merely swallowed hard and asked for her assignment.

Hugh went straight to his room, packed his bag—the same occupation Constance had found him in less than a week before, yet in its spiritual significance antipodally different—laid out traveling clothes, dressed himself in decent black for the service, and went downstairs to the room which had been reserved for the immediate family. Most of them were gathered there already and his entrance, quiet and matter-of-fact as it was, stirred a sensation of uneasy curiosity. It was not that he was different from the son or brother they knew, but that having been different, he had suddenly and almost unbelievably become his natural self again. What could have happened, since breakfast, to work a transformation like that? Had be been able, somehow, to pitch overboard, altogether, his obsession about that girl? It seemed the only explanation there was. And yet. . .

His mother's eyes hardly left his face during the service and they sought it whenever his look was turned away during the ride out to Graceland cemetery. The only time she wept was at the grave-side when she heard his voice come out, clear and steady through the murmur of the others, upon the Lord's prayer. A dozen years ago, when formal religion had been a much more real element in her life than it was now, she had entertained a day-dream, hardly genuine enough to be called a hope, of his becoming a preacher. The memory of it recurred to her now poignantly and at the words, "And lead us not into temptation, but deliver us from evil," a great sob shook her and she clung to his arm. The figure her fancy saw, down there in the grave, was not the old man who had lived his life out to so satisfactory an end, but this boy of hers that all her dearest hopes had centered upon.

Because what the others had only uneasily and vaguely guessed, she had understood to the full. She knew. And when, after their return to the house she heard him ask his father for a few minutes' talk, and saw them go away together to the up-stairs study, she went up to her own room and waited there, with the door open.

It was more than an hour later when she heard her son's steps coming along the hall, but she did not speak until they slackened outside her door. Then:

"I'm in here, Hugh," she said.

He was pale, she noted, but entirely self-possessed, and he had a smile for her that brought the tears again. She dashed them bruskly out of her eyes.

"I've just been telling father that I'm going away," he said.

"To her." She did not inflect the words like a question, but he answered as if it had been one.

"To Helena; yes," he said. "I've got to find her first, but I'm confident I can."

"To marry her?" This was a question.

"If I can persuade her to. It will amount to that, anyhow."

There was a little silence before she spoke. Then, "I'm not going to beg. You've been through everything that can be said, I suppose. It's decided, isn't it?"

"Yes," he said.

"Come over here and kiss me, then, and go."

The tears welled up into his own eyes as he obeyed her. At the end of the embrace she said:

"Come back again, some time, Hugh."

That was all.

XIII

The whole summer of nineteen twelve was a troubled one for the Corbett family, but the blackest period of it was the fortnight that intervened between the day of old Gregory's funeral and the day when Hugh's mother got a letter from him informing her of his marriage to Helena.

It was at the end of this fortnight that Frederica Whitney, having run down from Lake Geneva for a day or two, called up Constance on the telephone. She found her at the Corbett house in town, after having tried Lake Forest first, and asked if she could come to see her.

"Let me come to you wherever you are," Constance said. "This afternoon?—If you're alone, that is. I don't want to see anybody."

Frederica, it appeared, was at the Blackstone. Her own house was such a barn when there was no one in it.

"That's nice," Constance said. "Then, when we have shut the door and turned off the telephone, we can just sit down and talk. It's been ages since we've had a chance."

It was an old, comfortable, mellow sort of friendship, this between Constance and Frederica. They had never put it in jeopardy by subjecting it to any high emotional tension. They were too much alike—took each other too easily for granted, to do that. Both of them had been sensibly brought up; both had married well, and not only in the worldly sense of the phrase. Frederica was a genuine beauty, and a moralist might be inclined, therefore, to allow her somewhat less credit for the even amiability of her disposition, than he would give Constance, who had attained it without that attribute. It was characteristic of Constance that since very early girlhood this sheer physical loveliness of Frederica's was a thing she had enjoyed without a tinge of envy.

They talked for a while on the occasion of this meeting, with only half their minds, about what Frederica had come up to town for, the health and occupations of their respective husbands and children, the growth of their babies—Frederica had one a few months older than Constance's—and, presently, of the occasional satisfaction there was in getting away from them all, of finding themselves in the sitting-room of a hotel suite (It was a pleasant room, so high up that there was nothing but the horizon of a very blue lake to look at) without even one's familiar servants about.

"I have been envying you, this last two weeks, not having any family," Constance admitted with a sigh which was the beginning of genuine confidences.

Frederica was not precisely a waif, but both her parents, as well as her husband's, were dead; her married sister Harriet lived in Italy, and her brother Rodney's marriage, which had taken place only a few weeks before, gave her a sort of isolation, which to poor Constance looked like heavenly peace.

Frederica nodded sympathetically. "You poor dear!" she said. "I can imagine. Of course I have always envied you, having such a lot, so that one more or less wouldn't matter so much. And never more than for a while after Rodney had told me he was going to marry Rose."

"Oh,—*Rose!*" said Constance.

"Of course," Frederica conceded, "I felt all right about that as soon as I'd fairly seen her. Or almost. She is a perfect dear! And I think it's going to work. But when he told me about her—somebody I'd never even heard of. . . Well, you know, Connie, the decenter a man is, the nicer and straighter and cleaner, like Hugh and Rodney, the more likely he is to fall in love, in his innocence, with just anybody. That doesn't seem fair, but it's so. And Rod was the only brother I had. Of course it was a relief to be able to take my own line—not to have Harriet around, for instance. And I suppose that's what you haven't been able to do."

"I believe I could have rescued him," Constance said. "—Jean and I could have—with half a chance. But the others absolutely hounded him into it."

Frederica's eyebrows indicated that she had made a mental note of that reference to Jean for future examination. For the present she passed it by.

"How bad is it, Connie?" she asked. "All I've had is the gossip. Has he married her?"

"He went off to find her," Constance said. "And if he can, he will. She ran away and left a note, and he followed, the day of the funeral, to New York. He seemed to know that was where she had gone. I suppose he hasn't yet, or it would be in the papers. It will be, of course, when he does. That's what we're waiting for.

"It's simply been—well, Carter says, 'hell with bells on,' at home. Mother grim and Greg solemn; Anne simply in fits. She's almost funny, she's so—desperate. I wish she'd go home. But she thinks it's her duty to stay around and rub it in. She couldn't be half so ashamed and tragic if she'd eloped herself—with the chauffeur.

"As for Bob, he makes me almost hate him. He's so pleased down inside at seeing us worried about somebody else besides him. Complacent,—that's it. As if he'd been right all along, and we hadn't understood him—and he'd told us so."

Frederica had noted an omission from this catalogue.

"It must be awfully hard on your father," she said.

And, for a full minute after that Constance was silent. "That's—awful!" she said at last, and the gravity of her voice gave the worn-out word its full significance. "Of course he had a terrible quarrel with Hugh when Hugh told him, the afternoon of the funeral, what he was going to do. Like an old-fashioned father in a book, I guess. Turned him out—cut him off without a shilling, and all that, and never speaks of him at all."

"Hugh has some money of his own, hasn't he?" Frederica asked, and Constance nodded absently.

"Oh, a little. We got a hundred thousand dollars apiece from grandmother; and a few odds and ends. And then he's had a good salary ever since he went to work."

But her tone showed this was a digression; not what she was thinking about.

"There's something else with father," she went on. "It's worrying all of us and we don't know what it is, except. . . Well, of course, nothing was done about grandfather's estate until after the funeral. That was natural. There were so many other things to do and think about. But it's been two weeks since then, and we're sure father's gone down and opened up the boxes at the bank. But he hasn't said a word to anybody about what he found there—grandfather's will and all—and nobody's dared ask him;—speak to him hardly. Greg's bothered about that more than he is about Hugh, I believe."

She had only a wry little smile for Frederica's look of outright consternation.

"Oh, it wouldn't be very nice, of course," she conceded, "to find that grandfather had left everything to a theological seminary, or an aquarium, or anything like that. Well, in the first place, I don't believe he did. But, if I had my choice between that, with Hugh back again safe and sound, and—the other thing, I'd take that."

Frederica looked thoughtful. "I don't know," she said at last. "It may not be as bad as you think—about Hugh, I mean. Evidently the girl isn't an absolute harpy, or she wouldn't have gone away. She'd have sat tight and made sure of him while she had the chance. You've never seen her, have you? I suppose she might be somebody—really straight and—fine, in a way. Even if she *is* a socialist and her father a murderer. And if she is, it would give a sort of—gorgeousness to Hugh's caring for her. . ." She broke off there and asked, "What is it?" in response to a sudden look which Constance directed at her.

But Constance said, "Nothing." And, after a momentary silence, Frederica went on with her well-meant attempt to look at the bright side; to suggest, at least, the possibility that there was a bright side to look upon.

Constance didn't dispute the possibility. Almost anything might turn out better, in the event, than a first look at it would lead one to suppose. For that matter there was a bright side to the consideration of Helena as the merest mercenary adventuress. Because then the marriage would go to smash all the sooner. But Constance doubted if she was that exactly.

"There is nothing, though, to her having gone away," she went on. "She'd made some sort of mistake with him. He looked ghastly that night I took him home with me. And, from what he said, I gathered it was all over. Going away might have been the surest move she had for making him follow. And it's maddening to think that but for a little bit of bad luck—grandfather's not living another week—it needn't have happened. Because, out at home there, Jean and I. . ."

"Jean!" Frederica echoed. "You don't mean you have told that child. . . !"

"About Hugh's affairs? Of course not. We took pains not to, naturally. Only there's something about her. . . Hugh's seen it from the first. He's always been happy playing around with her. Rather gravely, you know. She's the sort you can treat that way."

"Is it a sort?" Frederica speculated.

"I think so," Constance said. "It's the simple ones; that just are what they are and never try for effects. Jean's like that. You can't imagine her posing—about anything. She adores Hugh; has ever since the first time she saw him, back at Anne's wedding, that was. It wouldn't occur to her to try to hide it—any more than it would to try to play it up. There it has been, that's all, for anybody to see that wanted to look."

"But, Connie!" Frederica protested, "you don't mean you're treating a thing like that—a seventeen-year-old child's romance—seriously!"

"I wish I could remember back when I was seventeen," Constance said. "Maybe it wouldn't help much if I could. Only I'm not sure life was such a joke, then. Anyhow, I have worried about it. I could imagine—I thought I could—the look that would come in her face when I had to tell her. Well, and last night at dinner Mother Crawford got started talking about it—what a fool Hugh was making of himself, and how it was his father's fault for having brought him up the way he did—oh, and a lot more. Frank tried to stop her, but he couldn't. I suppose she had forgotten the child was there, or thought she was talking over her head. Cynical, hateful cackling, that's what it was—if she *is* my mother-in-law.

"And Jean! It was wonderful to see the—the pure anger that came up in her face. I almost hoped she'd turn loose, but of course she didn't. She made some sort of excuse to get away from the table and her grandmother never noticed. I found her up in her room afterward; not crying—just white.

"Freddy, she's known all about it—has ever since she came back from San Antonio. I don't know how. Pieced it together, I suppose—from things Frank has rapped out and so on. And she thinks it's splendid—what you meant, I suppose, when you said, just now, that there was a sort of gorgeousness about it. She takes the girl absolutely for granted. If she hadn't been fine and good, Hugh wouldn't have fallen in love with her. She adores him more than ever for his having had the courage to defy everybody and go off to marry her. She asked me if I wasn't proud of him, too. And, somehow, with her looking at me like that, I was ashamed not to be. I believe if I hadn't satisfied her, she'd have left us—gone back to Roger and Ethel. Without any flourishes, you know—just gone.

"But I did, somehow, and we had a long talk. She said one queer thing. She'd actually tried to tell Hugh that she was on his side. It was when they were out on the sand, the morning of the day grandfather died. She'd been telling him some of her perplexities, it seems, and then she said she thought it must be wonderful to have things to do that there wasn't any doubt about—clear things that didn't tangle up. She meant that thing of his. That's how she saw it, you see. She couldn't come any closer than that, but she hoped he understood."

There was a ruminative silence for a while, and then Frederica produced a diversion by commenting upon old Mrs. Crawford's presence at the funeral. She must have come straight home from the boat on learning of old Gregory's death.

Constance nodded. "She never liked grandfather," she observed, "but somehow they got on. Both old-timers, of course. And then she is pleased to have outlived him—though she must be years younger, really."

It was at the end of another long silence, a while later, that Constance got up to go. "What I can't get away from," she said, "is their faces—Mother Crawford's, there at the dinner table last night, while she was thinking up and saying all those witty malicious things—so pleased with herself because she had never been a fool—and Jean's afterward. And Hugh's at the funeral. I sat where I could watch him all the way through. There was a sort of—clarity in it, just as there was in Jean's last night; as if he knew what he'd have to go through—the price of it all, you know, and wasn't afraid to pay."

"It makes me feel fat and soft and cowardly. I don't know whether there is something the matter with me or not. I've been through more or less, of course. There's the babies. I tried to make myself believe, last night, that that was the same thing. But it isn't exactly. It isn't quite—facing a thing in advance. And then, it's expected of you. The thing I mean is what people call being a fool. I've never done that,—no more than Mother Crawford. The question is, whether I would if the thing was there to do. Jean would, there's no doubt of that. Oh dear, if Hugh could only have waited a few years!"

At that, in order not to cry, Constance took her leave swiftly, and went back, to see if there was any news, to her father's house.

She met him in the hall and was struck by a change in his appearance. He looked—shrunken, somehow, like a man who has just given up a losing fight. Rather surprisingly to herself, she stopped and kissed him, though he would have gone by with an absent nod.

"I haven't seen you before today," she said explanatorily.

He gazed at her a moment rather blankly, then said: "I am just sending off a telegram to your brother, He has informed us that his marriage has taken place, I am sending for him to come home at once."

"To come home!" Constance echoed incredulously.

A grimace of pain convulsed his face and he turned away from her. "Go to your mother," he said. "She can explain." He left her standing there and went away to the telephone to send his wire.

The mysterious cause of Robert Corbett's behavior during the fortnight between the funeral and the day when Hugh's letter came in, was amply explained by the facts which Mrs. Corbett had ready for Constance.

In a perfectly natural—and only human—way, Robert Corbett had been looking forward for many years to the day when he would be the head of the family. He had never had any genuine love for his father. The difference in the texture of their two minds forbade it. What took, satisfactorily, its place was the traditional filial respect and obedience. It is hardly just to blame him for feeling vaguely aggrieved over the long postponement of his coming into power He had no sense of inferiority to his father. A thoroughly logical, unimaginative intelligence always finds it hard to appraise at its true value, an illogical intuitive one. When old Gregory's intuitions led him wrong, as they did on an average of one time in three, the cause of the error was always nakedly apparent to Robert. On the other hand, when the old man went right, his rightness looked to Robert mysterious—a matter of blind luck. If the son had ever been put in a position of full responsibility, where he stood or fell by his own unaided efforts, he might have learned better. But the father never gave him a chance. This was one of old Gregory's many mistakes.

Robert, then, had lived along for the past twenty years, anyhow, in the unshaken conviction that he could pilot the Corbett ship as competently as his father. Another conviction, parallel to and supporting it, was that some day he would get the opportunity.

The fundamental principle of old Gregory's life was the perpetuation of his clan. He wanted the line to run unbroken for many generations. It was the only sort of immortality he genuinely believed in. His fortune, which was another way of saying his power and his place, was a part of himself. Again and again his son had heard him speak caustically of the folly of his dead contemporaries who had allowed the enterprises that bore their names, to fall into alien hands. Robert was as sure as he was sure of anything in the world, that his father's will, when it was opened, would be found to have transferred the power intact to him.

He had come home from his father's grave the head of the family— patriarch of the tribe. And, to him, in that hour, had come Hugh full of his mad determination to marry the revolutionary firebrand whose doings had already caused the tribe immeasurable annoyance and humiliation, as well as more ponderable losses, and in the event, had resulted in his father's death. To marry an enemy like that was more than folly. It was apostasy.

The question of the rightness of his decree of banishment upon

Hugh, asked itself and was, without misgiving, affirmatively answered. The question of his power to enforce the decree never presented itself at all.

It was the next day that he read his father's will. Old Gregory had dealt his son's pride many a blow, but never so heavy a one as this from beyond the grave. The will was thought out with a thoroughness of detail which the old man was capable of, but seldom exacted of himself. It had been drawn by one of the leaders of the Chicago bar, and so clear and unmistakable was the intent of it, that it was like a window let into the old man's mind.

About half the value of the estate was comprised by common stock, practically the entire capitalization, of Corbett & Company. The other half was a miscellaneous list of investments, nearly all very high-class: municipal and railway bonds, and a few standard stocks. About the only speculative investment he appeared to have made, was a lot of steel common which he had bought in the twenties. In the main, his idea had been that whatever profits he took out of Corbett & Company, should be put where he could get them out again at need.

It was from this outlying part of the estate that his bequests to various charitable and religious institutions were made, a few old friends and servants—foremost among these, Hannah—provided for, and the claims of all the members of his family but three, satisfied. These three were his son Robert and his two grandsons, Gregory and Hugh.

The other moiety of the estate, that is to say, Corbett & Company, together with its various subsidiary enterprises, was put into a trust, the trustees being the three heirs just named, the trust to terminate with the death of Robert. There were provisions for the appointment, in case either or both the sons pre-deceased the father, of other trustees to take their places. The income of the trust was to be divided equally among the three of them while Robert lived. At his death, it was to be divided between Gregory and Hugh.

The old man had never believed, then,—this was the upshot of it,— that his son's hands were strong enough to steer the ship alone. Robert was never to exercise the power, never to occupy the place in the eyes of the world, that old Gregory had exercised and occupied. The Great Seal was to be placed, during his lifetime, in commission.

And his one decree, Hugh's banishment, was by this instrument, revoked. Hugh had now as much authority as he; was expressly entitled to his seat at the council-table and was made, in his own right, a rich man.

It was this last consideration that had been the cause of Robert's silence during the whole of that intolerable fortnight. It was his belief, the wish being father to the thought, that this woman who had infatuated his son, had done so from a mercenary motive. Hugh had started in pursuit of her under the belief that he was cut off from the family fortune, that he had no income except the small one his maternal grandmother had left him, and no prospects except those that he could carve out for himself. There was no doubt that Hugh would acquaint the woman of these facts. He was likely, indeed, in his honesty, to paint them blacker than they really were. Anyhow, he would not appear to her the rich prize she had set out to capture. It was possible, Robert thought, a chance worth taking, that she would refuse him—set her sails for richer booty that might be on the horizon somewhere.

So, locking up the steel boxes as he locked his lips, he waited and clung to his hope—not a very buoyant one, to be sure—as desperately as though it had been better. Hugh's letter, of course, made an end of that.

XIV

Hugh and Helena had settled transitorily in a family hotel whose front windows commanded a glimpse of Gramercy Park. It was not very cheap nor very dirty nor very old, though it was a little of each; not quite impossible, in a word, from any one of a dozen points of view; and its position—almost on the Park—gave it a faint tinge of desirability. The pair happened upon it and out of an intense preoccupation with vastly more important matters, established themselves forthwith in a suite comprising parlor, bedroom and bath and an entrance hall whose dimensions were determined by the width of the doors.

It was not until the eighth day that Hugh came out of a brown study to a sort of microscopic awareness of the dirt in the splintered cracks of the hardwood floors, the vicious ugliness of the furniture and the sodden rugs, the gaping deficiencies of the plumbing. Whatever else they did they must get out of here. But, of course, they were going to, anyway. That much had been decided—at all events. Hadn't it? But "decided" was not the conclusive word that, in his bachelor simplicity, he had supposed it to be.

Were they happy—this strangely mated pair? Hugh—left that morning with his thoughts for company—had glanced at the question somewhat nervously, then answered it with a vigorous affirmative. Only the word wanted a little defining. Happiness was not a mere vegetable contentment. It was not, even, the negation of its opposite. A certain amount of unhappiness was, probably, a necessary ingredient of it. Otherwise one would take it too much for granted to be thoroughly aware of it. Even an occasional violent quarrel—with its ensuing reconciliation and the broadening of the basis of mutual understanding—was, he supposed, a thing no husband and wife could be said to be truly happy without.

He and Helena had not had, though, so far, quite a fair chance. Hugh had known, of course, that their marriage would cause a certain amount of newspaper comment, but he had been fairly dazed by the cloud-burst of publicity that they were caught out in—had hardly come out of yet. Those were, it should be noted, the forgotten—almost unrealizable—days before the war; days when there was nothing much for the papers to print but politics and baseball. So the marriage of a Chicago multi-millionaire (since in current journalese every man who can afford to ride in a taxi is a millionaire it was necessary to use a more grandiloquent term for the grandson of a genuine one) to the daughter of a famous anarchist—martyr or murderer according as one looked at it, was worth black head-lines, double leaded columns, interviews by prominent clergymen, and photographs—genuine where possible—of the newly married couple getting into cabs, eating breakfast and so on.

At first Hugh writhed under this. It was not the publication of facts, however private and intimate, that distressed him, but the successive refractions of these facts through the minds of a reporter, a re-write man, and a head-line concocter, so that when they appeared on the page they had all the banal horror of a third-rate moving picture scenario. But he grew philosophical when he saw how little his wife minded it. The people it hurt the worst, of course, were not under his eye—nor in his thoughts more than he could help.

The hullabaloo had, rather absurdly, one really important result. On the second day after the news of their marriage was published, a special messenger came to the hotel with a note to Helena from the editor of a newspaper magazine saying that he was delighted to accept a story of hers which she had submitted to him a few weeks ago (It was the very story she had read to Hugh, as it happened), that he was enclosing herewith a check for two hundred dollars—hoping she would find the amount satisfactory; and finally, that he earnestly wished she might find time to come to his office for a talk about future work.

That check meant an enormous lot to Helena, intrinsically, since it was by far the largest lump sum she had ever received; but infinitely more as a symbol. It was the realization, she told Hugh, of the dream of her life. Everything she had done since the law took her father away from her, had been in preparation—unconscious sometimes, to be sure—for a career as an author. It was by the printed word in the guise of mere stories that the seeds of the revolution could best be sown.

Well, she was an author now. She had got through the guarded gate into the sacred enclosure where they pastured. Her troubles were over. Why, she'd written that story overnight! And here was two hundred dollars in payment for it! The independence it gave her and promised to make perpetual, removed the last misgivings she had felt about her consent to a marriage with Hugh.

That consent had not been won from her, of course, without many concessions and promises on his part. She was to be allowed to live her own life absolutely, just as he was to be allowed to live his. But that promised independence might have turned out to be rather illusory, if it could have been enjoyed only at the price the old hard drudgery had exacted.

Hugh did not quite share her confidence in the permanence of this roseate state of things. He had got the idea from Barry Lake that making a living by literature was harder work than an occasional wild night of scribbling came to. But her childlike pleasure and confidence— the way she laughed when she hugged him and read the letter again and, absurdly, kissed the check, supplied a new note in the gamut of his emotions for her—a note he had hardly been aware before was missing. For the first time he liked as well as loved her.

If only they could have gone on like that, carrying out their plans for a flat of their own, here on the Park, perhaps—a chemist's job for Hugh—there wouldn't be any trouble about that—and a career for Helena; friends—her friends at first, growing in time to be his as well; adventures, such as the fomentation of a likely strike here and there, but with the sharp tearing edge of them taken off by the new security offered by a home—a husband—a practical income!

Helena's plans, you will note; but, for a few days, Hugh was able to share them with her. And then came his father's telegram and, on its heels, the lawyer's letter with all the astonishing corroboratory facts about his grandfather's will and the great place and responsibility it forced upon him.

The telegram, which was long and contained all the bones of the thing, was delivered to Hugh while Helena was out making her call, by appointment, upon that magazine editor. And she came back to him in a state of effervescent excitement over the interview. She was to be a regular weekly contributor. Her stories were to appear simultaneously in half a hundred Sunday newspapers. The rich and poor—that was to be the theme of them. Sharp-edged little sketches, with a punch, illustrative, Helena confided to her husband—though naturally she had not pointed out the fact to the editor—of the bitter injustice of the capitalistic organization of society; fat employers and their shivering employees; rich, worthless ladies and their maids, and so on. In fictional form, of course, but that didn't matter. The truth would show through.

It was a bad moment for the production of Hugh's telegram. But he was too candid to have held it back in the hope of a better one turning up later. So he handed it to her without a word, and only when she had read it through and looked up at him with a blankly incredulous stare, he said:

"I'm afraid it means we shall have to go back to Chicago."

The thing in all its bearings—in all its multifarious implications, was too much, of course, for her to grasp in a moment like that, and it was characteristic of her that instead of settling down to wrestle with the problem, as Hugh had been wrestling for an hour before she came in, suspending judgment until she had managed to see her way clearly all around it, she snatched at the obvious emotional aspect of the thing and ignored the rest. In ten minutes she had whipped herself up into a fury.

What did he owe that precious family of his! Wasn't it their own doing that he had had to choose between them and her? And hadn't he finally chosen her,—after having taken a good long while to think about it? Now he was talking of going back to them and dragging her back with him, to the sacrifice of her career, to say nothing of his own. That was what he wanted, was it, now that he had the chance? To settle down into a fat pompous respectability, with her for a domestic slave, the helpless butt for all the scornful indignities his purse-proud family would put upon her? He thought they'd have to go back, did he! Well, he could think again. As far as the money was concerned, he'd get that anyhow, wouldn't he, whether he went back or not?

He ought, it may be admitted, to have left it at that for a while, and given her time to cool down and visualize the thing for herself in her own way. But tactful indirection was no more an attribute of Hugh's than a capacity for straight serious thinking was one of Helena's. He steamed straight ahead like a liner into the teeth of the gale, with reasons, arguments.

That monstrous plant out at Riverdale whose direction old Gregory's will confided in part to him, was a sorer problem now than it had been last May when Helena herself had swooped down upon it and headed that little delegation of coremakers in Bailey's office. By that act of hers she had assumed a moral responsibility of her own, as grave as his. The strike she had started was still dragging bitterly on—half lost, leaderless, losing power from week to week. If it protracted itself into the winter the hunger and cold and despair would cause incalculable suffering. Now, as things had somewhat ironically fallen out, he and Helena had a chance put into their hands to do something. There was simply no question in his mind as to their duty in the matter.

Going back to the family would present, no doubt, some awkward and painful moments, though it would be nothing like as bad as Helena, really absurdly, made out. The rest of the family weren't monsters any more than he was. She'd find them perfectly tolerable, even at first, and eventually, he was sure, likable.

He was not able, of course, to complete a consecutive statement like that, because intervening gusts of her temper, every now and then, blew it all to rags. They didn't quarrel all the time, either, by any means, during the three or four days while the discussion went on. There were periods of what looked like the most tranquil calm, when, by their talk and actions, you'd have supposed that no difference between them had ever arisen; periods, too, when they made love to each other whole-heartedly. And then, in the wake of these latter, generally, the tempest would burst again as if its violence had never been checked.

They fought pretty much over the same ground, beginning as a rule, not where they had left off, but where they had last begun. Hugh did indeed make one suggestion in the belief that he had hit upon a valid compromise. They needn't live in Chicago—needn't try to amalgamate themselves into the family. They could go to Riverdale instead; live in one of the worker's cottages and upon workers' fare. That would be best all around, perhaps, in the guarantee it gave to both sides of the good faith of their endeavors. But the passionate conviction of Helena's veto upon that proposal abolished it so that it was as if it had never been.

It was her counter-proposal that they presently settled down to. Hugh could do as he liked of course. If he felt responsible for the management of Corbett & Company, why, he might go ahead and manage—so far as his father and brother would let him—which would not, in her opinion, go very far, nor take very much of his time. She would remain here in New York, going ahead with the work which had just opened up before her. Whenever his duties left him leisure, he could come back to her. She'd be frightfully unhappy during his absences, of course, but that couldn't be helped. She realized that she had no more right to dictate to him than he had to dictate to her.

And if he was going out there—temporarily, of course—why she supposed the sooner he went, the better. Perhaps when he came back he'd have a freer mind; be ready once more to be her husband and lover again, instead of the solemn slave of duty he was now.

At the end of that statement she came swiftly over to where he sat, knelt at his knees, pulled his head down to her and kissed it, and then for a while wept quietly in his embrace. Later they went down to dinner at the Lafayette, and, in a taxi, to *The Follies* afterward.

It was the next morning that Hugh sat, as I have exhibited him to you, alone in their sitting-room, trying to make up his mind what to do. Helena had left him, immediately after breakfast, in search of material for the next story. It hadn't come quite so easily as she expected, but of course there was reason enough for that. The note of their parting had been good-humored enough, though her farewell injunction, jocularly meant, to be sure, had been perhaps a trifle heavy-handed. If he went off to Chicago before she came back, he was to leave a note.

He did mean to start—for only a few days of course—some time within twenty-four hours. He had hoped to take the fast afternoon train, but of course would not now, unless she came back in time.

She did come in just as he was thinking about going out to lunch, flushed, bright-eyed with excitement over, she said, the successful quest of her story. She had a letter for him which the clerk at the desk downstairs had handed to her—not a business letter, but written on notepaper and addressed in a woman's hand, and the casual air with which she held it out was, perhaps, a little exaggerated.

He had been secretly hoping, for two or three days, for letters that looked like that; especially for one from his mother or Constance. The possibility occurred to him now that Helena had been hoping for them, too. The interchange of telegrams with his father accounted well enough, to be sure, for the failure of them. They had taken it for granted that he was coming straight back. But the handwriting on this letter was one he did not know and he opened it curiously, aware that Helena's eyes sought and did not leave his face. This is what he read:—

Dear Hugh

"Your new happiness makes me very happy, too. I don't believe I need tell you that. I tried to tell you, that day we built the sand-castle, how much I hoped it would come out right, but I was afraid to. Now that it has, I can.

"Will you please give my love—my *real* love—to Helena. (Will she let me call her that?) If you come back to Chicago soon (next week) I shall see you. But if not, it will be a long time because father has been detailed on a military mission to England and mother and I go with him. It is all very unexpected and exciting, only it makes me feel, somehow, a little homesick, too. I *hope* you will come before I go.

Lovingly always,
JEAN

He did not read it aloud, but when he came to the end, handed it over to Helena, indescribably warmed by the simple affection of it, just as he always was by the sight of the child, or the thought of her.

He watched his wife's face while she read, for a reflection of the same feeling there. But it was not what he saw. She asked, rather trenchantly, when she reached the signature, "Who's—Jean?" and the sharpness of the question took him by surprise.

Who was she, anyhow, besides just—Jean? He actually had to cast about for an answer. "Jean Gilbert?" he said. "Why, she's old Mrs. Crawford's granddaughter."

His wife laughed and tossed the letter contemptuously on the table. "I know who she is well enough," she said. "She's the girl they wanted you to marry and that hoped to marry you herself. Sends her love to me, does she? I know the kind of love *that* is."

Hugh stared at her. It was as if she had spat in his face.

"She's a child!" he managed to say at last, and it was not until she heard his voice that she looked at him. "She's my sister's niece. She's. . ." But he couldn't manage to go any further.

By now Helena was gazing at him as if behind his eyes she read some secret. He turned away. Already his anger was passing. His wife's mistake was perhaps excusable enough, but her gaze followed him as if it meant to extort a confession. He could find, somehow, nothing to say. Then, suddenly, with a rush, she went into their bedroom and slammed and locked the door between them. He made no effort to induce her to let him in. Went over and sat down in a chair by the window.

He was not angry at all now. Only a curious blankness had settled over him. He was like one waking and finding himself in a strange place, unable to explain how he happened to be there. Who was it who had just slammed the door? Why didn't the sleep from which the sound had awakened him, discover him in his own bed in his father's house?

It was more than an hour later when Helena came out in a silken negligee,—her tears washed away, all her strange exotic beauty enhanced by the misty tenderness with which she came to him and asked to be forgiven.

He did forgive her easily enough and she curled up in his lap and slid a caressing bare arm around his neck. After a while she said:

"I'll go back to Chicago with you, Hugh, if you want me to. Only you must wait a week or two till I can buy some clothes. I'm going to try to be a credit to you."

XV

Getting Helena's clothes, such as would make it possible for her to be a credit to him, turned out to be only one of a number of things to delay Hugh's return with her to Chicago. It was the better part of a month before they really packed up and went. Hugh surprised himself by taking these successive postponements as good-naturedly as he did.

He felt strongly, to be sure, the urgency of getting back and beginning the thing that Destiny appeared to have marked out as his life's work; life's struggle, he expected it would amount to; the effort to bring it about that the bulk of his grandfather's great fortune should be administered—well, in the general direction of the millennium, (Hugh allowed himself a deprecatory smile over this way of putting it, but it expressed about what he meant, just the same) rather than for the mere aggrandizement of its possessors.

The first campaign on his hands would be the settlement of the strike. He was under no illusion that this would be an easy thing to do, that any comfortable short-cut to peace, prosperity and good-will awaited discovery offhand. It would be a long pull and, if the task were to be accomplished before winter added its own miseries to those the strikers were already suffering, there was not a day to be lost.

Still the fact was, though he felt sheepish about admitting it, that each new postponement Helena proposed, was a reprieve for him. Now that it was a settled fact that they were to go back again, he was enjoying this transitory irresponsible existence in the shabby family hotel just off Gramercy Park. He had, pardonably enough, gone a little slack and indolent after the emotional tempests of the past three months, and it was in the comfortable mood of an idle observer that he surveyed his wife's activities and acquainted himself with her friends.

These friends of Helena's were a bewildering lot to Hugh. There was apparently no end to them. They lived in little colonies—nests and warrens were words Hugh was tempted to use—all over the metropolitan district of New York. The first thing that struck Hugh about them was their variety. There were Russian Jews, Irish, Italians, English, French, surprisingly few Germans (Hugh asked Helena about this and got the information that the Germans were mostly orthodox socialists) and surprisingly many simon pure Americans—Yankee-Americans. The variegation of the cultural backgrounds they represented made a veritable crazy-quilt. But the insoluble riddle to Hugh lay in their similarity. The possession of some quality of mind, which he could not formulate nor define, made all these madly diversified people exactly alike.

To take an illustration at random: there were Stone, whose father was a Baptist minister in a small town near Dubuque, Iowa, a homely, lean, slow-spoken chap; his wife, Hilda Nikova, a white-faced, eager, wire-drawn little creature, who had never been outside the Pale until, at eighteen, she had been smuggled across the frontier by friends, after the raid that had sent her father and three brothers to Siberia; and their great friend Minetti, a Milanese factory-hand. These three could argue, when together, by the hour, finding minutiæ to disagree about, to be sure, but in complete agreement about essentials. These essentials were not so much facts, Hugh noted, as modes of feeling.

The thing they were all effervescing with just then, was the waiters' strike in New York City. Hilda was one of the leaders of this. She and her husband were financially pretty well off, for he was an article writer of good repute, able to sell his wares to the standard magazines at rather better than standard prices.

Hilda wrote, too, by spurts, but for weeks now she had been devoting herself with febrile enthusiasm to the organization of the waiters. She had gone from one hotel to another, staying as a guest in each, until an indignant management put her out, making converts, inventing ingenious methods of sabotage (nothing could be more discouraging to guests than soap in the soup, and this was one of the most innocent of Hilda's devices) and passionately addressing little meetings of the faithful in secret and unlikely places.

The strike had come off and was going on nicely, getting a huge publicity, of course, as that sort of strike was certain to do; and Hilda was in high feather about it. She didn't believe there was a hotel left in New York where they would permit her to register. And while, of course, it was not possible that all unfair eating-houses in the city should be picketed, a sufficient number were to make a very impressive demonstration.

But then a most unfortunate incident occurred. The pickets around one of the hotels, one night, picked up a scab waiter, ran him off into a quiet side street, and, to put it bluntly, kicked him to death. It was not until the next morning that the discovery was made that this victim of direct action was not a waiter at all, not a scab; he was a clerk, as a matter of fact, in the employ of an express company, and the sole support of a mother and two young sisters.

Hilda was deeply distressed about this mistake—genuinely upset about it—a state of mind in which all her friends sympathized, finding what consolations they could, but without making much headway in that direction with Hilda. But the next time they saw her, she was comforted. It wasn't so bad, after all. The coroner's inquest had revealed the fact that the man was tubercular anyway; hadn't had more than six months, probably, to live. The economic loss was not great—practically negligible. And the man's real murderers, as any one could see, were not Hilda's too-impetuous pickets, but the stock-holders in the soulless corporation whose wage-slave the unfortunate man had been.

Hugh's incredulous stare, leaving Hilda's big-eyed, delicate little face to travel round over the others, saw that they all took it in exactly the same way.

Well, there it was, the thing he couldn't define, that made them alike; big, slow, kindly Stone; sharp-nosed, pale-eyed little Shayne, the Irish schoolmaster, Minetti with his thick neck and his kinky auburn hair, Albertine Ellis (Albertine's delight was to be as mysterious as, with her wide-set narrow eyes, she looked. But she forfeited this effect with Hugh by speaking with the unmistakable Pennsylvania twist his ears had grown familiar with in Youngstown)—they all weighed that incident in the same kind of balance.

All the same, Hugh admired most of them enormously. Each of them represented some sort of triumph over a hostile environment—a thing which made him feel very humble. He marveled over their vast— so it seemed to him—knowledge. They didn't emotionalize much—not for each other, that is. When one of them got up on a street corner soap-box it was different, of course. But among themselves they dealt in facts; or at least what passed unchallenged for facts. Often these were minutely statistical, even when they were dealing with subjects whose statistics would be, one would think, difficult to compile. They were fond, too, of "inside facts"—the sort of facts that never by any possibility found their way into print—not even in the articles which Stone himself wrote for the magazines; though his talk was a perfect mine of them.

Another thing that kept Hugh humble was their ability to speak foreign languages. Hugh could read metallurgical monographs pretty well in German and in French, but nothing could have induced him to attempt a spoken sentence in any language but his own. You may remember how Helena's proficiency in languages had impressed him. These others, though by no means as remarkable in this direction as she, still managed to make themselves understood satisfactorily across all sorts of linguistic boundaries. And even when they talked English, the scope of their references took in literatures that Hugh had never heard of. He would walk home with Helena after an evening of this sort of thing, feeling, as he had once confessed to his mother, like an ignorant schoolboy.

He was getting on with Helena. There was less rack and strain. There were fewer tempests. There was a warmer, kindlier affection between them just now than there had been at any previous stage of the affair. She was about as near perfectly happy as it was possible for one of her temper to be. In this little group where I have just indicated her,— there were half a dozen others that would serve as well for illustration— sitting at a table in an Italian restaurant down on West Thirteenth Street, perhaps, with Hilda and Albertine, Stone, Minetti and Shayne, with her husband for audience, she was quite at her best. Their idiom was one her mind was completely at home in; her father's phrases flashed like arrows; her mother's beauty kindled to an absolute radiance. She was the queen of them—their pet. She was aware of Hugh's pride in her, and basked in it.

She had, too, the satisfaction of being proud of him; of observing keenly how he impressed these friends of hers. She had immensely increased her prestige among them by marrying him—a paradox, perhaps, since most of them professed a deep repugnance to the institution of marriage, as well as a bitter hatred of capitalists. Logically, the marriage of one of their group to a conspicuous member of the capitalist class, might well seem a double apostasy. But it did not work out that way. It was something of a Roman triumph for Helena, this parade through the ranks of the New York radicals, with Hugh in the rôle of captive at the tail of her chariot. It inspired her with hope of another conquest; the conquest of his world, back in Chicago.

Even the new clothes she was buying were a source of unexpected satisfaction to her. The sums she spent on them would have made Anne or Constance smile, but they gave her a pleasurable sense of reckless extravagance. And Hugh's boyish delight in the effect they produced, giving her beauty, for the first time in her life, a fair chance, kindled a new warmth in her heart for him. She had looked forward to their marriage with honest misgiving. But it seemed, just now, that the great adventure to which she had always regarded herself as predestined, was beginning auspiciously.

She wrote with immense diligence all the morning and sometimes on into the afternoon, getting ahead in preparation for those first weeks in Chicago when her time would not be so completely her own.

Hugh never could get over wondering at the ease with which she did it. She would sit, on one foot, in the Morris chair, a little portable typewriter he had given her in her lap, and click off six or eight pages in the most casual manner, interrupting herself, half a dozen times an hour, to read him bits she was particularly pleased with, or to chat with him for a minute or two about anything that happened to occur to her.

She asked him on one of those mornings, observing that he was rather at a loose end, why he didn't write, too, and his response was the obvious one that he hadn't anything to write.

But presently he did sit down at the table, pulled up a block of her copy-paper, got out his fountain-pen, and drifted off into an abstraction. When, at the end of her own stint, she came around and looked over his shoulder, the page he had marked "one," was otherwise completely blank. She laughed, patted his head admonitorily, and told him that if he was going to be an author, he'd have to do better than that.

But he stayed in that afternoon when she went out shopping, and went at his task again. He kept at it, in fact, for three or four days, and he excited Helena's curiosity to the highest pitch, and her resentment a little besides, though she pretended this was not so, by refusing to let her read what he was writing, or even to tell her what he was writing about. He mollified her, though, by the confession: "I had to promise myself you shouldn't see, in order to get going at all."

What it had occurred to him to do, was to put down, in plain words,—well, what he thought about things. There had been a chemical change in his ideas since that night drive back to town from Riverdale in his mother's limousine, when the reagent of Helena's story had been applied to them. The precipitate hadn't settled yet. Perhaps filtration through the medium of black words on white paper, would accomplish this result. It occurred to him later, that in case he succeeded the result would have an objective value as well as a subjective one. There were his father and Greg waiting for him, not knowing what to expect, nor what mad impracticalities they might have to combat. He'd always found trouble in talking consecutively to either of them. He quarreled with

Greg; he was polite to his father. If he could send, on ahead, a *précis* of his new opinions, it might save a lot of useless beating of the air.

The person his mind addressed, however, as he sat there at the table, whittling out his paragraphs, was his mother, and it was in the form of a letter to her that the thing finally was written. He could always talk to her.

"The only way I can begin," he began to write at last, "is with negatives. I am not a socialist—not, at least, if a socialist is what I believe he is. A socialist, as near as I can make out, is a person who wants to abolish property, property being whatever is mine exclusively; whatever I can forbid others the enjoyment of, and dispose of as I see fit. What the orthodox socialist wants is to put all that into the hands of the State—lands, mineral resources, transportation, industries—everything. He wants the functions of the State expanded to include, with what they exercise already, all the functions now exercised by privately owned capital. He hopes to bring that about by political action; by electing socialists to office; by passing socialist laws, all directed toward that one accomplishment. When that revolution is accomplished, the parasites of capitalism who, without doing any work themselves have been riding on the backs of the real producers of wealth, will be destroyed and the wealth they have appropriated will be turned back, through the State, to the constituents of the State, who produced it.

"I am not a syndicalist, either. The syndicalists want to abolish property, but they want to abolish the State as well. They regard the ideal State of the socialist with abhorrence as a bureaucratic tyranny infinitely worse than the present capitalist-controlled State would dare to be. They believe in direct action rather than political action, because in all political action they see a corrupting force which destroys its aims, however good they may be. The direct action they mean to take is the general strike; which would leave the workers of each industry in possession of complete control of that industry. All they would permit in the way of a general organization afterward, would be a sort of loose federation with consultative powers, but no real authority.

"The reason why I am neither a socialist nor a syndicalist, is that I do not believe, yet—although I mean to keep an open mind about it—in the abolition of property. I do not believe that property can be abolished as long as people generally, retain a possessive sense—as long as the words 'mine' and 'yours' mean anything to them. It won't do any good, that I can see, to try to abolish the meaning of the word 'yours' until you can abolish the meaning of the word 'mine.' And as long as it's in human nature for a man to feel that it adds to his importance—to his prestige—to his validity as a person, to see things that are *his* around him, the word 'mine' will go on having an important meaning. It seems to me that that possessive sense is the principal actuating force—the main source of energy of the whole machine; and I have no confidence, as yet, that a socialist, or a syndicalist machine would run any better without it than this one would.

"I haven't any label, then, nor any groove to slide down into. I must feel my way along as best I can. The point I start out from is the conviction that I haven't played fair; that the cards have been stacked before ever the game began, in my favor. And, along with myself, of course, I include everybody who belongs, roughly speaking, to the privileged class.

"That fact has been under my eyes for a long time and there have been moments when I have come near enough to seeing it to worry me. But I never should have seen it, I suppose, without this look I have had lately, at the other side of the shield. I have been getting acquainted with people the cards were stacked against, who have won—something anyhow—in spite of that; people who, but for the possession of extraordinary talents and energies, would have been submerged altogether. I am just beginning to get some conception of the courage it takes, the resourcefulness and self-denial, and the amazing plain endurance, to get one's self up from the depths they started in, to a decently lighted world.

"I have been seeing myself, lately, as I and my class must look to them. It makes so little difference whether we're any good or not. We float along at the top all the same. We have no excuse for not being immensely better than they are. All the apparatus for making the most of ourselves is put into our hands from the beginning. But even if our hands are too indolent to take hold of it, we're carried along anyhow. The race is jockeyed in our favor. We ourselves are the starters and the judges.

"I take my own case again for an example. I am a good metallurgist. I was worth, on a competitive basis, as much salary as grandfather paid me at Youngstown. But before I began earning that salary, I had had enough money spent on me to have provided a pretty good educational equipment for a dozen men. And mine was taken away from the other eleven. They were working out at Riverdale, while I was in school and college, for from six to twelve dollars a week. And now they're striking in the hope of getting twenty-four. Besides all that, I had the tradition of success to push me, and the assurance of an opening to pull me, so that short of being utterly worthless, I couldn't have failed. And if, being utterly worthless, I had failed, I'd have been 'taken care of' anyhow. Somebody down below would have had to pay my way—pull my oar for me.

"So it's no wonder, seeing me like that, and thousands of others like me, riding along on the top, that they are fighting mad; that they rage at our fatuous complacence—at our silly Pharisaical philanthropies; that they hate us less when we're outspoken in our intention to get and keep all we can, than when we talk self-righteously, as the Progressives are talking in this campaign, about passing prosperity around; meaning thereby, sending out the crusts and bones, when we have done dining, for them to gnaw. I don't wonder that they're more concerned to tip us out of the saddle somehow, and let matters come to an equilibrium afterward as happens, than they are in building up an Utopia of exquisitely abstract justice for everybody, ourselves included, that can be put into effect without pinching anybody's fingers. They aren't in a mood to care if some of us get hurt, nor to reject promising looking methods because those methods don't conform to our alleged standards of fair play. What do they know about fair play? Have we ever taught it to them?

"All that is rather emotional, I suspect, and not much to the point, the point being, so far as I am concerned, what I am going to do about it—I, personally, and I as one of the three trustees of Corbett & Company.

"I am not on their side—not on the side, that is, of the real radicals. I don't believe in the abolition of property except as it gets gradually abolished through erosion by a newer sort of social ideas. So I shall not advocate the surrender of our ownership of Corbett & Company to our operatives, nor the direction of it to a committee of them.

"What I would like to surrender, would be the entire labor management into their own hands. What I would like to see formed is a strong union, embracing the whole industry.

"I would be in favor of our insisting that every wageworker in the plant belonged to it. I would like to see it strong enough and responsible enough, so that we could enter into a definite contract with its officers for furnishing the entire wage-working man-power of our establishment. An organization like that should have in its hands the administration of what goes under the name of welfare work; insurance, cooperative buying, and so on. Our entering into such a contract would entail, I think, the admission to our board of directors of representatives of the union; the complete accessibility of our books to them, the discussion of our policies with them, and the reversion to them of a certain share of our profits.

"On the other hand, it would of course be essential that the union should be a responsible organization against whom a contract could be enforced in the courts and from whom damages could be collected.

"What I seem to be groping toward as a compromise between our present industrial autocracy and the revolutionary republicanism of the syndicalists is a sort of constitutional monarchy. Once it got established, I should expect the gradual tendency of it to be in the direction of limiting and wearing away our authority and ownership and the building up and making more real of a genuine popular control of the industry. But that movement would be gradual and in step with the common social sense of the nation."

He broke his promise to himself when he had got as far as this, and showed the thing to Helena. And he watched her with an anxiety that was only half humorous, as she read it. He could see that it was not making a favorable impression. She smiled occasionally at first—a rather patronizing smile, as a school-mistress might over the naiveté of a bright boy's composition. But the smile gave way to an angry flush at the end.

"That's a trick," she said hotly, "and an old trick, at that. '—A contract enforcible in the courts.' It's not worthy of you. But it won't work. Our people aren't flies to walk into that spider-web. They know who writes your laws and who hires your judges, and they won't be fooled."

Hugh sighed and did not attempt to answer her. That sensation of blankness which had come over him first the morning when she flew out against Jean recurred, and not for the first time since that day. It always did recur when she imputed bad faith to him. It wore off, though, within an hour or two.

He did send his little paper, with his father's name instead of his mother's at the top, just as he had written it.

"This isn't, of course, an ultimatum," he concluded, "nor even a program. I realize that the working out of any such scheme as I have outlined depends more upon the men out there at Riverdale, and on you and Greg, than it does on me.

"I am not an impossibilist. I have very little interest in anything that won't work, and I hope you'll find, when it comes to dealing with one fact at a time as they present themselves to us, that I will be reasonable. It is with the idea that it will enable us to avoid the more nagging sort of personal arguments that I am asking you to read this and hand it on to Greg; also to mother, if you don't mind.

"I am sorry about our delay in coming on. It has seemed unavoidable. I promise now that I, at least, will be on hand within a week.

Your affectionate son,
HUGH

XVI

I f Price, the Corbetts' butler, had been, instead of a real butler, one of those ironic and garrulous philosophers that Mr. Bernard Shaw would have us believe they are, his report of the dinner in the big house the night Hugh brought his bride home, would be worth having. Perhaps it would anyway.

It was an occasion they had all, naturally enough, been dreading for days. Not so much that Hugh—their own familiar Hugh—was bringing back with him, for domestication at their hearth, a chimera—a hippogrif—a snaky-haired Medusa, as that this violently exogamous act of his threw a doubt on his being their own familiar Hugh. If he had gone off to Mecca and announced his conversion to Mohammedanism, they could hardly have awaited his return with deeper misgivings.

None of them acknowledged this feeling to any of the others; it was too much an affair of the marrow of their bones to be talked about. They didn't talk much about Helena, either; though Carter, at the breakfast table on the morning of the fatal day, started something. A telegram had just come in from Hugh saying what train they were on and predicting their arrival in time for dinner.

"Greg had better go to the station to meet them," Carter observed. "He's the only one of us that knows her."

That startled his father out of a deep preoccupation and he shot at his eldest son the question, "Do *you* know her?"

"Oh, Carter's trying to be funny," said Greg disgustedly. "I saw her once. You knew about that. Down in Bailey's office the day the strike began, when he told her she was discharged and had better leave town— and she made an I. W. W. speech and threatened us with the guillotine. She had on a dirty apron then, and was all streaked up with sweat and coal dust. And now," he added morosely, "she's my sister-in-law! Will I be expected to kiss her?"

"Oh, well," said Carter *sotto voce,* "Hugh's probably washed her by now. And I don't suppose she always bites."

That was the end of Carter, for his father, in well-justified wrath, obliterated him. "She will hardly," he observed, "indulge in any such unspeakable vulgarities as that."

His wife could see, though, that this was a mere manner of speaking. There were no vulgarities, no horrors, that he put beyond probability as attributes of his daughter-in-law. They all had a nightmare prevision of a sprawling, outrageous, grotesquely clad, shrill, denunciatory creature, gesticulating over the dinner-table, in the enforcement of the polysyllabic jargon of anarchy; and of a horribly translated Hugh, gazing an infatuated assent to it all.

By the time they were fairly seated at the table, they all felt like rubbing their eyes after a bad dream. The incredible spectacle, up at the head of the table—to none of them more amazing than to the participants in it—of Helena at Mr. Corbett's right hand, talking pleasantly about the weather and the accident that had delayed their train; using, if warily, the right forks and never breathing fire at all, left them all feeling, in the light of their anticipations, limp and a little ridiculous.

I don't at all mean to say that the evening turned out to be an intrinsically enjoyable one, or even comfortably unembarrassed; nor that the ensuing fortnight, while Hugh and Helena were looking out a house and settling themselves into it, marked the beginning of affectionate relations between Hugh's wife and his family, or the subsidence of their profound regret that he had married her. The relief and gratification they all felt were purely superficial.

It does not do, however, to underestimate the importance of surfaces when you are dealing with a crystalline structure like a family. It was something for the Corbetts to discover that Helena if she was not quite all that is meant by the word presentable, was equally not impossible.

And it meant a lot to Hugh that, coming up to bed that first evening, very late, after a long talk with his father and Gregory, he should find Helena neither in tears of humiliation nor in a tempest of rage; but, on the contrary, amiably inclined to a cigarette and a review of the evening.

"I didn't know we were going to be so long," Hugh said, referring to the conference in the library, "but I felt sure you'd get on all right with mother and Connie."

"Oh yes," Helena said indifferently, "we got on all right, though it was rather dull."

This was a disappointment to Hugh, since Constance and his mother were the two members of the family he had felt surest Helena would like. Both were straightforward, warmhearted, open-minded women, and he didn't see what more Helena could want than that.

"I can't make your mother out exactly," she said. "What sort of person was she when your father married her? She was one of the people, wasn't she?"

Hugh laughed a big laugh at that. "She's the aristocrat of the bunch," he said. "She had a great-aunt who never got over the fact that a grand-niece of hers married the son of a man who worked with his hands—as grandfather did. He was a wheelwright, you know. No, if mother hasn't any manners, it's because—well, in a way, she's got beyond them."

A flush of annoyance in his wife's face warned him away from that theme, which otherwise he would have found it amusing to expand upon. He could see how it was well enough, though. His mother shocked Helena. Her monumental disregard of many of the first principles of drawing-room deportment, might well enough have seemed at first to Helena—self-consciously on her own very best behavior—simply as a personal affront, a calculated method of exhibiting disregard. And even the correction of this mistake by the observation that she treated every one like that, would not make matters much better. There *was* a sort of swagger about that attitude, Hugh admitted.

"But how about Constance?" he asked.

Connie's manners, of course, were beyond reproach and, in the two minutes of private conversation they had stolen in the drawing-room after dinner, she had given Hugh a reassurance, which he hardly needed, as to what her attitude toward her new sister-in-law was going to be.

"I think she's lovely," Constance had said. "Jean was right about her all along. I hope I can make her like me. *Really*, I mean. If you see me doing anything wrong, you must tell me."

So it was with genuine astonishment now that Hugh discovered that his wife regarded Constance as haughty and superior. The only one of them, she said, who was what she had expected them all to be.

"You're all wrong about that," Hugh protested. "If she seemed like that it was only because she was trying so hard. . ."

"Not to," Helena put in.

Hugh had, as a matter of fact, pulled up on the brink of that very phrase. But he had seen, before he made use of it, that it was not what he meant exactly. "Trying so hard to make friends," was the way he finally finished the sentence.

Helena's little laugh of dissent, urged him on to quote—or paraphrase, what Constance had said to him in the drawing-room.

"Oh, she wants to make up with you," said Helena. "That's plain enough. And for the present, she thinks that's the way to do it."

That left him without a reply.

But Helena, of her own accord, went on in a pleasanter vein. "Gregory seemed pleasant, though I didn't talk to him much. And Carter's amusing. But the one I really like is your father. He was lovely to me."

Hugh could not but have been amused by the spectacle at the dinner table of this *rapprochement*. Because he knew how purely an affair of surfaces it was. One moment of contact between his wife's real opinions, and his father's, would produce an explosion that would destroy it. But so long as the surfaces they presented to each other fitted together so smoothly, there seemed to be no reason why that contact should take place. His father's mannerliness was, naturally enough you could see, just as grateful to Helena as his mother's blunt ways were distressing. She played up to him—tried to reach his level. (Recalled forgotten and once despised precepts of Grace Drummond's.) By doing so, she kindled in Robert's heart a spark of genuine liking for her. He saw how hard she tried, and applauded the effort—found it admirable. His little acts of meticulous gallantry and consideration touched her and got a sympathetic response from her. (They never, by the way, had got just this response from any of his own family.) And then, of course, it didn't do to forget that Helena was really beautiful. Beauty in women was a thing Robert was always susceptible to.

Hugh, though his sense of the humorous aspect of this attraction was irresistible, still felt grateful to both of them for it. Down in the library his father had made what apologetic amends a father can make to a son, for the injustice he felt he had done him. Their quarrel, as a quarrel, was buried.

"You've made it up between us," he told Helena now. "There's no doubt about that, after what he said about you down there in the library. I wish you might have been there to hear."

He smoked a while in thoughtful silence. "You know," he said at last, "I'm awfully sorry for father. I don't believe I've ever understood him very well; seen things from his point of view. We're all a heavy-handed lot, and he's sensitive. That will of grandfather's was a horribly ruthless sort of thing, and it's left him—crushed. It seems unfair that the opinions and prejudices of an old man can go on binding after he's dead. Father's attitude toward Greg and me the minute we began to talk business, fairly made me wince. We've each got an equal authority with him, of course, under the will. But, all the same, we're just his two boys.

"And then, he's all broken up, too, about the strike. They're trying to settle that—did you know?"

"Who are?" Helena wanted to know. She bit down a yawn as she asked the question.

The governor, Hugh said, had appointed a conciliation board, and though neither side—none of the three sides, to put it more accurately, for it was a triangular affair by this time—had agreed to accept its findings, it was holding daily hearings. So far, Hugh gathered from his father and Gregory, the negotiations did not appear very promising.

"It's a real chance for me to do something, I believe," he went on presently. "It means working like a dog, of course, just getting up the facts to begin with. They're not going to stand in my way—father and Greg, I mean. Really, it's wonderful, considering how wide apart our opinions are, how comfortably we've got on together tonight. Greg and I haven't talked as much and quarreled as little in an evening, since I can remember. I suppose it's partly relief on their part, in finding me reasonable.

"Of course, I've got to have the facts before I can give Greg an argument. He's full of them. He was telling me about the molders tonight. They won't come back, he said, except on a closed shop basis; which means that we can't employ or discharge anybody without their consent. Well, there's no harm in that, if they'll give us men who'll deliver a competent day's work and let us discharge ones who won't. But Greg says they don't mean to give us a day's work. He says their limit on what a man can turn out on a molding machine is only a little more than what he could do by hand—somewhere from a third to a fifth of what he could do easily with the machine. If that's true—and Greg thinks it is, of course—why, it's all wrong."

Helena's only comment at this point was an audible yawn.

"Oh, I know it's late," Hugh said. "We can't really go into it tonight. But I'm full of it just now. It seems as if I had a chance of understanding both sides and bringing them together. Only, I need your help in the thing. There are men out there—your friends—that I want to work with. If you'll persuade them that I'm not an enemy—not a benighted bigot it's no use talking to. . . You will, won't you? You can? That's not what *you* think I am?"

She extinguished her cigarette in an ash-tray that stood on a night table, smiled, yawned and stretched all at once, and then, without dropping her arms, held them out to him. He came into them readily enough.

"You're a dear anyway," she said. "Yes, I'll do what I can, of course. Come along to bed." Then, a little more brightly, "I've changed my mind about how we're to live. I don't want a hotel, nor an apartment, either. I want a house. I hadn't an idea how nice they were."

He laughed. "We won't run to a house like this," he warned her. And she said she should hope not. She just wanted something with stairs in it, and separate rooms for all the separate things one wanted to do. "And a bed like this," she specified. "I never dreamed there was such a thing in the world. You'll go house-hunting with me tomorrow, won't you? It's too crazily absurd that I should be living here."

"It's too wonderful that you should be living here," said Hugh.

She made no reply to that observation, but it occurred to her to wonder—it was a very vague and transient wonder, to be sure—how long he'd go on feeling like that.

XVII

Hugh and Helena managed, rather easily, to suit themselves with a house. They found a high-shouldered, rather dignified old place not far south of Chicago Avenue, and east of Rush Street, which gave promise of meeting all their needs pretty adequately. The neighborhood was accessible, physically at least, to Hugh's family and his old friends, so that their going into it lacked anything like a gesture of repudiation. At the same time, there was nothing about it to discourage Helena's friends from the belief that she remained, in spirit, one of them.

It was in a state of decent repair, and they made no attempt to remodel it, beyond tearing out a partition or two on the top floor to give them one big room, which Helena called a study.

They both made a point, rather self-consciously, of wasting as little time as possible over the selection of it; and over the process of installing themselves there they were even more expeditious.

This latter part of the job was left entirely in Helena's hands, since as soon as the lease was signed, Hugh went off to Riverdale and pitched in, as he said, to the strike. She went at it, much as she went at the business of writing a story, with immense assurance, and, on the whole, competency. She rejected, without even the pretense of qualifying regrets, Constance's offer of assistance here. It can not be said of her that she knew in advance what she wanted, but she had what served as a substitute for that knowledge, the ability to make an almost instantaneous selection among objects offered for her choice, and to regard any choice, once made, as final. In an amazingly short time she had her household in running order.

The result she got was by no means bad—certainly not atrocious. But a resemblance might have been detected in it to her literary productions. Done in complete ignorance of all imaginative niceties, it lacked, just as her stories did, the mysterious quality of atmosphere. There was no projection into it of her own picturesque, and, in some aspects, fascinating personality.

The thing that surprised and distinctly amused Hugh about it all was Helena's intense practicality when it came to spending money. There were a hundred cents in every dollar, regardless of the number of dollars there were, and every one of them had to bring in all that it was worth. That he was not disposed to criticize the results she got, does not argue, necessarily, a lack of sensitiveness in him to the atmosphere of his surroundings. A house of his own was as new a thing to him as it was to Helena, and he took a rather boyish pleasure in it. The few hours he spent in it, after long and, from the first, discouraging days out at Riverdale, had a sort of holiday glamour about them.

Riverdale was depressing. The strike had got to a stage where no party to it hoped for any advantage. It was kept up simply by the rancorous determination that no advantage should be conceded to any one else. The strings all sides harped on in all their public statements, were the same old strings they had plucked from the beginning. But the notes they gave forth were frayed and flat.

It was, as Hugh had said, a three-cornered fight. The deepest bitterness it had engendered, existed between two groups of the strikers themselves, the I. W. W. element, which had begun the strike and had been, from the first few weeks, in full control of it, and the trades-unionists, who, weak at first, had been gaining strength from the beginning. The fanatical all-or-nothing policy, which the syndicalist creed of the I. W. W. commits it to, is, as a matter of fact, much more effective during the first fortnight of a strike than it is during the second and third. When it comes to settling down for a long pull, to organizing, gathering up advantages and making a good trade, the old, profoundly experienced Federation leaves the radicals nowhere. They had got to work at once, organizing unorganized trades, and stiffening up what rudimentary organizations they found, paving the way to the parley, the long process of trade and compromise which they knew must eventually come.

To the industrial unionist the fundamental idea of a trade union is aristocratic, reactionary and abhorrent. He says—and with a certain amount of truth—that the advantages which these skilled workers win for themselves with their closed-shop agreements and limited apprenticeships, are won, not at the expense of the common enemy, the capitalist, but at the expense of the great body of unskilled labor which can not, in the nature of things, organize itself so effectively and is, therefore, robbed like Peter, to pay Paul; works its endless hours and pockets its pitiable pay to make up for the exactions of the labor aristocrats.

The sight, then, of the molders' union out at Riverdale, negotiating a separate treaty of peace, roused a furious resentment among the radicals. If the molders went back and one or two of the other trades followed them, the strike would be broken indeed.

Hugh agreed with Helena's friends, the two or three radical leaders whom he prevailed on her to introduce him to, in regarding this outcome as wholly unsatisfactory and little better than disastrous. The hours he spent attending the hearings of the conciliation board, seemed to him utterly wasted. The thing was nothing but a horse trade—a game of haggle and bluff, a series of compromises with this union and that, between the most that Gregory could be induced to grant and the least that each particular trade could be induced to accept—a result hardly worth working for. The resultant peace from such a treaty as that could not be more than temporary. It would be full of destructive internal strains, injustices and inequalities. The real desideratum—a decent living wage to everybody, and a decent profit over the top for the company, the modeling of the whole mass while it was still plastic, so that in cooling and hardening it should not break down anywhere, was as far out of Greg's contemplation as it was out of the unionists'.

At the first hearing or two of the board that Hugh attended he had been profoundly impressed by Gregory's ability. It was the sort of situation that keyed Greg up to his best, and his best was very good indeed. He was amazingly informed, instantly ready, and in addition, he was, or seemed to be, candid, good-humored; fairer, more conciliatory, immensely more open-minded than any of the representatives of the strikers. In his determined fight against a deliberate limitation of output he seemed to Hugh demonstrably right. He found it hard to account for the implacable and almost derisive hostility with which the piece-work schedules, which Gregory offered as a counter proposition, were received.

But before Hugh had spent many hours analyzing figures for himself—raw figures, original documents such as old cost sheets and pay-rolls, he perceived that his brother's compilations and summaries were not as artless as they purported to be. They were not false any more than an expert's testimony on the stand, in answer to the carefully stated hypothetical questions of the side that has retained him, is false. But they were, in many cases, profoundly misleading.

"Well," Greg said with a wry smile when Hugh taxed him with it, "you have a real eye for business figures."

This was in his office at the plant one night—the same room that had witnessed their quarrel on that memorable evening in May, when Hugh had rescued Helena from Paddock's kidnapers.

"I'll confess," the older brother went on, "that I have never given you credit for it. I don't believe there's a man in the organization, barring

Bailey, who could have—got the goods on me like that. You're perfectly right as far as you go. I haven't a word to say."

"All right," said Hugh. "Now tell me where it is that I don't go. What is there beyond where I stop off? What's your idea? You're an honest man. What are you doing with crooked figures?—Well, misleading figures, then. In a sense they're straight, of course."

"Thanks for that," said Greg grimly. "Why, the idea is that I am making a fight for our property. I'm sticking to my own side of the argument. I'm not pretending to be the umpire. I'm after, in so many words, the best trade I can make. Because I happen to know, by experience, that the best I can get won't be any too good. We operate, when all's said, on a damn narrow margin of profit. If we can't show a profit, we're out of business. It's a question of what the traffic will bear. What I lose in one place, I've got to make up somewhere else. If one bunch out there are in a position to force me to pay them more than they're worth, I've got to make some other bunch take less. As a matter of fact, what they're worth, from Bailey down, is what they can make me pay for what I have to have. That's the long and short of it."

"What I am trying to get at," said Hugh, "is that the business has got to stand the payment of a decent living wage to every operative who has to live by it. If it won't, in this department or that, then there's something fatally wrong somewhere; either in the labor or in the organization. And the responsibility for finding where it is wrong, and making it right, is on us. That's what we're here for. That's all that justifies us in riding along comfortably on top. If we aren't equal to the job, it's time they tipped us out. You *are* the umpire. That's my view of the thing."

They wrestled over this difference half the night. But it was a fundamental one and they were as far apart at the end as at the beginning. They did not quarrel in their wonted fashion at all. Their nearest approach to it was when Hugh asked Greg, apropos of the question of higher efficiency, whether he had read Taylor's book on *Scientific Management.*

"Don't talk that to me," Greg said hotly. "Talk it to Holden and Mapes." These were the representatives, respectively, of the molders' and the machinists' unions. "Or to Helena's friends, Parkin and Jim Lea. See how they take it."

"That's about," Hugh answered, "what it's in my mind to do."

"You mean," Greg demanded with an intent look at him, "that you're thinking of 'going outside the fence' again?" He did not go on to say that that last excursion of his brother had been unhappy enough in its outcome to stand as a warning against another, but the thought vibrated palpably in the air.

But after a rather breathless little silence they took up the argument—once more impersonally, and they managed to keep that note to the end.

"I've got to have a try at the thing on my own," Hugh said as they parted. "I won't embarrass you more than I can help, but I suppose I shall more or less. I think you're half right—or maybe a little more. And I think you're the only man in sight who's got the ability it needs to swing the thing. That's why I've been trying so hard to get you to see that that trust of grandfather's involves more than his money." He grinned and added, "Though perhaps he didn't realize that himself."

"You bet he didn't," said Greg. "Well, there's no use chewing the rag any longer, I suppose. Good night."

Both felt something ominous in the friendliness of that parting. It showed how deep the difference cut. After that, when they met they avoided all mention of the business—chatted pleasantly about safe subjects, family trivialities—old times, and so on. And they separated as soon as they comfortably could. Hugh had gone outside the fence indeed.

Hugh got nowhere at all with Mapes and Holden. One brief and rather acrimonious session with them was enough to convince him that there was no thoroughfare there. They were special pleaders, like Gregory, and their aim, like his, was the best trade they could get. Both were clever, without penetration. They challenged Greg confidently at his own game, and it was hard to resist the feeling that if they were out-maneuvered, they deserved what they got.

With the other two, Parkin and James Lea, Hugh found himself, emotionally at least, in sympathy. They were vaguely adumbrating a great idea. They were fumbling with the lock, it is true. But it was the right door they were trying to open.

They were a curiously contrasted pair. Parkin, small, wiry, compact, with very large, bright eyes, a jutting nose rather finely modeled, a long pointed chin and, above a high narrow brow, a head of fine, wavy, upstanding hair, was an out and out fanatic. There was a strong touch of mystical asceticism about him. Given a different environment and he might have been a very High Church clergyman in a slum parish. He'd have made an admirable model for an artist who wanted to paint a haloed saint in the manner of the primitives.

Lea was a middle-aged, and not very prepossessing man, committed to the sort of a large, low collar that goes with a thin neck and an Adam's apple of great prominence and mobility. His countenance was habitually solemn, but there was a fugitive gleam in his eye and a quirk to his mouth—it extended itself indeed to an involuntary occasional twitch of the tip of his nose—suggesting that if one could get at what he was really thinking about one might learn something. Hugh developed, in time, a genuine liking for them both.

The three of them, with Helena, spent hours—nights almost— in the big, half-furnished room up at the top of Hugh's new house, threshing matters out. They smoked and talked, ate sandwiches and talked, drank—beer or coffee at preference—and talked, around and round interminably.

Others were present, too, at these "conferences," but they merely formed a sort of fringe, various in identity and never really important.

Parkin, the most voluble of the four, never really argued; never met an issue or controverted a statement. He did not surmount an opposing fact; merely used it as a point of departure for a tangential flight in the direction of infinity.

Lea liked to argue, though there was a humorous unscrupulousness in his choice and use of weapons.

As for Helena, she preserved, most of the time, a curious aloofness to it all, as of one listening to familiar music, though sometimes she swooped superbly to the rescue of one or the other of her partisans— never of Hugh—and when she did, she combined the prowess of both: Parkin's flaming zeal and Lea's resourcefulness.

What Hugh pleaded for—and what he never got—was a constructive program that would meet the existing case—a present, immediate aim, which could conceivably be accomplished. There was a set of ascertained, or ascertainable, facts to be dealt with. These were being dealt with now in a way they all agreed was wrong. There was no need of any further proof of that. The thing he wanted to discover was a practical way of dealing with them that was right.

"Oh, there's no use in trying to get together, Corbett," Lea said at last one night, "deciding on a program and all that. We don't want the same thing. There's the short of it. You want peace and we want war."

"War for its own sake?" Hugh demanded. "Perpetual war? War isn't a thing you can live on."

"Put it at this then," said Lea. "That you want peace before we've fairly begun to fight. You want peace that'll leave you in possession. You want a peace that'll leave you your Packard, while we're still tramping through the mud. Well, what we want's a Ford for everybody! And we mean to fight until we get it."

"You won't get it by fighting," said Hugh. "Because it isn't there to get. Did you ever take the trouble to look up the dividends that Corbett & Company has paid in the last ten years? It's averaged just over eight percent annually, on a five million dollar capitalization. That's four hundred thousand dollars a year."

"Well, that looks pretty good to me," said Lea with a grin.

"Does it?" said Hugh. "Then you're weak on arithmetic. Divide that up among five thousand employees. It comes to eighty dollars a year. That's a dollar and sixty cents a week. That's what you'd get if you brought off your revolution—turned us out completely and took over the business yourselves. You'd get it, that is, if you were capable of running the job as skilfully and efficiently as Greg does. And that's what some people would probably call a rash presumption."

"Of course you're talking nonsense," said Helena, uneasily—the other two men were simply staring from each other's faces to Hugh's. "I don't see just where the catch is, but. . ."

"Why, it's in that little word dividends," said Lea, with a sudden return of assurance. "Dividends is profits they don't take the trouble to hide. It's the lamb after they've done shearing it. There's what they call overhead and expense, and depreciation, and God knows what other juggling tricks."

"And fat salaries," put in Helena. "Bailey with his twenty-four thousand a year."

Lea laughed triumphantly. "That'd make a neat little addition to your dollar sixty a week," he said.

"Ten cents," Hugh told him. "Just under ten cents, on the basis of an even five thousand employees."

Parkin had been getting up steam, and now he launched forth, annihilating Hugh's pettifogging trivialities in a great gust of oratory. There were just two bed-rock facts: natural resources, coal, wood, iron and so on, which belonged, by rights, to all mankind. And there was labor; the toil of blood and sweat which made those gifts available for man. The rest was all lies and tricks.

Hugh listened helplessly until the gale spent itself. Then he said: "I wish I could give you all a lesson in elementary bookkeeping. All our books are for is to enable us to keep track of the facts so that we'll know how much we dare divide in dividends. I'd hate to see that plant after you'd run it five years without charging off overhead and depreciation. And as for salaries—well, if we couldn't see Bailey saving us twice what we pay him, we'd let him go. You people don't want to look at the facts. That's what's the matter with you."

"The matter with you is," Parkin said angrily, "that you're a capitalist at heart as well as in fact. You've been wearing your sheepskin very prettily, but you've shown us the fangs and the claws tonight."

"I suppose that's the only possible line to take," said Hugh, "when you're afraid to face the facts."

"The only line is the battle line," said Parkin, and the other two nodded appreciatively over this rejoinder. "Our first word is fight, and our last word is fight."

"And the fact is," said Hugh, "that the thing you talk about fighting for isn't there. Personally, you don't fight, you know. You talk. And for talking purposes, it suits you to assume that there's a sort of rich easy paradise that you could enjoy if you could just break into it. It's a fool's paradise. That dollar and sixty cents a week is a fact. It makes you angry because it's ridiculous. It isn't big enough to fight for, and if you did fight for it, it would disappear altogether; come out with a minus sign in front of it. The only way to make it bigger is to stop fighting and cooperate. Force capital to cooperate with you. Yes. And give you your share. Yes."

"Our share," said Parkin furiously. "Our share is all there is." And, as he got up to go, "I feel a fool for having wasted my time with you."

Between Hugh and Helena, after the others had gone, the wrangle protracted itself far into the night.

"Anyhow," she said to him, "by your own admission, you're stealing a dollar and sixty cents a week from each of those slaves of yours."

His answer was that he admitted nothing of the sort. "Grandfather put his life into that business; a perfectly extraordinary amount of energy and imagination. And—well, something that was more than that. Honor, if you like—devotion. Any sacrifice that it demanded of him, he made. There have been times, any number of them, when it made him sweat blood to get the money to meet his pay-rolls. Well, he got it, and he met them. Would a squabbling committee of the men have done as much as that? Not in a thousand years. I'll tell you what that dollar and sixty cents a week is. It's insurance that they'll get the rest."

"Well, there's no doubt whose side you're on now," Helena said. "Your family'll take you back with open arms, when they hear you talk like that."

It may be admitted that Hugh ought to have read, that night, the handwriting on the wall. It would have saved him a very bitter experience—an almost embittering experience, had he done so. But his fighting blood was up. He had got the bit in his teeth again.

He shut himself up for a week, got his material ready, and wrote a series of what he called speeches. He had printed a vast quantity of leaflets. He placarded the town of Riverdale and hired the only sizable hall in the place, for four evenings. And there, under no auspices but his own, on a stage ungraced by the countenance even of a polite chairman, he tried to force a recognition of the facts which, for him, made up the truth.

He had no grandiose hopes of a sweeping success. But if he could rally a party—even a small one, that would set out marching in the right direction; along the only road that was a thoroughfare, he would have felt his effort well repaid.

But the thing was a colossal fiasco. He had no experience as a speaker, and no innate sense of oratorical values. All he had to recommend him beyond the bare content of his ideas, was a genuine earnestness. And this, a bad stage-manner went a long way to disguise.

Besides, he had a great deal too much to say. The thing he contemplated offering to the rough-and-ready audience out at Riverdale, amounted to an attack on the whole system of current political economy and the sketching in outline of a new one.

For the first two nights his audience packed the hall—an idly curious, mildly derisive audience which flared up every now and then in overt hostility. The things he was saying affronted both camps of strikers; the trades-unionists and the radicals, about equally. And while one side booed and hissed, the other ironically applauded. The next moment, perhaps, the tables would be turned. It was only when he ranged his guns upon his own class—his own family, as with complete candor, he sometimes did—that his audience united. And even then they mocked as at one who, unwittingly, was giving himself away.

None of his clan was present in the hall. But reporters were, from most of the city papers. It was a capital news story, of course, that one of the Corbetts—the wild one, who had recently married the anarchist's daughter—had run amuck again. There was no deliberate unfairness in their selection, for their reports, of his attacks upon his class and tribe, to the exclusion of all else. It was simply that they were good reporters. Hugh Corbett, as a renegade, was news. As a constructive critic of the program of labor, he was not.

By the third night the novelty of the thing had worn off. The hard array of facts was getting dull. And then, besides, there was something more important to think about. The conciliation board had made its report that day—a report which was bitterly resented, especially by the radical wing of the strikers. So Hugh's audience that night only half filled the hall. It yawned and stretched, shuffled its feet, and began, before he had half finished, to melt away.

It was the next morning—a Saturday, as it happened—that Gregory published a total rejection, root and branch, of the recommendations of the board.

It is probable that if he had waited, every one of the strike committees would have rejected them as well, and the onus of the rejection might thus have been put on the other foot. But Greg was a Napoleonic rather than a Fabian fighter.

All that day it was easy to see that there was a storm brewing in Riverdale. Not since the first violent week of the strike had the mutterings and threats been so loud.

Hugh began speaking, that night, to an audience of not more than a hundred persons: a few crochetty idealists with panaceas of their own, a few old people who liked the warmth and the bright lights of the hall, a sprinkling of sociologists and settlement workers; hardly one genuine striker among them. But by nine o'clock, it having begun to rain, a mob came surging in from the street, not a frenzied mob at all—not actuated by any very clear idea; at most, by an ugly impatience that that fool was still spouting in there—that rich young man who didn't know his luck and, for some unaccountable reason, saw fit to bite the hand that fed him. They went in to stop his talk. And they did.

There was no disposition to offer him violence. Nobody tried to clamber up on the stage. They stood there, in the aisles and on the seats, and howled him down. When he saw that that was their intention, that they meant to stay there as long as he did, and wouldn't hear a word, he put his papers in his pocket and, with a nod and a rueful smile, which they greeted with a humorous cheer, acknowledged his defeat. He showed no hesitation about coming down from the stage right into the thick of them, and with them—among the last of them—made his way toward the door.

Half the crowd, perhaps, had got out of the hall, when, simultaneously with the boom of an explosion, the building shook and a good deal of the glass in the windows overlooking the street—in the direction of the one exit, that is to say—fell with a crash. The confounding suddenness of it, together with the fact that danger seemed to lie in the direction of the doors, produced an instant of spellbound silence before the panic could break. Hugh was quick enough to take advantage of it.

He said, casually almost, but in a voice that easily filled the big room, "That's not this building. It's in the plant across the street. You're perfectly safe if you go out quietly." Then as the surge of excited voices began welling up around him and showed that the danger of a stampede was not quite passed, he shouted a joke.

"Or if you want to stay in here," he said, "I'll finish my speech!" There was a laugh, a fusillade of satirical but good-humored replies, and the crowd made its way safely down the stairs and out of the building.

Hugh's guess that the explosion had taken place in the plant was verified when he got out into the street, by the crimson flames which were already leaping up from one of the buildings inside the fence, and two hundred yards, perhaps, to the westward. The paint-shop, of course! There was a high north wind with a little fine rain in it,—not enough to amount to anything, but the direction it blew from meant that the town was safe.

As for the plant, a part of it anyway—the old part—was certainly doomed. With the furious start the fire had got from the intensely inflammable nature of the material it began upon, and driven before a wind like that, it would be irresistible—would burn its way clean across until it was stopped by the river. None of the more modern buildings, however, was in that track. The plant had expanded westward. What with their position and the fact that they were built supposedly of fire-proof materials, they stood a good chance to escape. The building to make the fight for was the old administration building, which stood just west of the Charles Street gate; between it and the paint-shop. All the offices were here; all the records. By a fight it might be saved.

All that went through Hugh's mind while he was breaking through the crowd in the street and making his way down to the door marked "office," where he had left his mother's car, the night he rescued Helena.

For the next few hours he was nothing but one of the Corbetts.

XVIII

The man who set off the bomb—it took six months of detective work to bring the crime home to him and get a confession—proved to be not one of the strikers at all, but an ex-employee whose dismissal dated back three or four years. His mind had perhaps got a little unbalanced from long harboring of a grudge, but he had been shrewd enough to see that the strike held out a promise of immunity from suspicion for all except the strikers themselves.

So far as immediate results went, the job came off just as he had planned it, and one can fancy him drifting along with the crowd in Charles Street, feeling very safe from detection, and smiling grimly in the folds of an upturned ulster collar, over the stupendous harvest of havoc his hatred would reap. But the ultimate results confounded his calculations. It turned out that he had done Corbett & Company a service. The fire swept clean an area of about forty acres that had been encumbered by old buildings unfitted to the work that had to be done in them, a liability rather than an asset in that the cost of their insurance ran to staggering figures. All the new buildings, which—as Hugh had supposed they would—escaped or withstood the fire, had been erected in accordance with a plan which involved eventually tearing the old ones down.

It was, evidently, a statement of Robert Corbett's in the newspapers on Monday morning, to the effect that the losses were fully covered by insurance, and that work on the new buildings—whose plans already were drawn—would begin immediately, that first brought this consideration to the mind of the criminal. He sent an anonymous letter to the Chicago chief of police, hinting that since the fire was so advantageous to Corbett & Company, it would be well to investigate the possibility of their having set it themselves. It was this letter which gave the investigators the first of the clews that resulted finally in his capture and confession. But long before that happened the new buildings were up and in operation and Gregory had a plant that was, in every detail, the last word in efficient shop engineering.

Another important advantage the company got from the fire was that it ended the strike. The temporary necessity of closing down the whole plant—a necessity none could dispute—resulted in a change of feeling; a reaction, not logical perhaps, but certainly psychological. Everybody had had enough. That flaming night provided a needed emotional climax. After that it was time to turn over a new leaf. Concessions could be made without, as pidgin-English has it, a loss of face. And everybody made them. The details of the treaty need not be reported here.

The only person among those this story is concerned with, to whom the fire did a serious disservice, was Hugh. Preposterously, he was held responsible for it.

There is a genuine truth in the apparently frivolous phrase, "If I say it three times, it's so." It is the fundamental principle of modern advertising. To put it more seriously, it is the repeated impression that remains.

The newspaper-reading public had already had Hugh pictured to it as an irresponsible fanatic, on the occasion of his marriage, a scant two months before. So, when the papers took him up again—told how he was preaching socialism and anarchy (there is an ineradicable doubt in the reportorial mind as to which is which) out at Riverdale, denouncing his own family as oppressors of the poor, recklessly rousing the strikers to a renewed resistance and intensifying their animosity—already bitter enough against any form, however moderate, of capitalistic control,—it did not occur to anybody to question the fairness of these reports, or to doubt whether, as a matter of fact, Hugh had done these things. Of course he had done them! It was just the sort of thing that a man capable of flying off and marrying an anarchist, would do.

Then, on top of it all, Hugh was the victim once more, of a coincidence. The occurrence of the bomb outrage and the fire, on the very night of the last of his speeches, produced the inference, as inevitable as it was unwarranted, that it was the speeches which had incited the planting of the bomb. That young fool ought to be forcibly restrained. If his family were wise, they'd have his sanity looked into, and shut him up in a private asylum somewhere. He'd be murdering somebody the next thing any one knew.

In the family the feeling was deeper, though the expression of it, of course, was much less violent. They acquitted Hugh of any inflammatory intent in those speeches of his. And even, after they'd cooled down a bit, of any direct casual connection with the fire. Mrs. Corbett bluntly told Gregory that his own rejection, that Saturday morning, of the findings of the conciliation board, had more to do, in all likelihood, with the planting of the bomb, than any of Hugh's vaporings.

"I don't know exactly what he said, of course," she admitted, "but I know, in a general way, the run of his ideas, and there's nothing about them to set the world on fire. Besides it's a safe guess that his talk was miles over their heads. He says himself that they were bored to death before he was half done."

"Oh, very likely," Gregory conceded. "But the fact remains that for him to hire a hall out there and try to talk at all, with public feeling in the state it was just then, was simply idiotic."

"He's got twice my brains," he went on reflectively, "but the fact is he can't be counted on. He's proved that twice now. In a good many ways he's the best of the lot. I know grandfather thought so. But he does things, every now and then, well—that one of us simply can't do."

That, finally, was the family's verdict. It was possible to go on being fond of Hugh; impossible, indeed, not to. And one might admire him— his talents, his capacities, even his Quixotic altruism. But they could not regard him any longer as, in that deep-lying clan sense, one of them. He had, in his own phrase, gone outside the fence once too often.

There was nothing formal about the verdict of course. Except in that one curt phrase Gregory had employed in the talk with his mother, just reported, it was never expressed in words at all. And it was weeks before the realization of it finally came home to Hugh.

The fire nearly cost Robert Corbett his life. He had driven out with Gregory in the rain, late that Saturday night, in response to the alarm that had been immediately telephoned, of course, to the house. They drove out in Gregory's open roadster and Robert had spent the rest of the night, and a good part of the next day, on the scene. The fatigue and long exposure proved too much for him. He caught a bad cold, neglected it in the excitement of those ensuing days, and came down with a furious double pneumonia which narrowly missed killing him.

That was, of course—and most unjustly—added to the tale of Hugh's responsibilities. If any human agency was fairly chargeable with the misfortune, it was old Gregory, now in the grave. No profound spiritual shock, such as the revelation in his father's will had been to Robert, is without a corresponding physical reaction. And in this case, the reaction had been palpable. Robert Corbett had not been the same man since the day after his father's funeral; had not walked so straight, nor breathed so deep. The man he had been would, in reasonable likelihood, have thrown off the exhaustion of that night of the fire, just as his sons did.

As it was, he pulled through and surmounted the primary stages of convalescence as rapidly as the doctor hoped he would. But at the point where, dressed and able to be about, he began attempting a normal well man's routine rather than an invalid's, he was sharply halted. One tentative morning at the office, though Bemis drove him out and back most tenderly in a closed car, proved altogether too much for him.

So he settled down, with what grace he could, to a regimentation of naps, eggnogs and walks—if the day was fine—as far as the park. Sometimes he walked south instead and dropped in on Helena. On Helena rather than on Hugh, because Hugh was seldom at home in the middle of the day. His wife professed ignorance of his exact whereabouts.

"I think he goes to one of the libraries," she told Robert, and added, after a pause, "to write."

"To write!" Robert echoed. "Do you mean a book?"

Helena's brows puckered ruefully. "I don't know," she confessed. "He doesn't talk to me about it."

"Why doesn't he write at home?" Robert wanted to know. "That's what that study of yours is for, isn't it?"

Helena said with a smile, "I think it's in order to be away from home part of the time, that he's writing the book."

In his gallant, mannerly way, Robert ridiculed this conclusion. But he professed himself able to understand how, granted that a book was to be written, or any other sort of serious work undertaken, Helena's husband might well find a distraction at home that it was prudent and even necessary to flee from. He felt sure he would find it so himself.

Helena, who loved this sort of thing, replied appropriately, that she would certainly find it necessary to turn *him* out of the house during the working hours, and their mild little flirtation moved pleasantly along these lines, until Robert took his leave. But, going, he said:

"I'll come again tomorrow, if I may, and I wish you'd tell Hugh that that is my intention. If he feels that he can neglect his book for that hour, I would be glad to see him."

Helena suggested as an improvement on the plan, that he come to lunch, and promised to produce Hugh as a part of the feast. "A celebration of your getting well," she said.

A shade crossed Robert's face at that. To any one who took, as Robert had always taken, the Corbett physique for granted, his present state of semi-invalidism was a source of real humiliation. He brightened up resolutely, however, and told Helena in just the courtly way that pleased her, that he would come.

Hugh came to lunch next day, as Helena had promised he would, and—what she had been far less confident about—took his part very pleasantly in the talk; lent himself to the vein of it with a light-heartedness of which she had forgotten he was capable. She wished he might be a little more like that when they were by themselves. That curious insensitiveness of hers saw, heard, felt nothing of the thing that underlay the surface gaiety; the nervous tensity not far from fear in her father-in-law, or her husband's melancholy. She was surprised into a start of overt displeasure when Hugh, as they finished their coffee, said: "I think father wants to talk with me. Shall he and I go into the library, or stay here?"

But when she read acquiescence in Robert's more regretfully worded phrases, she left them abruptly.

There was rather a long silence after she had gone. The genuine pity Hugh had felt for his father ever since that first night after their return from New York, was much more poignant today than it had been before. It was not only the physical weakness that he saw, though that alone would have been pitiable enough and, in the light of what Hugh had expected from Helena's reports of him to find, was almost shocking. But the other thing which Hugh had felt from the moment when they shook hands; the timidity—the air of deprecation, of a sort of wistful apology, wrung his heart and, at the same time, made him feel warmly indignant at the two Gregorys. It was they who had done this thing, between them.

But these were feelings which it was impossible for Hugh to express. They would be difficult, I suppose, for any son to express to a father. They are no part of the conventional filial attitude.

It was Robert who presently broke the silence with a remark—palpably not connected with the subject he had come to talk with Hugh about,—concerning Hugh's book. Helena had said he was engaged in the writing of one.

"I doubt if it ever turns out to be a book," Hugh said. "I read more than I write, and I unlearn more than I learn, I guess. Like the frog jumping out of the well."

"You're fortunate," Robert said, "in being able to do your unlearning early in life—before it is too late to begin."

"There is much," he went on, "that I'd be glad to unlearn. But I only made that discovery simultaneously with the one that I am an old man."

"Old!" said Hugh. "You're not sixty."

"It is not a matter of years, I think," said Robert. "My father was never old in the sense I mean."

"It's not age with you," Hugh said bluntly, "it's illness. You're much farther from well than I had any notion of. You're hardly any stronger, if at all, than the last time I saw you."

"It is a slow process, I suppose," said Robert.

"It needn't be as slow as this. Shouldn't be, either." Then, as the idea occurred to him, he went on. "Why don't you go away? This is an infernal climate for an invalid to wrestle with. Why don't you and mother go to Santa Barbara for the winter? I don't see why no one thought of that before."

"That. . ." said Robert, and paused. Hugh noted with astonishment, that his father's hand was shaking.

"That," Robert began again, "is what I have come to speak to you about. Doctor Darby says it would be advisable, and your mother is anxious that we start at once. Before the weather gets any worse."

"Of course," said Hugh. "Why not?"

"Gregory feels," said Robert, "—we—we both feel, that in certain contingencies, it might be necessary that I be here. In default, that is, of an arrangement that might be made. . ."

At that the light broke over Hugh. His father saw the puzzled look in his face give way to a sudden flush and stare of comprehension.

"You want me to resign from the trust?" said Hugh. "So that with you away there'd be no danger of my interference? But can I do that without going to the courts?—Or was that the idea?"

He was almost inarticulate from the effort he had to make to keep the note of anger out of his voice.

No such drastic action as that, Robert hastily assured him, was necessary, or had been in contemplation for a moment. Only, with himself away, unable to cast a deciding vote on any question that might arise, unable so the medical verdict was, to take, for many months, an active part even in the consideration of matters of business policy, it had seemed to Gregory—and to himself as well, Robert loyally added—that some embarrassing, and possibly disastrous situations might arise from the fact that the two remaining trustees possessed an equal authority. If Hugh would be willing, for the present, to waive his legal right to interfere—in a word, to recognize his brother's authority as paramount—Robert could go away with a quiet mind.

"I'll write Greg a note to that effect, of course," said Hugh hastily. "Or if he prefers to draft it himself, I'll sign it."

"My boy!" Robert Corbett cried; and a more poignant feeling found expression in that pair of words than Hugh had ever heard from his lips before. "Your word is all we want. It is not your honor that we are in doubt about."

The sight of tears in his father's eyes stung Hugh to a sharp resumption of self-command. He said, in a voice that sounded about as he meant it to:

"I can't blame you for doubting pretty much everything else about me. I hadn't any idea of harassing Greg. But it's no wonder he didn't want to be left to my mercies." Then, in spite of himself, his tone took on an edge. "All that I don't see is why Greg put the job of—belling the cat—up to you."

"It was his idea to speak to you himself," Robert explained. "I insisted that it be left to me."

Hugh nodded, and presently got himself going upon the theme of the wonderful climate of southern California and the benefits his father would derive from it. He hadn't much idea of what he was saying, and it is doubtful if his father had. All that mattered to either of them was that the talk should be kept going, somehow, until the car should come to take the invalid home.

"What was it all about?" Helena asked when Robert had gone.

She had been waiting in the hall to bid her father-in-law good-by, as a dutiful hostess should. Her question was natural enough, too, as Hugh admitted while he resented it. He had hoped to escape Helena altogether; to get away by himself. He *must* get away by himself, where he could relax that iron grip he had been keeping, on thought as well as on word, ever since his father had voiced the family's decree of exile (that was what it came to) upon him.

In Helena's presence, under her intently regarding eyes, the need for that unrelaxed grip was greater than ever. He did not trouble to ask himself why this was so. It was already clearer than any reasoning process could make it, that it would be intolerable that his wife should even suspect the nature of that fiat of Gregory's. (It was Gregory's, of course, though the others had concurred in it.) Just as intolerable as that the family should discover—his other secret.

"Didn't you hear what I said just now?" his wife's voice broke in upon him. "You've stood there staring for five minutes. What was the wonderful secret?"

"Secret!" he echoed. Her picking up—like that—of the word that had been in his own thoughts, startled him.

"The secret," she explained in open mockery, "that I had to be turned out of the room for you two to talk about."

He got himself together. "I'm sorry it seemed like turning you out. It was only that they've decided that father ought to go away. For the winter. To southern California. He isn't getting well as fast as he should. He wanted to talk with me about it."

She laughed, angrily—and it may be conceded that her annoyance was pardonable. "If you can't tell better lies than that you'd better not lie at all."

"It happens not to be a lie," Hugh told her. Then he roused himself to improving the plausibility of it. "There are things that have got to be decided about the estate before he goes. That was what we talked about. Particularly, father wanted to be sure that my views coincided with Greg's about the possibility of his going at all. As soon as I'd assured him they did, we fell back on the climate and sea-bathing and orange-grove—that sort, of thing."

Then, with a look at his watch,—"I'd like to get another couple of hours at the library. . ."

"Don't go!" she commanded shortly. "I've got something to say myself, and it may as well be now."

She led the way into their drawing-room and, as he followed, said: "I wish you'd sit down." She did not herself, however; but walked across to the little white marble mantel piece and took her station there instead.

It always irritated her, he had noted, to have to talk to him when they were both standing. His great height deprived her of an advantage she did not like to do without. Her only way of neutralizing it, when he insisted on remaining upon his feet, was by herself lying out on something. But there was no couch in the drawing-room.

"I won't go on like this, Hugh," she said when she was ready. There was a kind of dangerous quiet about her as she stood there looking down at him. This was not going to be merely one of their routine quarrels. A realization of that kept him from speaking when her pause gave him a chance to do so.

"You're entitled to ask 'Like what?'" she went on. "You know. But I don't mind telling you. You've been perfectly nice and polite. There's nothing I could go into your rotten divorce courts with. You're treating me in a way that would be perfectly satisfactory I suppose, to. . ."

His eyes met hers and she hesitated; afraid, the literal truth was, to say the name that was on her lips.

". . . to any of the girls of your own sort who'd have been glad enough to marry you. But I won't go on living with a man—half living with him—who makes me feel as if I was something he was saddled with. You've kept it up long enough. Ever since the morning after the fire out at Riverdale. If it's just that you're angry over the things I said then, why it's time you got over it. Beat me, if you like. You ought to have done it then, if you felt like that. But then get over it.

"If you're not angry about that any more, and if there's nothing else that you have got angry about since—something that I don't know about—if it's just that you're sick of your bargain; that you don't like me—don't like to see me or hear me talk, or—put your hands on me, why you can say so and let that be the end of it. I've done all I know to make up for that morning."

She waited until he should speak; and it was plain to him that he must speak quickly lest the silence should answer for him. He must say the right thing, too. A good many seconds were recorded by the glass-domed anniversary clock whose revolving pendulum swung so lazily, before he found his voice.

She was almost altogether right; that was the plain truth. Certainly right in her complaint. Right in saying that his anger—if it was anger—had had time to cool. But was she right in her surmise that all desire for her was dead in him? Partly. It was a queer thing that had happened to him on that morning she had referred to. Something had gone snap like a frayed violin string, and would not, he thought, ever be played upon again.

There had been nothing much about that quarrel of theirs to establish it as a different thing—put it in a different species—from those they had had so many of and had so easily forgotten.

He had come in, wet, smoke-blackened, pretty well tired out after the fight they had had to make to save their office building from the flames. He was tired in spirit, too; and with reason enough. In a mood, if ever he had been, that wanted understanding and gentleness and comfort and security, to come home to.

But what he had found at home was very different. Helena, with a disposition to irony—a note she never managed very well. She had had a night of it too.

She had finished a short story in the middle of the evening, and was waiting up for Hugh's return from Riverdale in order to read it to him. About eleven o'clock came a telephone message, not in Hugh's voice, but relayed under his instructions, that the plant was afire.

With a little more energy, she would have dressed and gone out to Riverdale herself. For it was exactly her sort of thing—spectacular, terrifying, destructive. She liked to fancy herself haranguing a crowd, lit by the glare of it. She made them a wonderful speech. She saw their massed faces; heard their cheers—glowed, throbbed, quivered with it all.

(But while her spirit was indulging in these flights, her silk-clad body was reclining among the cushions of the *chaise longue* in a fire-lit room, her only physical reminder of the tempestuous world, the squalls of rain that audibly lashed the windows.)

About two o'clock she got another telephone message; this from her mother-in-law. Since the message had been sent under Hugh's instructions, Mrs. Corbett had assumed that it was meant for Helena, and called her up. Hugh was not to be expected home that night. The fire was being dealt with as successfully as one could hope.

It was natural that Helena should have taken this occasion to express the proper regret concerning the disaster; natural, too, that the sincerity of it should have sounded, even over the telephone, rather dubious. It was also natural that Mrs. Corbett, who had been getting half-hourly bulletins from Riverdale since midnight, and was fully capable of figuring out for herself the advantageous aspect to Corbett & Company of the attempted injury, should have communicated these considerations to Helena. It is not too much to say that she rubbed them in with a gusto that far outran discretion. Nothing was afire, or going to take fire, that wouldn't in the course of the next year or two have had to be torn down anyhow. What it boiled down to was the greatest piece of luck that had befallen Corbett & Company in many a long day. She did not go the length of saying that Helena's anarchists would need to be a lot wiser before they could hope to make an effective war upon society, but this implication was vibrant in what she did say.

Helena did not go back to her long chair after that. She spent the rest of the night, or most of it, pacing and prowling about her pretty room, like one of the big cats her movements so often reminded people of. And when she finally went to bed, it was not to sleep.

Her process of reasoning was precisely that which the criminal afterward tried to impress upon the chief of police. Since the thing turned out so advantageously to the Corbetts, they—Gregory that is to say—must have done it. Of course he had done it! Why had she been such a fool as not to have seen it from the first? It was what these contemptible capitalists were always doing when strikes gave them the slightest excuse.

And the thought of Hugh out there, risking his life, perhaps, to check the conflagration his brother had let loose, gave her a sensation of contemptuous pity. That was the mood in which she received him about ten o'clock Sunday morning.

"Of course," she said to him when he told her how little damage, except to the strikers themselves, the fire had done. "You could trust Gregory to see to that." And when, with a stare, he asked her what she meant, she told him in words of one syllable.

It was not until he refused to hear her arguments, that she grew angry. Then she whipped up one of her familiar tempests.

"I'll give you my personal guarantee," he said finally, "that Greg had nothing to do with it. He's exactly as incapable of that as I would be."

"Well," she said then, "how do I know that you weren't in it too? Perhaps it was your brother's idea that you should hire a hall and make those speeches and try to get them angry enough so that it would seem likely they'd do such a thing."

It was then that the string snapped. He realized, of course, that this last was not a serious accusation;—was simply a stroke of the claw, meant to tear anything that could be torn. His anger suddenly left him. He sat back a little more comfortably in his chair and looked at her; saw her now with a new pair of eyes.

He saw into her, through her. He saw her ignorance, her crudity, the shabby, glib—indolence of her mind. Indolence! That was the fundamental characteristic. She never really bored in, took hold. Hard things were to be avoided—got around anyhow. Her beliefs were matters of choice, not necessity. She didn't—literally—know what honesty meant. And the love she had written that wonderful letter about was just a matter of sensation; stroking with, or being stroked by, a velvet paw. And hate—well, it came pretty much to the same thing—

only with claws unsheathed. The two could alternate, with her mood, upon the same object.

So, when the present paroxysm of anger reached its climax and ebbed swiftly, as it always did, into a mood of repentant humility, when she stretched out her arms to him and invited his head to her breast, he just sat where he was and went on looking at her with no more emotion than a faint distaste. He felt like a fool.

Well, that about expresses the state of mind he had been in through the weeks that had elapsed since, whenever he reviewed, as he had hardly failed daily to do, his emotional history since the outbreak of the strike last May. The dreams he had dreamed of that other—illusory—Helena of his. The agonies he had suffered for and through her. The tragedies he had made of her spells of bad temper; the enigmas he had wrestled with.

There was no tincture of self-pity about this. It was his own doing, all he had done. He had had plenty of good counsel, there was no denying that. Even from Helena herself. Equally it was clear that the thing must be seen through. To run whimpering back to his family with the acknowledgment that he had been a fool, to let them so much as suspect that he had come to see what they had seen so clearly from the first, would leave his self-respect without a leg to stand on.

From now on that chamber must be kept locked and there was none to whom he could confide the key.

But what Helena had just brought home to him, here in the drawing-room, after his father had gone home, was that she had to be reckoned with as well as himself. A mere cold endurance was not good enough; would not turn the trick. She was right.

She was more than right. She was admirable, bringing him up with a round turn like that. He had been posing during these past weeks; that was what it came to. That Olympian aloofness of his, hadn't been quite the real thing. There had been hours when he had wanted her hotly. Was the thing that had held him back from her quite so highly idealistic and superior as he had supposed? Or was it just plain vanity?

Anyhow, the prospect of her leaving him, which with every appearance of good faith she had just held out, dismayed him. He looked up, and across the room at her, with a smile.

"I *have* been on a high horse," he said. "I must have been infernally irritating. I have been acting like a prig and a fool. I expect I have a tendency that way. But don't go off and leave me now. Give me another chance. I have an idea I'll do better."

Among all the alternative possibilities she had contemplated, she could not have included that one. For a moment she looked as if she couldn't believe her ears. Then, raggedly, she said:—

"If you mean that, come over here and kiss me."

But he stayed where he was in the big chair. "You come over here," he said.

That talk with Helena produced, for the time being, fortunate results; and in more directions than one. The attitude she enforced from him toward herself, the conviction she brought home to him that a half loaf, or less, might still be enjoyed in default of a whole one, and that a beautiful and, occasionally, loving woman could be lived with after a tolerable fashion even though she were not the little sister of one's soul;—all that helped him to a philosophical acceptance of his partial alienation from his family. It shook him out of the exalted mood of the past weeks; brought him down to earth.

He stood alone; that fact must be faced. He had no unreserved solidarity with any person, such as his wife; with any group, such as his family; with any organization, such as Corbett & Company; even with any system of political and social ideas. For it was clear that he was neither a conservative, a liberal nor a radical. By a series of revolts he had cut himself off, successively, from them all. He stood alone.

Well, then, let him walk alone. That was well enough to say. Only in what direction? Where?

He struggled along with what he called his book—though he realized it never would be one—for a few weeks more. And then, quite fortuitously, he got the clew he needed. It was so plain that it seemed incredible he could have been blind to it so long.

To Helena's Sunday supper parties (Helena was launching a social career which shall be dealt with later) there came, occasionally, one of the professors from the University, a sociological knight-errant who loved to splinter a lance with any antagonist and on either side of any dispute. One night he brought a friend along—obviously by way of giving him a look at the animals. This friend, Allison Smith his name was, on being brought up for introduction to Hugh, stared at him in undisguised bewilderment. He seemed more, rather than less disconcerted, when Hugh, instantly calling him by name and shaking hands with the appearance of the keenest pleasure, explained to the cicerone that he and Smith were two old comrades in arms. They had watched out some nights together down in the University laboratories.

And when the cicerone tactlessly demanded of his friend: "Why didn't you tell me you knew him?" all Smith, in his daze could say was, "I didn't know I did."

He went on to explain, after the laugh this brought, that he remembered Hugh perfectly. Had failed merely to identify him with the Hugh Corbett he had been hearing so much about lately and had been brought around to meet.

The fact of that identity seemed to go on troubling him. His companions, right and left at the supper-table, found him absent-minded. When he could, after supper, he made a chance to talk with Hugh.

"I can't get over it," he said. "I never dreamed of associating you. . ."

"You knew my name down there, didn't you?" Hugh asked, a shade impatient over the fuss the man was making about a trifle. "There were a half dozen of us, of course, and I suppose you mislaid it."

"I knew your last name—yes," said Smith. "I don't know that I ever heard your first name mentioned. And anyhow. . ." Then, with an intent look up into Hugh's face, as though the mystery were still too much for him. "Why, my God, man! You're a *metallurgist!*"

At that Hugh understood. Smith had been hearing about a freak—a crazy, windmill-battling Don Quixote, at whom curiosity justified the trouble of taking a look. Coming to take that look, he had found, incredibly, a metallurgist—a man whose mind, and whose professional attainments he knew the quality of, and respected.

"I have been in strange pastures lately, for a fact," said Hugh. "I'd about forgotten that I was a metallurgist. And I am inclined to think that's all I am really."

"It's enough," said the other curtly, "if one's as good as you. You haven't a laboratory of your own then?"

"Not—yet," said Hugh.

"I wish," said Smith, "if you could find time this week, you would run down. I've got. . ."

And from this point on, in the evening, for a solid two hours, oblivious and utterly unintelligible to any of the company but themselves, these two talked.

BOOK III
THE LABORATORY

XIX

It is three years, almost to the week, from that Sunday night supper of Helena's (to which the controversy-loving sociologist at the University brought his metallurgical friend for a look at the animals) to the point where we again pick up the thread of Hugh's life.

It is not because they were unimportant years for him, that we pass them by in this chronicle. It may be questioned whether, to the omnisapient eye, any one year in a man's life is more important than another. Even his static phases contribute, likely enough, as much to the final sum of him, as his kinetic ones. But they make heavy going for the biographer.

These three years of Hugh's were not static, for he had by no means stood still during the lapse of them. Considering him as a man of science—and that of course is how the world will consider and remember him—those years will very likely be written down as the most important and fruitful years of his life. But his scientific achievements are—necessarily as well as preferably—outside my province. For the record of them, I refer you to his own contributions to the *Journal of the Non-Ferrous Metals Institute.* There, if your mathematical, electrical, chemical and crystallographic knowledge is sufficient to enable you to understand what it is all about, you may follow in detail the earlier and less revolutionary of his investigations among the ternary alloys of the white-metal group.

It is the story of the man and not the scientist that I am trying to tell. And even with that, I am dealing only in a partial and episodic way; with the critical angles of his life, to borrow a figure from his own science; with those points at which it changed direction—the points at which new influences intersected it, rather than with the planes of uninterrupted development. Most biographies, I suppose, have to be limited to about that.

We saw him first at the time when the capture of the burglar by little Jean, on the eve of Anne's wedding, brought him out of his laboratory at Youngstown, and put him down at Riverdale, where, his grandfather calculated, he could get the humanitarian nonsense out of his system.

We took up the thread of his life again at the outbreak of the great Corbett strike, where Helena Galicz came into it. That phase ended when he said to Allison Smith: "I believe a metallurgist is all I am really."

From that moment on for three years, almost to a week, the thread lies straight. And if, as indeed was true, the man himself as well as the metallurgist, changed in those three years, it was a change so gradual and constant, that it can best be seen in retrospect as with the eyes of one whom an unfaded memory and a long absence provided with the data for measuring.

It was in October, nineteen fifteen, that Jean Gilbert, with her mother, came back to Chicago from England.

Major Gilbert, we may pause to explain, had, on the outbreak of the war, been sent to Paris, attached, not to the Embassy, but to a special military mission the War Department had established there. He was recalled in May, nineteen fifteen, to make a personal report to the Chief of Staff and was, immediately thereafter, reassigned to his battalion. On his return to America, his wife and daughter had gone back to England to Ethel's older sister, Christine, both of whose sons were in the army. They lived down in Surrey, and the sight of Zeppelins, going over to raid London became a familiar one. Their village had got a casual bomb or two one night, and an old woman they knew had been fatally hurt. Ethel and her daughter, along with Christine, had been working all those months as volunteer nurses' aids.

They had attempted to return to America earlier than they did. On the afternoon of August eighteenth, they sailed from Liverpool on the *Arabic,* but that ill-fated liner had already made the last voyage she was ever to complete. She was torpedoed, without warning, and sunk, by a German submarine, just before nine o'clock the next morning.

The two women were on deck, having just finished breakfast, when, directed by the exclamation of a fellow passenger, they saw an apex of foam glinting along toward the side of the ship. The next moment, almost masthead high, a great column of water spouted up, and they experienced palpably, as well as audibly, the shock of an explosion. And, very promptly thereafter, the curt blare of a bugle. They both remembered that ringing assertion of authority as immensely reassuring, and were inclined to credit it, in part at least, with the failure of anything at all resembling panic to manifest itself.

The life-boat to which they had been assigned before the ship sailed, was one of the fortunate ones that was launched without accident, and the crew (they had no officer) pulled away from the side safely before the final plunge. Jean saw the captain on the bridge—incredibly high, he looked, as the bows rose farther and farther out of the water. She looked as long as she could endure it; then covered her eyes. Presently she heard, with a gasp, as of relief, from some one, "She's gone!" and from another, "It's just seven minutes."

They then rowed back over the area marked by a litter of wreckage—human and other—where the ship had gone down; and managed to rescue four men, all members of the crew. This was a task attended by great difficulty and considerable danger, since no one in the boat was capable of directing operations, and there was a heavy swell, breaking every now and then in whitecaps. The last man they got aboard, one of the stewards, was badly hurt; an arm crushed and all of his side stove in. Jean and her mother did what they could for him, but it was, of course, little.

They had been in the boat about three hours, and for the last two, trying to row, when they sighted a patrol-boat coming to the rescue. Within a mile of them, they saw her sharply alter her course and, for a moment unaccountably, open fire. Then some one said:—"It's the submarine. They can see it. Waiting around to sink her, too."

It was then, for the first time, that Jean realized the human malice and hatred that lay behind the attack; saw with her mind's eye the complacent face, with a hungry, half-satisfied smile in its beard, watching, through the cobra-hood of the periscope, their little bobbing cluster of boats; awaiting the arrival of a rescuer that he might make his crime complete. That sense of the thing that was waiting to strike again, was, as she remembered afterward, the sharpest emotion of all. It was enforced by the haste with which they were bundled aboard the patrol-boat and by the intense alertness of the watch.

But the gun-fire had been accurate enough, perhaps, to make a further attack seem too dangerous. Another patrol-boat came up presently to help, and all the survivors were got safely aboard. At seven o'clock that night, they were landed at Queenstown. Mrs. Gilbert and Jean embarked again, six weeks later, and this time made a safe voyage home.

Their disaster and narrow escape from death on the *Arabic*, had one personal result in their lives, which was quite unlooked for. It brought about a reconciliation, long overdue and just about despaired of by Jean, between old Mrs. Crawford and her daughter Ethel.

The old woman had a life-long habit of going first—of being put first in the consideration of all about her; finding other people's wishes and intentions pliant to her own. She had allowed herself to grow genuinely fond of this straight-standing young granddaughter of hers, before she realized how unconquerable a thing the child's original loyalty was. When she did realize the quality of it, she could not but respect it—loved Jean all the better, of course, for her possession of it. But she charged the exasperation it cost her, to the account of the original rebels, Roger and Ethel.

But her encrusted vanity was not hard enough to withstand the shock of the event of the nineteenth of August. On the very day when the evening papers reported the news, (she was at Bar Harbor that summer) she had had a letter from Jean telling of their intention to sail on the *Arabic* rather than on the dangerously overcrowded American liner, which was leaving the same day. And it was a dazed, distracted and utterly pitiable old woman who waited twenty-four sleepless hours for the reassuring cable that finally came.

Jean wrote two letters to her grandmother in the interim before they sailed again, and what in the first one had been a mere undercurrent of uneasiness about her mother, became an outspoken anxiety in the second.

"She won't admit that she's ill. And there's nothing that I can really put a finger on. It's like something elastic that has been stretched too hard. What she counts on doing when we get home, is going straight to Columbus or whatever border town will be nearest to father. I hope I can persuade her not to. But wherever she goes, there's no question of my not going with her."

Jean's blunt refusal to consider a separation from her mother on any terms, missed the effect it once would have had, of rousing old Mrs. Crawford's anger. Within an hour of the receipt of Jean's letter, she electrified Frank and Constance by informing them, by telegraph, that she meant to spend the winter in Chicago and to have Ethel and Jean with her. She didn't want her own house—an old mansion on Rush Street usually inhabited by her son and his wife during the winter months when they were not up at Lake Forest—but an apartment, furnished, in one of the newer buildings on the Drive. There was one belonging to Constance that would do.

Constance and her husband agreed that Mother Crawford's scheme was an ideal one from every point of view. To the old lady, herself, whose existence had—there was no disguising it—been growing lonelier and more barren from year to year, it would give a new interest and concern;

an object for the renewal of those social activities she had so reluctantly relinquished. It would literally mean a new lease of life for her. For Ethel it presented the one conceivable alternative to the monotonous and intensely familiar privations of life in some border town, enlivened, to be sure, by her husband's occasional visits but, conversely, made duller and deadlier by his long absences. After what she must have been through in England during that past few months she would be in no condition—Jean's letter made this clear—for a trial like that. A winter with her mother, well served and attended, a renewal of comfortable old friendships, enough amusements to enliven the time and enough leisure to relax in, ought to make her ten years younger. "That's about what she needs taken off, too," mused Constance. "The last time I saw you two together it didn't seem possible that you were twins. She might have been fifty then. And she's only forty-one now!" Lastly, and with no need for explanations, it would be most awfully nice to have young Jean about again.

So the two of them put their competent shoulders to the wheel and got just the apartment their mother wanted. Constance spent days over such matters as bedding, silver and table-linen, and in good time—well ahead of time, as was her way—had everything ready.

There was a bombardment of telegrams from New York, whither Mrs. Crawford had gone to meet the returned travelers—a bombardment that did not slacken—intensified itself rather, after the receipt of the good news of their safe arrival. They weren't coming at all. . . They were taking the fast train this afternoon and must be met at the station with a wheel-chair. . . It would be at least a fortnight till they could think of coming.

Finally they did come, with no premonitory telegram at all (the message had been written, it afterward appeared, but not despatched) well within the fortnight that had last been prophesied.

The consequence was that the four of them (Mrs. Crawford had her maid along) descended to the station platform about four o'clock one wet afternoon, and slowly followed their convoy of red-caps up the length of it, without seeing either of the familiar faces that might have been expected to be waiting for them. There was no need of the wheel-chair. That collapse of Ethel's had proved as brief as it had been sudden. But Jean eyed her mother rather closely as they walked along. Old Mrs. Crawford, brisk as ever, had got ahead, on the heels of the porters.

At a distance of fifty paces, one would have said Jean and her mother were sisters. Ethel had never lost the rounded slimness of outline her daughter had inherited from her. They were just of a height; wore the same sized gloves and shoes and could—and frequently did—exchange garments indifferently. But if, at a distance, Ethel looked younger than her years, she paid for it as you came nearer—added not only the twenty years that was her due, but easily another ten. Approaching strangers got a surprise that was often visible to Ethel herself, and that she winced at. Her hair, which you had taken from afar for a decided blonde, betrayed when you came near, the indeterminate ashen color that looks older than white. And the face it framed was haggard with lines. Her skin—you knew it must have been lovely once—had lost its tone; was flaccid now, where three years before it had merely looked weather-beaten.

It was not really Ethel's fault that she looked like that. An army officer's wife, living nomadically in an alternation of violent climates, all the way from Fort Laramie to Zamboanga, can keep her looks, to be sure, but only by making them a primary consideration. Ethel, long ago, had decided that this price was too high, and deliberately sacrificed them, along with a lot of other things, to her love for her husband, and his, as constant as possible, companionship.

The effect of illness on a face whose one remaining beauty had been that it looked hale and sound, was particularly cruel.

Ethel said, aware of her daughter's solicitude, "I'm all right. Don't keep looking at me. Of course I'd have been glad of the sight of Frank."

"It was in this same station," Jean said, "that he didn't meet me. When I first came on, you know."

Involuntarily, she caught her breath in a little gasp over the surprisingly tight grip of an emotion that took hold of her throat, as her glance went down the concourse to the big bulletin board where, on that other occasion, Hugh had been waiting for one of Anne's bridesmaids. Wouldn't it be—nice, if he were there now, waiting for somebody else?

She smiled; first over the ridiculous inadequacy of the adjective, and then at the emotion whose force made it inadequate; at the absurd—the utterly idiotic tears which she felt flushing up into her eyes. Heavens! Hadn't she got over that?

They took a couple of taxis straight to the Rush Street house.

That their arrival was unexpected was instantly apparent and almost as quickly explained by the non-receipt of Mrs. Crawford's telegram. But a sense that it was a little worse than unexpected—that it made, in so far as a really welcome event could, a *contretemps*—was not so quickly accounted for. Constance was taking a nap when they came. She was called at once, of course, and came flying down, very negligee, to welcome them. Frank was summoned home from the office; the children were hastily rounded up to be admired and kissed; the inevitable trivial first questions were asked and answered all in a jumble, anyhow. But then there came a lapse. The same things got said twice and with uncalled-for emphasis. Constance was—trying too hard.

Ethel, less able than the others to go on ignoring a thing like that said, presently, "We've come at the wrong time. You've got something planned. You mustn't let us be in the way."

Constance hesitated over a total denial; then gave it up. "There isn't a thing, now. Not for hours. Only Frank and I have got a party tonight, and I was hating the thought that we'd have to go."

"Why go, unless you choose?" her mother-in-law inquired, rather dryly.

"We're giving it. Oh, not here," Constance hurried on to explain. "At the Blackstone; and not till after the theater—though we'll have to go to the show first, because that's really a part of it. It's—it's for Rose Aldrich. It's the first night here of *Come On In.*—The thing she made the costumes for, that was such a hit in New York all last season. She's here now with Rodney, and we're having this for a sort of celebration. It's very exciting, because Rose has promised that Lester Vernon and Ivy will both be there. They're the stars in her show, of course. We're all wild enough over the idea of meeting him, wondering whom of us he'll dance with, and so on, but it's nothing to what the men are about her. I suspect Carter's begun dressing already. I really frightened Frank, asking him what he thought would happen if he kicked her ankle. They must be worth about a million dollars apiece, those ankles."

"I remember Rodney Aldrich well enough"; Ethel said, "and I seem to remember his having married somebody. But do I know her?"

Constance shook her head decidedly. "Nobody did," she said, "until Rodney married her. That was three years ago last summer—just about the time you and Jean went to England. She's led us a life since. First we all fell in love with her, and then we all hated her, and now we're all making up our minds that we love her better than ever.—All but poor Frederica, who hasn't quite got over it yet."

Constance had been talking a little harder than she was in the way of doing, from a realization that her mother-in-law was getting ready to say something disagreeable. A very audible sniff from the old lady could not, at this point, be disregarded.

"She's a young woman," Mrs. Crawford explained to her daughter, "whom we had all supposed to be a person of sense and breeding, who ran away from an excellent husband in order to be what is called, nowadays, a chorus girl. In my day she'd never have been allowed to come back."

"She didn't run away,—exactly in order to be a chorus girl," Constance good-humoredly protested. "She was a chorus girl for a while, while she was learning to make stage costumes. She's made a perfectly wonderful success of them."

A critical moment in old Mrs. Crawford's life had been that when she made the fancied discovery of a resemblance between her wit and that of George Meredith's heroines. She had assiduously been modeling her conversational style upon that of those classical ladies ever since.

A smile of hard, glittering brilliancy now appeared on her face, and she said: "Rose Aldrich made a sow's ear out of a silk purse and then set about trying to make silk purses out of sows' ears. And, since they are filled with gold, no one will examine the tissue too closely."

The completeness of her satisfaction over this dubious piece of wit, was made evident by the number of times she repeated it during the ensuing season. Before she had half done using it, she had worked herself into a thoroughly good-humored acquiescence in Rose's reinstatement in society.

A bolus like that always sticks in the throat of conversation—momentarily, anyhow. And there was a little pause before Jean changed the subject.

"I don't even know," she said, "who the Vernons are that are so exciting."

"You *have* been away," said Constance. "It doesn't seem possible that you haven't heard of them. They're the most wonderful ballroom dancers in the world. They're simply—fabulous. Anybody who's taken three lessons from either of them, can make his fortune teaching for the rest of his life."

She checked herself rather abruptly. The girl's smile had come responsively enough, but there was something a little remote about it.

"We have been away, that's true," she said. "Or else we haven't got back yet, I don't know which."

"I know," said Constance. "It must be bewildering. After all you've been through. We're going to try to help you forget it." She added: "I wish you'd come tonight." She turned to Ethel. "We'd love to have you, only I know I mustn't ask." She also invited her mother, with a humorous lift of the eyebrows and, on seeing the grim smile which was all the answer she expected, she turned back seriously to Jean.

"Won't you come, really?" she repeated. "We'll have an early dinner and get your mother safely put to bed before we need go. And we can manage another seat at the theater perfectly. Frank shall attend to it as soon as he comes in. Everybody will be there, and we'll make Rose have Lester Vernon dance with you."

Jean went to the party, though it involved something of a scramble for her trunks, and a scant allowance of time for dressing, and she did not get home till after four.

At that hour she stole burglariously to her room, hoping to avoid rousing her mother whose chamber adjoined hers. The precaution was futile, however. At the end of ten minutes the communicating door opened, and Ethel in robe and slippers, appeared.

"You are a mouse," she said. "I couldn't be sure whether you were really there, or whether it was just fancy. And I'd been listening for you for ever so long, too."

She cut short her daughter's contrite, "Oh, I shouldn't have gone!" with a decided negative.

"I have had a splendid night's sleep between ten and two. And if you hadn't gone, I shouldn't have had anybody to talk to now. You don't mind, do you, telling me all about it?"

"Mind!" said Jean. "Doesn't everybody love to talk after a party?"

So they repulsed the maid Constance had sent around with a whispered offer of services. Ethel volunteered to solve the intricacies of Jean's hooks and stipulated for permission to take down and brush out the girl's hair.

"I love to do it, you know," she said. "I pretend it's mine."

"It is, for that matter," Jean observed. So, once she had got out of her "things" and was comfortably robed for the night, she settled down on a little foot-stool between her mother's knees, and began— "at the beginning," according to Ethel's instructions—an account of the party.

She told about *Come On In;* how funny Mr. Vernon was, and how adorable his wife; the wonder of the costumes Mrs. Aldrich had designed;

the brilliancy of the assemblage in the hotel ballroom afterward. "Only no uniforms, of course; that seemed queer."

"There were lots of people there that I knew, and all of them were lovely to me. Gregory Corbett and his wife. She's the widow he was in love with so long. I only just met her, but she must be nice, because he is now.—I mean, nicer than he used to be. He used to seem a little self-satisfied and dull. And then there was Carter." She smiled and sighed at once. (The pair were seated before the long dressing mirror so that they could see each other's faces while they talked.) "How I used to hate Carter for making me feel like a little girl; being so lordly and superior and cock-sure. I used to try to pretend to laugh at him for it, but I never could be quite sure I really did."

"He's different now?" her mother prompted her when she paused.

"Not very," said Jean thoughtfully. "Oh, he's different to *me*." A fugitive smile came then, just before a look of deeper seriousness. "He makes the puzzle all the harder to understand. He, and some of the others like him. There were a lot of them there tonight. He's beautiful, mother! Clean and hard and slim, with that same kind of wholesome brightness about him. He *is* the same kind as those over there, even down to his little tricks and ways. He's rude just the way they are. The kind of rudeness that's like a fresh bath-towel—makes you glow. It's the same race—the same blood. He *isn't* too proud to fight! Only he doesn't see. It's just as if all that, over there, had never happened; was just our own little nightmare, yours and mine.

"It's funny," she went on after another pause. "Who do you suppose the exception was, mother? There *was* one there.—The dancing man, Mr. Vernon. We did have a dance together—danced a dance, I mean—without saying anything much. And at the end of it he complimented me on how well I did, in a rather tired sort of way. I suppose he says that to all the women he dances with. Even those he has to haul around like sacks of potatoes. I said I was surprised that I could dance at all, because I hadn't for so long. Because of where I had been; there at the hospital in Brighton.

"He was just going away when I said that, but he changed his mind and found a place where we could sit down. And then, the first thing I knew, I was telling him all about it; things you and I haven't been able to talk about to anybody. We talked straight through two dances, and later he came back and we sat out another. I think I was quite unpopular for a while. I heard one girl say, going by—and I know she meant me to hear—that she had never really understood the fable of the dog in the manger until now.

"He says he's going over. He's under a contract that he's trying to carry out, but he can't stand this sort of thing much longer."

Then, "Oh, I know," she said; "they haven't had it brought home. If Carter could just have *seen* that bent old man puttering around the wreck of his house, trying to save little useless things out of it. Going to tell his wife how much there was, to cheer her up. Trying to make her understand. And she dying there—half the bones of her body broken. On purpose, mother! Because there wasn't anything anywhere around for those bombs they dropped to hit but just little cottages like that. On purpose so that everybody in the world should cringe and shrink when a German went by. They don't believe that, yet, over here.—If I could bring a Zeppelin over Chicago tonight, by wishing it, I think I would. Then they'd know.—They've got over minding about the submarines. People were asking me tonight why we *tried* to come home on a British boat.

"Oh, it's wicked of me to be talking to *you* like this. Why didn't I to them! I wanted to, but somehow I couldn't. The words stuck in my throat.—Of course quite a lot of them have gone. There are thousands of Americans, Mr. Vernon says, in the Canadian battalions. Nobody important for the papers to make a fuss about. Just, regular people— old-time American people, without any attitudes or moral superiorities; not beyond being angry when they're struck in the face."

The mother's hands rested a moment on the girl's shoulders—all the remonstrance that was needed. "That wasn't fair," she admitted instantly. "Carter—I can see him—all ablaze, and yet with just that wonderful impudence that *they* have;—that makes a sort of sport even out of the ghastliest of it It *is* the same blood. . . I'm starting around again."

She broke off there, but her mother, looking in the glass, could see the thought that was, indeed, going round again. With an effort of her own, she changed the subject.

"How did you like Rodney Aldrich's wife?" she asked.

Jean brightened. "Oh, I really liked her a lot. We didn't talk hardly at all. But what we did, went to the spot in a way. She didn't ask me if it wasn't nice to be back in America again, nor say how 'horrible' it must be over there, nor any of those deadly things. I can't remember anything that she did say, except that she was going to California for a month, in a few days, but that she hoped she'd see me when she came back. I hope she does. She'd be a wonderful person to have for a friend, in case you happened to need one."

Her mother laughed. "That's quite a conclusion to come to from her having said she was going to California, instead of asking you how it seemed to be back home."

"It wasn't anything she said, of course," Jean admitted. "And there wasn't anything particularly she did, except—well, the way she looked at me. As if she really saw me, and didn't mind my seeing her. It isn't often you get a chance to exchange a look like that with anybody; with the wrappings off, you know. She hasn't been in the war, but she's been—somewhere that came to about the same thing. You can tell when they have, somehow. Don't you think so, mother?"

Mrs. Gilbert assented rather absently. She was tired. Her face—if Jean had looked up to see it—had gone a little slack. She would have been glad, to tell the truth, of a simple recital of gaieties without any implications. She asked: "Who else was there? Any of the people I used to know? John Williamson, or Heaton Duncan? Or William Forrester? The Whitneys were there, I suppose. I always liked Martin."

Jean was able to identify and report about a few of them, and they got at cross-purposes about some of their younger brothers, or older nephews. Ethel wasn't old enough, of course, for any of the sons to come in and confuse identities. Finally she asked:—"Anybody else?"

"No," Jean said rather decisively, and with a restless twist of the body at the same time. "Nobody. I mean," she added—for her mother's quick look invited explanation—"I mean the person I went there specially to see wasn't there. That was Hugh!"

"Hugh Corbett?" Ethel asked,—superfluously of course, because she knew well enough; merely because something had to be said. A sentence like that last one of Jean's, if left hanging up in a silence, gets charged with a kind of electricity.

"Yes," Jean said. She leaned forward now, out of contact with her mother's body, and rested her elbows on her knees. "I've wanted to talk with him ever since we landed in New York.—Oh, before that, of course. All last summer. Everytime *Punch* came out with a new cartoon, or the president sent over another note protesting about the interference with American commerce. But it was worse in New York. Of course we kept saying to each other that what we saw, there in the hotel and all, wasn't the real America; was just the drunken scum, throwing money away and making it back again faster out of its 'war babies.'"

"But I've wondered all the while—haven't you?—whether we really understood, after all. Whether there mightn't be something we didn't see. I've wanted to know how it looked to—well, to Hugh. When he has explained it to me, then I'll know."

"He's still infallible, then?" Ethel asked, with just the light breath of affectionate amusement that she wanted in her voice. It was not quite spontaneous. She was rather more alert than she wanted the girl to guess.

Jean smiled in response to her mother's tone, but she answered, quite seriously. "Yes. Well, that's reasonable, mother. He really thinks through things—without knowing when he starts where he's going to come out; and there aren't many people whose minds are good enough for that, even if they wanted to. And then he's not afraid of anything in the world. Not of any of the things Carter wouldn't be afraid of—nor of any of the other things that he would.

"So, of course," she went on after having waited a moment to see whether her mother wished to dissent from either of these propositions, "it was to see him and—*begin* talking with him, anyway, that I went to the party tonight. And I could have—wept, almost, with disappointment, when I saw he wasn't there."

"Why wasn't he?" Ethel inquired. "Did you ask Constance about him?"

"Not Constance," Jean answered. "But—his wife was there. Mrs. Williamson introduced me to her. She said Hugh was in his laboratory with some experiment he couldn't leave, but that she knew he'd be disappointed when he found he'd missed me by not coming."

"Oh, I'm curious about her," said Ethel. "Tell me about her. I've wondered how that would come out. Do you like her?"

Jean was not very prompt with her reply. "I think I will," she said, finally, "when I have had time to get used to her a little. She's rather—strange, at first. There's something sudden, that flashes up and then goes away, that's rather—frightening. She's really beautiful. Everybody seemed to admire her a lot; especially the men. She had on a very—stunning gown. I'd been wondering all the evening, until I met her, who she was. And of course it was a little bit surprising to find out. I thought she was surprised, too, at me. But she meant to be nice to me, I'm sure. She asked me to lunch for day after tomorrow;—Wednesday, that is; it's tomorrow already. She says she can't absolutely promise Hugh, but that she thinks he'll come. I hope he comes, of course; though I don't suppose there'll be much chance for a real *talk*, anyway."

"Jean," her mother said, after a pretty long silence, "don't you think it might be well to be a little careful. . . ?"

"Not to fall in love with him again, you mean; the way I did four years ago." This was not inflected like a question, nor was there any humorous mockery in the voice. "I'm sure there isn't any danger of that," she went on. "I did then, of course, and I'd be sorry for myself if I hadn't. I think any child would. There's something about him—about the way he says and does things—I don't know what it is—but it's romantic. And for anybody that wasn't quite out of the world of fairy stories yet. . ."

"Prince Charming?" asked Ethel. "I'd hardly have thought that of him."

"He was Cinderella's prince, wasn't he? No, not him. Nor Snow White's, either. Nor Beauty's prince, that was Beast before she kissed him; nor Sir Launcelot—quite—nor Ivanhoe, though they're nearer. Mother, we're getting silly. Let's go to bed. They'll be blowing reveille in a few minutes, down in Texas."

XX

The glimpse you have had of Helena at the Crawfords' party, in a stunning gown and much admired, according to Jean's report, especially by the men, will have indicated to you—and truly—a social success which considerably outran the earlier prognostications of the Corbett family.

A number of causes were contributory to this fact; the chief of them being, perhaps, her ability to maintain, without effort, a set of social standards that were, quite simply, her own. There was not the smallest streak of the snob in her; no disposition at all to be overwhelmed by name or place; to make her, on the one hand, cringing, subservient, genteel; or, on the other, uneasily self-assertive.

She had, back in the days before she married Hugh, a nucleus of friends and admirers, in a set that loosely gets spoken of as "Bohemian"; not all extreme radicals, but mostly—a group that sometimes inundated Alice Hayes' flat, and made itself as much at home in half a dozen other places.

Helena's marriage, and her commodious, informal establishment, made her at once the focal figure of this group and gave her the power of contracting or expanding it, where and in whatever directions she pleased.

The direction she took—and I do not think this fact is one to be regarded with surprise—was away from the real revolutionaries and toward the intellectuals and esthetes. She had been, back in the days when she made that hawk-like swoop upon Riverdale, a real revolutionist. She had shared, that is to say, the economic pressures of the class she was fighting for. Hunger, cold, the tyrannical operation of the law, were personal and not abstract possibilities. She honestly hated the rich as her own actual oppressors. And her efforts to accomplish their downfall were made with no lurking reservation that it did no harm to try, since the thing could not be brought about within her lifetime anyway.

But upon her marriage with Hugh, all the surfaces of her life—the whole crystalline organization of it—changed. And the shape of her ideas changed to match, though of the extent of this transformation, she remained unaware. That she now had charge accounts at the big stores, enjoyed the privileges of her husband's clubs; that she could drive whenever she liked, in taxi-cabs, and eventually had a car of her own, may seem irrelevant and inconsequent facts; but they were not. They made up a new fabric of realities for her and in doing so, they made, of what once had been her grim realities, toys.

Without taking that truth into account, it would be hard to explain the importance in her life, during the first year after her marriage, of young Boyd Barr. Encountering him at any time prior to her marriage, she would have passed him by as not worth a second look.

There is a very strong disposition in Chicago—by no means confined to the rich, though best advertised and most effective among them,—to Do Something for Art. I don't know whether it is fairer to say that Boyd Barr seized upon this disposition, or that it seized upon him. At any rate, they coincided very nicely, and the result of this coincidence was a slim, well printed magazine bound in cartridge paper, and called the *Red Review*. Barr, under pseudonyms, was most of the contributors, as well as editor under his own. He had managed to create the illusion in a small sector of the public mind, that it would be—well, one of the minor failures of civilization, and, locally, a reflection on Chicago's pretense to enlightenment, if the *Red Review* were allowed to perish. So, though chronically in a sinking condition, it was perpetually being saved. Repeatedly it had announced its own demise and held a little funeral service over itself. But the pathos of this act always stimulated somebody, in the extreme instant, to rush to the rescue with the two hundred and eighteen dollars—or whatever the amount might be— that would enable it to go on.

Barr took Helena on as a disciple; criticized her writings, and was amazed at her aptness in responding to his suggestions. He printed some highly explosive free verse of hers in the *Red Review*, and proudly proclaimed her his discovery. He collaborated with her in a short horrible play or two, whose production they superintended at the Drama Workshop—an earnest organization of amateurs, every one at least a potential playwright. And he devoted himself seriously to building up her Sunday nights into a real salon.

He had a pretty good social sense, understood that the success of any company depended on the correct proportioning between audience and performers. And a wide acquaintance in most of the social strata from the very top to the very bottom, enabled him to mix his ingredients nicely. Of those mysterious nomads who drift vaguely about in any big city, lecturing on strange things, reading strange poetry, dancing esoteric and philosophical dances, collecting funds for distant and rather incredible enterprises, he selected the more desirable and brought them around to Helena.

At the end of a year of this sort of thing, they parted—in great bitterness on his side—over her peremptory and rather contemptuous refusal to become his mistress.

He had, it may be owned, some grounds for feeling aggrieved. She had avowed, from the beginning of their acquaintance, an attitude toward marriage as widely latitudinarian as his own, and she had made no pretense to a consuming passion for her husband. Such a pretense would, indeed, have been idle. The relation between this married pair had attenuated itself, visibly, under Barr's eye. He was justified, though mistaken, in supposing it to have been from the first an affair of convenience on her part and of infatuation, rapidly waning, on her husband's. (He had not become a frequent visitor at the house until after the fire and the quarrel that resulted from it.) But whereas, at the beginning, Hugh's presence at all Helena's parties had been something to reckon upon and he had often made a third in their discussions, of late his necessary presence at the laboratory, at unlikely as well as likely hours, had been pleaded so often as to be taken by Barr for nothing but the baldest fiction. A man of more masculine temper might have felt nettled over the good-humored indifference with which this husband consigned a beautiful young wife to his company; but Barr hadn't much of the sort of pride that would have been affronted by this, and cheerfully made the most of the opportunities it offered. The woman's contempt was another matter, though, and he writhed under it.

The whole blighting force of it was not turned upon him until, very unwisely, he taunted her with being at heart, after all, merely respectable. That untrammelled spirit she boasted, was nothing but a pretense. She might like to think she was a hawk, but when one opened the door, it appeared that she preferred the cage.

For a moment Helena's eyes glowed dangerously; then she chose the more cruel method of good-humored ridicule.

"Just because I don't want to fly away with a chippering little sparrow like you?" she asked. "Hugh would cut up into a dozen of you. Go away and get over your sulks. And then, whenever you like, come back. You're nice enough to have about; I won't deny that. Except when you're out of temper. And then you're ridiculous. Hugh's never that, at least."

He never did come back; and, presently, he moved away to New York, taking the *Red Review* along with him in a hand-satchel. Whenever he talked of Helena after that,—and at a certain stage of intoxication, he invariably did—it was as of a vampire who had sucked his life-blood and then cast him off.

He is not, perhaps, a deserving object of sympathy. Especially if one stops to consider the different outcome of their companionship that he, from the first, had meant and foreseen. But this remains to be noted; that she did not finally turn him off until she had got all the profit out of him that he could be made to yield. When he went away, she was perfectly competent to walk alone along her chosen path. Even her— now celebrated—Sunday nights never missed him. Indeed, it was not until he had gone away that full recognition of herself as a personage, was granted. She was too wise to put a successor in his place.

Her prevalent mood during the next two years, was self-satisfaction. And it would have taken a bold prophet to deny the solidity of her grounds for it. The change in her from the awkward girl in the ill-fitting dress, who so plainly had not known what to do with Hugh when he called on her that first Sunday afternoon in Alice Hayes' flat, to the woman in the stunning gown whom Jean found at the Crawfords' party, amounted fairly to a metamorphosis. If the process was not one of true growth, at least it was the easiest thing in the world to mistake for it—an immense enlargement and variegation of her world, a pushing back of her personal boundaries, a wider currency for her word and deed. She was continually and pleasurably busy. Opportunities for a great number of sorts of activity crowded her threshold. She had only to select among them and invite them in. But her literary work remained the favorite.

She had, to be sure, given up, back in the days of Boyd Barr's tutelage, her syndicate arrangement with that New York editor, and the consequent sharp decrease in her earnings that resulted from this, necessitated her accepting an allowance from Hugh. True Art had never got adequately paid for since the capitalist system had been established.

Of late, she had been planning a novel—an immense affair; a great, grimly ironic cross-section of the human comedy from the top crust— which her new acquaintance with smart society would provide the materials for—all the way down to the bottom, where her own childish and adolescent memories were a sufficient reservoir.

(Planning a novel, it may be noted, is one of the most comfortable occupations in the world. There is a fine spacious leisureliness about it, since it is obvious that a work of that sort can not be hurried. Gathering material for it patently involves all sorts of stimulating excursions; it entails a rigorous exclusion from one's daily routine of all harassing duties and entanglements. In a word, it transfuses doing whatever one likes, with the glow of a good conscience. And it can be kept going, in the absence of the need of money and of skeptical friends and relations, almost indefinitely.)

Helena wrote sometimes, when her mood invited it. But, as she always told Hugh when she read these fragments aloud to him, they were merely preliminary studies or notes. The moment for committing herself concretely to beginning it, seemed to get no nearer. She saw nothing ominous about that. At any rate, never admitted, even to herself, that she did.

This, as I have said, was her prevailing mood. But there was another; tolerably rare, and fortunately brief—at longest it never lasted more than a day or two, and often an hour, sometimes a mere moment, saw the beginning and the end of it. But while it lasted it stabbed like a neuralgia. Always it was out of the jungle of memory that it sprang upon her. Sometimes it came when, after a particularly gratifying success of hers, she let herself attempt to measure the distance she had come, in a deliberate retrospect; back to the meager, big-eyed slum child, with the idle immigrant father, sitting beside him in the back room of some saloon, listening with strange, uncomprehending excitement, while men talked about the General Strike and the Social Revolution. How amazing a flight from that to this.

And yet—here came the stabbing doubt—what would that Helena have thought of this one?

Sometimes it was a mere coincidence—a chance resemblance— real or fancied—of a face, that evoked a concrete memory. This was what happened late one snowy afternoon, when, driving out on West Chicago Avenue to get Hugh at his laboratory, her car was held up by a blockade of traffic. There was a strike on at one of the factories out here, it seemed, and there was what would be spoken of the next morning in the police reports as a mob in the street—a crowd of people, that is to say, eight-tenths of them merely curious, listening while a girl made a speech from the upper step of a doorway.

One of the pickets she must have been—a slight young girl in a round little plush hat that had taken on, from the melting snow, the drowned look which that fabric exhibits when it is wet. Her neck was bare of any sort of scarf. She had on no outdoor garment beyond the boyish jacket that went with her suit. Between excitement and cold, she had to talk with her teeth locked together, and she was saying her say as fast as she could, since the arrival of a policeman, coming along, hand over hand through the crowd, was going to terminate it. Helena's car moved on again just as the policeman reached out a hand for the girl.

The little vignette that had actually been beneath her eyes hardly reached her consciousness at all. What she really saw was another impromptu street-corner meeting, on a Christmas Eve, addressed by a girl even younger than this one—sixteen almost to the day. The snow had been coming down in big flakes and clinging just as it did now, and that girl had shivered, too, and talked through locked teeth, and the feet inside her sodden shoes had felt as cold and dead as lumps of marble. She had been frightened, that girl, and yet exultant in her fear; begging, but proudly. She was collecting the money to get her father, Anton Galicz, out of jail—the authorities having neglected, for once, to lock her up with him.

It was that Helena's eyes that now encountered this one's with a questioning stare that stabbed. No need to ask what that flaming young proselyte to her father's gospel thought of the befurred thing in the motor-car. The excruciating fact was that the woman in the car still professed the same gospel as the girl on the soap-box. A repudiation of it, the admission of a new enlightenment, which could afford to look back tenderly upon it as a generous but misguided fanaticism, would have excused—explained, anyhow, the abyss between the two; but it had never been made. There was no shield that the burning contempt in the girl's eyes could not penetrate. It was hours before that ghost would look away. And it was never completely laid.

There were other ghosts, too; ghosts of other Helenas; especially of a later one—of an older and much less remote Helena; a Helena that was her mother's daughter much more than her father's, and yet, though the mother's side may have been said to have won the victory, no less contemptuous—asking a question that rankled even more bitterly. Was this relation that Helena Corbett had settled into with her husband the great thing that that brave young adventuress, riding about the world on her high horse, had dreamed of—guarded her virgin altar for?

Well, of course it was not. Had it ever been? Even in those very first days, when she had tried so hard to believe it was? Before that long train of quarrels that had been set off by Robert Corbett's telegram, had begun? Once more the answer, plain enough now, was no. It never had been that great, wonderful dreamed-of thing. Why not? Was it the fault of her dreams that the reality had fallen so far short of them? She had adopted that long ago as a sort of provisional explanation; the more easily since her married life was so crowded with new and absorbing experiences.

For the first year Boyd Barr had kept her busy with that new world of his; new ideas—new terminologies, at any rate—new people, new attitudes; a new ambition toward literature. She had spent another year, after her break with him, making it all her own; discovering her ability to walk alone; making minor personal conquests here and there, as she needed them, to render her new position secure; settling herself firmly in the saddle and acquainting herself with the paces of the new horse her marriage had given her to ride. But by the beginning of the third year the novelty was exhausted. The adventure had become as tame as a drive round Lincoln Park. Her novel had palled upon her, though the first chapter of it was still unwritten.

It would, of course, always remain unwritten. All those postponements of hers, excused in the interest of collecting new material, all those "preliminary studies," were merely so many indolent evasions of the effort it always takes—the immense expenditure of energy it wants—to transform the easy dream into the hard concrete reality.

That indolence, which Hugh, in a clairvoyant moment, had once attributed to her, was, indeed, the besetting vice of her character as it is, I suppose, of most restless people. They are apt to be spoken of, in contempt, sometimes, and sometimes in admiration, as idealists. They dream, with passionate persuasion, some of them, of a kindlier, easier world, that this hard one of ours ought somehow to be transformed into; but the fact remains that they dream. They do not, as Hugh put it, bore in; take hold.

To Helena, the realization that marriage was no longer an inexhaustible wonder-box of new experiences, brought back the old restlessness, the old resentment—smoldering just now in the absence of any wind to blow it into a flame. Once more she began wondering why the thing which she had expected to prove the emotional climax of her life, should have quenched down into this that it was.

She and Hugh got on well enough. They seldom quarreled any more. They chatted amicably over their meals even when they were alone, and to her friends—even the wildest of them—he was always courteous. His rather dry humor, though her inability to understand it sometimes exasperated her, never roused the old angry suspicion that the enigma was a cloak for malice. He never tried to interfere with her liberty. And, as the saying is, they lived together. But was this all she was entitled to? Was a tepid, half contemptuous liking, punctuated by moments of only half satisfied passion, the best thing there was to hope for? Or was there, still before her—the great possibility?

That last question must, I suppose, have been latent in her mind from the first, strongly enough to have prescribed one line of conduct. Hugh had, at the beginning, been eager, impatient, for a child; wanted a lot of children. She had met this wish of his with no blunt denial; avowed no permanently contrary intent. But she was unremitting, and successful, in her precautions against being overtaken by maternity. After the first few months her husband had ceased to talk about it; seemed to have forgotten.

It was at the Crawfords' party that she was roused to an amused realization of a change that had taken place in her own attitude toward her husband. She had asked Violet Williamson who the girl was who was sitting out all those dances with Lester Vernon. "Why, that's Jean Gilbert," Violet had said, a little surprised that she didn't know.

Jean Gilbert! Helena drifted off into a retrospect. What a lot that name had meant to her once! How bitterly jealous of it she had been! She had never doubted the accuracy of that first surmise of hers on reading the girl's congratulatory note to Hugh; his anger had only confirmed her in it. The girl who had meant to marry him; the girl his family had wanted him to marry. As a mere abstraction—she never had been anything more than that—she served Helena, for months, as an emotional objective. Hugh's silent moods were often enough assigned to a regret that he had not married that other girl. Even his indifference to other women, when she had satisfied herself of its genuineness, could as easily be attributed to a sentimental longing for the absent Jean as to a loyal devotion to herself.

That feeling had worn away to nothing long ago; she hadn't thought of the girl for a good two years. Only the process had been insensible, for it was not till now, when Jean was identified for her, that she was aware it had taken place. She had made a mountain out of a molehill that time, to be sure. Hugh in love with that child? Preposterous! Why, he wasn't capable of being in love—enough to matter—with any one. With no one more than with herself. What he gave her was all he could give. What he wanted from her was all he could want. From anybody!

It would be amusing to see what he'd make of Jean now that she was back. He'd sentimentalize over her in his own queer ineffectual way, no doubt—if let alone. Well, she was welcome to anything she could get from him.

It was utterly characteristic of Helena that she should leave out of account altogether the possibility of any deeper feeling on the girl's part. From the first, she had never questioned her assumption that to Jean, Hugh had represented merely an opportunity she had not been clever enough to grasp.

She had never considered the women of her husband's world as capable of the experience of a real passion, and the occasional instances to the contrary that had been brought home to her since her better acquaintance with them, had always been dismissed as exceptions. They flirted, of course, just as Jean, over there, was obviously flirting now with the dancer, but the proprieties could always be relied upon to intervene—in time. You may remember how this attitude of hers had tinged the love letter she had written, years before, to Hugh. She did not suppose, she had said, that the girls he knew were in the habit of boasting their virginity to a lover. Perhaps there were no prophets of Baal about their altars. Or perhaps the true fire never came down from Heaven. She didn't know.

Something—a mere momentary flash of the old hostility—had leaped up when she first met the girl and talked with her; enough, just momentarily to have troubled Jean, and been reported afterward to her mother. But it had died down as swiftly as it had arisen, and from that point on, her professions of pleasure over the girl's return and of a hope that they would see a lot of each other, had been, in their own fashion, genuine. She did hope she could get Hugh home for lunch on Wednesday. She relished, only half maliciously, the notion of launching an "affair" for him. His sort of affair!

Jean, arriving with military punctuality for Helena's lunch at one o'clock on Wednesday, was ushered by a maid into a drawing-room whose only occupant was a stranger to her. Having noted a man's hat on the settee in the hall, she had entertained the hope of Hugh; and before the bulky figure in front of one of the bookcases could face around, she had time for the absurd thought, "He *can't* have changed as much as that!" The man was not by inches as tall as Hugh; was very blond, blue-eyed, broad-faced. His head was an only slightly modified cube; his trunk a parallelepiped. He had rather the look—attractive to some persons no doubt—of a well-bred bull.

He said, in an accent which she bristled at as German: "Miss Gilbert?" And then introduced himself by the name of Bjornstadt. "Our beautiful hostess," he explained, "does not count punctuality among the virtues. So I am under her instructions to make you at home until she shall be dressed."

There was no doubt of his being quite at home himself, and his conversational resources were more than adequate. But Jean had a struggle during the whole of the twenty minutes that elapsed before Helena came down, to get beyond monosyllables. If she had been coached about him, as he evidently had been concerning her, she'd no doubt have done better. He knew the main facts in her recent history and seemed determined, by questions, to elicit details. He set about, with considerable address, getting an account from her of the sinking of the *Arabic*. How much warning had they had? Was it true that the ship had changed her course in the attempt to ram the submarine? What measures had been taken prior to the "accident," to provide for the speedy embarkation of the passengers in life-boats?

Then, finding this theme unfruitful, he spoke in a friendly, familiar way, about England; remarked that it was months since he had visited that country, and wanted to know how, in her opinion, the English were taking the war.

Well, he mightn't be a German; probably, since his name was Bjornstadt, was not. But he was a foreigner, in the sense in which no Englishman, nor Frenchman, ever could be to her again. And these were matters which she simply could not bring herself to talk about freely with a foreigner.

Then, too, his smiling assurance and the florid gallantry of his manners, rubbed her fur the wrong way. She felt—was still young enough to feel—that any manifest disapproval of him on her part, would be ridiculous. She could not be sure, toward the last, that it hadn't begun to take him that way. His demure observation that but for having been told who she was, he would have taken her for an English girl, struck her as indicating that.

Helena's eventual descent, in a rather dressy hat, did not improve the situation, either. Rather, indeed, the contrary. She seemed as foreign as he.

"It's very bad of me to be late," she said. "I had counted on it that, for this once, Hugh would not be. I hope Bjornstadt has kept you amused." She paused there for a glance at him—her first since she had entered the room—and added: "And that he hasn't been flirting with you too violently. It's a harmless weakness of his with pretty girls."

He protested, with manifest amusement, that this injurious charge was wholly unfounded. "I assure you, my dear lady, that our conversation has been decorum itself."

She cut him off with a brusk nod and asked him to ring the bell. "We won't wait lunch for Hugh," she said. "There is simply no telling when he'll come, since he's as late as this."

Jean was, really, a pretty good cosmopolite. She had had enough experience of the world to have taken this sort of situation easily enough; to understand that this paraded air of intimacy between a married woman and an unattached man need not necessarily be stretched to bear a sinister interpretation. She didn't go the length of so interpreting it today; not, certainly, in her formulated thoughts. But it embarrassed her painfully. She just wished with all her might that she hadn't come. Suppose Hugh didn't, at all! And she had to sit through lunch with them. . .

"He comes!" exclaimed Bjornstadt, who stood where he commanded a view out the front window. *"Mirabile dictu,* he is here."

She was amused, thinking it all over afterward, to realize that once more, just as so often in the old days, he had rescued her; not by doing anything in particular—just by coming in and being Hugh.

It was as mysterious as a trick of legerdemain, the way the very atmosphere of the room changed when he entered. His greeting to Jean was practically all hand-shake and smile; both completely satisfactory. He must have said something, of course, but she wasn't able to remember what. Then, his smile changing quality a little, amusement replacing the affection there had been in it, he turned to the other guest.

"Count," he said, "make a note for your book on America, that men sometimes come home for lunch. Once in—how many times is it?— five?" And lastly, in a good-humored but thoroughly domestic tone, he asked for an exegesis of his wife's hat. "Does it mean that this lunch is a party? Or only that you're going out right after? You're not taking Jean, I hope."

"She's very welcome to come if she likes," said Helena. "Bjornstadt is going to talk to our Wednesday class about Free Trade."

Jean took it from that that she needn't go unless she liked, and she believed that if she elected not to, Hugh would stay for a while and talk to her. She was happy again. What a silly she had been to worry about this Swedish count—if that was what he was? Hugh, being Hugh, his very same, dearly-remembered self, was a match for a dozen of him.

In this suddenly changed mood, she even enjoyed the lunch, though the talk, to which she contributed very little, would have distressed her had not Hugh—himself a listener most of the time—been sitting there at her left hand, taking it all so calmly.

Helena and Bjornstadt discussed the war; but in a set of terms almost bewildering to Jean. America was responsible for it, of course, Bjornstadt said, through having begun, within the last fifteen years, to export a greater value of fabricated articles than she had imported. She had more than built a dam. She had turned back the tide. And the result was an inundation. So long as America had remained an unlimited reservoir for manufactured products, there was room in the markets of the world for England and Germany to go on expanding side by side. Now that the reservoir had, so to speak, overflowed, these two great industrial rivals must fight it out for survival. France, Belgium, Serbia and the rest, were mere incidents—pawns in the great game. And well within the next hundred years, he noted calmly, the survivor—whichever it happened to be—would fight it out with the United States for the industrial empire of the world. "All that," he concluded, "in the absence of the adoption of my panacea, Free Trade."

Hugh's remark at this point, that the English certainly stood committed to Free Trade, amused Bjornstadt very much.

"They're the cleverest people in the world," he said, "at giving their own material advantages the labels of high moral principles, and then imposing those labels on the world. The United Kingdom has what it calls Free Trade, yes. But the great dominions, Canada, Australasia, the South African Union, and the colonies dotted all over the map, have they? And how can trade be free, while Britannia rules the wave; controls all the great trade-routes; has the power any morning to say, this door shall be shut, or that be opened?

"Take your own case, you Americans. You had dug your Panama Canal. But, when your Congress attempted to exempt your coastwise ships from the payment of tolls, your president informed them that he dared not to do it. England had given orders to the contrary.

"They're two well-matched antagonists," he said, referring once more to England and Germany. "The English, subtle but careless. The Germans, infinitely patient and thorough, but unimaginative. It is interesting to speculate about the outcome, but difficult to prophesy."

Helena, who had agreed with him in explaining the whole struggle on an economic or capitalistic basis, was impatient of his attempt to draw nationalistic distinctions. They were all alike, all over the world; the capitalist class, in trying to enforce its advantages; the proletariat in submitting in a dull blind resentment that would not remain acquiescent forever to its tyrannies. She was glad of the war since it brought the great revolution nearer.

When the cigarettes came around, Jean hesitated, then declined one, and, catching Hugh's glance, she explained: "I did over there, of course. We all did. When we came off duty at the hospital,—the nurses themselves, and we aids, too, who'd only been washing up and holding basins and things—cigarettes were more what we needed than anything else. Even the nuns in a convent we used to take supplies to in Belgium, had to take to them. But back home here, it's rather pleasant not to."

The remark produced a rather electrical little silence, with the realization it enforced, even on Helena, the least sensitive of the three, that to the young girl, who had sat through all their talk so quietly, the war meant something utterly different from anything their comfortable philosophy took account of. It meant blood sopped up in sponges, limbs with the splintered ends of bone protruding through the sodden flesh; screams of an unconquerable agony, and Death coming as a white sister of mercy. The girl who had sat so quietly listening, knew what this was but the bare beginning and routine of.

It was Helena who broke the silence. "It will take you a little while, I suppose, to get used to all this again. We ought to try to make you forget."

Jean shook her head—not in dissent, but unconsciously, in the effort she had to make to follow the line her hostess had taken.

"That's grandmother's idea," she said. "I'm to have a very gay season, beginning with a regular coming-out party, and doing all the things a débutante does, afterward. And Uncle Frank is finding me a horse, so that I can ride again."

"That's what Hugh is always talking about, but never does," said Helena. "I wish you could persuade him to do it. If he had you to ride with, perhaps he'd stop urging me."

"You ought to ride," Bjornstadt said to Helena. "If not for your selfish pleasure, for the delight others would take in the spectacle."

Helena said it would be a spectacle, no doubt of that, and vividly expressed her ineradicable aversion to horses. And from then on, until she and the count left the table, the talk ran on in this lighter vein.

"I don't know how long it is," Hugh said, when he and Jean were left alone—the question of her going along with the other pair had not been raised—"since you and I have seen each other, but somehow it doesn't seem as long as it must be."

"It's three years and three months," she informed him, without any pause for reckoning; and he laughed. She smiled contentedly back at him without asking why, and added: "I thought Count Bjornstadt was you, from his hat being in the hall, and when I saw him, I thought how could you have changed as much as that, before I was sure he was some one else. I'd been warning myself, you see, that you couldn't possibly not have changed a good deal. That's how long it seems to me. And when you came in and weren't changed at all, you were almost as surprising as the count had been."

He didn't laugh at that, as her tone had invited him to; went grave for an instant instead. "Connie said once," he told her, "that you'd always be the same. Would never turn into a young lady. It's very nice to find that she was right. Of course, it's because you are the same that it's hard to believe such a lot of time has gone by. Time—and other things. What you said a little while ago about not smoking, now you were back home again. . . I wish you'd tell me more. About what you've been doing over there. It's hard to understand how you can have come through that—and be like this."

He could see that it was with an effort that she collected herself for the recital. But before he could withdraw the request, she had begun—a little dryly at first, with a bare chronicle of important facts.

It was not until she began describing Paris to him, as it had been during those days just before the battle of the Marne, when the government had moved to Bordeaux, and all who meant to flee had fled, that she gave herself up, without reservation, to the narrative—began living it for him again.

"There was the most wonderful spirit there during those days," she said. "Every one you saw, on the street—anywhere—was your friend; was like one of your family; had a sort of bond with you that nobody who wasn't there could have. I don't know whether we really believed, any of us, that the Germans were going to be stopped, but we knew we meant to see it through."

It was during those days that she made friends and went to work with a sturdy young *vicomtesse*, who was organizing a relief for the Belgians, civil and military, in the still defended strip of that stricken country.

"You mean you've been under fire!" cried Hugh, when she described to him how they went in with three motor-ambulances full of supplies to a village that had been under bombardment, and how, just as they had gathered the wounded together in the little convent garden, the fire had opened again; and the struggle they had had getting these helpless ones into what insecure shelter there was; the long wait in the dark, and then the flight back after the bombardment had thinned to the normal sprinkling of occasional shells.

"There was always that," she said, "in all the places where the people were that we were trying to help. Nothing ever hit very close to me. Yvonne had her ambulance hit once, when she had four wounded soldiers in it. But she found it would still run and drove straight along, not knowing whether they had all been killed or not. None of them had been, it happened.

"The hardest thing I ever did," she said presently, "was giving that up—that work. But what mother was doing was simply killing her. She was in one of the French hospitals, and father said, when he was ordered home, that we must either come with him, or go back to England. And Aunt Christine wanted us, so we went there. We went right on working, of course, but it wasn't so—ghastly. You could get away from it. The English are like that, you know, with their 'Business as usual,' and *Punch*, and Bairnsfather."

When he asked, bluntly, "Why did you come home?" she hesitated over her answer.

"It was partly for mother," she said at last. "She couldn't stand it. I don't mean the work. She could have gone on with that just the way Aunt Christine did—if father had been an English officer. Or if we'd gone into the war—after the *Lusitania*. Oh, it wasn't the way they treated us personally. Nor even that they said such very bitter things about America. The people who talked the worst were the other Americans over there. We used to boil at that. But our friends—English friends—were just puzzled. They wanted us to tell them why we took it like that. And, of course, we couldn't. Because we were as puzzled as they. It was a feeling you might call—homesickness, that really was too much for mother. That on top of all the rest. I think she'd have collapsed altogether, if I hadn't brought her home.

"It isn't fair, though,"—this, after a little pause—"to put it all off on her. Because it got me in just the same way. I felt as if I couldn't endure it, not to come back—here to Chicago—where the people I knew and loved were—and learn to see—what it was they saw. I thought if I could just talk with *you*—have you explain it all to me, then it would all come straight."

Her emphasis on the pronoun made it impossible to believe that she had used it in any but the singular, personal sense. His "With *me!*" was not a question, but a mere cry of surprise; almost of consternation, one might have said.

She nodded. "You've always understood things, better than any one else I know. And you're not a selfish mercenary monster"—her inflection was humorous, but the affectionate, contented warmth in her voice made of every ugly epithet almost a caress—"and you're not a hypocrite, pretending to be very noble because he's really afraid. Nor any of the things they say we are. You're—Hugh. Mother laughed at me the other night for saying that when you'd told me, I'd know; but it's true. When I can see what you see, then I'll be contented to wait—for what you're waiting for. That's—really—why I've come home."

It was so long before he made her any answer at all—just sat there with his gaze focussed upon his empty coffee-cup—that at last, in a troubled voice, she prompted him.

"If it's something you're—afraid that I wouldn't like to hear, something that you think will hurt me. . ."

"No, it's not that," he told her. "It's that you have come to the wrong person. I don't know what to say to you. I haven't thought it through."

"You haven't thought!" There was simple incredulity in that almost voiceless echo.

"At least I've tried not to think. I've tried, as well as I could, to let it alone."

There were a good many silences as he went on, but not one of them did the girl break in upon.

"Most men, I suppose—outside the really great ones—come to the point sometime, where they acquiesce in their limitations. It's just age, or indolence, that brings some to that, and they come to it so gradually they don't know they've done it. But a man may be brought to it—the way I was—by an experience, or a set of experiences, so that it's a more dramatic recognizable thing; so that he goes inside some sort of fence, once for all. Says to himself: 'I'm all right so long as I stay in here. Here's where I belong.' There's a certain sort of thing that I seem to be able to understand—get at the truth about. Not living things; inorganic things—metals. It makes more of a world than you'd think, even the small sector of it I have marked off for myself—a world I won't live long enough to explore anywhere near to the end of, if I go on till I'm a hundred.

"When the war broke, I said: 'That's another of the things that's outside my fence,' just as I'd found that sociology and politics were outside my fence; just as the big strike we had out at Riverdale was, only immensely more so. I could keep out of it, even if I couldn't altogether keep it out of me.

"I had to get some sort of working basis toward it, of course. I've tried to say that my own personal feelings didn't count. I was an American of Scotch and English blood—nothing else, so far as I know—and we've been here since the Revolution; but that didn't make me any more truly an American than my polisher, Schultz, out at the laboratory—or than my friend Bausch, at the University. Bausch had his argument. I, if I wanted to argue, had mine. And, in both cases—I could see it plainly enough in his, and he, I suppose, could see it plainly enough in mine— the line of that argument wouldn't be determined by any pure reasoning faculty we had, but by what Rodney Aldrich speaks of as our visceral sensations. Bausch is an American. Perley, his assistant, is a Sassenach-hating Irishman, and he's an American. My wife's half Hungarian-Jew, half Pole, and she's an American.

"So, I've said, the America of the school-books, doesn't, just now, exist. It has in the past, and it will, I suppose, again. All the nations—even the greatest—have had phases like that. All we are now is an agglomerate of individuals and groups. We'll get into something, sometime perhaps, like the arc of one of my electric furnaces, that will burn everything out of us that won't fuse into one national consciousness. I waited for a while—'watchfully'—to see whether it wasn't coming; but it seems it's not. Not for a while. Anyhow—I've said—it's no concern of mine."

That, evidently, was the end. And still she did not speak.

"Not much to have come home for, was it?" he said with a rueful sort of smile.

"Well, it's something," she said. "Something I hadn't thought of."

"Jean," he asked suddenly, "when *was* three years and three months ago?"

"It was the day your grandfather died," she told him, her color brightening a little as she spoke. "We spent the morning down on the beach at Lake Forest, building a sand-castle. You wouldn't remember it, but I do. I told you some of my troubles, and you helped—a lot. The telephone message about old Mr. Corbett came in right after lunch."

"Not remember!" he echoed, with a curious smile that filled her, for an instant, with the panicky fear that she might cry. "Yes, I remember very well. Three years and three months! And that was the man you came back to talk to! You will wonder, when you get home, whether Bjornstadt wasn't really that man, after all. He's fully as like him as I am."

"You've not changed," said Jean confidently. "It's only—things that have. I must go. I've stayed hours. But—sometime, will you take me to see your laboratory?"

Hugh nodded. "I'd like to do that," he said.

Taking leave of her at the door, he asked: "If I get a horse, will you really ride with me?—Mornings, before breakfast?"

"Yes," she said.

XXI

"Mother!" Constance exclaimed. "Here!—At eleven o'clock Sunday morning!"

She had come down to her sitting-room from a visit to the nursery, to find Mrs. Corbett planted, with every effect of permanency, in a big armchair. This was along in November, three or four weeks after Helena's lunch.

"I thought I recognized the cigarette out in the hall," Constance continued, "but I couldn't believe it could be you."

"I parted from your father at the church-door," Mrs. Corbett said. "I started out, right enough, but I had a change of heart. He wasn't left solitary. Greg and his wife were along. They'd called for us. And they all looked so much more religious than I felt, that I came on and took a chance on finding you. I'm glad I did. I haven't seen you for a dog's age."

"Well," Constance demurred with a smile, "yesterday, for a minute. And at dinner Thursday night."

With a brusk exhalation of a cloud of smoke, Mrs. Corbett dismissed these instances of her daughter's as trivial. "Oh, I knew you were still here—or hereabouts," she said. "But what I wanted was a chance to stretch my legs and go over things a bit with you. You're not just running off anywhere, are you? Nor expecting anybody to come running in? Where's Frank?"

"Gone to church," said Constance. "He took Philip" (this was their nine-year-old) "and went round for his mother and Ethel."

"It's the men, with us, who do most of the religion, isn't it?" commented Mrs. Corbett; "—your father and Greg and Frank. It's odd about Gregory," she added. "I wouldn't have expected it to take him that way; especially since Eileen, up to the time he married her, was what your grandfather would have called a Free Thinker. Of course that meant nothing with her. Any man she married she'd swallow whole. The puzzle is, why did marrying her make Greg religious?"

"Well, you never can tell," said Constance. The domestic nature of the occupation she had found for herself on settling down for her mother's visit, may be charged with the sterility of this reply.

Evidently Mrs. Corbett thought so, for she observed: "That's about the sort of thing you'd expect a woman darning socks, to say. You *can* tell sometimes."

Constance nodded and allowed the sock with the darning-egg in it to drop in her lap. "Poor old Hugh," she sighed.

"The last time he dropped in on us," her mother said, after a ruminative silence, "—it must have been a month ago—I didn't know whether to cry or swear; did both, as a matter of fact, after he'd gone. He was like a ghost. I don't mean pale. He's well enough as far as that goes. Like somebody, I mean, come back for an hour from a long way off, looking on. Fond of us as ever, of course—more so, for that matter. He never used to be especially affectionate, and he is now. And interested, in a way, in the things we were doing and talking about. But just as a ghost would be, who'd have to go back in an hour or so, to another world—or hell, of his own, that he couldn't tell us anything about. I was bilious that day, and I suppose I exaggerated. But I didn't make it up out of whole cloth."

"No," Constance agreed. "He's like that when he comes here. Not tragic, though. The children simply adore him."

"Of course not! He's not a fool. It would be better for him if he were—a bit of one. If he hadn't brains enough to see through her. . . He did that, I'm sure, years ago. Or if he had Greg's temper to frighten her with now and then; or Bob's selfishness to keep her worried. The devil of it is, she couldn't have got either of them in a thousand years. It had to be just Hugh."

"Oh, I know; it isn't fair," Constance agreed.

"I suppose we weren't any too wise," the older woman reflected, "but I don't know just what we could have done. You separate two people like that, and you find that absence makes the heart grow fonder. Or, you throw 'em together, and they don't sicken of it as you meant them to. What we tried was a little of both. Oh, I suppose it was hopeless from the start. Poor Hugh! That's about all there is to say."

None of this was new ground, and both women had been talking and listening a little absently. But what Constance said now, had a sharper edge, and Mrs. Corbett's manner became less reflective and more alert as she heard it.

"I wouldn't dare let Jean hear us talking like this."

"Do you happen to know where Jean is this morning?" The older woman's question did not sound quite as casual as the substance of it indicated.

"Why, I think she's gone off somewhere with Carter," Constance said. "I called her up last night to see if she was coming in to lunch today, and she said she didn't think she'd better promise, because he was taking her for a drive out into the country, and she didn't know whether they'd be back."

"That's it, then," Mrs. Corbett said. "He'd had his breakfast and gone off in a great fume long before we were down. But I didn't know whether it was because she was going somewhere with him—or because she wasn't."

"Well, she was; this time."

A moderately sensitive ear might have heard a slight stress, both in the mother's speech and in her daughter's, which made the alternative which had not eventuated, into more than a negative thing.

Mrs. Corbett lighted a fresh cigarette, and settled back into her chair a little more comfortably. "It's being a wonderful experience for Carter; finding a girl who won't come at his whistle. They won't even give him time to whistle—most of them. If I'd wanted to marry him off, I'd have given a tip, to some one of the half dozen, to hold off a little."

"Oh, they don't need tips," said Constance. "They know, well enough; only the poor little things can't help it. They make their plans and resolutions, but the sight of him's too much for them, and they all come fluttering round just the same."

"How is it that Jean keeps her head?" Mrs. Corbett followed that question with a look.

"Why, that's natural enough, mother. When you think where she's been, this last year—what she's been through. All you have to do is look at Ethel and talk to her—see what it's done to her—and then remember that Jean's been having the same experiences. You can't wonder that she isn't so very excited about dance teas and silly suppers at the Casino, and amateur movies; nor very thrilled over Carter, either. I think it's natural that she likes—older people better, just now. If Carter had good sense, he'd stop being so solemn and intense and proprietary about her; go in for being comfortable and brotherly. That sort of thing would bring her round before very long—I'm sure. I wish he'd see it."

"What does she say about Hugh?" Mrs. Corbett asked, after a nod of agreement and a thoughtful inhalation of smoke. "She knows more about that ménage than any of the rest of us, certainly. Doesn't she think he's to be pitied? Or, does she want to do it all herself?"

"I take that back!" she added hastily. "Shouldn't have said it. That's just the eternal feline, Connie. The child is all right, of course. What does she say?"

"Oh, just as you guessed first; that he isn't to be pitied. She never said anything to me but once, and that was when she was indignant over something Carter had said—she didn't quote it—about Hugh. She said the people who treated him as if he had made a failure of his life were mistaken. She said she was sure he didn't feel that way about it himself, and that he'd be certain to, if he had. Might even, well enough, if he hadn't.

"I didn't ask her what she thought of his marriage; because, after all, that speaks for itself. She wouldn't go to their house if she didn't like Helena. And she'd hate her if she thought she was treating Hugh badly.

"I've wondered since," Constance went on, "if she could be right. I suppose the whole thing we see, might just be self-consciousness, coming from the rows—over the business as well as over Helena—and making us all see things that aren't there."

"Self-consciousness!" fumed the older woman. "Is it self-consciousness that he hasn't any children? Or that he lives like a hermit all of his days, and half his nights, in that laboratory of his? Or his wife's goings on with one man after another—poets and foreigners and such? What does she mean, do you suppose, throwing that child at Hugh's head the way she's been doing? It isn't like anything we've ever known of her. Constance, why doesn't the child's grandmother put her foot down on that? I don't understand it. Do you?"

"I think so," said Constance. "Admitting, that is, that there is anything for her to put her foot on—and I don't think there is, really. What worries Mother Crawford is the fear that Jean will rush off and marry somebody before this winter's half over. Carter—or anybody. She doesn't want her to. She wants Jean to play with for a while. You can't blame her, really. And any interest the child takes in—ineligibles— so long as there's nothing for people to talk about—and there isn't, of course—is so much to the good."

"Oh, I suppose it's just that I'm getting suspicious with age; like an old mule," her mother said, getting ready to get up to go. "Only I wish that that pair of children would come home from their ride and tell us they were engaged."

It had, upon them both, something of the startling effect of a stage-trick when, pat upon her words, almost, the "pair of children" came in.

But the part of Mrs. Corbett's wish that really was the whole of it, was evidently not to be fulfilled. Whatever else might have happened during that drive, Jean and Carter had not engaged themselves to marry. Indeed, their manners were so good that Constance was, for a while, in doubt whether anything had happened at all. Without any undue insistence upon their explanation, they accounted for their unexpectedly early return, by the Sunday crowds in the highways. It was as bad as summer; no possibility of anything but plodding along in a smoke-smothered procession. Jean inquired if her invitation to lunch, here at Constance's, still held good, and Carter, having observed that his mother was on the point of going, urged her to let him drive her home. Then every one would think they'd both been to church, he said. You had to know the color and shape of Carter's roadster to appreciate this joke. His mother grinned at it and, to his surprise, said she'd go with him; adding that she only hoped her husband would be where he could see her coming up to the door.

It was the way Jean's eyes kept seeking out the boy's face, that directed Constance's observation to the fact that he had gone pale, now that the flush of the wind had left his face. And the suspicion this phenomenon awakened was confirmed by the way the girl took leave of him.

She said, evenly enough, to be sure, but in a voice colored beyond disguise by a strong emotion, "It was a lovely drive, anyway. Thank you—for asking me." She held out her hand to him and after a perceptible hesitation, he took it.

That made it all as plain as print. Carter had asked and been refused. And there had been no half-tones about the refusal, either; no uncertainties nor pleas for time. That note of affectionate deprecation would never have got into her voice if there had been the slightest chance for him.

"Better luck next time," he told her blithely; and went away with his mother.

There was a little silence after they'd gone, then Jean asked: "How long is it till lunch? Have we five minutes before the others will be coming in? I want to ask you something."

"Come up to my room and take off your hat," Constance suggested. "I'll go along. Then it won't matter if they do come in."

"Oh, it's not as bad as that," said Jean. "Still, I suppose I am blown away, rather."

She had stood before Constance's mirror two or three minutes, busy with minor improvements, when Constance prompted her by saying: "Ask away."

"I ought to have done it down-stairs," Jean said. "It's got too important already. Why, it's just this: oughtn't I to ride with Hugh, mornings, the way we've been doing?"

Constance was a little startled, the question came so pat on what she and her mother had been talking about.

"What put that idea into your head?" she asked.

"It was put there," said Jean, "that's the point. I mean, it didn't come there by itself."

"By your mother?" Constance asked.

And Jean's "No!" had so much surprise in it that she went on to explain. "Of course if mother felt anything like that, why—that would be the end of it. I mean of the riding. I wouldn't ask anybody else."

"All mother ever did," she went on, "was to warn me, the night we came home, against falling in love with him again—the way I did when I was a little girl. And I haven't done that."

There was such perfect candid conviction in the girl's face and voice, that Constance laughed.

"Why, it isn't the sort of thing people would talk about," she said. "I mean, socially it's correct enough. So what it comes down to is what Helena thinks about it. If she objected to it, or even if there was anything to give you the idea she didn't like it much, why, I'd stop."

"Well, that's what I thought," said Jean. "It was her own idea, you see. She doesn't like to ride, and Hugh had been urging her to—for company. And she said—why not me? Oh, and she meant it, you could tell!"

A flash of her mother's uneasiness came over Constance. "Do you like her, Jean?" she asked bluntly.

The girl nodded. "I suppose it's because he does that I do, really," she said. "There were a few minutes, the first day I went to their house, before I knew he did, when I hated her. But I have felt awfully silly about that since. I think she's awfully fond of him, and I'm sure he is of her. They do it their own way, of course; but then, aren't people entitled to?"

There was one more question Constance wanted to ask. But it was a flagrant impertinence, and she did not. Was it Carter who had put that notion into Jean's head? She felt pretty sure of the answer.

Coming down-stairs together, they met Frank and his boy bringing Hugh in for lunch.

"We found this man in church, of all places!" Crawford explained.

"And Phil captured him single-handed and brought him along. Why, hello, Jean! I thought you *weren't* coming."

It was obvious—demonstrable—that there was no prearrangement in this meeting between Jean and Hugh. Constance was hotly indignant with herself for having let the fleeting shadow of that thought cross her mind. It only showed what a mean, suspicious, ornery sort of mind she had.

It was in the reaction from this feeling that she watched her brother all through lunch. He sat between the two little boys, Philip and Francis, and they pretty well monopolized him. How he would have loved to have some like that for his own! He was defrauded there, anyhow—whatever Jean might say. Only perhaps it wasn't Helena's fault. None of them were enough in her confidence to know. He had had a lonely time.

The undisguised pleasure that had lighted his face at sight of Jean, had troubled Constance for a moment even while it had warmed her heart to him. The trouble went away, though, and the warmth remained. If the girl could give him an hour, now and then, of unalloyed happiness—why not? That consideration governed her attitude toward a project that came up while they were still at lunch.

Frank had said, down the table to Hugh, "I didn't know you knocked off work at the laboratory on Sundays," and Hugh's answer had been that he didn't—because they were Sundays. "Taylor and Brigham and Schultz are all out there now, busy as bees. They do all the hard work. I'm lazy. I only turn up when things are getting exciting."

This drew a running fire of the sort of jokes that always are provoked by such a remark; about how they were beginning to learn the truth at last, and what a convenient thing a fortified mystery like a laboratory must be. As good as a Bluebeard's chamber.

Jean asked, "Has any one ever seen it? I asked to, ever so long ago, but I've never been taken."

"There's no time like the present," Hugh said promptly. "We'll go this afternoon. As many as like," he went on in answer to Frank's "All of us?" But Frank had not asked this seriously. He was already committed, as his two sons vociferously reminded him, to another expedition that afternoon.

Constance, though, happened to be free till tea time, and had to make up her mind whether to go or not. She wanted to see the place, quite apart from the consideration of Mrs. Grundy, but that old maternal feeling of hers, which she had never lost for Hugh, and which was stronger than ever in her today, led her to plead letters to write. The "Have a good time," with which she despatched the pair, amounted to a blessing.

They set off afoot, since it was not more than a mile to the laboratory, and a walk was just what they agreed they wanted. A walk out West Chicago Avenue!

XXII

He had mentioned at lunch where Helena was that day—down at her laboratory, the Drama Shop, where they were putting through the dress rehearsals for a bill of one-act plays that were to be presented the next night. So there was no question of her going with them this afternoon.

But Jean said, just after they had left the Crawfords' house: "Do you suppose Helena had rather we waited until she could go, too? Because we can do anything else; just walk."

"No," he said, "it's no treat for Helena. She's been there dozens of times. She goes there," he went on reflectively, "about the way I sometimes go to church. Not understanding, a bit, what it's all about, but getting a sort of wonder out of it; especially when she's a bit low in her mind. A big bare copper bar, for instance, as thick as my arm, that you can put your hand on—it feels perfectly cool and dead—and yet it's got enough electricity going through it to burn you to a cinder if you got in the way of it. You can see a pot of steel boiling like water in the white arc it makes. That sort of thing."

"Is that why you went to church today?" she asked. "Because you were low in your mind?"

"Not a bit," he said. "Today I was following the line of least resistance. When Helena found me this morning with a day off that didn't coincide with hers, she packed me off to find you. By the way, she wants me to bring you to supper tonight if you can come. I went over to your apartment and was told that you were off driving with Carter and that your mother and Mrs. Crawford had gone to church. It was obvious that I couldn't follow you so I followed them."

At that she gave up as something there was no use trying any longer—for the present, at least—to account for, the notion that he dreaded a little taking her out to the laboratory. She had become aware of it the moment she asked, there at the lunch table. It hadn't anything to do with Helena, so much was clear. And it didn't relate to any special state of mind he was in today. Well, she wouldn't fuss about it; would go along as if she hadn't noticed any more than he had meant her to. It's a poor sort of friend that insists on being too penetrating—and on showing how penetrating he is.

Silences were of course a part of their conversation. His omission to comment upon or to inquire about her truncated excursion with

Carter told her, plainly enough, that he suspected an emotional crisis somewhere in the neighborhood. And she felt pretty sure that by not mentioning it herself she was giving him a strong inkling of what had happened. But that couldn't be called violating a confidence, could it? Anyhow, it was all very comfortable and pleasant.

Almost any sort of laboratory will give a layman, who has been brought to see its wonders, a disappointing surprise for a first impression. He has anticipated something entirely mysterious, just as the sensation-seeker in a notorious cabaret has anticipated something entirely disreputable, and is shocked to find most of the patrons sober and decorous enough to pass muster anywhere.

The first room Hugh took Jean into, in the ordinary three-story red brick building whose street door he unlocked, had the same sort of machinery in it that she had seen in the shops at Riverdale. (She had seen Riverdale thoroughly. Gregory, who had taken a sudden warm liking for the girl, since her return from England, had collaborated with Carter in the personal conduct of her excursion through as much of it as she could see in an arduous day; a sight well worth the labor, it may be mentioned, for the huge, thoroughly modernized plant was taxed to its utmost capacity by floods of war orders, running nights and Sundays, and paying a scale of wages that Gregory would have regarded, two years before, as fantastic.) Only, at Riverdale, each of these prosaic machines had gained a dignity, through being repeated, through a vanishing perspective, down endless aisles. In this little room they were all cluttered up—meanly. It might have been the repair shop to a garage.

Hugh saw her trying to look interested, and laughed at her. "Not much, compared to Gregory's lay-out, is it?" he commented, but without any ironic implications; nothing but pure amusement, in his voice. So she laughed too, contentedly, at herself, and followed him through into another room that took up the rest of the ground floor.

"These are all testing-machines of one kind and another," he said; and walked over to the only one of them that was running. "That's doing pretty well," he observed, after a glance at an instrument which looked like an automobile speedometer. "It's a fatigue-test," he explained. "We're trying to tire out that little shaft of metal turning round in there with the weight hung on the end of it. When it breaks, the machine will stop, and a look at the revolution counter will tell us how long it lasted."

"I didn't know that metals got tired," Jean said. "Do they all?"

He nodded and turned from the machine, which was an ordinary-looking lathe, only with a few trimmings, to another, more mysterious—with more the laboratory look.

"Here's the classic test," he said. "It's for tensile strength; how much pull a thing will stand before it pulls apart. The interesting thing about that machine is the way we measure the amount of pull we put on the piece we're testing. We fasten the piece to one end of that big steel bar there, and apply the pull to the other end of it. And the force of the pull is measured by the amount that the bar stretches. When the pull is taken off, it goes back to exactly the length it was before."

Jean was inclined to be incredulous. Did he mean that a great solid piece of cold steel like that would actually pull out longer and then fly back like a rubber-band?

"You could stretch it yourself," he said, "enough so that one of our instruments could measure it."

"They stretch and they get tired," she mused. "It makes them seem more alive, somehow, than I ever thought they were."

"You're getting the idea," he told her.

It was this idea that grew steadily more fascinating and more marvelous during the whole of the next two hours. She saw beautiful photomicrographs that betrayed the strange crystalline structure of this metal and that. She learned, from watching Schultz at his polishing, how incredibly sensitive they were. "He's been hours at that," Hugh said, "and he could have put a good commercial burnish on it in two minutes. But under the microscope it would be nothing but a smear. And squeezing it in a vise, or getting it hot by running his wheel too fast, would change the structure of it completely. He's as tender with it as if it were a baby, you see; and when he's through with it and we've given it a little rest, and etched the crystal outlines with a little weak acid, then it will be possible to see what it really looks like."

She had explained to her the great horizontal microscope through which he studied his specimens and took their photographs; the very light he used for the purpose had to be cooled by passing through water. And she saw the electric furnaces—strangely harmless and insignificant-looking considering the fiery energies they contained—and the mysterious thermocouples that registered the exact degree of heat.

"You can't exaggerate the importance to us," Hugh said, "of being able to produce and regulate and measure temperatures. From the moment a metal begins to freeze. . ."

She exclaimed over the word.

"Solid metals are only frozen liquids," he told her. "They freeze at higher temperatures than we're accustomed to, that's all. And it makes an enormous difference in the characteristics they'll show, whether they've been frozen slowly or suddenly; how much leisure they've been given for adapting themselves to a new state of things. And they go on changing—reorganizing themselves—away below the freezing point; long after they're solid all the way through; after they've stopped being incandescent; after they're cool enough to hold in your hands.

"That's why they're such tyrants," he added with a smile. "I hook up a thermo-couple to an electric bell in my bedroom over there, to call me when a specimen I'm studying has got down to a certain temperature. It won't wait for me. It will be in a phase, just then, that it won't repeat. So, if I want to see, I have to be there to look. It will never be just like that again."

"Why, they're human, in that!" she exclaimed; but he would not accept the word.

"They've as many moods and varieties and mysteries—as a poet's conception of a woman. But if one's imaginative and patient enough, he'll get down to the truth, at last. There's always a law there. And when you've found it, it will always work."

Then, suddenly, "Come in here," he said. "There's something I want to show you." He led her back into his library, where he had shown her the photographs.

He unlocked a safe, that was built in under his bookcases, took a small steel strong box out of it and under her eyes, at the desk, unlocked this. It contained ten or a dozen pieces of lead-colored metal of various sizes and shapes. He picked out one of them, a roughly rounded disc, and handed it to her.

"It feels like lead," she said, looking at it curiously. "What is it?"

Before he answered, he took it from her and tossed it on the desk. It rebounded with the clear ring of silver.

"It's like nothing we've ever called lead before," he said; "not in its physical characteristics, that is. But chemically, I'm practically certain, there's nothing but pure metallic lead in it. Only, I've managed to catch a different phase of it from any that's been found before. I've persuaded the molecules to arrange themselves in a new way. And the crystals, to a marked degree, have a similar polarity. It's immensely harder than lead, but it's quite as plastic."

He made a thoughtful pause there. Then, with a smile reflecting some emotion she could only guess at, he added, "If I can ever really get it, and publish a description of it, I suppose I'll be entitled to call it Corbettite."

"If you can really get it?" she questioned. "Haven't you got it there?"

"I can't do it everytime," he said, his absent gaze turned to the window. "A year ago, I felt nearer it than I do now. Then every experiment brought me nearer to it—made the possibility that had only seemed barely worth playing with at first, come out clearer. But then, when I carried it further along, it began to take—freaks. That's not the right way to put it, of course. It was acting, all along, according to its own laws. Only, I'd got into the domain of some law that I hadn't discovered. I'd think I was doing the same thing everytime, but some factor I hadn't taken into account, would be different. I haven't found it yet. Half the times I try, I can produce a material like that. The other half I can't."

"That must be perfectly maddening," she said.

"You can't be mad in this work," he told her. "Resentments and impatiences may effect something when you're dealing with your kind, but it doesn't do to indulge them with metals. When you come into their world, you've got to subscribe to their laws and ways. It wants a degree of patience to make a metallurgist, that would seem contemptible in a man. But a metallurgist, who was nothing else, wouldn't care. In so far as I am one, those bits of metal in that box are the biggest fact in my life. I may spend the rest of it hunting for the secret they're still holding back from me. Another man may find it while I am still looking; or the day after I am dead. Or, I may find it myself, tomorrow. And, I suppose, a pure scientist—if there were such a monster in the world—wouldn't care about that, either."

She turned away from him suddenly, and went over to the window; heard him locking up the box again and putting it back into the safe, without turning round. Then,

"What will Corbettite do," she asked, "when you have really found it?"

"That's what I try to pretend I am not interested in," he said. "—More honestly, what I try not to be interested in."

At that she pressed her hands to her eyes, turned and stared at him. "Why?"

"Well, if you're looking for something you want very much," he explained, "you're likely to think you see it when you don't. Here's a parable for you:

"Do you remember that room out there, that you said was like a refrigerator?—The room I told you had a separate foundation, independent of all the rest of the building so that the vibrations wouldn't be communicated to it? We can control the temperature in that room to a fraction of a degree. I have worked in there, for hours at a stretch, in a sort of modified deep-sea-diver's suit, helmet and all, getting my air through a hose from the outside, and having my warmth and moisture carried away through another. A man's body, you see, is only a sort of glorified donkey-engine, radiating heat, breathing out carbonic-acid, and there are close experiments that these factors have to be eliminated from. Well, a perfect scientist ought to wear a sort of spiritual diving-suit like that. He hasn't any business with hopes. Don't you see?"

But he did not wait for her reply. "Why, that stuff," he said, with a sudden change of manner, "is incomparably the best anti-friction metal in the world. I've babbitted an ordinary standard bearing with it and run it dry—without oil, I mean—for six hours at three thousand revolutions, without getting it hot. That's as fast as an airplane motor runs. It had a glaze on it, when I took it out, that must be, I think, the most nearly frictionless surface that ever has been made, on anything."

"You mean," she asked, in a manner of strong excitement, "that if an airplane pilot ran out of oil. . ."

"He'd hardly need start with any," said Hugh. "It ought to add ten hours, I should think, to the flying-life of a plane."

There was a silence. The girl dropped into a chair and clasped her hands in her lap. She hoped he wouldn't see that they were trembling. But she was safe enough. He had drifted off into an abstraction; stood there in the window, his hands in his trousers pockets, gazing out at the thickening twilight.

Finally he said, "Greg was out here a while ago. I didn't show him 'Corbettite,' but I gave him a look at everything else. He was interested all right. But just before he went away, he said, 'You ought to have a lot of fun out of this. It must cost you as much as a steam-yacht.' And I don't blame him for taking it like that. The thing is so near like the most wonderful toy in the world, that I sometimes almost wonder, myself, if it isn't."

"Was that why you didn't want to bring me?" she demanded in sudden enlightenment. "Because you thought I'd take it like that?"

"I didn't think you would," he said, "but I wanted you so much not to, that I had to—stiffen up a little to put it to the test."

She made no attempt to tell him how she did feel about it. There was, plainly enough, no need of that. They set out homeward, presently, and walked all the way with no more than a casual absent comment on the people they passed and the dust blowing up the street and the gulls over the river. And at last, on her part, even that died away.

"I've simply paralyzed you this afternoon," he said at last, when they stood in the doorway of the apartment building that she called, just now, home. "I don't wonder. You've had metallurgy enough to make anybody's head swim." And then, with a closer look at her, "Why, Jean! What is it?"

"It's nothing. It's just what you said; that I'm—paralyzed. Only not by metallurgy. Not by the new world you've been showing me. By the new things you've given me to think about—and understand—begin to understand, anyway—about my old one. It's the—parables you've been showing me. Oh, not the one about the diving suit. Because you *don't* wear one. I'm very glad of that. Good night."

Hugh walked slowly home, pondering upon those parables which she said he had shown her. She had given him new things to think about his old world; no doubt of that.

XXIII

That first visit of Jean's to Hugh's laboratory had no immediately visible and dramatic results. It was not really until months afterward, that he found himself dating events from it as from a new era. The comparison to a water-shed suggests itself. These do not always lie along craggy summits. The Corbetts, going out from town to the plant at Riverdale, crossed daily, from the St. Lawrence Valley into the Mississippi, and back again at night. But not one of them could have told where the divide was.

That question of Jean's about Corbettite—What will it do?—had not so much suggested a new idea to Hugh as it had fertilized, given a germinant power to an idea that was already in his mind. He had answered, to be sure, that a scientist had no legitimate concern with the practical applications of his science. But, even as he spoke, he doubted whether this were the final answer. That doubt was pregnant with a revolutionary change in him. The talk with Jean over those bits of strange metal in his strong-box; the picture which one of her vivid questions lodged with terrible concreteness in his mind, of an aviator, miles up in the frosty air, his motor stalled because a bearing had got hot enough to bind, became, as he could see afterward, one of his "critical angles."

But the development along the new plane was slow; at first, almost imperceptible. If this fact makes you impatient with him, if you ask why he did not at once, realizing the great need, adopt the new motivation; why he did not say there and then to the girl who was watching him so breathless?—"From now forward, this laboratory of mine shall be nothing but an instrument to serve my country's and civilization's needs."—I can only ask you to remember when it was that this scene took place.

As I write, in January nineteen eighteen, the nation seethes with a great impatience. "Why are we not ready? Why, with the enemy's great offensive imminent, are not our armies holding their sector of the lines in France? Why are our men in the training-camps at home, still without rifles, guns, machine guns; even without shoes to march in and overcoats to keep them warm? Where are the ships, the railroad equipment, the vast supplies?" We've been nine months at war, and when a complacent secretary assures us that we have done well, we stare

HENRY KITCHELL WEBSTER

at him in angry incredulity and demand his head. This, as I write, in January nineteen eighteen.

But how well do you remember the winter of nineteen fifteen and sixteen? Jean and Hugh, walking home from the laboratory, might have talked about the Peace Ship,—the *Oscar VIII*, wasn't it?—that Henry Ford was taking over to Stockholm. They were going, he said confidently, to have the boys out of the trenches before Christmas.

The question of peace or war was, except in its financial aspects, a platonic one with us, all peril of our being involved in it having been averted by the president's diplomacy. Germany had been brought, by easy stages, to an "assumption" of responsibility for the lives of American citizens lost on the *Lusitania*. Another note or two would secure the substitution of the word "acknowledges" for "assumes" and a formal disavowal of the act of sinking her. Von Papen and Boy-Ed of the German Embassy, who were shown to have had a hand in the sinister disorganization of our war industries, strikes, fires, explosions, were bruskly sent home; so *that* was all right. The Mexican difficulty recrudesced suddenly, (it was on the seventh of January that nineteen Americans were taken from a passenger train by Villa's bandits, and murdered in cold blood) but the State Department, determined not to involve the nation in the fate of a numerically negligible group of commercial adventurers, met it by warning all American citizens in Mexico to come home where they belonged, or to remain at their proper peril. We were not going to be tempted out of our blessed state of peace, into a war with anybody.

A different and more active leaven was at work in the mass, of course. It manifested itself, on the surface, in some strange bubbles; the children's chain of dimes to build a super dreadnaught—a feature of the news in January nineteen sixteen—for an example. The possibilities of "preparedness" as a new sort of pork barrel began to dawn on the consciousness of certain congressmen. It was in this month of January that one of the gentlemen from Illinois introduced a bill for the construction of "an armory factory" at Quincy, "to cost not more than five hundred thousand dollars"; and a more urban colleague of his sounded out the newspaper offices as to what they'd think of "another West Point for Chicago."

In the main, though, it was a consternating thing for the politicians— this discovery of a new and dangerously vital issue so few months before the great quadrennial conventions. On the twentieth of January

Colonel Roosevelt published his letter to the Security League coming out for universal military training and a real army, and the Republican wheel-horses settled ruefully into the traces to the task of finding some one to beat him. Volunteers sprang up by dozens, favorite sons from most of the Republican states, like the harvest of the dragon's teeth. But they showed little more initiative than the army that confronted Cadmus. Patriots, of course, every one, but what with the German vote here and the pacifists there, the safest thing for each of them to do appeared to be absolutely nothing. A yearning arose for Hughes, about whose political opinions one not only knew nothing, one would, with absolute certainty, continue to know nothing so long as he continued to sit on the bench.

On the Democratic side the doubt was just as painful. How much vitality had Mr. Bryan? How many people believed in his comforting assurance about the million men who, if need arose, would "spring to arms" between sunrise and sunset? How many people wondered what arms they would find to spring to? The secretary of war, Garrison, was working hard with Congress for his "Continental Army" of half a million men. The president, announcing that he favored "adequate defense" set out on a speaking tour. In St. Louis, where the German vote is very heavy, he was reported as having declared that the United States must have "incomparably the greatest navy in the world,"—the implication being that England, rather than Germany, was our most probable enemy—but this phrase was hastily retracted and "incomparably the most adequate" substituted for it. Within a few days of his return to Washington, the administration formally repudiated the Continental Army scheme, and the next day, February eleventh, Garrison resigned. It was in that same week, however, that *The Chicago Tribune* announced in head-lines "Prepare Wave Sweeps House"; two Navy Bills having been passed without opposition; one for the increase of the number of cadets at Annapolis and one for the enlargement of the Mare Island Navy Yard. Over in the Senate, Penrose announced the threat that if the government persisted in its project for manufacturing its own armor for battle-ships, the mills would raise the price of it to two hundred dollars a ton.

We had, of course, other things to think of that winter than war and politics. Business went on booming, a fact we celebrated on New Year's Eve out here in Chicago, with an unparalleled consumption of alcohol; six hundred thousand dollars, so *The Tribune* announced next morning, having been spent in the down-town restaurants, and the lid, supposed to come down at one A.M., forgotten.

The anarchistic attempt to poison the new Catholic archbishop and about half the notables of Chicago with arsenic in the soup, at a banquet in the University Club—an attempt frustrated by the unexpectedly large attendance and the consequently necessary dilution of the soup, tickled, somehow, our sense of humor, and had the effect, I think, of leading us to treat somewhat more skeptically than otherwise we should have done, other terroristic manifestations which were extraordinarily prevalent that winter. There was anyway—still is, for that matter—to our Middle Western American minds, something fantastically humorous about the importing from the realms of romance into sober reality, of such concepts as plots, conspiracies, spies and foreign agents. The somewhat hysterical nature of the attempt we have been making of late to deal with such matters soberly, is an indication that we don't at bottom really believe in them.

There was the familiar series of appeals, that winter, for various sorts of war relief; the most compelling of these, Paderewski's plea for Poland. He gave the thousands that heard him play Chopin and talk about his stricken country an evening they will never forget. Jean's *vicomtesse* came in khaki to get help for the Belgians, and two English girls with a moving appeal for the adoption of French war orphans at ten cents a day, thirty-six dollars and fifty cents a year. A shop—waited upon by débutantes—was opened in the loop, with a reception, for the benefit of the French wounded. The opera gave a gala benefit for the Italian Red Cross, and the cripples of Parma. Take it by and large there was enough activity of this sort to make hard sledding for the United Charities, who thanked God for a comparatively mild winter.

The theaters regaled us with "glad" plays and funny farces; we found *The Follies* better than ever, and we were greatly excited about the Russian Ballet even after the question whether we were, or not, to see Najinski was answered in the negative.

We—in a much more inclusive sense—were presently absorbed, given an immense emotional outlet, when, in the middle of February, they found a young high-school girl up on the North shore, dead in the snow out in a lonely patch of wood; dead of cyanide poisoning; and when a young university student was, within a day or two, arrested and charged with having murdered her. There was nothing parochial about this affair. The whole country rang with it for months.

The great German offensive at Verdun began on the twenty-fourth of February.

It was Carter who brought home the war to the Corbetts. He went to New York in January, to be best man at a classmate's wedding; made a trip to Washington the day after the ceremony, came home with his passports to France, and informed his family that he was going to enlist—in the air service, if they would take him.

This was a bomb for the family. Carter was their baby, you see, and it had never been their habit to take him seriously. They had always petted him. He had "gone to work," of course, according to the family tradition, at the end of the traditional year abroad that followed his graduation in nineteen twelve; but even Gregory, though he grumbled over the kid's outrageous hours and the negligible value of his labors out at the office, did so merely as a matter of form and not in the expectation that his remonstrances would effect any improvement. To Greg, as to the rest of them, Carter's pyrotechnic social success and his insouciant way of dealing with it, was a matter of undisguised amusement and hidden pride. The elder Corbetts, barring Bob (whose derelictions they had taken somewhat too seriously, perhaps) had run rather solid and stiff for ornamental purposes, and a bit of pure decoration, like Carter, finished them off rather well; showed what they could do, in that line as well as in others, when they tried.

It was taken as an amusing piece of retributive justice that to Carter, after whom three seasons of débutantes had sighed. . . —No, I'll admit they don't sigh these days. . . had toiled in vain, should have befallen, at last, the magnet's experience of falling in love with a silver churn.

The family's amusement would have been less genuine but for their unanimous affection for Jean. But they were fond of her, and they remembered Carter's lordly ways with her, back in the summer of Anne's wedding; and they agreed that it was a good thing for him to get a little of his own back. The progress of the affair had been visible enough to all intimately placed observers, though nobody was in possession of any authoritative confidences. It needed only half an eye to see that he had asked and been rejected, that Sunday morning when they went out for a drive in his car. It was really rather touching—even while one smiled—to note the way they treated each other afterward; the "cousinly" good will and affection (they weren't cousins, of course, in any degree) which they so scrupulously and delicately stressed. She'd come round in time—though the boy couldn't be expected to see that.

He had no rival in the field. Unless one wanted to apply that term to poor old Hugh.

So the boy's studiously casual announcement that he was sailing within a fortnight to enlist in the French army was a thunderbolt. He deprecated their astonishment. It was a notion he had had in mind for ever so long, but his visit to New York had clinched the thing. "They know there's a war going on better, down there, than we do, somehow. People talk about it more. It seems closer. 'Burge' Smith is over there already and Carrol Wayne says he's going. Before long I'd have to begin explaining why I didn't go. It's a great chance, of course, to learn something about airplanes; might come in handy if *we* ever get into anything."

It was not Carter's habitual way to explain the things he did. But this explanation, or minor variants of it, he was a little unnaturally ready with. It couldn't be said that he recited it, still less that he launched it defiantly at people's heads, though each of these exaggerations contained a grain of truth. At all events, if anybody entertained in the inner recesses of his or her mind, any other explanation of Carter's going for a soldier, it was not going to be Carter's fault.

Whatever explanation one chose to assign, there was a sort of splendor about the boy during those days, that put an end to the possibility of maintaining the old smiling attitude. If he was going because, loving Jean, she didn't love him back, then his love for her was a bigger and deeper thing than they'd supposed. He got a new heroic stature in their eyes.

And then, before they could readjust themselves to it—believe it, fairly—he was gone. There were a number of projects for giving him an appropriate farewell—dinners and such—but he prevented these by leaving a week ahead of his announced time.

At a dance that he and Jean attended, he carried her off into a corner and told her.

"I'm off in the morning," he said, "so this is good-by. Nobody else knows. Oh, it's been my date all the while. I told 'em an extra week to save fuss. All the sob stuff. It'll be easier—for everybody. Don't you think?"

"I suppose so," she managed to answer. There followed a long silence. She leaned back against the pillows in the cushioned recess he had found for her; not voluntarily; all her body had suddenly relaxed—gone limp. She wondered, fleetingly, whether it would be in her power to shut one of her half-open hands—or lift it. He was leaning forward, elbows on knees, hands clasped. He was as taut as the strings across a violin bridge, and trembling. They hadn't been alone together, like this, since that Sunday morning in the car. They *were* alone. Other couples, coming hopefully to the doorway, would see the white of her frock and of his shirt, and go away—enviously.

"I'm glad you've told me, though," she added, after a while.

"I had a reason," he said. "Not what I'm afraid you'll think. I—I didn't do it to try to cash in on—being a little tin hero." He heard her gasp of protest and added, quickly, "Oh, I know that isn't what you think. I oughtn't to have been afraid. It would be such a cheap, second-rate thing to do, and you don't suspect people of doing cheap things. I suppose what I really was afraid of was that I might do it. It wouldn't be the first time that I'd done a thing as cheap as that."

There came no reply from Jean. Her gaze was fixed on his clasped hands, and his wrists. They were so slim and fine and strong. Carter was the "little" Corbett; not more than five feet nine inches tall and weighing at this time around a hundred and fifty pounds. A watch, some one had called him once, in a family of eight-day clocks. The yearning in the girl's heart was to mother those hands of his in her own, until they stopped trembling. But, of course, that wouldn't be fair.

"It's one of those cheap things," he went on at last, "that I want to talk about. I brought you here so that I could take it back. I wish I could really take it back—unsay it—undo it, so that there wouldn't be a memory of it in your mind at all. You know what I mean, don't you? The things I said about Hugh, that last time we were together. I was jealous of him. I've always been jealous of him, I guess, ever since that night you caught the burglar. I didn't know I was in love with you then, but, of course, I was. That was why I tried so hard to—show off; why it was such a grind on me that you never were impressed. It made me sore that you took to Hugh. I wouldn't have felt that if it had been Greg. It always seemed to me that everybody ought to admire him.

"Well, and when you came back and I knew I was in love with you—which I did the minute I saw you, there at the party Frank and Constance had for the Aldriches—then the jealousy was all the worse. I remember when I came up for a dance with you after you'd been sitting out all that while with Lester Vernon. I didn't mind being cut out by him, for the time being. I was all set for that. But you began right away asking me about Hugh; why he wasn't at the party, and—how he looked and what he was doing. I don't know exactly why it made me so sore, but it did.

"Well, and after that, the only time I ever saw you angry, was once when I said something, in a half joking way, about his being the family failure. Of course it was a rotten thing to say. I knew he was—cleverer than Greg, or any of us; and had a great deal more advanced ideas and all that, so it was a kind of natural spitefulness to try to say: 'What's all that got him, after all?'"

"But you didn't say anything like that," Jean reminded him, "the time you're talking about. That day in the car. You said you'd come to see what a—what a wonder he was. You warned me that I'd fallen in love with him. Without knowing it. And that with him married, especially, you said, to Helena, that was thin ice. There wasn't anything cheap about doing that, if you thought that was what I'd done. It was brotherly of you to warn me. It was just about the kindest, finest—hardest thing you could do."

He made a little grunt of dissent. "I was jealous," he said, "furious. I wanted to hurt—him or you—both of you. Well, that's what I want to take back. This is what I want to say."

It took him a minute or two, though, to articulate it.

"You know, Greg," he said at last, "has always been, ever since I can remember, a kind of ideal of mine. He is yet, I suppose. If he did a thing, it was right. All along, through school and college, when things came up—and they do come up all right, even when you're just a kid; I don't suppose a girl can understand that, really—I used to try to think what Greg would have done about them. How he'd look and feel about them, if he knew I'd done them—or hadn't done them. If he did them, they were right. That was enough for me. Now, I guess I can make you understand.

"You're like Greg to me—in a different way, of course. Anything you do—whatever you do—anything you could possibly do, is right; is what I'd want you to do, if I were here to—talk to you about it. That's all I want you to remember about me."

It would have been possible to smile over that, of course, but Jean couldn't. "That's terrifying," she said very gravely. There was a note almost of awe in her voice. "You mustn't think of me like that."

"Must or mustn't has nothing to with it," he insisted. "It's a simple fact that I do. But it's got nothing to do with you. You're my—well, my ideal, just because you happen to be yourself. So all you have to do to live up to it, is just to go on being yourself." He added, in a deliberate effort to get away from heroics, "You should worry!"

"All the same, . . ." she protested; then let the sentence die away. "I've thought a lot, since," she went on, presently, on a different theme, "about what you said that day. Not wondering if I was in love with him, because I knew I wasn't. But wondering how it was I knew. He's—in a way—the same sort of—ideal to me that Gregory is to you. I mean—there's nothing I couldn't tell him, nor that I couldn't imagine his telling me; nothing, on either side that the other wouldn't be sure to understand. And there's something so safe and secure about that feeling, that of course I love to be with him, and have him talk with me. Well, I know now how it is that in spite of all that, I know I'm not in love with him. Carter, you can't be in love with any one, can you?"—it was one of those downward inflected questions that demands a corroborative answer—"*in* love, you know—that way—without being jealous of them."

"Search me!" he answered restlessly. "I couldn't. That's sure enough."

"Nobody could," she asserted. "At least a little. Some way. And I'm not. I mean more than that, really. There's nothing about him that I want, or wish I might have had, for *mine*. I'd be glad if everybody he knew felt about him the way I do. I was glad when he married Helena—though, of course, I was too young then, I suppose, for what I felt to count. But when I came back, I was glad, completely glad, to find that his marriage had been happy. Because it has been. You're all wrong about that. I don't think you understand him very well—any of you."

"Maybe not," he said vaguely. Then he roused himself and said it again. "He gave me a surprise, the other day, anyhow; the first time he saw me after he knew I was going to France. I've always thought of him as a cold unemotional sort—nothing in his mind but ideas. Well, I was wrong about that."

"What did he say?"

"Oh, I don't know. You can't repeat things like that. When I started telling him why I was going, he said the rest of them—of 'us' he said—might have some explaining to do, but that I hadn't. It was mostly the way he looked at me. And took hold! He had me by the shoulders. I'd no idea he was as strong as that. He's stronger than Greg, I think. I felt like a baby."

"I'm glad that happened," Jean said. After a little silence she went on. "And I'm glad you've given me a chance to tell you—about things. So that I can be sure you understand. You do—don't you?"

"Sure, I do. You needn't worry about that."

They sat there a little while longer without saying anything. Then, suddenly he sprang to his feet and stood before her, with something soldierly in his attitude, new in him though long familiar to her. She rose, too, and faced him, standing as straight as he.

"Well, it's good-by, then," he said. "I'm going home now. Packing to do."

She was trembling now, and when she saw the quiver of his compressed lips, her eyes filled with tears. The appeal in his eyes was as easy to understand as it was impossible to resist. She swayed toward him.

But he held her off. "Not unless you want to," he said.

She took him by the shoulders and held on while she got the better of a sob. "But I *do!* It was only that it seemed—not fair. As if it seemed like meaning something that—that I wish it did—but it doesn't."

He smiled, a little wryly, but on the whole a very presentable smile. "I shan't misunderstand—now," he said.

So she kissed him, and for a moment, afterward, clung to him and put her head down on his shoulder while she drew in a steadying breath or two.

"I wish you'd make me a promise," he said. "When I come back, whatever may have happened in the meantime—whomever you may be married to—will you let me have another time like this? And kiss me again, like that?"

She nodded.

Her handkerchief had disappeared somewhere, so he let her have his to dry her eyes with. "You look all right," he then assured her.

The music of a new dance came faintly to them from the ballroom. "That's a peach of a fox-trot," he said. "Shall we dance it?"

They did dance it through. "Tip me off," he had said in his old authoritative way, "if you see any of these birds trying to cut in on me," and with her cooperation this tragedy was avoided. He left her with her grandmother at the end, with a nod and an unceremonious little gesture of farewell. "Till next time," he said.

BOOK IV
THE WHITE ARC

XXIV

There were two messages on Helena's telephone pad when she came home about six o'clock one sharp February evening. One was from Hugh, to the effect that he would be home for dinner at seven. She shrugged over that; he had some plan evidently, the mood having taken him, for a domestic evening.

The other message, beneath which the maid who had taken it had written and underscored the word *Immediate,* was simply that she should call a certain number and ask for Mr.——, the maid having so completely failed to understand the name as to be unable to write down even an approximation to it. But for one fact, Helena would have dismissed this with the simple decision that the mysterious Mr.——, who wanted her so urgently, could try again.

The one fact that prevented this summary treatment of the matter, was the name of the telephone exchange, "Canal." That took her back five years or more; back to days when the name Corbett meant nothing to her; back to a different and painfully incredible Helena—a figure of half-forgotten romance. She had called Canal often enough in those days. It meant a district down on the southwest side. Blue Island Avenue is the backbone of it. It was strange that a voice from there should have attempted to speak to her—tonight, of all nights.

She rang for the maid. "What was the name of the man I was to call at this number?" she demanded. "Why didn't you put it down?"

"It was a foreign sounding name," the maid said. "I couldn't understand it. I asked him to spell it, and he started to, then hung up."

"What did it sound like?" Helena persisted.

The maid was reluctant even to attempt it. But the flattening of her mistress's brows and the darkening of her eyes—sure warnings of a storm—led her at last to venture desperately: "It was Cal something. Or Gal. . . Galley."

"Not Galicz!"

It was no wonder that the intensity of the exclamation (it was not loud, but it hissed from Helena's lips like a rocket) startled the maid. But she assented to it unequivocally.

"Yes, madam. That was the name."

"That's impossible!" Helena said, as the maid flinched under her stare. "Impossible nonsense! Why did you say it?"

"It was madam who said it," the girl retorted. "I may be mistaken, but I think the name was that."

"Very well," Helena told her. "You may go."

It was all but downright impossible that any one genuinely entitled to that name should be trying to get in communication with her. Her father had been dead five years, and he had never, in all the period of her most intimate association with him, had any communication with his family in Poland. It was in the highest degree unlikely that it was one of them who had got track of her now. Still, she didn't doubt that her maid had identified the name correctly. Some one in desperate need of her, and knowing that it was a name to conjure with, had used it—some one from the other side of the abyss that her marriage had cloven across her life.

It was strange that it should have happened tonight—falling in with the current of her mood like that.

One of the numerous "circles" she belonged to had met that afternoon in a studio on Chestnut Street. It was an antimilitarist group, organized to combat the propaganda of the munitions-makers and their bellicose dupes who were shouting for preparedness. They circulated anti-enlistment blanks and read each other papers urging disarmament, the embargo, the abandonment of nationalistic emblems, the rewriting of school histories, non-warlike toys for children, and so on. Like all such gatherings they were a heterogeneous lot: a few genuine non-resisters, a considerable number of pro-Germans and other Anglophobes, a lot of thoroughly good-hearted people who thought that war was horrible and ought to be stopped, and a sprinkling of genuine dyed-in-the-wool radicals who interpreted the whole world disaster in terms of the capitalist conspiracy.

Helena was under a promise to read them a paper that afternoon. She had put off writing it until the last moment—as she always did—and had been dismayed to find, when finally she sat down to it, that she couldn't get herself started. An impish mood of derision of her prospective audience was upon her and would not be shaken off. Before a big audience in a hall—especially an audience with any fight in it, she could have trusted to the spur of the moment, but she had found out from experience that a group of forty or so, most of whom she knew, sitting on little folding chairs and expecting tea afterward, could not be dealt with that way.

So, as a last resort, she had rummaged through an old trunk of hers in the attic and found a paper on "Patriotism" that she vaguely remembered having written—oh, ages ago; back in the days before the Riverdale strike.

It was part of her perverse mood that, beyond making sure that the thing was all there, and that it was legible, she did not read it before she set out for the meeting. She had thought it was good when she wrote it, she knew, and it would be amusing to see what came of it now; what sort of impression a little real, undiluted radicalism would make on this kid-gloved, well-fed studio tea.

Its effect on them was about what she had, somewhat derisively, expected. They were nearly all shocked—all but the few radicals, who enjoyed the spectacle. But almost all of them—all but a few evangelical pacifists (who loved the flag but wanted it to float as a symbol of peace)— swiftly concealed their dismay with understanding nods and little riffles of self-conscious applause. The chairman expressed the sense of the meeting admirably when she spoke of it as a very bold paper, startling, no doubt, to many of them and containing some statements to which they could not all agree, but, in its uncompromising and courageous honesty, sounding a note which merited their deepest thought.

What Helena had not foreseen was the effect the reading of it had upon herself. It shook her as she had not been shaken in years. It brought back, with a flaming vividness that scorched, the living presence of the girl who had written it—who had so fierily meant it with all the red hatred that was in her heart. Hatred of the State that had oppressed and tyrannized over her; that had martyred her unforgotten father. Hatred of all its manifestations; contempt of all its lying symbols.

To Helena, the present Helena, Mrs. Hugh Corbett, who sat there before them so secure, so "prominent," so smartly clad—whose chauffeur already waited in the wintry street below to convey her, when she wished, the thousand yards or so she was from home, or wherever else her fancy might direct—the reading came, more and more, to seem a betrayal, a profanation, a casting of pearls to swine. She longed to crumple those faded sheets into her bosom, where their heat could burn; to stand up and tell these piffling fools what they really were, and then rush away, by herself, where she could breathe.

Of course she did nothing of the sort. She read the paper through. She acknowledged, suitably, the chairman's thanks. She even managed to talk a little, though absently, with some of her friends who came crowding up afterward to tell her how wonderfully "daring" and "thrilling" and "basic" it all was, before, declining tea, she escaped and went home—in her car. But the mood she was in was her blackest; a smoldering, absent reverie which her servants knew and walked warily to avoid waking her out of. No wonder she shrugged, impatiently, over Hugh's message that he was coming home to dinner.

But this other thing! This name, Galicz, coming up so mysteriously out of nowhere, on this very night when she was more nearly Anton Galicz's daughter than she had been in years before! It couldn't be made to seem like an ordinary, every-day coincidence. It had the feeling in it of a touch of the finger of Fate. For a matter of minutes after her maid had left her alone, she sat, staring at the telephone on her desk as if it had been an unfamiliar instrument of magic. Then, impatiently, she snatched it up and repeated into the transmitter the number on the pad. And on getting her connection, "I was to ask for Mr. Galicz," she said.

There was a momentary hesitation from the other end. Then, "This is the Popular Drug Store," a voice said, and went on to give her the address of it. "In the matter of your account with us, we'd like you to see us about it, personally, tonight, before nine o'clock."

She exclaimed "What!" in perfectly blank amazement, whereupon the voice repeated this utterly preposterous message, word for word.

So repeated, however, it took on another color altogether; made her heart leap to a quicker rhythm and tightened her throat. Again it took her back over a span of years. It was long since she had experienced the necessity, in talking over a telephone, of guarding against hidden listeners, but she had done it many a time.

She checked herself on the verge of a protest that she owed no account at any "Popular" drug store, and asked, instead, for the address again. It was characteristic of the old almost forgotten phase it had evoked in her, that she memorized it without writing it down.

But the next moment, her every-day, present self getting the upper hand, she cried impatiently. "Oh, it's absurd! I must know more about it than that. Who is it that wants to see me? What does he want to see me for?"

"I can not discuss it," the other said. "It is a question simply whether you will come or not. Before nine o'clock."

Helena said: "I don't know whether I will come or not. I don't know whether I can."

Whereupon the man said, "Good-by," and hung up, thus cutting off a question she meant to ask; whether on coming to a decision, she should call up again?

During the half-hour that elapsed before Hugh came in, she prowled about her room in restless agitation, dropping into chairs and getting out of them again, starting to change her dress, and then giving over the idea not knowing what she was going to dress for. It was not that her mind hung balanced between two decisions. She was always, at any given moment, decided. But two contrary decisions alternately had possession of her.

To Hugh's wife, to whom he was presently coming home for dinner with a notion of taking her somewhere—to a musical show, perhaps— for the evening, the idea of carrying out that mysterious rendezvous at a little west-side drug store, was absolutely fantastic; a hoax almost too stupid to be offered for his amusement at dinner; the baldest sort of popular magazine melodrama.

But the other Helena who had written the paper she had read this afternoon, was fighting for—and occasionally winning—full possession of her. When she was in possession, the supreme, fantastic, mad unreality was not the cry for help that had come to her ears with such carefully guarded mystery over the telephone. It was the rich husband who was presently coming home to dine with her and take her to the theater afterward. It was this pretty room of hers; the maid who would come in answer to her ring to help her dress in an evening frock. It was the bare momentary consideration on her part—on the part of Helena Galicz, of letting that cry for help in her father's name, go unanswered.

If you doubt the power of it to take hold like that, remember what she was. You have known her not quite four years; only since that May morning in nineteen twelve when she came into Bailey's office at the head of that little committee of core-makers. When she was upon the point, that is to say, of her great departure into Hugh's world. She was then twenty-four years old. She had lived the whole of her life, since the beginning of her consecutive memories, in a world of violence and intrigue, in a guerrilla war upon organized society. She knew, at first hand, police courts and jails. She knew what it was to be shadowed, spied upon, kidnaped. Her friends—most of them—up to the time when Hugh transplanted her, were enlisted in the same cause and fared as she—or worse. To the Helena who, in the limousine, that night at Riverdale, had mangled Hugh's left hand with her teeth, there would have been nothing romantic or improbable about a cryptic telephone message from a drug store, from a friend "in trouble." It would all have been as natural, as much a part of the day's work, as it was preposterous and fantastic to Hugh Corbett's wife.

The struggle between these two utterly irreconcilable personalities for the possession of her, was still undecided when he knocked at her door and, upon her invitation, came amiably in, helped himself to one of her cigarettes, and stretched out at ease in her long chair. Ordinarily she liked him to do this. Her commonest grievance against him was that he didn't do it often enough. Tonight, this comfortable, domestic complacency of his irritated her.

"You telephoned," she said. "Anything special?"

"Not very," he told her. "I thought if you hadn't anything else tonight, we'd drop in on father and mother. They are starting off for California early next week. And they're missing Carter like the devil, of course. So I thought it would be a good thing if we could try to cheer them up a bit."

"You can go if you like," she said. "I don't believe I will."

Hugh looked deliberately round at her. "Special reason?" he inquired. "Or a general one?"

"Oh, I don't know," she said. "I'm not much in the mood—tonight, anyway—for sitting around in a family party, rhapsodizing about Carter—what a wonder he's suddenly got to be now that he's gone to war."

He didn't lash out at that as she more than half wanted him to; quietly took it to ruminate on, instead. "It does make a difference, though—a thing like that," he said at last. "You've got to revise all your estimates by it. It's one of those touchstone things. We all get tried by 'em once or twice in a lifetime and show whether we're true metal or not. He was, all right. Not only what he did but the way he did it. First water, absolutely. One of those blessed—straight things that there's no doubt about."

At a sound she made then, not classifiable but clearly indicative of dissent, he looked sharply round at her. "—Or do you mean that you are in doubt about it?" he concluded.

"Not in doubt, a bit," she said. "It's plain enough to me. He's going off to wear a pretty uniform and learn to run an aeroplane. When he can fly pretty well he'll go out, some night, and drop a lot of bombs on some innocent men and women working in a factory, that happens to be in Germany, and then come back and get a medal for it—instead of getting hanged for murder. He has nothing against them. They've done nothing to him. He's doing it for fun. Or, if you like, for spite; because a girl he'd taken a fancy to wouldn't marry him."

Still he didn't get up from his chair. "That's a pose," he said. "It's like a little girl making faces. You don't mean it." Then he looked round at her again. "Come!" he urged. "Be human! You can be when you like."

His invincible good humor infuriated her—naturally enough, considering what it meant, how little she mattered to him if she could hurt no more than that.

"You've been getting human, lately, if that's your word for it. Sentimental would be mine. You're sentimental about Carter because your Jean wouldn't marry him. Of course you knew she wouldn't. She'd rather go on holding hands with you. A platonic flirtation. Where there was no chance of her getting—the real thing offered to her."

Before she had got as far as that, he was on his feet, staring down at her, his look black with sudden rage. But she went on.

"Oh, I know, I started it. I thought it would be amusing to see you two—the pair of you—together. The sort of imitation affair you'd have. The only sort either of you is good for. Well, I've had enough. I'm sick of it. I'd like the real thing better. Go and make love to her. . ." With a grossness not to be reported, she went on to make her meaning clear.

Once more, as in that other crisis in the relations of these two, his inhibitions interfered. Long before she had done speaking, the terrible desire of every fiber in him was to wreak his rage upon her bodily; to clench that bare throat of hers in the grip of one of his hands; to beat her; to trample upon her. How near he had come actually to doing it, became the theme of a sort of nightmare wonder with him occasionally thereafter. Possibly the fear of his own strength had something to do with holding him back—the thought that if he touched her he would not stop until he had killed her.

And then, there was the stupefying suddenness of the thing. The cigarette he had lighted before he dropped into her long chair, wasn't half burnt yet.

But, more than either of these, the thing that held him helpless, speechless, staring—as he had stared at her on that former occasion—as King Polydectes had stared until he turned to stone at the Gorgon's bloody head—was the paralysis of sheer horror. Horror of what she was, and meant, and saw; of her wanton defilement of a lovely thing. And, as on that other occasion, it was not until her "Oh, don't go on standing there! Go! Go away!" that he could leave her. He went, then, without a word.

She sat, just as she had been sitting when he came into the room, holding one bare arm in the other hand. She stayed like that, stonily still, for a moment after he had gone out; then suddenly and viciously dug into the soft flesh of that arm until the nails brought blood. Another moment and she relaxed, caressed the wound with her mouth and sucked the blood away. Her eyes were smoldering but she smiled, a curious, sullen, defiant sort of smile.

I do not think she can fairly be called perverse. Love and pain are messages that run along parallel wires and in many, if not most, quite normally constituted people, strange inductivities are set up between them. That craving in her for pain and struggle was a fundamental want in her which Hugh had never satisfied. Never, since their first accidental encounter, had he exerted any force upon her. Again and again through the weeks before their marriage and the months that followed it, she had tried—only half conscious, I suppose, that that was what she was trying for—to provoke him to do something violent to her, to use his strength against which she should struggle in vain. She knew he had it; it maddened her that he would not use it. If ever he had beaten her, choked her, taken hold of her, even, hard enough to bruise, her love for him would have become a whole-souled, complete, satisfactory thing. Giving it up, at last, as hopeless, her love for him, while it persisted, became a rankling, unsatisfied, contemptuous thing. And the contempt accumulated.

Mrs. Corbett was all wrong, of course, in her interpretation of Helena's motive in throwing Jean, as she said, at Hugh's head. The notion of trapping Hugh into a compromising situation which would give her the whip hand in dictating the terms of a divorce was one which Helena, to do her justice, would never have entertained for a moment. Her real motive, which Mrs. Corbett would hardly have understood had it been explained to her, was, substantially what she had just avowed to Hugh. Watching the pair, reflecting upon the sort of use they made of the opportunities she gave them, gave that contempt of hers something to feed upon.

She had not plotted out the consequences farther than that. She had no intention of springing her mine on Hugh; certainly not when he came in tonight. Their quarrel had been as surprising to her as to him. Only surprises didn't effect her in the same way. Her mood, created by the paper she had read that afternoon and by the telephone call after she got home, was dangerously explosive. His mood had exploded it. The materials of which she had made their quarrel were nothing to her. She had begun it quite at random.

She was, in a word, a much simpler person than he. It was her temperamental habit to let herself go, just as it was his to hold himself in. And she was as incapable of understanding his inhibitions as he was of understanding her excesses.

Well, she had done it now. And she guessed it was just as well that she had. She was glad of it. This was about what that defiant sullen smile of hers meant. She'd given him his last chance. If he wouldn't resent a vile insult like that to his precious Jean, he would never resent anything. He had gone away, she tried to tell herself—though not, I think, with very genuine conviction—like a whipped dog. It suited her mood, anyhow, to think so.

She had an extraordinarily pleasurable sense of satisfaction and well being. She wanted to do something. Something exciting. What was it she had meant to do?

Her eye fell on the telephone pad. She had, for five minutes, forgotten all about that. She would go, of course.

She dressed in the plainest suit she had, a pair of stout boots and an untrimmed beaver hat. She inquired if her husband had gone out, and on being told that he had, said that she wasn't coming down to dinner. He was out tramping the streets, she supposed. Thinking! It amused her to find that she was in a good humor with him again.

With a smile a little rueful, a little impatient, a little mischievous, she scrawled, without sitting down at her desk, a note to him.

"I didn't mean it, of course. Not that that makes any difference, I suppose."

This she took into his bedroom and laid on his pillow.

Then slipping on a storm coat, she went out, walked over to State Street, and took the street-car, on the way to her rendezvous.

XXV

When she got down-town, the sight of a lunch-counter reminded her that she was hungry. So she went into it, ordered an oyster stew, sat down in one of the wide-armed chairs, and ate it. She hadn't been in one of those places in years. It had romantic associations, too. A man in love with her had once threatened to kill her in one of these nice clean, white-tiled lunch-rooms. They had come in about four o'clock one wet winter afternoon, when the place was pretty well deserted, for the warmth of it, and a chance to sit down and talk—as they had done, in whispers.

She couldn't have been more than nineteen when that happened—the better part of ten years ago. And yet, it seemed more real to her tonight, than the house she had just left; than those rich, complacent Corbetts, whose name she bore; whose secure, upholstered life she had, in a dream, been living. What a dream!

She paid her punched check—twenty cents—at the cashier's desk. And, after going out and walking a block or two—it had begun to snow—boarded the car that would take her to her destination. It was not crowded but it had been recently; had the familiar smell.

She had a long ride before her and she settled to enjoy it. Her fellow passengers interested her—stimulated her curiosity. The savor of them excited her; a man with a beard, a woman with her head in a shawl, a Yiddish newspaper, a conversation in Czech between a man and woman in the seat behind her. The effect upon her was that of going back to meat upon one who has, for a reluctant while, been a vegetarian. After the car got out of the down-town district and threaded its way to its eventual thoroughfare, her gaze was constantly out the window. The foreign language signs on the shops greeted her as old friends. She experienced the thrill—not of an adventurer, but of one returning, after long wanderings, home.

She did not leave the car at the corner her drug store was on, (it was on the far side of the street and the car stopped on the near) but rode by and took a preliminary look at it from the window.

It was a dingy old wooden building with a ridge roof, the gable facing the main thoroughfare. Through the half-glazed doors, she caught a glimpse, as she went by, of a glowing stove out in the middle of it. The upper story was flamboyantly painted with a doctor's sign, advertising X-ray cures for a catholic catalogue of camplaints.

She cast a sharp glance into the recessed doorway which gave access to the doctor's quarters, to see if any one were lurking there. She couldn't be sure, through the snow, but she thought not. At the next corner, she got out and walked back briskly and with no overt pauses for looking about, but with an eye which missed no geographic or human detail of the scene, either upon the opposite side of the street or upon her own. She saw no suspicious appearances anywhere.

It may be remarked that there wasn't one flutter of fear about her. Whatever else one may think of her, it is impossible to deny her courage.

Entering the store, she found one old woman customer being waited upon by the solitary clerk. She was buying a precious little bottle of ear-oil, guaranteed, it appeared, as a sure cure for deafness.

Helena asked for the telephone directory, and on having it pointed out to her, busied herself with it until the old woman went out. When the clerk came back, she said: "I am looking for a man named Galicz."

The clerk pointed to the telephone booth and she went into it, to find that it had another door opening into the prescription department behind the screen. He came round the other way.

"The man you want," he said, "is in the doctor's place upstairs. You can go through this door"; he nodded toward it, but made no move to open it for her, "and down the hall to the stairs, without going outside."

She obeyed this direction implicitly once more. The hall and the stairs were sufficiently lighted, and she made her way, without misadventure, to a door on the second story that had the doctor's name painted on it, and the invitation "Walk in"; which she did, thereby ringing a little bell.

Two or three patients were miserably waiting in this reception room, staring blankly at some terrifying and highly colored diagrams that hung on the walls; but the doctor, summoned by the bell, appeared immediately from the inner room. He was a brisk, bearded and spectacled gentleman in a frock coat and skull cap. Evidently he knew who she was, for he said: "You have an appointment, haven't you?" And, taking her assent for granted, he led her out the door she had come in by, and down the hall, to a room at the end of the building; indicated the door to her, and then went back as he had come.

She opened it, still without hesitation, and went in. She found herself, rather surprisingly, in a comfortably furnished room; carpeted, a solid drop-leaf table in the middle, with an old-fashioned hanging lamp above it, a shelf with books along one wall; a folding-bed, davenport and a wash-stand; a base-burner stove, and, between it and the center table, an easy chair with a man in it.

He had been reading a newspaper and smoking a pipe before she opened the door, and he looked deliberately around at her before he got up. He was collarless and in his socks. A fortuitous growth of black beard, two weeks old or so, covered his face. His eyes were a bright Irish blue. On the whole she liked his looks. It would be hard to say how old he was. In his early thirties, she guessed.

"You're Heleena, then," he said.

His pronunciation of her name was on the right note. Hugh and his friends had always stressed the first syllable. She liked his voice, too, though the tone of it had been by no means ingratiating; not quite hostile perhaps. Non-committal, anyhow.

She looked at him thoughtfully for perhaps a dozen seconds before she answered. "Yes, I'm Helena," she said, pronouncing the name as he had, "but I don't know you. You're no one I've ever seen before."

"That's true," he assented. "I've never seen you, either. But I knew your father."

A frown of undisguised suspicion creased itself sharply between her brows. "I knew every one he did," she said shortly, "from the time I was ten years old until they took him away from me."

"I knew him in prison," the man answered her. "My name's Frank Gilrain. I can convince you of the truth of that—if you're willing to be convinced. If you don't want to be, go now."

They stayed as they were, looking steadily at each other for a moment longer. Then, suddenly, rather giddily, one might have thought, she sat down in a chair. "Tell me about him," she commanded.

He took his time about beginning; relighted his pipe, and, after standing before her for a minute or two, twisted his easy chair around so that it faced her, and seated himself. From the moment he began to talk, she did not doubt that he was telling the truth.

"You wrote him some letters at first," he said, "but I think he never answered them."

"No," she said. "From the time they took him away, until they wrote me that he was dead, and that I could have the body, I heard nothing from him."

"He died of pneumonia," Gilrain said.

She nodded assent to that too. That was what her letter had said.

"He wasn't so unhappy there." This was after a silence; Helena staring, a thousand fathoms deep in reverie at the glowing stove doors; the man watching her with half shut eyes, through the smoke of his pipe. "He was a sort of philosopher. Said he was dead already when he came there, and so had nothing to worry about. He'd lived his life, he said, and given it.

"He had one bad time, but it didn't last long. He was a trusty almost from the first. One could see with half an eye that there was no harm in him. And when they found out what an education he had—what a power of languages he knew, they thought they saw a kind of special use for him; interpreter. And that was all right with him. But they wanted him besides, to read the letters that came in, in foreign languages, to some of the prisoners, and the answers they wrote back, to see that there was no harm in 'em.

"That put him beside himself with rage. He defied them. Started raising hell; so that they gave him the solitary. He starved himself until they had to put him in the hospital, and after that they eased up on him. He had no trouble after that. They gave him a job over in the printing office—there's where I got to know him—and he was there for the rest of his life."

He paused there with the deliberate purpose, one might have guessed, of giving her a chance to ask him what he himself had been in prison for. But nothing could have been further from her mind than that question. Indeed, she had no questions to ask at all, it seemed. She sat motionless, deep in thought, her dark eyes glowing, her brows drawn flat, a spot of color, bright enough to be visible even by the lamp-light, in the olive cheek that was turned toward it. A perilously beautiful thing to look at, she was just then.

Evidently Gilrain found her so, for he turned abruptly away from her.

"We all liked him," he went on again, "and he seemed to like all of us, in his dreamy way. But he must have taken a special liking to me, for he talked to me, toward the last, as he did to none of the others. It was two years I knew him, before he ever spoke of you; before I knew he had a daughter. But when he broke loose at last, he talked to me of little else; what a companion and a help you'd been to him. And, at the last, he said to me: 'If ever you're in trouble again, Frank, and can find where my Helena is, ask her to help you. Tell her you were my friend, and she'll do it.'"

The only response he got to that note was a sudden impatient shift of her body in the chair. He had finished speaking without looking around at her. He was, for the moment, profoundly disconcerted, and he concealed the fact by continuing to stare, in meditative silence, through his pipe smoke, at the stove door. At last, by way of forcing her to speak, he went on.

"Well, I am in trouble now. And I have found you."

With an air of rousing herself from a dream, she said: "I suppose you mean you're in trouble with the police. What do they want you for?"

"I don't know what the charge will be," he answered, "except that it won't be what they really want me for. They'll frame something on me that suits their purposes. They'll take damned good care not to let the *real* cat out of the bag. And they've got me here," he went on, his voice thinning to a sudden snarl of rage, "like a rat in a corner. All of my holes stopped; all my friends watched; a trap ready to spring on me wherever I turn. I haven't dared stir out of this damned room for four days. If the doc, here, hasn't crossed me, they don't know where I am. But what good's that, if I can't move hand or foot?"

"What is it," Helena asked quietly, "that they really want you for?"

His momentary silence after that question was asked, the deliberate way in which he rose from his chair and came around before her, gave his sudden snatching of her two wrists, and the agonizing grip he put upon them, the astonishing force of a thunder-clap.

"Now you answer some questions first," he commanded. "Yes, stand up, if you like!" for she was silently struggling with him. She hadn't screamed. He'd taken a chance on that.

"What are you, in the first place? Are you Anton Galicz's daughter? Or are you that damned millionaire's wife?"

"Let go my wrists," she panted.

As suddenly as he had seized them, he did. And, with a superb insolence, thrust his own hands into his trousers pockets.

Her eyes were blazing, green as a black leopard's. And his, also afire, devoured her face. He was the first to speak.

"It was James Lea told me to try you; said he couldn't answer for you any more, now you were married to a capitalist who was getting fat on war munitions. We agreed to try the old name to see whether you'd answer to it."

"Well, I did, didn't I?"

He nodded. "That's good as far as it goes. But what have you come for? Are you a rich lady out for a lark? Looking for a little harmless excitement to laugh with your friends about at your next dinner party?

That's not what you'll get from me, I promise you that. Or have you come out to make good?"

"You know little enough of me," she said. "But I know less of you. I know you've lied to me. Anton Galicz never gave you that charge—to seek out 'his Helena' if you were in trouble and she'd help you for her old father's sake. He wasn't a sentimentalist while he lived, and he didn't change to one on his death-bed. But that doesn't matter to me. I'm not a sentimentalist either. I'll make good, if the good is there to make. You tell me, without lying to me this time, what you've really done that they want you for, and if I like, I'll help you. If I don't, I won't. We'll start from there."

She was, as she confronted him there, blazing, utterly unintimidated by his flash of violence, the most beautiful, the most exciting, altogether the most desirable woman he had ever come to grips with. And his experience with them had been long. Varied, but nearly always victorious. His fists clenched inside his pockets, and his jaw set. Suddenly he turned away from her.

"You're the real thing anyhow. I'll give you that," he said. Then, "Don't you know what it is we're doing? Haven't you seen? Don't you read the papers? What are the capitalists doing—your own household pet among the rest? Getting rich out of the war. And getting ready to rivet their yoke on our necks so tight we'll never get it off. Making a bluff that the United States will get drawn into it, for an excuse for an army. What do they want an army for? To collect what they've loaned the Allies? That's part of it, but not half. When they'll really want the army is when the war's over. They'll want it to turn on us. To tell us workers, when they get ready to reduce wages again and starve us out, 'Now strike and be damned!' They want those machine guns they're talking about for our streets. It's plain for the blind to see. You can see it. You've heard them talking it.

"Now do you ask what we're doing? They haven't their army yet. They're in our power; that's where they are. They're afraid of us. They can't do without us. They're paying big wages. What they call big wages. How long will they go on doing that after they've got us where they want us? Now's our time to call a halt. They're afraid, already. Now's the time to put the terror into them. To show them what we can do. It won't take much. Dynamite a few more of their war plants. Burn a few more of their war harvests. Show them who their master is, *now*, before they get their army and their machine guns."

"That's talk," she said sharply. "Good talk, but old. I've been talking it myself, for months. I read a paper this afternoon at a perfectly polite tea that had all that in it, though it was written long before the war. Talk is easy, and not very dangerous."

"It's not talking I've been." The open derision in her voice stung him to that response, but he stopped there with a black scowl of suspicion. She met it with a smile.

"What have you been doing? And what are you planning to do? That's what I want to know. And I won't lift a hand for you until you tell me."

"I will tell you. I'm going to trust you. But I warn you first. If you think this is a parlor game you're playing, fast and loose, to take up for excitement and drop when you've had enough—get up and go home now; while you've the chance. I've never killed a woman yet, but I'll kill you if you welsh."

"Don't talk like a romantic fool!" she commanded. "Go ahead and tell me—if you've anything to tell."

"There's the strike out at the Acme place; that's the first. They were making three-inch shells out there; and they haven't turned a wheel for two weeks. Then there was the fire at the Peerless, and another at the Salisbury plant; and there was an explosion out at the Wadsworth Watch Factory, where they were making shrapnel firing-heads. That wasn't in the papers and you may not have heard of it. It didn't come off just as we meant it to, but it was enough to put the fear into them.

"That's the beginning. And it's just nothing at all compared to what I have got right in my hands ready to do, if these bloody English secret service agents hadn't drawn the net on me. It was all in my hands, I tell you, ready to spring! Plans all worked out; the stuff all cached; the men all promised. And now I'm stopped; tied hand and foot."

"What is it?" she asked. "—Money?"

He nodded sourly. "I've got it," he said, "but I can't get it. Oh, that's not what I've come to you for! It isn't pin-money I want. It's thousands."

"What kind of money?"

"Capitalist money," he grinned. "One of the big respectable brokers, here in town."

"A German?"

"What does that matter? You're an internationalist, aren't you? What if the poor boob does think he's serving his damned kaiser? He isn't in the long run. Once the revolution starts, it'll spread all over the world."

"He's suspected, I suppose, and afraid to pay you."

He did not answer at once. "That's not the worst," he finally said glumly. "If he thinks they've really got me, if he makes up his mind to write me off as a loss, because I'm too hot to handle—don't you see what he'll do? He'll beat them to it. He'll inform on me—to clear his own skirts. This fake doctor out here, who owes him money, will gladly give me up. That may happen any time, I've been waiting for it."

He laughed and showed her a small automatic revolver that had been in his pocket. "If that had been a man's step I heard coming along the hall with him just now, I'd have had this out."

"What do you want me to do?" she asked.

"I want you to get me out of here—clean. Where that yellow-livered Dutch swine hasn't got his thumb on me. Where I can talk turkey to him—show him that the string isn't played out yet. Put me where I can have two or three days free to turn round, before they can get the shadows on me again. That's what I want. Will you do it?"

He was standing before her when he asked that question. She, half sitting back against the edge of the table, gripping it tight with both hands, was looking up at him. The color was high in her cheeks again, and her breathing quick—visibly so—through her parted lips.

It may have been the familiar informality of the pose, the fact that she had let him come so close without altering it; the look, still defiant—not friendly, but almost smiling—about her upturned face; it was something, at any rate, that he himself did not understand, and certainly made no effort to analyze, that took possession of him. For, a full minute after he had asked that question, she having given him no indication whatever what her answer would be, he seized her suddenly in his arms and tried to pull her up into an embrace.

She fought him off furiously and, breaking away—the struggle lasted no more than a very few seconds—struck him, with all the force of her open hand, across the face.

"You fool!" she panted. But she smiled. Then, while he still stood staring, as much amazed at himself as at her—"Sit down there," she commanded with a nod toward the chair, and without waiting to see that she was obeyed, she herself sat down in another one; erect, intent on her own thoughts—businesslike almost; altogether as if that momentary interlude between them had never been played.

"Yes, I'll help you," she said. "I can do all you ask me to; maybe more. I want a little time to think."

Evidently though, she didn't want long; for almost immediately, she began: "You're to spend tomorrow making yourself presentable. Get your clothes pressed. Do it yourself if you have to. Polish your shoes; that's important. Shave, shampoo your head; get some proper shirts and collars, and a hand-bag—some sort of decent looking hand-bag."

"What are you going to do with me?" he asked with a humorous touch of scorn. "Take me home with you?"

"Yes," she said. "That's exactly what I'm going to do."

"Hm!" he grunted dubiously. "How about your husband?"

She smiled a curious sort of smile. "He doesn't matter," she said. "It's the servants I'm thinking of." After a moment's pause, "You're to be an old friend of mine. I'll tell you who you are when I've made up my mind about it. There's time enough for that. You're getting into Chicago tomorrow afternoon, from the Coast. I'll tell my husband, tomorrow morning, if I see him, that I'm expecting you. Otherwise, I'll call him up and tell him. And I'll order my car to take me down to the Northwestern station, late in the afternoon, to meet you."

"I can't hang around a railroad station," he said.

But she ignored the interruption. "I'll tell my chauffeur," she went on, "that the train's likely to be late, and that he's to wait. Then I'll come out here. I'll come into the drug store at exactly six o'clock—it will be dark enough then. You'll be ready with your bag packed and your overcoat on. I'll buy something in the store and go out and stop the first through-route car that will go back to the Northwestern station. I'll manage to stand on the step for a second, asking the conductor a question or something, so that he'll start the car before he shuts the door. Then you can come out and jump on. If there's a shadow on you, you've a pretty good chance to drop him. He won't be able to get that car, and there aren't any taxis around here."

"He won't try to follow," said Gilrain. "He'll see the valise and telephone the men at the railway stations to pick me up."

"They'll watch the ticket windows and the train gates," said Helena, "and we won't go that way at all. We'll go in the side door and through into the cab-entrance, where my car will be waiting all the time. My chauffeur will drive up the minute he sees me. He'll think your train has just come in, so it will look all right to him. There! Do you see anything the matter with that?"

It was not a real question; just a flourish of triumph at the end of a good performance. An invitation for applause. But after he had been looking at her in silent cogitation for a while, she repeated, "*Do* you see anything wrong with it?"

"It's all right, I suppose, if your husband will stand for it. He'll ask a lot of damned awkward questions, of course, but we can manage that, like enough."

"He'll ask no questions," she assured him curtly. "Why shouldn't he stand for it? Do you think I've been giving an account of myself to him all these years, like a concubine in a harem? I've had guests, before."

He stared at her with a new look. "You have, have you!" he exclaimed coarsely, and made as if to laugh. But it was almost ludicrous the way the sudden cold intensity of her gaze checked that laugh before it had fairly begun. His haste to withdraw the implication in it, amounted to a scramble.

"It's great, of course," he said. "It's made to order, completely. Once I can get word to Bertsch. . ."

"Hermann Bertsch, the Board of Trade man?" she asked.

He nodded. ". . . I'll make him sing a different tune," he concluded.

She smiled. "I think I can manage that. I'll tell you tomorrow, when I've thought it out. We've done enough for tonight. Now I'm going home."

She rose so quickly on the words and began her preparation for the street, that she was half into her ulster before he could get round the table to help her, and then she managed, without seeming to try, to evade his hands. Her arms free, once more, she whipped round and faced him, her own hands warily busy with her buttons. Again her upturned face challenged him insolently.

"Anything else?" she asked.

"Look here!" he commanded. "I want to know—and I mean to know—before you go out of here—what you're doing all this *for*. What your game is. You've got some game, that's plain enough. And by God. . ."

But in the face of her smile, he couldn't go on with that. His bluster sank away into silence.

"Why shouldn't I do it?" she asked. "I'm as good a revolutionist—as you." And then, swiftly, "You've got it all straight haven't you? Clean and presentable, with an overcoat and a hand-bag, and your shoes polished, tomorrow night at six. Six by the correct time. Good night."

He dropped back into his chair after she had shut the door behind her, and wiped the sweat off his forehead with his sleeve.

"What a woman! What a devil of a woman!"

XXVI

Where Jean and the Corbetts both went wrong about Hugh was in judging his scale of values. The family's idea of him was pretty well expressed by his mother when she told Constance he made her think of a ghost. They attributed his detachment from them, his way of coming back now and then, looking on at their doings and listening to their talk, like one no more concerned in it than an unearthly visitant would be, to his unfortunate marriage. He had simply acquiesced, they thought, in the inevitable. He saw there was no good trying to break out of his domestic world—or hell, as Mrs. Corbett bluntly put it. He wasn't the sort to whine or bid for sympathy, so he just shut up and took his medicine. They respected his reticence and felt sorry for him.

Jean, avoiding that error, fell into one of her own. She saw, plainly enough, even in her first visit with him, that he was not pitiable. He was emphatically not, in her eyes, a man dumbly resigned to an unhappy fate; he wasn't making the best of a bad job. At first she smiled confidently to herself but later fell into a state of acute exasperation, at the way the family sighed about him. She boiled whenever they spoke in a comfortably superior way about "poor old Hugh," or contemplated his blighted possibilities. He wasn't a failure and he had his own reasons for knowing it. Any one with eyes ought to be able to see that! If he had made a mess of his life wouldn't he be the first person in the world to feel it? Wasn't his liability to error in the opposite direction? To conceiving himself a failure when really he was not? Of course it was!

She was right so far. Where she went wrong, was in the inference she went on to draw from a perfectly correct observation. Because she found him unbeaten, confident, elastic as of old, she assumed that his audacious marriage had, in accordance with her hopes, turned out well.

The truth was that his marriage was neither the blighting thing the family took it to be, nor the well-fitted keystone that Jean, perceiving how well the arch stood up, believed it. It was, and had been ever since the partial reconciliation a few weeks after the Corbett fire, unimportant. "I believe a metallurgist is all I am really," he said to Allison Smith. "It's enough when one is as good as you are," had been Smith's answer. Not true, of course, but true enough to have served as a working hypothesis for three years.

Just as he admitted his failure as a humanitarian, as a prophet of a new industrial order, as a social philosopher, so he admitted his failure as a lover. He did not try to account for it, nor even think of it as accountable. Where the failure of one of his alloys to exhibit the qualities he had expected of it was a matter of the most vivid interest, subject of endless experiment, the failure of this human alloy was dismissed with the reflection that it was, most likely, his own fault.

He had told Helena once, in one of the very earliest talks they had together, that the common ground people needed for friendship—that was what he had been talking about then—was their instincts. What mattered between them was the sort of things they did without thinking—in unforeseen or difficult situations. Well, it seemed that with him, love as well as friendship needed that sort of common ground, and it was precisely here that she failed him. Her sudden flares of suspicion, her readiness to attribute mean motives, to impute bad faith; her evasions; the dishonesty, not of her intentions but of the very fiber of her mind, chilled him beyond the power of her beauty and her passion to warm. When she would let him like her he could love her—satisfactorily enough. When she assailed him, taunted him, turned one of her rages loose upon him, he went off to his laboratory and let her alone for a while.

It was not an ideal relation, certainly, but, he fancied, not uncommon. At all events it was nothing to whimper about—let alone erect into a tragedy.

It would have been a tragedy of course, but for the laboratory. This was the factor which Jean, as well as the Corbetts, had failed to evaluate. In this domain his energy and his imagination found a full and satisfying expression. His two assistants, Taylor and Brigham, both thoroughly trained metallurgists of the professorial type, regarded him with awe—with a sort of childlike wonder. They were children to him. He saw at a glance glints of undiscovered truth in the data they spent laborious days and nights collecting for him, that were beyond their comprehension even when he attempted to explain them. Over some constitutional diagram of theirs in three dimensions, representing a series of incredible alloys, his eyes would light up with as vast a surmise as that which held those Spanish adventurers silent upon a peak in Darien. Both of them had grown through a period of incredulous skepticism about him; both had come to work for him under the impression that he was a mere rich amateur whose hobby would afford them a heaven-sent opportunity for the pursuit of their own researches. Taylor had spoken of him once as a crazy alchemist. Eventually both of them compensated for this phase of hostile doubt, with an absolutely slavish devotion.

And it was no wonder; for he had not only the imagination, but the technique of a genius. His resources were endless. Any fact that he wanted, no matter how apparently indeterminable, he could devise the means for tracking down. And about these methods, too, there was often a sort of inspired simplicity that made them laugh like schoolboys.

That was his real world. Until the day when Jean came, for the first time, to lunch, and asked him to explain America and the war to her, he never fully left it. That was why his mother spoke of him as a ghost. That was why his wife's rages, her contempt, her flirtations with other men, came and went, and left no marks upon him for Jean's eyes to see. Even the reverberations of civilization's supreme struggle against a fanatical and barbarous kultur, though they troubled him somewhat, came to his ears but faintly—inside his fence.

What happened when Jean came back to him, with memories of that struggle visible in her eyes, with her questions and her confidence that he would be able to supply the answers to them, Jean a woman, but with all her old unquestioning affection for him revealing itself as candidly as the child's affection had done—what happened to Hugh then can be stated in the simplest and tritest of phrases. He fell in love with her.

It was as natural as that a hungry man invited to a feast should eat. What is, I think, not much more surprising, though perhaps less easily explicable, is that he should have fallen in love with her without being aware that that was what he was doing.

There was, to begin with, nothing about the process to suggest comparison with his only other experience of the same sort—his affair with Helena. That had been an agonizing thing, full of doubts and struggles, racking enigmas, irreconcilable desires and revulsions. He had been like a child driven by some mysterious but unescapable authority, to an adventure into the dark—a dark peopled with hobgoblins as well as with enticing mysteries. He had not dreamed that falling in love would be like that; but he had found that it was. His experience, now, with Jean, was much more like that old dream of his than his first experience with reality had been. In the absence of that first experience, he would have been quicker to identify the second.

A stream may run very swiftly and yet smoothly down an unobstructed channel. It is the opposing rocks that make the turmoil and the tumult.

Well, in the channel he and Jean had slipped into so easily, there were no warning rocks—no jealousies, no misunderstandings, no oppositions of will or intent—no questions even. Indeed, the very essence of their relation was a kind of fathomless confidence and security.

He had, to be sure, dreaded her return from England—a surprisingly strong emotion, that had been. His memory of her had kept itself warm during the whole three years of her absence; had remained something singularly perfect—something with a quite unique charm about it. And the prospect of her return had, apparently, presented him with a dilemma. Either—and more probably—she would have changed to some one else, nice enough no doubt, but so different as to take all the life out of that treasured memory of his; or else, being the same, she would offer him the old undisguised affection. In which case, Helena. . . It was all too easy to foresee what his wife would do in a situation like that.

As you know, the event had falsified both of these forebodings. Jean came back amazingly unchanged. The actuality of her, simply grafted itself upon the stem of the memory, and went on growing as if it had never been severed. And Helena, amazingly, watered the plant.

It was characteristic of his way with his wife that he made no effort to understand her motive in this. He merely charged himself with having done her an injustice and liked her better for it. And then, as I have said, let himself slip into the current without the least notion how swift it was, or whither it would carry him.

There is this to be said for him: individual morality, its problems and its paradoxes, had never been a field of speculation for him. He'd always taken conventional rules and labels pretty much for granted. For a married man to let himself fall in love with another woman was, simply, disreputable. Decent people didn't do things like that. He was a decent person. Therefore, he wasn't falling in love with Jean.

They had passed none of the conventional danger signals. They didn't hold hands. He had never kissed her. He had never even hinted to her that his marriage was anything but successful and satisfactory. He had never been jealous of any of the men—beginning with Carter—who tried to make love to her; never tried to lessen the amount of time she gave to the social life her grandmother had launched her in, or to war relief work, in order to get more of her time to himself.

What had he done then? Ridden with her for an hour three or four mornings a week; taken her to the Orchestra concerts pretty often, when it happened that Helena didn't want to go and that Jean herself had the evening free. Come home in the afternoon, sometimes, to find her at tea with Helena and walked home with her afterward.

On the surface that was all. Of what lay beneath that surface, he was brought to realization, literally and truly for the first time, by that outbreak of Helena's on the night when he came home with the suggestion that they drop in on his father and mother to cheer them up a bit now Carter had gone to war. When she said to him, "You're sentimental over Carter because Jean wouldn't marry him. You *knew* she wouldn't," she shocked him into the beginning of understanding. Because, so far, what she said was true. He had not been jealous of Carter, because he had known all the while, with a confident though inexplicable certainty, that he had nothing to be jealous of. He had time to get as far as that before the blind rage shut down on him.

It was hours later before he began thinking again.

He spent those hours tramping the streets at random, his mind a chaos. But around eleven o'clock he found himself standing before the great St. Gaudens Lincoln, in Lincoln Park, and in that majestic presence he got himself in hand again; not through any self-conscious moralizings concerning the deeds or words of its great original, merely through the noble beauty of the thing itself. It quieted and steadied him, somehow, just as a phrase of Beethoven would have done; re-established the scale of things; made of his rage a mere outburst of childish petulance. Now he could think again.

And he must think because, sometime before morning, he must have come to a decision what he would do. Already he perceived that here was a situation he could not deal with by merely retreating from it. There was no possibility, here, of another withdrawal, "inside his fence."

How often he had done that! From his family, from the men he ought to have kept for friends, from his humanitarian experiments at Riverdale, from his grandfather's trust—from his wife. Oftenest of all, from her. Countless times from her. What was the matter with him? Cowardice? Or a kind of monstrous self-sufficiency?

Well, for the present, that didn't matter. Coward or not, this time he must see it through.

He was in love with Jean. The rising and blowing away of the fog of his rage against his wife, left that fact confronting him as the cliffs of Cornwall confront, now and again, a mariner who has lost his reckoning. How had he managed to stay blind to it so long? Had he really been blind to it? Why, she was the light of his life! She was food and drink to him! Manna in the wilderness. Wherever he turned, he turned to her. Whatever he did was done with some sort of unconscious reference to her. The whole fabric of his life was woven with the gold threads of her. The pattern of it remained pretty much what it had been before, but the texture had changed.

Looking back he could see where one day had drawn a line across it; the day Jean had come to lunch. That Swede—whatever his name was—that Helena had been going on with at the time, was there. And talked free trade. And then Helena had carried him off and left them alone. And on his asking how long it had been since they had seen each other, she had answered—just as the little Jean who had been Anne's bridesmaid would have done—that it was three years and three months. It was as if the sun had come out!

What sort of self-hypnosis had he resorted to that he did not see then—that very day—what it was that had happened to him? Well, he had come out of his trance at last.

He was still confused, bewildered. The problem he must wrestle with and find some sort of solution for before morning, had not even got itself stated yet; but one fact shone out above the welter, like a beam from a light-house; he was in love with Jean. Helena's final taunt—as much of it as was aimed at him—troubled him not at all. It had been her contemptuous notion all along that there was something—submasculine about his feelings toward the girl. That his relation with her was something less than real; a philander, in the manner of Rousseau. Well, that was simply one of Helena's mistakes.

There was nothing incomplete, nothing left out of his love for Jean. The whole of him went into it; spirit, mind and body. There was nothing of him now, that was not crying out for her, aching for her. And it was nothing new, this sensational, bodily want of her. It had been there, all along. Only—transmuted somehow; in a phase he hadn't recognized.

What an ignorant fool he'd been! Love was one of the elemental facts of life—and what did he know about it? He'd been content to deal with it in the fractional currency of romance; traditional sentiments, their mintage worn away with much handling, and very likely counterfeit to begin with. One of these precious bits of coinage he had been contentedly jingling was the adjective "brotherly." Had his sister Constance, whom he loved as much as, in the way of mere affection, it was possible to love anybody, ever changed the rhythm of his heart one beat? Had it ever thrilled him *not* to take one of Anne's hands in his!

There was time for all that, but not tonight. He was in love with Jean. What was he going to do about it?

He brought up at his laboratory at last—it was mere instinct in him to turn thither—and shut himself up in the library, the room where he had brought Jean one day and shown her his little samples of Corbettite. He took off his wet boots and set them to dry; got into slippers and a shabby old coat, lighted a pipe, and sat down, soberly and unhurriedly, because he had half a dozen hours yet before morning, to think it out.

All the way out Chicago Avenue, he had trudged to one refrain: Jean mustn't know. This was his starting point—his axiom.

It was going to hurt horribly to keep her in ignorance. Well, that would be his penalty. Honor prescribed it. When you stated the case in general terms, that became clear enough. Here was a married man in love with an innocent young girl. It would be a matter of mere elementary decency in him to guard that secret from her; to make—without flinching—any sacrifice that the guarding of it called for. She had given him her affection freely, in good faith—confidently. He had betrayed her confidence; embezzled the trust fund. Their friendship was bankrupt. That was bad enough. But to try to involve her in the fraud. . . !

He dashed both fists down savagely on the desk before him. This was bosh—maundering. It was getting him nowhere. What was he going to *do?*

Let their friendship go by default? End, without explanation, their morning rides—their concerts—their little excursions? Leave her wondering, dumbly, what the matter was?

But she wouldn't wonder dumbly! She'd come and ask him what the matter was.

Go away then, without a word—disappear? *Leave her to Helena's mercies!* Helena, with that flicker in her veiled green eyes!

No, by God, not that! Not a chance of that! She must be warned to keep away from Helena. And at once! He must see her tomorrow and warn her somehow—tell her something that would serve.

Well, there was the first step decided upon. He would see her tomorrow—tomorrow morning. He knew where she was. He always knew where she was; from day to day, from hour to hour, almost. She had gone up this afternoon to Lake Forest.

Tomorrow was Philip's birthday (Constance's oldest boy, he was) and he was having a party whose specifications he had been allowed to draw for himself. The house in Lake Forest was opened up for the occasion, and six or eight small boy friends of his, including his younger brother Francis, invited from Friday afternoon to Sunday morning. There was plenty of snow up there for forts and battles, a gorgeous slide down the ravine road, a pond to skate on, and larks in the big empty house; trimmings in the way of a birthday cake and a candy-bag and so on. Miss Muirhead, their governess, a strapping middle-aged, out-of-door sort of English woman, had volunteered to convoy the party. Philip, who adored Jean, had invited her to come. Not casually; seriously, after deep thought. And Jean, appreciating how fine a compliment it was, had accepted, whole-heartedly. She had gone up, with the others, on the four-twenty train, this afternoon. Hugh knew all about it.

He hunted out a time table and looked up morning trains. There was a fast one at eight o'clock. Another point settled. He'd take that train and walk the mile or more that it was out to Frank's. He'd find the party. No trouble about that; they'd be making noise enough. Sledding down the ravine road, they'd be, most likely. Or trying their luck with snow-shoes.

And Jean would be there among them, with snow in her tumbled hair, breathless. . . She would see him coming, and bright as her eyes would be, they would still brighten—change, somehow, with welcome at the sight of him. That welcoming glance of hers had never failed him; never, from the very first day.

With another look she'd see that something serious had brought him there. That clairvoyant understanding of his moods had never failed, either. He wouldn't have to say that he must speak to her alone on a matter of importance. In all his misery, he grinned over the notion of saying anything like that to Jean. No, she'd rescue him from Philip and Francis, who'd be clambering all over him like young bears, and manage somehow, without any fuss, to carry him off, somewhere, where they could be by themselves. And then she might say, "What is it, Hugh?" Or she might—and it would be more like her—just contentedly wait for him to begin, when and how he would.

It was all clear enough up to there. But then. . .

It was too clear, that was the trouble. He could see her face—the lovely clear profile of it. She'd have dropped down beside him, somewhere.

And looking at it all his excuses, lies, elaborations, melted of their own absurdity.

It was no use. He couldn't do it—tonight. Tomorrow, when he had found her, when they were alone together, then he'd have to do it. Perhaps, from somewhere, he'd get—help. From her own dear self, very likely. From her straight-looking clear eyes, which never suspected baseness or disloyalty. He couldn't, in the light of them, dishonor her with the avowal of an illicit love. The moment, then, should serve its own need.

He drew in a great breath of relief and his body relaxed in its chair. For that night's remaining hours he simply let himself dream. Looked over, like Moses on Pisgah, at the green land he was not to enter.

An episode from earlier in the evening came back to his mind. Back when the fog of his rage had lain thickest on him, he had encountered, somewhere in Lincoln Park, Rodney Aldrich and his wife. He had marked them for a pair of lovers before he recognized them, and, the sight being unfriendly to his mood, he would have gone by without looking at them. But Rodney stopped him with forcible friendliness, and made him talk a minute. At the time nothing they said had really got through to his mind at all. Now, though, there came to him the memory of a certain intense satisfaction in Rodney's voice when he said—in answer to a perfunctory question of Hugh's, it must have been—"No, she's back with me—for the present, anyhow." And from Rose, with a sort of satisfactory richness in her voice, "Oh, yes, I do skate. But I'm not this winter."

Looking back, now, he understood. They were going to have another baby. They already had two, hadn't they? And had been married just as long as he. And were still lovers. And yet, a year ago, his friends had been pitying poor old Rodney over the failure of his marriage, and wondering what he'd bought that house for.

Was there, in Time's resources, the possibility of a transformation of life like that for him? Not a possibility, perhaps, but material for tonight's dream.

There was snow in her hair when he found her; snow in her woolly green sweater, on her short green corduroy skirt, on her leggings. She must have been rolling in it. She was all alone, in a dead winter silence as well as solitude—not a boy nor a sound of one in the landscape, anywhere—when he, where the road rounded a projecting clump of hemlock, came upon her. She was approaching him across the virgin snow, but, ludicrously, backward and seriously preoccupied with her tracks, taking great care to put her toes down first, and as the snow in the road had muffled his footfalls, she remained unaware of his presence there until, irresistibly, he laughed.

Then, "Hugh!" she cried. She had started, but managed to preserve her balance, with outstretched arms, like a rope-walker, and she did not turn; remained rooted where she was. To his, "What in the world are you doing?" she answered with a deep-throated little laugh of her own. "Wait," she commanded. "Let me think." But while she thought, she explained. "I'm a German spy, and I've drugged the secret-service men and escaped; from the dungeon—that's the cellar, where they are. They'll come out of the drug"—there was a reference to her wrist watch—"in fifteen minutes. And track me down. They've already done it once, much too easily. They were disappointed in me. So I changed to another pair of shoes—Constance's—to make different tracks, and tried again. This time I want to make it worth their while."

Then she laughed again. "Come over here and pick me up and carry me somewhere. Can you?"

"Yes," he said.

She untied her sweater belt, dropped it on the snow and trampled upon it. "There must be marks of a struggle," she explained as he came to her. Then she held up her arms for him.

He picked her up just as he would a small child. "Where shall I take you?" he asked.

Her answer was breathless—came with a gasp. "I don't care. You're carrying me off."

Just as he started with her, she shifted her position in his arms a little; settled herself closer and relaxed, as a child does when the arms are familiar and strong. His heart gave a great throb at that.

All the way across the field, he carrying her with great swift strides, neither of them spoke another word.

At the wooded edge of the field, the declivity into the ravine was steep, but not quite precipitous.

"I think I can get down here with you all right," he said very evenly. "But if you'd rather not chance it. . ."

"I'm not afraid," she said.

And gathering her a little tighter in his arms, he plunged down the descent with her. As an athletic feat it taxed even his great strength. But at that it was not as hard as he wanted it to be. The exultant rhythm that was beating in his veins challenged the impossible.

Coming out on one of the lower reaches of the ravine road, he did not pause, but strode on with her, out upon the snow-buried beach; floundering, now, knee deep and, beyond concealment, breathless.

But he did not stop until he reached the lea of a little breakwater. It was here, years ago, on a sun-drenched summer morning, that they two had built a castle in the sand, while the nightmare that he had brought down there with him, receded—almost blew away.

He stopped, but he did not put her down; nor did she make the expected movement to release herself; lay as she was, quite still. Looking down into her face, he saw that her eyes were shut, and there were two tears welling up from under the closed lids. And at that, the whole of his heart came out in a muffled outcry upon her name.

"Jean!"

Her eyes sprang open, wide with wonder, and searched his face. There was awe in them, but not fear. Then,

"Put me down—now," she said.

She steadied herself a moment—clearly this was a physical necessity—after he had set her upon her feet. But she was not faint. The color had come flaming into her face.

"I meant it," she said laboriously, "just as part of the game, when I called you. But it wasn't quite honest, because I had time to think before you took me up, that it would have done just as well if I had walked behind following in your tracks. Only, I wanted you to carry me." Then, getting control of a sob, "But I didn't know it would be like this."

"No," he said. "I didn't know either."

An ivory colored timber of the breakwater projected through the snow. She sat down on it and buried her face in her hands. "I'm not crying—really," she said at his exclamation of remorse. "It's just—excitement, I guess." Then, "We can—talk about it a little—can't we?"

"That's what I came out to do."

He dropped down beside her on the beam. "I found it out last night. In a quarrel I had with Helena. Over something detestable she said about you. I wanted to kill her for it. And then I knew. I don't know why I haven't known all along. I have, in a way, of course."

She looked round at him with a quaintly rueful smile. "I have, too," she said. "Of course I have, or I wouldn't have spent so much time arguing to myself that I wasn't." She drew in a long tremulous breath. "Well, I'm glad we know now," she added. "Both of us. It would be worse if one of us knew and the other didn't."

"I meant to keep you from finding out," he said. "I spent hours last night thinking up cock-and-bull stories that would warn you to keep away from Helena and explain my going away. . ."

There came from her a little indrawn gasp of pain at that.

"Oh, my dear!" he said.

"It's all right," she reassured him. "I didn't mean to flinch like that." Then she managed another smile. "In a way," she explained, "it's a good thing it's us it has happened to. We'll both—stand it."

After a silence, she asked a question. "Had Helena seen? Was that why she was angry? I suppose I must have blinded myself to that too. I thought all along she liked us to be together."

"She did," said Hugh. "For her own reasons. It was an expression of contempt really. She threw us together, so she explained last night, with the idea that we weren't capable of feeling anything beyond what she could afford to be amused about."

"That was one of Helena's mistakes, wasn't it?" the girl said dryly.

There was another pretty long silence after that. It was Jean who broke it.

"I'll do anything you want me to," she said. "Nothing I could give would be giving. I'm given already, you see. All of me. All there is. If it's right for one of us to go away, why, that one will go. And if it's right for us to be together, why, we'll be together. The main thing is for us to do what we mean to do. Not cheat ourselves because we want to so much, in little picking, stealing ways. I suppose while we're deciding what we really mean to do, we'll have to be apart."

He uttered a half suppressed groan of pain. "Yes," he said. "With you close to me like that, I can't think of anything—I don't know anything but. . .

She pulled off her woolen glove and slipped her cold little hand into his and somehow it pulled him together again. He bent down and pressed his lips into the palm of it. "I've never even touched it before outside the regular polite ways. But, oh, my dear, you've no idea how many times I haven't done it."

She smiled dissent to that. "I've known everytime, I think," she said.

Suddenly he pulled her up into his arms; bent down and found her lips, in a long embrace.

At the conclusion of it she slipped back to her seat beside him. "I'm glad that happened," she said presently. "I suppose, if we have to, we can—live on it for a long while. Years. Or forever, maybe. Though I can't manage to believe that, can you? But it's settled one thing, anyway. We can't go on—half together and half apart."

"Yes, it's settled that," he said.

But it was surprising, after that, how easily and quietly they slipped into talk; one of her hands in his once more. There was no tragic note about it, though it was their separation they mostly talked about.

Jean, it happened, could go away very accountably, without any fuss, and without awakening any surmises. Both her mother and her grandmother were getting restive; the older woman to escape the cold, and the younger woman to go back to her husband. Their two desires intersected at San Antonio, and both of them had spoken tentatively to Jean about the project. All it needed was her own enthusiastic approbation of it.

"That's as good as California," she said. "If it was New York, we'd always be riding back and forth for little glimpses of each other. And it's got to be a real separation to do any good. And you can't go away. You've got to stay and discover Corbettite."

"It's a funny thing," he said. "I quit the laboratory yesterday afternoon, more discouraged about it than I've been in six months; went home with the idea that I was just about ready to give up; thought that about the best thing I could do was to follow Carter over to France. Well, it's certain that I haven't thought about it since, because it was as soon as I got home that Helena and I had our row. But I've got an idea now. I had it last night when I went back to the laboratory. I know, because I remember slamming the door on it. I've a notion it's a real clew. It must have just followed along, somehow, in the trail of the other discovery."

She laughed happily at that. Then, "I don't know why I'm not crying," she said. "I would be, if it was anybody but you that I was in love with and was going to have to—do without—for a while."

Voices of the long-forgotten secret-service men now became audible up on the crest of the bluff, and presently, here and there, a head peered over. They'd been baffled by the tracks it seemed and resorted to drag-net methods.

"We'll surrender," Hugh called up to young Francis. "Though I'd have got her away in my submarine if it hadn't been for the ice. You stay up there and I'll bring her up by the road."

He agreed with her about the strangeness of the paradox she had been talking about when the boys appeared. He felt the same way about it. Curiously happy, content, elated, secure—even in the face of their parting. "I don't know anything about love," he said. "I suppose it must be a thing one can study and get to be an authority about. But there must be two kinds of it, anyway. One that can only hurt. And one that can only—bless. Even—even, Jean darling, when we give it up."

They were around the corner, by now; at the foot of the ravine road. The whole pack of little boys was audibly coming down, pell-mell, but they were still a turn or two of the road away.

"Once more?" he asked. "They aren't here yet."

"It doesn't matter. This is good-by."

So their lips met once more.

XXVII

O h, wait just a moment," Hugh heard Brigham saying, evidently into the telephone. "I think this is he coming in now." Then, turning around and seeing that he had guessed right, he told Hugh that Mrs. Corbett was on the wire for him.

"My mother, or my wife?" Hugh asked, and learned that it was Helena.

This was around three o'clock on Saturday afternoon. He was just back from Lake Forest—from Jean—from his great voyage of discovery!

He didn't want to talk to Helena yet. Didn't want to think about her. But this was one of those compulsory situations which leave no choice. Had he come in at any other moment, except when his wife was actually on the wire, he could have avoided her with a blanket instruction that he was going to be very busy and should not be called for anybody. He had done that often enough before now.

But it wasn't possible to say to Brigham, "I won't talk to my wife." He said, "All right," instead; hung up his hat and overcoat to give Brigham time to get out of the room, and sat down before the instrument. The last time he had heard her voice, it had cried out in frantic exasperation: "Oh, don't go on standing there! Go! Go away!"

There was none of that quality in it now, as it came over the wire. She meant it, apparently, to sound good-humored and casual, to match her words. But his ear detected a suppressed excitement in it—a sort of reckless hilarity—a ring of challenge.

"I tried to get you earlier," she said, "but they told me you weren't in."

He answered that they had told her the truth. He had been out all the morning. She then asked if he meant to be home to dinner, and he told her no.

"That's just as you like, of course," she said. "But I'm expecting a visitor—an old friend. Quite a good friend. He's getting in on a train from the Coast, late this afternoon. I don't know how long he'll stay, but probably several days."

"All right," Hugh said. "Nevertheless I shan't be home to dinner. I'm starting a piece of work here now that will keep me pretty constantly occupied for some time. I don't know when I shall be home."

"Do as you like about it," she said satirically, then added: "If you'd come home last night, you'd have found a note from me on your pillow."

Then, after an instant's silence, he heard her, "Good-by, Hugh," and the click of disconnection as she hung up.

He pushed the instrument away, but remained staring at it for a moment in an uneasy abstraction. Something admonished him that he'd gone wrong. The sensation was so sharp and clear that it was as if he had been spoken to in audible words. "Go home. Have it out with her now."

All the way back to town on the train, an idea had been knocking at the door of his mind, without ever getting full admission; the idea that he must, of course, come to some sort of understanding with Helena. It was unthinkable that he could continue on terms of marital intimacy with her, and, sometime, if not at once, that fact would have to be made explicit. The situation, in so far as she was involved in it, was one to be faced and dealt with, not merely retreated from.

He had recognized this visitor on the door-step as one fully entitled to admission and serious entertainment. Only not now; not today. Today he had something else to think about.

He was not thinking about Jean. The new ozone that he breathed was Jean, the exultant rhythm of his pulse was Jean, and the new light that transfigured the world. But the engine of his thoughts, running swifter and more smoothly than ever it had run before, the full dynamic force of his imagination, was at work on Corbettite.

It was odd about that. He had been working for months, with a patience he had described to Jean on the day of her visit to the laboratory, as something less than human, without gaining a single step. He had gone over the old ground again and again; repeating experiments, checking old data, methodically sweeping the whole area of possibilities as an astronomer sweeps for comets. This was a familiar experience, of course, but it had never been so hard as it had been this winter. Life had got a new urgency. His fence no longer shut out the world. That was Jean, of course, though he didn't know it. Disappointment had a new poignancy. The successive frustrations of his search became more nearly intolerable. The impulse he had avowed to Jean, down there on the beach, to chuck the whole thing and go to France, to do something— serviceable, was one that had often assailed him.

But he had stuck doggedly to the task that seemed to be his, whipping his tired mind back to work as often as it revolted. It should know no rest during the longest working hours it could be made to endure, until Corbettite was a fully accomplished—fully understood thing.

But out there in Lincoln Park last night, in all the chaos of his rage and bewilderment, in the very vortex of the tempest, as he had stood for a moment staring at the spectrum refracted by a swirling cloud of snow-crystals round an arc-light, something, in a flash, came to him. He ignored it so completely that his only conscious and memorable mental process on reaching the laboratory had been, as he described it to Jean, the slamming of a door upon it. Something was there, but he would be damned if he would look at it now!

It was not until Jean told him that she must be the one to go away— that he must stay and complete the discovery of Corbettite—that he thought of it again. And even then, he did not take out his clew and look at it. Simply reminded himself once more that it was there, with an increasing confidence, born of the strange exultation of that moment, that it was good.

He stayed to lunch with the birthday party. Not at all because of the inferences which his failure to do so would have suggested to Miss Muirhead, but simply because he wanted to. It had been a hard thing to do, of course. But it was the sort of hard thing he gloried in doing. He took an immense pride in devoting his attention, whole-heartedly, to the little boys; in offering suggestions for their afternoon's entertainment, that were received with riotous joy and the tempering regret that he could not stay to share them. He looked at Jean and talked to her, without a stolen glance, or a veiled meaning.

"It's a good thing, in a way, that it's us it happened to," Jean had said, "because we'll stand it." She was as confident of him, that meant, as she was of herself. Well, that confidence should be justified.

It was Philip's suggestion that the whole party, including Miss Muirhead and Jean, should escort him to the train. And, with unanimous consent, this thing was done. On the station platform it happened while they waited that some mild diversion drew away the rest and left Jean and Hugh for a moment alone. There was no exchange of whispers; no fugitive contact of hands; not even a meeting of eyes. Just an infinitely gracious silence. That was their parting embrace.

The train came in, he mounted the steps of it, and his parting look and wave of the hand, and his shouted good-by, went out impartially to all of them.

His mood was antipodally remote from the melancholy despair of the traditional lover bereft of his mistress. He even afforded the recognition of this fact a smile. His whole being was an instrument newly set in tune, and tuned to the very highest pitch. Last night he had dreamed. Today the reality had outrun his dreams. The great need in him was for something hard to do. Corbettite met that need. He had gone to work upon it before the train was fairly out of the station.

The new surmise that had, unregarded, found lodgment in his mind last night—for all the world like some migratory bird blown in on the tempest—suggested, made necessary, a revision of all he had done; put a whole series of experiments—the labor of months—beside the mark altogether; called for a new set of determinations.

It was maddening not to be in his laboratory now, this moment, with his diagrams and tables within hand's reach (he was going to it, of course, as fast as the train would carry him) but it was marvelous how his memory helped him, bringing him, with photographic fidelity, whole pages of computations. Such mnemonic feats are not so very uncommon. Hugh knew an orchestra leader who said that when he conducted from memory he saw the pages of his score photographed like that. Only it was a power he had never supposed he possessed. But he had never worked in an illumination like this before. If it would only last!

So far as he could see, the new idea was right. It grew, not like a plant, in however rich a soil, but in long ramifying leaps, like a pattern in frost crystals on a window pane. It might, of course, prove to be nothing more than that. Under the pitiless light of experiment that it must be subjected to, it might melt away to nothing.

The man he once had been would have pretended—and honestly tried to feel—a complete indifference concerning the result of those experiments. The cause of purely scientific truth would equally be served by disproving his new theory or by proving it. But Hugh had forgotten the very existence of that man. The hope that his hypothesis would stand the test was almost agonizing in its intensity.

A necessary corollary to every discovery is the finding of the means for putting it to the proof. Columbus would have dreamed in vain of that western passage to the Indies, if he had not found his ships. In some cases, of course, the means are ready at hand, and obvious of application. In others, paradoxically, it is the means that lead to the discovery. The mere having of the ships results in the finding of America.

But this case of Hugh's fell in neither of these categories. His was one of those staggering hypotheses that no man of science would consider seriously until it was demonstrated up to the hilt. And this demonstration demands quite a different set of qualities from those which produce the hypothesis itself. A philosopher might have reasoned out Corbettite—the new Corbettite. Hugh, having imagined it, had still to make it. A matter of technique, that was, of ingenuity and resourcefulness and skill. Mechanic, chemist, electrician—he must be all three, beginning where the philosopher in him left off.

Fortunately for him, he was all three. And he attacked the task with an exultant confidence. Even while he sat there in the train, he was scheming out the means in terms of metal, crucibles, electric current and chemical reaction, for determining this factor and eliminating that. And, by the time his taxi reached the laboratory, the preliminary experiments were all decided upon. He was absolutely incandescent with eagerness to begin.

That being his mood, it seems to me that the wonder is, not that Helena's veiled hints and warnings, her note of challenge, her contemptuous "That's as you like, of course," failed to bring him home, on guard against the thing she appeared to be meditating against him, but that an uneasy thought of her should, even for a moment have broken in upon his preoccupation. Not that he failed to heed the voice that spoke in his ear after he had pushed the telephone away, but that he heard it at all, and for a moment, sat staring at the instrument, before, springing up, he called his two assistants and began telling them, swiftly and eagerly, what they were to do.

XXVIII

The relation between Constance and her mother did not impress either the family or their friends as an especially intimate one. There was no element of dependence in it on either side, and the family manners didn't run to endearments. But the fact remains that well within a week of the time when Mr. and Mrs. Corbett started to California, Constance was missing her mother frightfully. There were times, simply, when nobody else would do; things that no one else could be trusted to a candid talk about.

She had her husband, of course. In most perplexities he was admirable; well poised, resourceful, clear as a bell. But this thing he'd take either too lightly or too hard. If he didn't dismiss it as nonsense— well, there was no telling where he'd stop. He might prove a bull in a china shop.

Frederica? Somehow it didn't seem the sort of thing she *could* confide to her, oldest friend as she was. And anyway, what good would it do? Freddy would be shocked, of course, and then encouraging; might manage to persuade her that there was nothing to worry about. All very well in case it turned out that way, but in that event, she might as well have kept her trouble to herself. But if it turned out the other way—a sickening, ghastly mess that some action of hers might just possibly have averted—mitigated, anyhow. . . No, not Frederica.

Gregory was the obvious person to turn to, of course, but—thank heaven!—he was in New York. When he came home, which would be within the next few days, he would almost certainly do something. Eileen would tell him how it looked to her—she was simply aghast about it—and he would go charging down on Hugh; a bad matter made worse! Indeed one of the most urgent aspects of Constance's perplexity was whether she shouldn't do something merely to forestall Greg. "Do something!" But what? What did she want to do—or what prevent? Given carte blanche by the Almighty to deal with this situation as she chose, how would she deal with it? It shocked her to realize that she didn't know.

This was not at all like Constance; not like, at least, the Constance her friends knew and she herself—save for once in the proverbial blue moon—took for granted. Common sense and good humor were her outstanding qualities. Her mind—a good dependable sort of mind—

was not at all given to speculative excursions. Current social usage, current morality, had about the same place in her conscious life of every day that the fences beside the road have in the consciousness of the driver of a motor-car. You can't drive over them, of course, nor through them, without coming to smash. But then, why should you want to try? The road runs between—doesn't it—with plenty of room for all reasonable purposes? And the sight of a wrecked car here and there— if this be not straining my tenuous figure too far—the sight of a car that had disastrously tried conclusions with the fence moved her not to indignation nor to unmixed pity. Puzzled her, rather, as a case of unaccountably bad driving.

Fortunately, though, this was not quite the whole truth about her. She was redeemed by an occasional divine misgiving. Do you remember a talk she had had, years before, with Frederica Whitney? That was when Hugh had gone to New York to find that anarchist girl he was infatuated with, and to try to persuade her to marry him. She'd told Frederica how the thing looked to Jean, and had enlarged upon the look in their two faces—the child's and Hugh's; contrasted it with the look in Mother Crawford's face—old Mrs. Crawford, who never in her whole life had made a fool of herself.

That same old perplexing argument—upon the merits of making a fool of one's self, granted the occasion, was again distracting Constance. And it concerned itself with the same three people who had thrust it upon her before, Hugh and Jean and Helena.

This time, however, the triangle was sinister. It was a double triangle, too. There was a man of Helena's in it. It was this aspect of the situation that all the scandal was about. It was this that had horrified Eileen and that Gregory, coming home from New York any day now, might be expected to try to deal with in his own fashion. Even without complications it was ugly enough; by no means just "another of Helena's episodes."

Helena and her flirtations had been a fruitful theme for gossip, since the very early days of the marriage—since the days of Boyd Barr and the *Red Review*. Helena was always making a fad of somebody; usually a sojourner, who, if he did not actually live in her house during the whole period of his stay in the city, at least made himself very much at home there and was to be found about the premises at the unlikeliest hours.

The prevalent notion was that you were always likely to stumble upon some sort of masculine exotic when you went to Helena's. She had always made a great parade of them; rammed them down the throats of her friends, insisted that people read their poetry, or go to their lectures and exhibitions. Her manners toward them were usually familiar—would have been judged intolerably so, but for the fact that familiar manners were the new thing anyhow. And they were often, these men of Helena's, flagrantly sentimental about her. And all that, taken in connection with Hugh's hermit-like ways, made a lively topic for talk.

But she had never, in any of these affairs, gone beyond a certain loosely drawn but quite visible line. It was always possible to talk about them jocularly—with an air of jocularity, anyhow.

But this new thing that was happening at Hugh's house, didn't fit on in that series at all. No one knew who the man was who had been there all the week. He had been there though, it appeared, ever since late last Saturday afternoon. And nobody knew where Hugh was, except that by Helena's own statement, he had not been at home since Sunday morning anyhow. Helena in that time had hardly gone out at all; had broken or defaulted most of her engagements. She had told a few insolently transparent lies about where she was going and where she had been. Not many people knew, to be sure, quite how bad it was. No one, Constance thought, outside Eileen and herself. But even the glints of the situation, which their friends had got, had been ugly enough—not to start gossip going, but to stop it short. It was as bad as that.

What Eileen and Constance knew was absolutely damning. It was no wonder pretty little Eileen was aghast. Where was Hugh? What was he doing? What was he thinking of to let his honor be outraged like that?

Yes, it was bad enough. But it was not what horrified—fascinated Constance. Constance was afraid she knew what he was thinking of.

It had been on the Sunday morning after Philip's birthday that she began looking at Jean and wondering what it was about the girl that made her different. She couldn't satisfactorily express it to herself and attempted, intermittently, to make herself believe that it was all her own imagination stimulated by her worries about Hugh and Helena, which had already, that morning, begun. The effect produced by that childish observation of Philip's shouldn't be taken as evidence of anything. Frank had been right to treat it—as he had—with a chuckle of pure amusement.

The birthday party had come back to town, packed into one big motor-car, and, arrived at the Rush Street house, the little boy had begged Jean to come in, as a last protraction of the party. When she went home, it would all be over. Jean, after learning by telephone that her mother and grandmother were both at church, consented to assist in the recital to Frank and Constance of the glorious deeds that had been done at Lake Forest; the battles and stratagems in the snow; the nocturnal pillow fights and feasts, in all of which, it appeared, Jean had fully participated. She could hardly have been a whole-hearted ally of Miss Muirhead's.

The fact that Hugh had turned up, on Saturday, for lunch was of course elicited, the fertility of his suggestions dwelt upon, and a passionate regret expressed that he had not been invited for the entire period of the party and had callously insisted on going home again so soon after his arrival.

Constance didn't take that circumstance very seriously; told herself it was just like Hugh, and was disposed to let it go at that. That was not, at all events, what started her looking at Jean. It did remind her that she had been looking at Jean and seeing something different about her ever since she came into the house. It was after a short reflective silence on Philip's part, that he threw his bomb. He had his hands in his pockets and stood looking at Jean.

"Why don't you get married to Uncle Hugh?" he asked. "I wish you would."

I don't suppose it was more than a second before Constance undertook an explanation of how the monogamous arrangement of society stood fatally in the way of the project.

"Well," Philip insisted, "I wish you would, anyway."

Whereupon Jean—with a smile, to be sure—asked, "Why?"

But evidently her question rang true to Philip; did not strike him, that is, as one of those adult attempts to betray him into saying something that could be laughed at, for he made a serious attempt to answer it.

"Well, of course," he said, "if you and Uncle Hugh lived together by yourselves—not with grandmother or Aunt Helena—why, that would be an awfully nice place for me to go to visit."

This was said a little dubiously, as if it were, after all, a secondary consideration, the primary one remaining to be formulated. But he got no further, for at that point, Constance, having got her breath again, interrupted vigorously. Frank, as I said, did nothing but chuckle.

Well, perhaps that was the way to have taken it. But Constance found she couldn't dismiss it like that. It was nothing, of course, that Jean had remained speechless for rather a long second after Philip threw his bomb. She might well enough have gasped, or flushed, or laughed a little self-consciously. She had done none of those things. Her silence hadn't seemed like the result of shock at all. It almost gave Constance the impression that she was considering the child's question seriously. That notion, unbelievable as it was, was fairly rammed home, a minute or two later, by Jean's serious, though smiling, "Why?" She had wanted the boy's answer.

It was then that Constance got, for the first time, and full in the face, the horrifying surmise that had been tormenting her all the week. She dashed it, indignantly, out of her mind. But it attacked again and, within the next twenty-four hours or so, had dug itself in.

Her mother-in-law's bulletin, the next morning, had for its chief item the announcement that the project for a move to San Antonio had been revived—this time by Jean herself, who had been very half-hearted about it before. Now she was talking impossibilities, such as a start that very week. Within a day or two! Of course it would be at least a fortnight before they could hope to start.

This was significant, and became more so when it appeared later that Jean had persisted in her attempt to hasten their departure, even to the point of irritating her grandmother into a doubt whether she would go at all. This wasn't a bit like Jean. Obviously something had happened.

There was nothing exalted, though, or entranced about the girl's actions. She went about where she was supposed to go, responded alertly enough to all the social demands that were made upon her—conversational and other. Constance noted that Hugh had dropped out of her talk, that she had not seen him since the birthday party, nor had any communication with Helena. She must have heard some of the gossip from her grandmother who simply battened on fare like that, but she never came to Constance with it, and when Constance approached the subject once or twice, definitely veered away.

These facts, as far as they went, were evidence. There had been some sort of explosion and Jean had been involved, if no farther than merely by her knowledge of it; a rude expulsion from the Arcady she and Hugh had been wandering in. Her unobtrusive breaking off with Hugh, her withdrawal from Helena, her proposed retreat to San Antonio, all fitted neatly into that pattern.

But that look of hers did not fit into it. It was not the look of one in retreat; not the look of one who contemplated the barest possibility of retreat. It was, on the contrary, the look of one committed, waiting for the hour.

It fairly took possession of Constance before the week was over. She didn't see why every one else hadn't noticed it—why they weren't wondering what it meant. Finally some one else did notice it. This was at the concert Friday afternoon. On the spur of the moment she had gone to sit in the Whitneys' box with Frederica and Rose Aldrich.

Rose was the lure here. There was something—romantic about that young woman. They had always found her so, ever since Rodney had electrified them all by marrying her. People spoke of her as thrilling, and with a very happy use of a much abused word. And now, as once before, approaching maternity heightened that quality in her. It had completed, for the second time, the conquest of Frederica. Sitting by her, you weren't likely to think about anybody else. And Constance, whose thoughts had begun spinning in a circle like a falling airplane, clutched at the invitation as a rescue—temporary, anyhow.

But it didn't work out that way. Rose sat where she could look across the circle into the Crawfords' box, where Jean sat full in view. Old Mrs. Crawford was there, too, falling asleep as she always did (she never missed the concerts when she was in the city; evidently got some sort of somnolent, remote pleasure out of them), and two guests of hers. But it was to Jean's face that Rose's look kept going back during the whole immortal, lovely length of Schubert's C-Major Symphony number ten, which made the first half of the program. In the intermission, she said to Constance something about what a beauty Jean was getting to be, and then asked, rather suddenly:

"Is she going back to France?"

"Why, no," Constance said, startled. "Not that I have heard of. Why?"

"I don't know," Rose answered thoughtfully. "It was just her look, I guess, that made me think of it."

So it wasn't imagination!

They rode home again after the concert, Jean and her grandmother, in Constance's car, and at the carriage door of the apartment, Constance said to Jean:

"Do you want to come back, after you have gone up with mother, for a turn in the Park with me?"

She made a point of asking it casually, so that the old lady wouldn't decide that she'd go too. But it was plain enough that Jean gave the suggestion a definite meaning and importance.

She nodded and said simply, "Yes."

When the girl was once more seated beside her, Constance said into the tube to the chauffeur.

"Just drive along north—toward Evanston." She was not quite sure what the little sigh Jean gave on hearing this direction meant, and asked: "That isn't more of a turn than you bargained for, is it?"

"No," Jean said, "I'm glad we've—plenty of time."

That settled the preliminaries then and there. This was going to be a real talk—a real coming to grips. Jean both understood and invited it. But for a few minutes, while they were rolling through the Park, Constance hung on a dead center. She had her opening thought out well enough, but she was in the clutches of a contradictory impulse. The youthful loveliness of the girl at her side, the fine straight grain of her, the spiritual—resilience, affected her somewhat as they must always have affected Hugh. Her impulse, mad of course, was to say; "Jean, dear, if you and Hugh are lovers, and don't know what to do, count me in on your side. I'll help. I'll do anything you want me to."

She entertained the notion for a while, in silence, as I have said. Then, with a movement of resolution, a stiffening of her moral backbone, she began as she had meant to begin.

"I see you haven't made any headway with your grandmother about going south."

Jean admitted she had not. "Grandmother's theory is, no matter how little there is to do getting ready for a trip like that, it takes at least two weeks to do it."

Constance drew in a long breath. "Frank can get *you* off," she said, "if I tell him to. If you want to go—now, tomorrow. We'll think of some excuse for your going ahead. Getting things ready for your mother. I suppose that wouldn't be a bad idea, really, considering how fragile Ethel really is. Anyhow, Frank can put it over."

"But that wouldn't do me any good," Jean said. "It's mother I want to get away with." She reached out for Constance's hand and clutched it tight. "I want to talk with her," she went on, an edge of released emotion in her voice. "I feel as if I *had* to talk with her. The doctors keep on saying she mustn't, on any account, be excited or worried by anything. But I thought if she could be back with father—with him to—hold on to, it wouldn't be so bad." She smiled and added, "Nor seem so serious to her. But you see, I couldn't go away alone—leave her here—to grandmother."

"Jean dear," said Constance, "would talking to anybody else do you any good?—To me?"

The girl was silent for a moment. Her clutch tightened on Constance's hand. "Not much," she said. "It has to be mother. For my—feelings, I mean. I do want to talk to you," she went on, "only not that talk. Because, of course, my feelings aren't the only thing in the world—even to me."

For the present then, her "feelings" were to be dismissed from consideration—packed in their box and locked away. That was the air with which she dried her eyes, put herself a little farther back on the cushions, and—her old childish trick which Constance remembered with a clutch of the throat—squared back her shoulders.

"You thought," she said, "that I wanted an excuse for getting away quickly—for running away. Is there any. . . Do you know any reason why I ought to run away?"

"I don't believe so," said Constance—rather dubiously, though. "Not if you don't know of any."

"I don't know whether it's safe to trust to that or not," Jean said after a little silence. "I haven't been very sensible this winter, I don't believe. I mean there are things I ought to have seen, that I haven't."

It was with an apparent effort that Constance went on. "Jean," she asked, "how much do you know about Helena? I mean about what she's been doing lately—this last week?"

Jean's eyes came round to her, wide open. "That isn't just gossip, then?" she asked, and added: "Why, grandmother said something the other night. But I didn't think it was anything anybody *knew*. And I didn't much want to listen. Not because I don't like gossip well enough. I had a special reason."

Constance ruminated over that a moment, not quite sure that she understood. What could the girl's special reason be? If she was in love with Hugh—and there wasn't much room for doubt on that head any longer—hadn't she a legitimate ground of interest in the reported misbehavior of Hugh's wife? But not in an unfounded rumor! It was not a pretext Jean wanted. Nor to be tempted with one. That was it of course.

"We do know," she said. "It's all true. We haven't spied on her. It was really by accident that we found out. Greg wanted to see Hugh before he went to New York. Tried to find him and couldn't. There was some paper it was important Hugh should sign. Greg told Eileen to find him and get it done as quickly as she could. That was Sunday. She drove out to the laboratory—found it locked up and nobody let her in—if any one was there. So then she went to his house. What she saw made it all plain enough. And then there are things that have happened since. I can go into the details if you want me to, but—"

The girl shuddered, then steadied herself. "I'd rather you didn't," she said.

Constance, after a reflective silence, her gaze fixed on the black ellipse of her chauffeur's cap, said:

"I'd have talked to you about it sooner, but—I had an idea you knew."

Jean echoed that wonderingly. "But how could I know?" she asked.

"I thought," pursued Constance, finding the thing more and more difficult as she went on, "that Hugh might have told you."

"But Hugh doesn't know!" Jean cried. "I don't believe he knows!"

"I think he must," Constance said. "Why else has he gone away?—Disappeared like that?"

"Gone away!" echoed Jean. "I didn't know he had gone away." The girl's voice wavered over that. Constance could hear incipient panic in it. But the old code and the old drill came to the rescue. She squared her shoulders, flattened her back, and repeated the assertion steadily. "I didn't know that he had gone away. Are you sure?"

"I'm not sure of anything," Constance admitted. "Only Helena says herself that he hasn't been home, and that's hardly a thing that she'd lie about. And when we try to telephone the laboratory, sometimes they don't answer at all, and sometimes they say that he's not there and that they can't tell anything about him. They'll ask him to call us, if he comes in. And he never does."

"Well," Jean said steadily, "I don't believe he's gone away, and I don't believe he knows. And I'm sure he hasn't gone away because he knows. That's not what Hugh would do."

"No," said Constance, "it isn't very accountable. But then, this that Helena's doing isn't very accountable either. You wouldn't think she'd do a—crazy thing like that, a perfectly reckless, abandoned thing like that. . ."

She didn't add the word "unless"; pulled up on the brink of it. But Jean caught the implication.

"You do account for it some way," she said. "You've got a theory. Tell me what it is."

Constance found that her throat had gone dry. She had never had to say so hard a thing before.

"Yes, I have a theory," she said at last. "That's the whole thing, really. What I wanted to talk to you about. You mustn't hate me for this. You wouldn't even be angry with me for it, if you knew how I felt.

"Jean, it worried mother—my mother, I mean—away back last fall, just after you came home, the way Helena seemed to be deliberately throwing you and Hugh together—'throwing you at his head'—was how mother put it. She thought Helena might be doing it for some detestable purpose of her own. I tried to laugh her out of it. I never liked Helena very well, but I didn't believe she was capable of anything like that.

"Well, I believe, now, she's capable of anything—of trying it, anyhow. And I've been wondering—if she succeeded. I couldn't help wondering. I don't see how she could have thrown away all she's got in the world, her position—everything, for a shabby little transient love affair. I can't believe she'd have risked it, unless she has something she thinks will protect her—some sort of threat against Hugh that would make him keep quiet—pretend not to see.

"And the only threat I can think of that would work that way, would be one that involved you—with him. . ."

She stopped there, not quite sure whether she had gone far enough. Did the girl understand? Did her life afford her the data for understanding a monstrous supposition like that? And if she understood, how had she taken it?

There was nothing in the silence to afford her a clew, and her courage faltered from looking round into the girl's face. Finally she said—and the words were almost a cry:

"Jean, darling, do you understand what I mean?"

"Yes, I understand of course," Jean said quietly. "I was thinking."

Then Constance did look round, amazed.

There was no look of anger or hurt in the girl's face; no expression of horror, or even of protest. The attitude of her body, the poise of her head, was tensely alert. Her gaze was fixed out the window in concentrated thought.

"I don't know how much one needs to make a scandal of," she went on, at last, in that quiet voice—"not very much, I suppose. And still less to threaten one. But there's nothing that Helena knows, or can have been told, by any one who's telling the truth, that's any different from what you know about us, yourself."

The phrase struck Constance as curious, but in an instant she understood. (Her own mind was keyed to a much higher pitch than her normal one.) All Jean saw, all there was room for in her mind at that moment was Helena. She was eying her as one might eye a movement in the grass where one suspects a snake. It hadn't occurred to her to protest her innocence to Constance. It was only from that latter point of view that the use of the phrase might have seemed evasive. So it was all right after all!

But just as the older woman was drawing in her first long breath of genuine relief, a gasp from Jean checked her. She looked round again in time to see a flame of color leap into the girl's face.

"Why, Jean!" she cried. "What is it?"

It was a matter of seconds before she got an answer. Then, "There's nothing that anybody knows—except what nobody knows but Hugh and me. Unless he told her—that same day that it happened. Saturday. After he went back from Lake Forest. I—I wasn't thinking about that."

There was a long silence after that. Constance had simply gone limp. As for Jean, she showed no disposition to add anything to the amazing admission she had just made, either by way of explaining or qualifying it. Her mind, so far as Constance could sense from the way she sat there, so still and so alertly poised, seemed to have gone back to the consideration of Helena once more.

Finally Constance said: "Jean dear, won't you go away? Just as soon as it can possibly be done. Tomorrow. Don't you think Hugh would feel better if you were safely out of the way? She's terribly dangerous. Especially if Hugh has told her—what—whatever there was to tell. And if she's threatened him with making a scandal of it. . ."

"I don't believe that's it at all," Jean interrupted. "I don't think he's seen her since they quarreled last Friday night. There was some terribly important work he meant to do at the laboratory, and I think he went straight back to that. I think he's been there all the time. And I don't think he knows what Helena's been doing. If I *knew* that was so, I'd go away. I told him I would go, and I think he'll expect to find me gone when he comes out of the laboratory. But I'm not going. Not as long as there's a chance that she's done what you think. If she's done that, he must fight, of course. And I must stay and help him. I'm about the only one who can. Why, it would be admitting I've done wrong, to run away!—Shall we go home now?"

Constance weakly assented. To say that she had got out beyond her depth is an utterly inadequate way of putting it. She felt as if she had come through a mill-race. But along with her sense of her own complete helplessness there came a curious confidence that her young niece was not going down to shipwreck. Storm-battered she was, no doubt, going to be; she would probably lose a sail or two. But the essentials of her were going to come through intact. When they clasped hands, it was Constance who was clinging to Jean, not Jean who was clinging to Constance. That was the way it felt to the older woman at any rate.

They didn't say much all the way home; not a word that bore on the subject that was in both their minds, until, the chauffeur having taken the inner drive through the Park and turned down Astor Street, they passed Gregory's house.

"I've been glad he was away," Constance said, "and dreading his coming back. Because there's sure to be an explosion when he does. But I'm beginning to wish he would."

"He came today, I think," Jean said. "At least, Eileen was expecting him this noon, when I saw her. He'd telegraphed or something."

It was with an equal mixture of relief and apprehension that Constance received this news. "I wish it were tomorrow at this time," she said, "and nothing—terrible had happened."

Jean left her with a reassuring hug and an affectionate kiss. It was a strange reversal of rôles, for a fact.

Nevertheless, the young girl paused outside the door of their apartment, for a steadying breath or two, and then she rummaged in her wrist-bag for her latch-key, in preference to ringing and having to face the maid.

She walked swiftly across the hall and down the corridor to her own bedroom. Arrived at this haven, she allowed herself just one moment's indulgence in the friendly darkness of it before switching on the lights, or ridding herself of her outdoor wraps and changing to a house frock for dinner.

This moment of "recollection" was broken in upon by the jangle of the telephone bell. She started at it and sat breathless, listening with

HENRY KITCHELL WEBSTER

strained ears. She had done that, poor child, since Sunday morning, everytime the telephone bell had rung. The apartment was very quiet, and the voice that answered—that of one of the servants—though faint, was audible.

"No, sir," it said, "Miss Gilbert has not come in. She returned from the concert and went out again. . . Oh, no, sir. She's not left the city. She's expected for dinner."

Jean snatched up the extension that was in her room—one of those little English instruments with the receiver and transmitter all in one piece. The way her face nestled to it was a caress. But she said steadily enough, "I've just come in, Mills. I'll answer from here."

There was a dead silence over the wire for an instant after the click which told that the other receiver had been hung up. And then, in Hugh's voice—the voice she had been so certain she would hear:

"I was afraid you'd have gone before this." And in the moment before she answered, "You're there, aren't you?"

"Yes," she said. "Only my voice wouldn't come, for a minute. You're there, too? At the laboratory? You haven't gone away, either?"

"Gone away!" he echoed. "I should think not! I haven't had my head out-of-doors since last Saturday afternoon. Jean, I've got it! I've had it ever since three o'clock Monday morning. Since then I've just been making sure. I swore I wouldn't call you till I was. But I've checked it every possible way. There isn't a doubt about it. The job's done!"

"Oh!" she said, breathless. "Oh, I wish we didn't have to—talk!"

Evidently it was as difficult for him as it was for her. At last he said, "Jean, can we see each other again? Once more before you go away? I didn't mean to ask that."

"We must," she agreed. "Not because we want to so much, Hugh. But we can't talk like this and there are things to say. I won't go—I can't possibly go—until I've seen you. I won't go at all if— if I think you need me here. No, not—that way. That's not what I mean. Need me for a special thing. If it's a question of—fighting instead of running away. Oh, Hugh—you don't understand, do you?"

All he understood, it appeared, was that there was some new emergency that he knew nothing about. "We can't talk like this," he said crisply. "I'll come straight over."

"No, it's not like that, either," she said. "It's not me. I'm all right. It's you. Hugh, don't come tonight. Go and see Gregory, instead. See him before you go—home. And if you don't find him, go to Constance."

He agreed to this, but made it a matter of sheer docility. "I want to see Greg, anyway, but I shouldn't have thought of tackling him tonight. I had a notion of getting about a week's sleep, first."

There was a vibrant silence then, two or three breaths long.

"I want a promise from you," she said at last, in a tone of deep seriousness. "Hugh, I want you to promise that—that you *will* come to me. When you're ready. Tomorrow or whenever it is."

"You want me to *promise!*" he echoed incredulously. "Promise to come to *you!*"

"Yes," she insisted. "Whatever happens."

It was in a tone of troubled wonder that the words she wanted came at last. "Yes, I promise."

That satisfied her, and with a little gasp she said, "Good-by."

There was one blessing in store for Jean that she had not counted upon; one sacrifice which she had resolutely braced herself to make, that was not demanded of her. The one almost unendurable aspect of the situation that had resulted from her discovery, there on the beach that Saturday morning, had been the necessity for keeping her mother in the dark about it.

They were companions—confidantes, that pair, as mother and daughter seldom are. It was something much solider than a mere intuitive understanding (that is a sword which cuts two ways) that this relation was built upon. It sometimes took a good deal of explaining, indeed, to get a situation fairly understood between them. But the point was that the explanation was always possible. They could have kept secrets from each other if they had wanted to. Indeed, I think it is the inability to do this, that often reduces two intimately associated, and it may be warmly affectionate, companions, to bare nerves and almost unendurable exasperations.

The bond between Jean and her mother was a profound—and quite unconscious—respect, in each, for the integrity of the other's life; of the other's right to a separate, individual entity. I don't know that a respect like that—reticence it almost amounted to—is accountable, but I'll venture to guess that in this case it was partly accounted for by the completeness of Ethel's love for her husband—by the extent to which he satisfied and absorbed her. The child, much as she had been loved, had never taken his place.

And then, being the grave, responsible little thing that she was, it had been possible to treat her as an adult, in matters of responsibility, before she could even talk straight. Jean had been enlisted as an ally of her mother's long before she could remember, in the business of helping make her father's arduous life run smoothly where it could. As a child of ten she had had problems brought for her help in the solution of that many a daughter grows to womanhood without having ever been asked to consider.

Confidences, then, between the pair, never having been forced nor pried into, were as natural a function as eating or breathing. And it is the simple truth that that strange elation of Jean's, about which she had so wonderingly commented to Hugh in the moment of their parting, did not leave her until the realization came that here was something she could not tell her mother.

Ethel's condition was far from satisfactory. For a while after their arrival in Chicago in the autumn, it had steadily improved. But this improvement reached its peak around the Christmas holidays, when her husband came north on a twenty-days' furlough. Since his return to the border, it had steadily grown worse. The doctor who was looking after her had taken the orthodox line—and stuck to it: rest and quiet, an exact regimentation of her days, and above all, no excitement—no shocks. And, of course, the less she improved under this treatment, the more rigorous the treatment had to be.

Anyhow, it was transparently clear to Jean, when she came home that Sunday from Lake Forest, that Ethel was in no condition to be told that her daughter had embarked upon a mutually avowed love affair with a married man. The only hope the girl could see— and it was a passionate one—was that which she had expressed to Constance. (There was not a trace of bitterness in the girl's prevision that Ethel, reunited to her husband—"with him to hold on to," would take her daughter's affair less seriously.) There was nothing to do but wait for that.

But accident intervened. As Jean hung up the telephone, after her talk with Hugh, she heard her name spoken quietly, and from near by, in her mother's voice. It came from the next room and the communicating door was open. She switched on the light and went in.

"Here I am," her mother said. She was stretched out in a long chair. "I didn't mean to be an eavesdropper," she went on. "I must have been asleep when you came in, and wakened rather slowly. I just enjoyed the sound of your voice for a while, before I realized what it meant. And when I did, it was too late to interrupt."

"I didn't think," Jean said. "I didn't remember even you. I heard Mills telling him I wasn't at home, and I forgot everything else." Then, dropping down beside her, she took both her mother's arms in a strong grip. "It's all right. mother," she said. "There's nothing—not one thing in the world for you to worry about. No harm has been done to anybody, and none is going to be. And I'm not unhappy. I've never been—really— happy before. Can't you just believe that?—Let it go at that?—Put it out of your mind and not be excited or distressed about it?"

"Oh, my lamb!" her mother said. "You haven't done me any harm. Take off your things so I can feel you, and light that reading lamp so that I can see you a little, and then come back and tell me all about it."

Jean obeyed the first of these instructions quite simply, like a little girl. But when she came back and seated herself once more upon the long chair beside her mother's knees, she was all of a tremble and voiceless, and she put her head down upon her mother's breast and cried a while instead.

Eventually, and in fragments, the story got itself told—the story you already know. And after it was told they talked about it for a while.

"People don't take things the way they're supposed to, do they?" Jean said thoughtfully. "Hugh and I didn't; and now you don't. I've done something that's supposed to be terribly wicked and dangerous and you aren't angry or shocked at all."

Then, "Mother, that isn't because you don't believe it? You don't think, because I could go on so long without understanding, that it's just a little girl thing and that I don't really understand even now? I wasn't jealous, you see. That was what I went by. I liked Helena because I thought he was fond of her. Because I thought she made him happy. I thought she was what he wanted. But when I found he wanted me. . .

"Mother, if it's wrong to love him, then there's nothing I could do that would make me any wickeder, in my heart, than I am now. I'm ready to do anything he wants me to do. Anything—that will make him happy. What becomes of me doesn't matter. It's like what the preacher said—'Rejoicing to be damned for the glory of God.' That's what I mean. You *must* believe it, mother."

Her mother quieted the girl's vehemence just with the pressure of her hands. Before she spoke, she smiled. "You come by it honestly, Jean dearest. Had you forgotten—or didn't you ever know—that you wouldn't have to explain that—to me? Why, lamb, I was just your age— almost to the week—when I defied my mother—told her I didn't care whether she disowned me or not—whether I ever saw her again or not, or any of her family or friends,—and ran off with Roger. We did it on what he had left of a month's salary, around eighty dollars it was, and the first thing we bought out of it was a complete outfit of clothes for me so that I could send everything I'd worn away from home back to mother in an express package. Neither of us was married to any one else, of course, but I'm not sure that that would have mattered much, granted that we'd had a chance to fall in love honestly and in good faith, first. I'd never had a father long enough to count. I'd been badly spoiled— indulged—brought up soft. But I'd have followed Roger barefoot and in rags, and gloried in it."

"I've known all that, of course, always," Jean said in a voice of wonder. "Only I never tried to think what it meant. I couldn't have understood it, I suppose, till now." She put her head down again on her mother's shoulder and clutched her in a tight embrace. "Then all you have to do is to remember, and you'll understand, too. Remember hard, mother!"

Ethel winced at that, but she resisted the girl's attempt to sit up and inquire into the cause. "No, lie still. It's all right. Only—'remember,' Jean! How old do you suppose *you'll* be at forty-two? Beyond love and the hunger for it? It looks different to you now, but looking back, from then, it won't."

It was getting close on the dinner hour and old Mrs. Crawford made a great point of punctuality, but they stole as many minutes as they dared just to sit there close—closer than ever they had been before—in the dusky silence. At the end of it Ethel gave Jean the one word of counsel she had to offer.

"Remember that when two people love each other—*completely*, it isn't possible for either one to make a sacrifice for the other. You're willing to do anything to make him happy, willing to be ostracized, disgraced, damned—for him. I know. But his happiness can't be had at that price. No more than yours could be, by letting his life be spoiled and broken. Any sacrifice you make, will be the sacrifice of both of you. No one told that to Roger and me. It was life that pointed it out to us as we went along."

XXIX

Eileen was in what her mother-in-law would have called a twitter over Gregory's return.

But this isn't fair. Quoting Mrs. Corbett for descriptions of Eileen is a temptation to which, I am afraid, I have yielded too often for justice. Gregory's widow (she'd been the widow *par excellence* in the family idiom for so many years, that the appellation stuck for a year or two after she'd married him) was not a sentimental little fool, and no one—not even old Mrs. Corbett herself—really considered her such.

What led the family to take her—as they did—rather less seriously than she deserved, was, in the first place, her looks. She was a pretty little thing (little according to their scale. She looked tiny alongside Greg) with a soft little mouth, a small sensitive nose and very delicately arched eyebrows. Add to that a pink-and-white skin, and hair of so very light a brown that it could still be described as golden, and you have established a strong presumption against her fitness for the business of a work-a-day world. It was not her fault that she looked from five to ten years younger than her age. (She was twenty-eight when she finally made up her mind to marry Gregory.) This was not an effect that she tried for at all and she sometimes regarded it as an out-and-out misfortune.

She was, it can not be denied, given to being a bit soulful and helpless. This was merely acquiescence in an attitude that people had been taking toward her ever since she was five years old—not much more her fault than the shape of her nose—but it explains the attitude of the family. The Corbett women were neither soulful nor helpless. Even Anne, silly as she was in many ways, knew how to operate a bank-account and read a time table.

Greg's attitude toward his wife is, naturally, to be distinguished from that of the rest of the family. He'd adored her blindly for many years, helplessness and all. He had spent uncounted hours doing her services that neither of his sisters would have dreamed of asking even of the most infatuated lover. Marriage produced a change—not disillusionment, but acceptance of a new duty. He went right on adoring her. That dreamy look in her eyes continued to be—in his—the most heavenly thing that could exist on earth. He loved her way of seeing pictures in the coals and in the clouds; her fancies; her glints of poetry. It is literally true that he thought of her as a sojourner from a better world. And, incarnating for him an ideal like that, she did redeem him from the mere dull materiality that he might have sunk into otherwise. Jean was quite right. He was—"nicer"—more human, for having married her.

But he came to see her helplessness in a new light. It was not that it irritated him—not that he begrudged the expenditure of his own time upon trifles, that it demanded. It was a sheer sense of duty that drove him to educating Eileen into a competent grasp of practical matters. She was none the less an angel now that she was his wife. But she was his wife as well—wife of the prospective head of the Corbett clan, prospective mother of the Corbett heirs. In the event—unlikely enough, to be sure—of his own untimely death, she would be under a heavy responsibility.

So, though it seemed to him a little like breaking a butterfly upon the wheel, he went to work, with a patience which his office associates wouldn't have credited him with, teaching Eileen to do things for herself.

He taught her to keep her household accounts so that they balanced, to put through long distance calls on the telephone, to wind her watch every night and see that it told the right time—as a preliminary to the art of punctuality. He entrusted her with things to put away in his safety deposit box at the bank, and made her clip her own bonds and deposit her own dividends, and the picture that these rumored activities made in the collective mind of the family, was that of David Copperfield and Dora. This was a gross injustice, of course, of which Eileen was well aware. She might well have resented it if she hadn't been the sweetest tempered little thing in the world. She'd really taken her job quite seriously and was learning it as fast as could have been expected. What was aroused was her pride. When Greg gave her an errand to do, she made a tremendous point of doing it, without bungling and without delay.

She had no idea how important the matter was that Gregory delegated to her upon his unforeseen departure for New York, Sunday morning. He had asked her to take a certain paper to Hugh, secure his signature to it, and mail it, registered and by special delivery, to an address that he gave her in New York. The fact that Gregory wanted it done, and that it was a matter of business, gave it, so far as she was concerned, a paramount importance. It never occurred to her to leave off trying when her first attempt to find Hugh, on Sunday, was baffled, nor did she think of telegraphing to Greg and asking for further instructions. She simply kept on trying to get that signature, day after day, at the house and at the laboratory. And though it is true, as I have said, that she was horrified at the discovery of Helena's misconduct, the thing that was still in the foreground of her mind, as she sat at home late Friday afternoon, awaiting her husband's return, was the fact that she had failed to get that signature. She was, absurdly, more indignant with Hugh for being inaccessible when there was something Gregory wanted of him, than over his failure to look after his wife.

Was Gregory coming home just because she had failed? Had the trip to New York been in vain? For the want of that signature was a fortune to be lost, as a battle was once, in the school reader, for the want of a horseshoe nail?

He was very glad to see her. That was plain enough. There was no lack of ardor about his embrace. Perhaps he didn't know that the paper hadn't been sent—supposed all the while that it was safe at its destination! She hadn't thought of that.

But no. He was worried about something, she could see; was preoccupied, anyhow—had something on his mind. She braced herself and made her confession. "I didn't get that paper signed, Gregory. I couldn't find Hugh."

All he said at first was, and without full attention, "Oh, that doesn't matter." Then, waking up a little, "You couldn't *find* Hugh! What do you mean? Where is he?"

"I don't know," she said. "Nobody seems to know."

"Oh, he must be somewhere. Did you try the laboratory?"

"I should think I did. I've been out there every day. It's locked. It's always locked."

"How about the phone? Don't they answer?"

"Sometimes not. When they do, they just say he isn't there."

"Did you tell them who you were?" he asked.

The thing that was wearing through Eileen's nerves was the fact that he seemed to be taking her failure so little seriously. She assured him, subduing her excitement as well as she could, that she had told them who she was and had made it clear to them that her errand was of first importance.

"Oh, well, don't you worry," he said soothingly. "It's not a matter of much importance, anyway. But I imagine they'll tell me where he is. I've really *got* to see him. Tonight, if possible."

He said it soothingly, but that was not the effect it produced. Her eyes filled up with tears, as she said raggedly:

"It wasn't important? And I've been having this perfectly horrible— detestable time with Helena. . ." She broke off there, a shudder and a sob all mixed together.

Greg took her in his arms, called her pet names, tried to comfort her, apologized for having given her an exaggerated idea of the importance of the business, all without success. And it gradually came over him that there was something in the situation that he didn't know about.

"What about Helena?" he asked. "You don't mean she's been rude to you?"

"Rude!" said Eileen with another shudder. "Oh, Greg, it's horrible! It's unbelievable. Would be, if I hadn't s-seen it!"

"Tell me about it," he said quietly, and just his manner of giving the command steadied her so that she could.

"I went there Sunday morning, after I couldn't get into the laboratory. I asked the maid for Hugh and she said he wasn't at home. And then I asked for Helena. She said she'd find her, and was gone quite a long time. She'd asked me to sit down in the drawing-room, but I hadn't, because I only meant to stay a minute.

"—Greg, you know that mirror up on the landing of the stairs in their house, built into the wall on the bias? Well, I heard her coming at last and looked up. I looked up when I heard her stop. There was a man with her. And before I could look away, he'd kissed her. It was very quick and furtive and—nasty. He took her by the neck with one hand. Hard. . . And when he'd done it, he tiptoed away. I heard him. And she came down-stairs, looking—oh, wicked! There was a smell of cigar smoke in her clothes and in her hair. It almost made me sick. She said she didn't know anything about Hugh, except that he wasn't at home. She supposed he was at the laboratory. I'd better try there if I wanted him.

"And she asked me if I wouldn't come in and sit down. She didn't say anything about the man being there. But, of course, I didn't. I wanted to get out into the air again.

"Greg, he's been there ever since. At least I think he has. I've been back at the house twice. I thought I *had* to go, if there was any chance of finding Hugh. Once I saw him, and once I only smelled his cigar again. He'd just gone stealing out of the room before I came in. And

Hugh hasn't been home at all! At least Helena says he hasn't. That was Sunday, and this is Friday."

She heard Greg say, "By God!" and read some unguessed intention in his dark face.

"What are you going to do?" she cried.

His manner instantly became cool again. "I'm going out for a little while," he said. "Don't you worry about it, dearest. Forget it, if you can. Don't think of it again."

She asked him, timidly, if he wouldn't surely be back for dinner.

"I don't know," he said. "Don't wait for me."

She had to stop to dry her eyes and powder her nose, before she could follow him down-stairs (she didn't want any casual servant she might meet, to see that she'd been crying, in the hour of her husband's return), and he was just going out the door in his big ulster and with his big thick walking stick hooked over his arm, when she caught her last glimpse of him.

A quarter of an hour later he rang his brother's door-bell and was promptly admitted by one of the maids. It happened he knew her. She'd worked for his mother once. So the first exchange of words between them was his "Good evening, Martha," and her "Good evening, Mr. Corbett." And then, "Mrs. Corbett at home?" he asked.

The maid said she thought Mrs. Corbett would be coming down for dinner in a few minutes, and volunteered to find her.

"No hurry," said Greg. She hesitated, and with a gesture offered to help him out of his coat. But he said, "No, I'm not going to stay," and strode across just as he was, into the drawing-room.

It all happened very quickly—quicker than it can be told, almost. Certainly before the man, who had been lounging very much at ease in a big leather easy chair before the fire, could get himself together to meet the emergency; almost before he could get to his feet, for he had sat quite still for a paralyzed moment after he had heard the maid say "Mr. Corbett," trying to decide what line to take. And anyhow, the apparition of Gregory—six feet and nearly three inches tall—huge and formidable enough even without that great ulster, and the heavy walking stick that was in his hand, was enough to account for a blink and a gasp. He hadn't visualized any such man as that, nor reckoned upon him. He had to swallow before he spoke. Then:

"Mr. Corbett?" he said. "My name's Gilrain. Frank Gilrain. I'm an old friend of your wife's. Go back to the San Francisco days. You've heard her speak of me, I guess. She says she—told you I was going to be here for a while."

"I'm not Mrs. Corbett's husband," Gregory said. "I'm her husband's brother."

There was an electrical intensity in the silence that followed this statement. Gregory, standing very still and looking steadily at the other man, was thoughtfully weighing, among other alternatives, the wisdom of dragging Helena's guest out to the front door and kicking him down the rather long flight of stone steps. And the guest, as was apparent from the way he clenched his hands and moistened his lips with the tip of his tongue, had a clairvoyant perception that this project was being considered. There wasn't the smallest question in his mind, any more than there was in Gregory's, that Gregory could do it if he chose.

But, into the silence came the sound of Helena's step on the stair and Gregory, with no preliminary motions at all, strode out into the hall to meet her. Gilrain, hesitating whether to follow or not, dropped back rather limp, into the big chair again.

Gregory said, with only a nod of greeting, "I understand Hugh isn't home. Can you tell me where to find him?"

Even to Helena, his sudden emergence through the drawing-room door, was formidable. Was Gilrain in there? Had Gregory seen him? She didn't know. It wasn't as easy to treat him with insolently smiling defiance, as it had been so to treat that slip of a wife of his.

"Why," she said, "I don't know whether he's coming in to dinner or not. He hasn't been home much lately. He's likely to be at the laboratory, I suppose." Then she came the rest of the way down-stairs and, in the interval, got herself a little better in hand.

"We're just sitting down to dinner," she said. "He may come. Won't you stay?"

"I think not," he said. "But, if I may, I'll telephone."

The instrument was at the end of the hall and he went back to it quickly, hardly waiting for his sister-in-law's curt, "Of course!" But even as Helena said the words, her eyes left him and sought the drawing-room doorway—looking for Gilrain, or signaling to him, he couldn't make out which.

He called the laboratory number from memory and got an immediate connection. It was Hugh himself who answered.

Gregory said, after telling who he was, "I want a talk with you tonight. At once. It's a matter of great importance."

"I've just this minute been calling your house," said Hugh, "to tell you the same thing. But Eileen said she thought you were already on the way out here."

"I came to your house, instead. I'm there now." Gregory paused there; then, with a significant edge to his voice, went on, "I'll come out to the laboratory, or I'll wait here for you, just as you please."

"Oh, come out here," said Hugh. "If you haven't your car with you you can pick up a taxi just round the corner."

Helena was still at the foot of the stairs when Gregory came back from the telephone, and Gilrain nowhere in sight; lurking round the corner in the drawing-room he must be. Some sort of communication had passed, no doubt, between them, while he was at the telephone. The woman had got herself thoroughly in hand again; color was in her cheeks and an insolent spark in her eyes. She looked wicked, just as Eileen had said.

"Is he coming home? Or are you going to the laboratory?" she asked.

"I'm going to him. Good night."

She said good night in reply, but did not move toward the door with him. She had not moved when he closed it.

The laboratory door was locked, but a man was waiting, down in the machine-shop, to let Gregory in and conduct him to the foot of the stairs. Hugh sung out from the head of them, "Come up."

It was symptomatic of something unusual in the atmosphere between them, that the two brothers gripped hands. Demonstrations of that sort weren't their rule.

Hugh's first words were, "I hope you haven't had dinner. Because I haven't. I don't believe I've eaten a meal this week. But I've ordered a real one tonight for the two of us. There's a little saloon around the corner, where they have a man that really understands steaks."

"No, I haven't dined," said Greg. "I'll be glad of a steak." Then he added, "You're looking first-rate."

There was not, it may be noted, the faintest doubt in Gregory's mind that Hugh knew the essentials at least, of what had been going on in his house during the past week. That conviction took possession of his mind the moment Hugh said over the telephone, that he wanted to see him that night, about a matter of importance. His remark now, about Hugh's looks, meant a good deal more than it said. There was a clear brightness in the younger brother's eyes, a ring of confident authority in his voice, that made it plain to Gregory that he had risen to the situation—had his plans—knew just what he was about.

"You wouldn't have said that, half an hour ago," said Hugh. "I've just had my first shave since Saturday morning." Then he called down the stairs, "Come up and set the table, Fred. We'll be ready for dinner as soon as it comes along." And at the man's "All right," Hugh led the way into the library. Fred came along, too, and with an expedition evidently the result of practise, set the table, producing his materials from a sort of kitchenette that opened off the library.

There was something curiously attractive about the library. There was not an article in it that made any esthetic pretensions, but the total of it produced an effect of homeliness and comfort. Eileen, in her mystical way, might have said that this was because a man was happy here—secure—content. Hugh himself produced an effect at variance with Gregory's habitual thoughts about him; an air, "of knowing what was what." One who saw him here, wouldn't think of sighing over him as "poor old Hugh." And he "did himself," as the English would say, rather well out here, too. This man Fred—whatever his other functions might be—was doing the work of a man servant very effectively.

His presence in the room made it, of course, impossible to talk, so Greg's eyes lazily followed him, with the sense, just faintly stirring, of recognition.

When they heard a knock on the street door down-stairs—the dinner, doubtless—and he went to answer it, Hugh asked: "Do you remember him?"

"I've been half thinking I ought to," said Gregory.

"He's Jean's burglar," Hugh reminded him. "He came out and asked for a job two or three months ago; had another one, but thought he'd like to work for me. I hadn't heard anything of him in years, but I was very glad to get him, of course. He's an absolutely first-class tool-maker and machinist, and he can make a shot at anything. He's the only one of us, except the night watchman, that keeps regular hours—seven to seven."

"You're not afraid of him, then?"

"I don't know anybody," said Hugh, "whose loyalty I'd rate any higher."

It *was* the dinner that had knocked, and the two brothers now settled down to do justice to it—a big thick steak apiece, a platter of fried potatoes, a pie and a pot of coffee. They could eat, those big Corbetts, and it was their habit to treat food seriously. Fred was dismissed as soon as they were fairly settled, sure that they had everything they wanted within reach, but except for an occasional word of friendly idle reminiscence, there was no attempt to talk until they had finished. Then Gregory lighted a cigar, and Hugh loaded his pipe.

"You've something you want to talk over with me, as well as I with you," Hugh said after a little silence. "Tell me your story first."

Gregory was, for a moment, profoundly disconcerted. It was true he had wanted to talk with Hugh. Had come home from New York intent upon that interview as the first step in a course he was determined, if possible, to follow. But it was also true that he had forgotten his intention so completely, since his talk with Eileen, that he could hardly, now, bring it back to his mind at all. Certainly, though, a discussion of Hugh's wife and of Hugh's honor should be begun by Hugh himself and upon his own terms.

So Gregory began, rather vaguely; but presently he got into his stride. The thing really was near his heart. Nearer than any abstraction except Corbett & Company had ever come to it.

"I've been talking to some men in New York," he said, "who know the real truth about what's going on over there—in France—I mean, as well as anybody does, and it looks pretty black to them. The French military authorities didn't mean to defend Verdun. They thought it was hopeless. It was the politicians who saw they didn't dare let it go; that the whole French morale would cave in if they did. So it's a desperate thing. They're probably going to lose it anyway.

"And the English haven't got up steam yet. They aren't ready to start an offensive in their sector that will take the pressure off the French. They won't be ready till next summer, and it looks as if that would be too late. If the French collapse, we'll have to go in, whether the man in the White House wants to fight or not. The Germans are simply playing with us in this submarine business. They're stalling to hold us off until they've finished up the French. Then they'll tear up their promises about respecting neutral shipping, and start sinking everything. Regardless. If we stand for that, and wait till they've starved out England, then they'll take us on by ourselves. The kaiser has said that, in so many words, to Gerard. Said he wouldn't stand any nonsense from us after he got his hands free.

"And where will we be then? Hog-fat with money, and without any defense at all. But it won't come to that! We're going to be in the war ourselves—up to the neck—before the year's out. Well, that's preliminary. I may be wrong about it. My dope may be wrong. But it's what I believe.

"Now, here's where we come down to brass tacks. There's an idea for a new kind of tractor for a military purpose. As a fighting thing, I mean; armor on it, guns in it. They'll want an immense lot of them. There's no question of a contract. The thing hasn't gone through yet. But if it does, they'll want 'em. My God, how they'll want 'em! And they'll want 'em quick.

"Well, my proposition is that we get ready. Take an absolutely blind chance. It'll mean a hell of a lot of money invested; new land, new buildings, new equipment, and that money'll have to come out of our own jeans. And—this is what I want you to understand—not a ghost of a guarantee that we'll ever get it back. Just a blind chance, as I've said. As a business proposition, it's indefensible. If it weren't that we three, you and father and I, own every share of Corbett & Company, I couldn't consider it.

"I remember your having said once, that you thought grandfather's trust involved something more than his money. That sounded wild to me then, I admit. I didn't see it at all. Well, I've changed since then. This war has begun to—get me. Especially, I suppose, now that the kid's over there. The old game of making our annual statement every year show better than it showed the year before doesn't seem quite the only game to play. There's a better one, and I want to get into it. But I've got to know, first, how it strikes you."

Hugh had not interrupted once. Gregory had been talking with averted gaze, a little self-conscious and ashamed over the betrayal of emotion he knew his voice was making. But now, looking up, he needed no words for his answer. Hugh's face was alight. A brightness of tears was in his eyes. He thrust a big hand across the table, for his brother's. "You didn't really doubt how it would strike me, did you?"

"Oh, I didn't suppose you'd care a damn about the money," Gregory admitted. "But I wasn't quite sure how you'd feel about the war. I thought, perhaps, you didn't believe in war."

"I've been pretty slow coming to see it—what it was going to mean to us," Hugh said. "Up to four or five months ago—well, it horrified me and made me blue—but it was something I kept trying to ignore. But then—I was waked up. And lately I've been thinking that when I could get free, over here, the best thing I could do would be to follow Carter. I think that's one way of waking us up; getting us ready. I'm not quite clear about it. That's one of the things I thought we'd—get to, perhaps, tonight.

"I've felt I had a job here, you see. But that's finished now. I think it is. I think that this last week has finished it."

He hesitated there, a little awkwardly. It wasn't as easy to tell about Corbettite to Gregory as it had been to tell it to Jean. The strong-box that had his samples in it stood upon his desk. He got up and fetched it—it was heavier now than it had been—and laid it on the table in front of Gregory.

"Open it," he said.

Gregory lifted the hinged cover. "What. . . !" he began. But literally, he could not command another word. Could only stare, blankly, across at his brother.

He hadn't had the faintest doubt that the subject Hugh was leading up to was his disastrous marriage. Everything Hugh had said, refracted, as it was, by that fixed idea of his, bore that interpretation. Even when he left the table and fetched the strong-box, there was in Gregory's mind, the wild notion that it would be found to contain letters, from or to Helena, incriminating evidence of some sort. It wasn't a notion he had time to develop or examine before he lifted the cover and saw the bits of dull metal which the box contained. The effect on his mind was that of a collision. For a moment it simply stopped.

Hugh had not sat down again; had gone back to the desk and was busy reloading his pipe. "It's a phase of lead, that stuff in there," he said, "with a completely different set of characteristics. It's as plastic as lead, but immensely harder. It's the ideal bearing-metal, I think. The tests I've made indicate that. I've been working at it for two years—on the track of it. Six months ago I was getting it half the times I tried. Now I can get it everytime. I know how it's done. It's only in this past week I've really made sure of it. But I am sure now."

Something automatic in Gregory's mind turned up the observation, "I suppose if you could make it in quantities, and cheap. . . How much does it cost a pound to produce it?"

"I haven't an idea," said Hugh, taken aback by this, to him, novel aspect of his discovery. "I suppose that what I've got in that box has cost me as much as so much gold would have."

Gregory's mind was coming to life. "And that's what you've been doing this last week, shut up in here so that no one could get a word through to you! Playing with that stuff! Man, don't you know what's been happening in your own house! Don't you know that your wife's got a lover. That he's been living there with her all the week."

Hugh's pipe dropped to the floor. Slowly his face went white. He sat back limply against the edge of the desk.

"Are you sure of that?" he asked. "Are you sure that's true?"

"Yes, I'm sure," Gregory said more gently. "As sure as it's ever possible to be in such a case. I'm sorry I spoke like that. I thought you knew. I thought that was what you wanted to talk to me about. I've just come from there, you see. From your house. I've seen him. He thought I was you. Thought I was the husband he'd dishonored. And he stood there looking at me like a rat in a corner, thinking I meant to kill him, I suppose. I'd have done it gladly enough, only. . ."

Hugh picked up his pipe, and, with shaking hands, lighted it. Then slowly went round to the swivel chair that stood before his desk, and sat down. After a minute he struck another match and held it to the bowl of his pipe, but did not draw upon it. And he did not say a word.

Silence was not endurable and Gregory began to talk. He told, in somewhat fuller details than I have reported, the story that Eileen had told him, his manner as dry and matter-of-fact as he could make it. All Hugh needed, he felt, was time and the reaction of anger would come. A glow of determination in place of this white passive bewilderment.

But the glow did not come.

"The man told me he was an old friend of hers," Gregory observed presently. "He pretended to think that she had told me all about him. Told you, that is. He thought I was you. He said his name was Gilrain." Then, "Have you ever heard of him?"

"Not his name," said Hugh. "But it's quite true that she did telephone to me, last Saturday, that she expected some one for a visit. She asked if I was coming home for dinner. I was just getting this new set of experiments laid out, and I forgot all about it."

"By God!" said Gregory under his breath. Then:

"Look here, Hugh! You've got to do something about this. If I can help, tell me what you want me to do. That's what I came out here for."

"I know," said Hugh laboriously, "and I'm much obliged. But you can't—help. I've got to think the thing out."

"Let me help with that."

"I can't. There's more to it than you know, or than I could explain. I'm getting my bearings now. It's coming clear what I have to do. I'll be all right. You go along home. I'll get on better by myself."

Gregory came over and sat on the end of the desk close beside him.

"Hugh," he said, "you aren't playing with the idea of letting her get away with it, are you?—The rotten idea that she's entitled to that if she wants it? That's well enough for these free-love swine that we read about. This is your wife—Mrs. Hugh Corbett! That's the name she's dragging in the dirt."

He paused there, waiting. Then, in a sudden blaze of passion.

"Damn you, Hugh! You had a right to pick her out of the gutter. But you've no right, now you've married her, to let her go back there."

Another silence. Then:

"All right. I'll go."

"You're all wrong," said Hugh, "but you've a way of coming out right, at the end. Wait a minute and I'll go along with you, if you're walking."

"Where?" Gregory asked.

"Home!" said Hugh.

XXX

The table linen under Gilrain's hands had the cool sheen of satin. The glass whose stem his thick fingers handled gingerly in the fear of breaking was full of the best champagne he had ever tasted. Wonderful food was before him.

Helena, across the table there, was incomparably the most beautiful woman he had ever seen, and more beautiful tonight than she had looked to him before. He had never seen her dressed like this before. Tonight she come down as if for a ball or a great dinner. Her sleeveless gown, cut very low, was of a curious shade of blue, dark yet bright, vivid yet variable. Even his untaught eyes discerned a harmony in which it took a part with the jade earrings she wore, and the jade pendant that hung in the cleft of her bosom, and her hair, and the dusky olive color of her skin, which darkened into mysterious shadows in the candlelight.

She was his, that woman. His mistress. Utterly his, and had been ever since that first night when she had brought him home with her. One of the easiest of his conquests. The incredible augury that had been in her smile after she had broken away from his hands and struck him, that night in the little room over the drug store—a week ago tonight, that was—had come to pass. It seemed that she had meant from the very first that it should. Her attitude now, as she lounged over the table, her bare arms stretched toward him, her clasped hands within easy reach of his, her shoulders contracted so that the silken line of her gown sagged even more than it was meant to do, was an insolent proclamation of their intimacy—a provocation to a renewal of it.

He had dreamed stories like that; but this thing had happened! To him! And yet the only real comfort he had, in this moment, the only wholly pleasurable sensation, was the pressure against his thigh of that little revolver of his.

They had sat down to dinner as soon as Gregory Corbett left the house. She had given him no chance even to suggest anything else; a mere direction to one of her servants had compelled him to follow her out without an audible protest. All through the dinner, too, the servants had constantly been about; hardly out of the room, so that he'd had no chance to talk with her. It hadn't happened like that before. It hadn't *happened* tonight. She had managed it—without appearing to. By some mysterious social resource that he didn't understand. His hurry had effected nothing. She had gone through the dinner with all the lazy deliberation of complete security. And that enormous brother-in-law of hers had gone off, the better part of an hour ago, now, to tell her husband what he so plainly suspected! What was her game? What the hell was her game!

Now, though, with the dessert and the coffee, the servants were finally dismissed. Now they could talk.

"You didn't make much of a dinner," she observed. "And your last night, too; when I had tried so hard to make it nice. I'm afraid Gregory spoiled your appetite." There was mockery but no real malice in her tone. A sort of lazy amusement, if such an emotion were credible in the circumstances.

"I've never seen the man yet that I was afraid of. I wasn't afraid of him. But *you* were—that was plain enough—when you saw him there."

"It took my breath, for a minute," she admitted. "I'd forgotten they were so big."

"They!"

"Gregory and Hugh. They're about of a size. If anything, Hugh's the strongest, they say. Oh, he could wring your neck as easily as he could mine, if it came to that."

It was with an uncontrollable jerk that he thrust back his chair and slid forward to the edge of it.

She laughed, outright; a hard laugh with the edge of a sneer in it. "But he won't," she added. "That's what he never does. He—thinks, instead."

He made an effort—not very successful—to drop back into an easier attitude, but her strange eyes no longer mocked him. They had darkened into a sober reverie.

Here was his chance—the chance he had awaited so impatiently—to talk with her. And it was high time. Every moment put him in deeper jeopardy. He knew what he ought to say; what he ought to do.

He ought to ask her for the money. His money. Bertsch's money. He ought to take it and go, without wasting another minute. And thank his stars if he was not too late. But this was not what he wanted to do. He had another idea—a bigger idea. One that would provide for this adventure of his an ending as strange as its beginning had been. Was it sheer rank madness—or the only sensible thing a man in his position could do? The only way that could be determined would be by putting it to the proof. The moment for putting it to the proof was now.

Well, then—but his throat was dry. He swallowed, and reached out for the glass of champagne. She spoke, and he started at her voice; pulled back his hand from the glass.

"I drew the money this afternoon," she said.

"What money? I mean—how much?"

She looked at him curiously. "Why, the three thousand dollars, of course. Thirty-two hundred, rather; to avoid the even amount I'd put in. You can have it, if you like, that extra two." She smiled. "My husband's contribution to the cause."

"They didn't make any trouble about it at the bank?" he asked. "Didn't act as if they suspected anything?"

She frowned. "Don't be a fool," she admonished him sharply. "What should they suspect?"

There it was! Another manifestation of that astounding fact; a fact he could not—even now—quite bring his mind to accept.

A clock—somewhere—struck the half-hour, and his muscles drew taut again.

"Have you got it here?" he asked.

"In the house, yes. Naturally, I haven't it—on me." With a smile and a gesture she indicated the scantiness of her corsage. "There wouldn't be space for it," she said; and added, "It's up in my room. We'll go and get it presently. Or now, if you're in a hurry."

"*You'll* get it now. And you'll bring it down here." He tried hard to get the confident ring of a command into his voice, but could not feel that he had succeeded. And his eyes, which had met hers boldly enough at first, had to shift away as those black brows of hers flattened down.

"You're afraid," she said. "You're still afraid. You're afraid Hugh will come back and find you here. Like a scene in a society play. Haven't I told you he won't come! Nor do anything if he does!" Then the note of angry impatience left her voice, but it took on a darker intensity as she went on. Her eyes found his and held them.

"Tell me if it is not true that I have kept my promises, so far. Every one of them. And more. If I have not—as you say—made good. I've done all, haven't I, that you wanted me to. More than you dreamed I would or could. Everything has been as I said it would be. Well, and now I say you are still safe here. Even though my husband knows—or guesses—everything. Unless you are a coward, you will trust me now. This is our last evening together. You are going away and never coming back. This will be our good-by. Come."

Without a look at him she rose and led the way, and without a word he followed.

Frank Gilrain (this was only one of the many names he went by, but it serves our purpose well enough) had been living by his wits for thirty years. He was a roving adventurer; had made as many strange voyages as Sinbad; knew, like the palm of his hand, many strange corners of the world. His operations were never very bold nor imaginative. He was a rascal of the merchant or broker type—a go-between—a tipster—a hanger-on in the fringes of things; a snatcher of minor strategic advantages. The rewards he got were what would have been called commissions, had the enterprises he was engaged in been reputable. All were fish that came to his net. He had held a few minor political jobs—one of these in the superintendent's office of the prison where Anton Galicz had served out his sentence. And his graft here had been the extortion of money from the families and friends of prisoners, on the strength of his pretended ability to secure concessions and privileges for them, and even a reduction of their terms. He had had a job in one of the bureaus of the Philippine government, and had done a little business in the way of selling concessions, which he could not deliver, to dupes who would be afraid to complain. He had knocked about in the Central American countries—a filibuster in a small way—a dealer in revolutions.

He had undeniable gifts; an extraordinary memory for persons, and a very quick perception of the possibilities latent in the positions they occupied, the strategic advantages that might be derived from them. He had a remarkable capacity for digesting gossip, trade talk, technical terms of all sorts. Give him a week's visit on a coffee plantation, and he could pass himself off as a coffee planter; a sea-voyage with a mining engineer, and three years later, if it served his need, he could talk like one. An amorous adventure of his had once taken him into an anarchist free-love colony, and the catch phrases of radicalism—the idiom of it, had been like his mother-tongue—one of his numerous mother-tongues—ever since. Whatever he pretended to be, he could always create the impression of being an insider; of possessing sources of confidential information. Indeed, he managed to believe, somehow, that he *was* an insider; that he really did know.

His courage was good enough—it had never really failed him—and he believed it impregnable. He had, as a matter of fact, a very high appreciation of his own gifts. And, in the light of them, had often wondered why the big thing he was always looking for, never came his way.

It never did. A few hundred dollars always seemed to be his limit. The thousand he was to have from Bertsch for this job, would be a high-water mark for him. He was always broke, that was the trouble; always in a position where he would have to take whatever the bigger men were willing to pay.

His experience of the past week had disconcerted him profoundly—stripped him of his old assurance. Nothing that had happened to him, since the night Helena had come to his room over the drug store, squared with anything in his previous experience. He had got into a topsy-turvy world—a wonder-land—a page out of the *Arabian Nights*, where effects he had always regarded as inevitable, didn't follow causes. Helena's proposal to take him home with her, openly, and keep him there; her casual assurance that he would not have to be accounted for, except as an old friend, to her husband—that was astounding enough to begin with. But it was nothing to the revelation that followed, when she outlined her project for getting Bertsch's money into his hands by a route which the sharpest-eyed watcher of the broker's affairs, never would suspect.

"We'll have him make out a check for the full amount—three thousand dollars, isn't it?—to my husband—to Hugh Corbett, and mail it to me here at the house. No one would look twice at a check like that. Any one would take for granted that it was a perfectly regular business transaction. Well, the check will come here to the house, and I'll take it to the bank and deposit it to my husband's account. And then I'll draw the amount in currency in any denominations you like, and bring it home to you. I don't see how that can go wrong."

The proposal sounded stark mad to Gilrain. It turned him giddy. Was she proposing to forge her husband's name to a check? And even if she did, wouldn't the whole transaction lie bare before his eyes?

"He'll never look," she said. "And I've the same right to draw against the account that he has. It's a joint account. My signature's just as good as his."

She had to go back and explain in detail, before she could get it into his head at all. Hugh's dividend checks came in quarterly. They were very big. His income was well over a hundred and fifty thousand dollars a year. He took what he wanted for his laboratory, she what she wanted for the household. When the accumulation in the bank got too unreasonably big, she called his attention to the fact—when she could get it—and they decided what should be done with it in the way of charities, investments and so on. It was she who made the dispositions they had decided upon. In was she who kept all accounts, did all the banking, got statements and went over the checks. She rather enjoyed that sort of work and he hated it. Not because he was a fool about finance. He understood it well enough, but he had more interesting things to think about. Incidentally, she was an excellent bookkeeper.

The explanation did not lighten Gilrain's bewilderment; deepened it, on the contrary, tenfold. Ali Baba, having pronounced his "open sesame," could not have stared more aghast at the treasures in the unguarded cave.

"See for yourself," she had said, with a laugh, and tossed him her check-book.

There it was in black and white. She had not been raving. And there she was!—A woman in that amazing position, with those amazing opportunities—the most beautiful woman he had ever seen, and in love with him! Utterly infatuated with him, she must be, to run even a momentary risk of losing a position like that, for him. A risk! You couldn't call it a risk! She was absolutely courting destruction, just as she had courted him.

Because that had been the way of it. It had not been on his part a pursuit and a capture. Not even his vanity could interpret the thing that way. The strangeness of the situation, his anomalous position in the household, the unfamiliar manners of this new social stratum he had got into, had intimidated him—held him back. The initiative had been hers. She had come more than half-way to meet him.

Well, then, wasn't it simple enough? Obviously she was mad about him. Wasn't it reasonable to suppose that, having already ruined herself for him, (She'd certainly done that. Think what the servants had seen; of the stories they'd have to tell to that blind fool of a husband when he came home!) wasn't it reasonable to suppose that she'd come the rest of the way at his whistle?—Run off with him and bring along, in cash, the money represented by those figures that still danced before his eyes—a substantial part of it anyhow, say a hundred thousand dollars? It would not be a theft. In the eyes of the law she could take that as easily as her husband. And with as little question. What a life he could have in a security like that! With a hundred thousand dollars in his pocket, he could tell anybody to go to hell, even the husband. There was the great idea.

Well, why didn't he carry it out? What was he afraid of? He did not know. The fear eluded formulation. But it was there. When he brought himself to the point of making that proposal to Helena, somehow his throat went dry and his hands shook—a sort of panic took possession of him. Was she really in love with him? It seemed absurd to doubt it. She'd certainly given proofs enough. Yet it was a doubt that never left off tormenting him. A misgiving that always rankled. Not even the utmost ardors of passion could drive it away. What was her game! That was the form it took. There was something behind it all—something that the strange look in her eyes, the twitch to her smile, the intonations of her voice, perpetually betrayed, but did not reveal. She was steering her own course. It was not he who had prevailed over her. He had not for one moment prevailed over her. Never once deflected the course. She was doing—had done from the very first—exactly what she had meant to do. And it was something, somehow, that had no reference to him. He was a dummy—a symbol—a servitor of her purpose.

There, formulated, is the misgiving which he, for himself, was unable to analyze; which reiterated itself with maddening monotony in the question, what was her game?

He had followed her to her room, that pretty up-stairs sitting-room of hers, with its gay chintzes, its soft pale rugs, and that long chair where she loved to stretch herself like a great lazy cat. She waited by the door and closed it after him. He turned an uneasy glance of protest toward it, and she laughed.

"Oh, I'm going to let you go," she said. "Only you've plenty of time. You weren't to meet your people till nine, you told me."

"Where's the money? Is it safe where you left it?"

She lay back luxuriously in her chair. "It's over in the top drawer of that chiffonier."

He could not interpret her nod in the direction of it as permission to go and look, and turned back, with a troubled helplessness, to her. Her look changed.

"I won't tease you any more," she said. "You shall take it if you want it, and go. Only I hoped I could make you forget it for a little while. A last little while. I didn't want you in such a hurry to end it all."

The moment was now. It could not be postponed again. The realization gripped him like a vise. He clenched his hands and steadied himself with a long breath.

"I don't want it ever to end," he said.

"Yes, but of course it must.—Mustn't it?"

"Not if you'd come with me," he said.

"Run off with you!" she cried incredulously. "Now! Tonight!"

"Tonight," he said, "or tomorrow morning. You could—join me somewhere tomorrow."

So far so good. The heavens hadn't fallen yet. That mysterious look was still in her face, but it was kinder, somehow—softer. He forced himself, clumsily, to begin making love to her. The old endearments—the old caresses; half heartedly, though, because of the fear. Neither did she respond to them as she had been wont to do; was curiously passive—reticent. It might have been the beginning of a love affair instead of the end of one.

"If it's no go," he broke out at last, "say so! Don't play cat and mouse with me!"

"I'm not," she said. "I'm thinking about it seriously. I think perhaps I'll go with you. Only I'm taken by surprise. I never dreamed of your proposing that. I must have a little time to think."

Once more he essayed the conventional lover's attitude—his pleas and protestations; what comrades they would be—what a wonderful life they would have together. He dropped down beside her and would have fondled her, but she turned from him impatiently.

"Don't try to come close now," she said. "Go away. Over there, and let me think."

After a little silence, she began to talk. Thinking aloud it was, rather—an attempt to visualize the sort of life it would be; the experiences that such a pair of adventurers would have to look forward to. That was the note of it. Adventure—daring! Sherwood Forest, not Arcady. A warfare upon the upholstered people of the world—the fat—the complacent—the secure—the respectable; like these Corbetts she had come to hate.

She had reverted to a former Helena—the stormy petrel—the adventurer. No longer on a high horse, though. A week ago she had looked upon life as an *impasse*. But was there a little door of escape after all? She had thought to pull down the pillars of her temple like Sampson among the Philistines. She had pulled them down. But was she alive after all? Could she become a new Helena once more, with a new life in front of her? Her courage had not faltered before pulling down the pillars. But was it equal to facing the road—a crooked narrow little road like that? A life of flying by night and living as one could, in company with this rather likable impostor, who, strangely enough, had fallen in love with her—wanted her?

She had been thinking aloud, as I have said. But Gilrain, over by the window, had not heard half of it, nor understood half that he had heard. He did understand, however, that she was hesitating—reluctant—doubtful of her own fortitude. And he thought, naturally enough, that he understood why. Hardship—poverty. She didn't realize her opportunities. Time was slipping away. That husband of hers might, any moment now, be slipping his latch-key into the street door. Still, unaccountably, the words stuck in his throat. But he got them out; not looking at her, though. He stayed at the window, his gaze ranging over the snowy moonlit roofs.

"We wouldn't have to be poor," he said. "Nor shady. We could be respectable. Don't you see? You could take the money—as much of it as you wanted to. All of it. They couldn't touch you for that. It's yours by law, as much as it is his. He'd get a divorce, I suppose, and then we could—m—marry, if you wanted to. And I'd be on the level with you. We could be real people."

He had felt from the beginning that he was talking into a vacuum. No sound came from her at all. She hadn't moved, he knew, from that long chair of hers. But he felt, with mounting panic, a sense of something behind him, gathering itself up for a spring. His words died away to a mumble and presently ceased of sheer inanition. But he did not turn until he heard her spring from the chair. Then he whipped round and his hand involuntarily sought the pocket of his coat. But it dropped at his side as the other one did. He turned white and leaned back against the high window-sill for support.

The face of the woman who confronted him was literally terrible. Her mouth wore a sort of smile.

"You dog!" she said. And again, after a moment, in a whisper, "You dog!"

His glance wavered away from hers and sought the chiffonier where she had said the money was. He must have that. Bertsch would hound him to death if he didn't get that. What a fool he had been. He'd known it would turn out like this. Known it all the while. There was a lump in his throat as if he were going to cry. What right had she to be in a rage like that? What had he done anyhow?

She had followed the direction of his look toward the chiffonier, and like a flash, was there before him, and faced him from there with her back to it.

He had followed her a step or two, but stopped when she turned. He was going to fling her out of the way and take that money and go. Of course that was what he was going to do. He was strong enough, wasn't he, to thrust a woman out of the way when she stood between him and something he wanted? He would be as soon as he could get over this trembling fit.

She said: "I'm going to tell you something. I hate my husband because I'm in love with him. Because I never could make him hate me. You can't understand that. But you're going to listen until I'm done. He never would beat me when I deserved to be beaten. Nothing I did to him made him even take hold of me to hurt. He would just stand and think. And then go away, looking as if I were something he didn't want to—touch.

"We quarreled a week ago, and I played my last card; said the last thing to him that a man could endure to have said. And he looked at me and went away.

"Why do you suppose I picked you up and brought you here? Why, because I wanted to use you—to do the thing I couldn't do alone—to make a final smash of it that he couldn't ignore; that that precious family of his wouldn't let him ignore. I had nothing against you. I half liked you. That wasn't why I made love to you. It was because having a lover was striking a blow at him. I wanted to see how he'd look when I'd told him what I'd done.

"But when you asked me to go with you, I thought I would. It amused me that you should have fallen in love with me. That you should ask me, the way you did, to go away from all this and share your life with you. Your shifting, mean little life.

"But I wasn't what you wanted. You wanted his money. That's what you've been making those eyes about from the first. And you didn't even want me to steal it with you honestly. You talked about the law to me! Talked about being safe and respectable. I didn't suppose that anything as base as you crawled on the earth."

"Come now," he said, "where is that money?"

She turned, snatched open the drawer and rummaged in it with both hands. It was full of soft lacy things. But his ear told him that there was something hard in there and heavy, and as her hand encountered it, the exploring movement was suddenly arrested and she stood most tensely still.

"You're no fitter to live than I am myself," she said.

His eye caught a gleam of polished metal. So that was what she had there! That was what she meant to do, damn her!

It was with one convulsive movement that he snatched the little revolver from his side pocket and fired it.

Then, frozen, breathless, he watched her fall. It was incredible how slowly it happened; how long it took. His eyes were on one of her hands that clutched weakly at the corner of the chiffonier. It slipped and clutched again, and at last relaxed.

He gave a sob of relief when she lay still.

He put the little revolver back in his pocket, drew in another long breath, went forward, skirting where she lay, and reached into that top drawer.

The money was there—a bundle of it. He thrust it into his breast pocket. His hand explored the drawer again. The revolver was there, too. He took it out and looked at it stupidly, as if he did not know what to do with it. Then he stooped, laid it on the floor near her hand, and tiptoed out of the room.

On the floor below he turned into the room that had been his, took up his bag and went on down-stairs with it. In the hall he put on his overcoat and hat. Then he went out. He had met no one.

XXXI

There was an incredible lot of blood. The pale silken rug on which she had fallen was sodden with it—a dark purple—and a sharply outlined continent of it lay map-wise on the floor. But that, the beginning of the horror, was also the end of it, for there was, about the attitude of the body, nothing of that convulsive distortion in which violent death so often grotesquely masks itself. It was still Helena lying there, dead and marble white, but as she had familiarly lain in life, utterly relaxed; utterly—somehow—satisfied. The eyelids had drooped shut. The colorless lips were parted.

Wondering—awed beyond the possibility of feeling any other emotion—Hugh softly crossed the room and knelt beside her and pressed his hand upon her breast where now the heart was still, to make his first acquaintance with Death. What a superb—finality there was about it! What a guarantee of good faith it gave! The only ultimate guarantee.

The natural emotions, grief, pity, self-reproach, eluded him altogether as he knelt there gazing at her. They—or the positive negations of them—would come in time to him, to harass or sustain. There would come, too, in the near approaching hours, a review of the strange stormy life they had led together; the attempt at a solution of its moral enigmas—the search for a clew to the meaning of it all. All he could feel now was a curious futility—a sense of having been outdone—left behind. There was something strangely triumphant about this last still relaxation of hers. He could read the sighing, contented, "It is finished!" upon her parted lips.

"We should only destroy each other, you and I." She had said that to him years ago, up there in Alice Hayes' flat, the day of his first visit. He had been talking confidently, like the sophomore he was, about the possibilities of their "friendship." She had seen clearly enough then. Had she ever been blind? Or, open-eyed, had she challenged the destruction she saw? Challenge! That had always been the note of her. And now, in the acceptance of this last challenge of hers, she had found—peace.

The last time he had seen her—a week ago—here in this very room—he had hated her; had wanted to kill her for the abominations she had uttered about Jean. That was what she had invited him to do—challenged him to do. And he had looked at her and gone away, hating her. But it was a futile hatred. He had not said a word; had not lifted a hand. A hatred she could smile at now. He glanced at her lips again to see if the smile was there.

The hatred was gone—the loathing—the horror of her, that he had brought with him tonight fairly to the threshold of this room.

There had been, indeed, a strong access of it in the last few minutes before he turned into his house. It had been sharpened to an edge. A face had thrust itself into his preoccupation just as he and Greg, walking back from the laboratory, were approaching the point where their ways would naturally have parted.

He had been a thousand fathoms deep, of course; had hardly spoken to Gregory in the whole mile they had just walked together. Indeed, had hardly been conscious he was there. But this face, the face of a man walking toward them, close to the building line, but coming just here into the luminous zone of a drug-store window, became suddenly and sharply visible to him—a pale face, dabbled, shiny with sweat. He had gripped Gregory's arm and commanded him to look. He had felt his brother's muscles turn to steel under his fingers, but Gregory had not spoken until after the man, walking straight along—not noticeably fast, doggedly and with rigid eyes, like a somnambulist—had passed. Then he had said what Hugh, somehow, had already guessed.

"That's Gilrain! That's the man!"

They had paused and looked back after him. And then, Gregory's eyes having asked a question which Hugh's sharp shake of the head had answered, they had walked on together.

Unidentified, the look of the man would have been repulsive. An abject surrender to panic is always that. But as Helena's lover—the creature her hands had caressed, her lips had kissed—the rat-like thing, huddling along in the shadows, dropped below the level of human accountability and vengeance altogether! Became the mere symbol of the loathing Hugh felt for his wife.

Gregory's, "Something's happened—for him to look like that! I'm going home with you!" was accepted by his logical faculties as reasonable enough, and he fell in with the quickened pace that Gregory took.

Indeed, this premonition mounted in a swift gradient to certitude as they entered the silent but brightly lighted house, looked into the dining-room where all was just as the two who had dined there had left it; the coffee-cups, the half-emptied glasses, the little silver ash-tray with the extinguished ends of two or three of Helena's cigarettes on it. Where were the servants who should have come in to clear away?

No, the tragedy, as such, had not been a surprise to Hugh, when from the threshold, he had looked in upon it. The bewildering thing had been the sudden recession of all the horror and disgust he had brought to that doorway with him. The tranquillity of a last supreme satisfaction was as legible in the white body he knelt above, as a seal set in hardening wax.

It came upon him, a haunting surmise with all the force of a demonstrated conviction, that the man Gregory had called her lover—the loathsome rat they had seen out there in the street—had no real significance in the affair; had been a merely casual instrument—the first that came to hand—in the accomplishment of her now completed purpose. Completed, no doubt of that! She had finished her course. She had kept. . . Some sort of faith, obscure to him, she must have kept, or the transubstantiation of death would not have left her beautiful, like this.

The surmise glanced forward again, lifted another horizon. This course of hers, this seeming devious course, and this obscure faith, had they a reference—some sort of constant reference—to himself? Was he the object of her perpetual challenge? Was it to him that she had been trying, vainly till now, to bring something home? And was it the belief that she had, at last, succeeded that had left that look of ineffable contentment on her parted lips?

He must solve the riddle, somehow. But not now. There must be things to do. A hundred things. Gregory must be somewhere. He rose and went to the door and called him; voicelessly at first, but again in a voice that sounded naturally enough.

Even Gregory, looking thoughtfully down upon her, gave her the grace of a long moment of silence, and it was with an evident effort that he roused himself, laid a consolatory grip on Hugh's shoulder and—took charge.

"There's no doubt but it's all over, is there?" His voice had the brusk deep tone one hears in crises. "She's quite dead?"

Hugh's "Yes," was a little startled. It had not occurred to him to doubt it. He added, "Yes, I'm sure."

"The doctor's the first thing, anyhow, I guess. Shall I try to get Darby?" Darby was one of Chicago's most eminent surgeons, but the Corbetts, antedating his fame, were among the few barnacles of a general practise that he had never scraped off.

Formalities, however necessary, were not in the focus of Hugh's mind at all. He assented indifferently to Darby. Gregory, however, did not move toward the telephone—stayed where he was, looking thoughtfully down at Helena.

"I'm glad it happened—this way," he said, indicating the revolver which lay beside her hand. "This way rather than the other. I mean, that she shot herself instead of. . ."

He broke off and looked closer; stooped down, stared, took up the revolver and scrutinized it. Then he put it back, accurately, where it had been.

"She didn't do it herself," he said in a changed voice. "She was shot—murdered. By Gilrain."

Hugh considered this in silence for a moment. Then gravely he said, "That doesn't change anything, really. It comes to just the same thing."

In the context of his own thoughts this comment was clear enough. Death was still, he meant to say, the completest expression of the thing she had sought; still represented, somehow, a triumphant accomplishment—self-inflicted or not. The murderer's bullet had been challenged—welcome.

But to Gregory—naturally enough—this was lunacy.

"Old man!" he expostulated patiently. "Try to think what it means. It means that the whole rotten story will have to come out. Every rag of it. It won't take two minutes for them to see that it isn't an ordinary burglary murder. They'll question the servants. Where are all the servants, anyhow? And they'll question us. And they'll have enough to go on, God knows, right there. The whole pack will be loose—detectives, reporters, photographers, sob-writers. They won't miss one dirty rag of it. If Gilrain's caught, there'll be a trial. If he isn't, there'll be a hunt for him. I don't know which will be worse. That's the difference it makes. Unless. . ."

"That mustn't happen," Hugh said. "That can't be allowed to happen. The thing wasn't the way it looks to you. There was something in it you don't understand. I don't myself, clearly. But she doesn't deserve to be dragged through the mud, and she shan't be! I'll protect her from that, anyhow."

Gregory nodded and gripped his brother's shoulder once more. And this time with a much more genuine feeling.

"It will want thinking out," he said, and then walked irresolutely over toward the telephone. "We can't have Darby, that's the first thing. We'll need a crook—a man we can buy. And we'll need the same kind of a trained nurse. And an undertaker and his assistant. There are four we'll have to buy, body and soul. And the servants, here in the house. All but Martha. She'd stand by, from loyalty to the family, I think. That chauffeur of yours. He'll have seen more or less, too. We've got to get them all. Because there can't be even a whisper."

Hugh had dropped into a chair. His face was whitening, his eyes looked sick, as the foul tide rose higher around him. But he nodded a dazed assent.

There was a moment of silence. Then, abruptly, Gregory turned away from the telephone and faced him.

"Hugh, it *can't* be done! It's impossible! Because of what they'll think. What every one of them will think, the minute the proposition is put up to them. They'll think you killed her yourself. They're bound to. And that means that, somehow, it would all come out, including our attempt to shut it up. And when it did, you'd be done for—don't you see? Because then it would be too late for us to tell the truth. My word wouldn't be any better than yours."

That, curiously, brought Hugh out of his daze. He rose deliberately from his chair, walked over to the window and for a little while, stood staring out over the snowy roofs. Then he came back to Gregory.

"All right," he said, "we'll let it go at that—let it look like that. That's disastrous, but not—filthy. And it's truer, somehow, than the other. It was I that killed her, you might say. She saw it all. It was all in her voice when she telephoned to me out at the laboratory last Saturday. Oh, I'm not raving! Or at least, not much. There's a sort of truth in it. Anyhow, Gilrain doesn't figure—except by chance. She'd have found somebody."

Up to that point he had spoken quite collectedly. But at Gregory's incredulous stare, he went to pieces.

"Oh, you don't have to understand it!" he cried frantically. "I won't have the other thing, that's all you need to know! I won't have it! I'll take it on myself."

"You won't," said Gregory. "It may suit you to get yourself hanged for murder, but don't your father and mother, and your brothers and sisters count for anything? Yourself! Good God, Hugh, isn't there anybody but yourself in the world?"

Hugh's face was that of a man in a nightmare. He had added one more name to Gregory's catalogue. He turned back unsteadily to his chair.

"You're quite right," he said. "I can't protect her that way. I'm—a little out of my head, I guess, in addition to being a fool. You'll have to take charge. I'll do as you say." Then:

"We don't have to leave her lying there, do we? Can't I take her and put her in on her bed?"

Gregory nodded, and refrained from offering to help. It wasn't necessary of course. He waited until Hugh had carried his burden into the adjoining room before, at the telephone, he went to work.

XXXII

A mere foot-note is all that remains to be made upon this tragic conclusion of Helena Corbett's stormy life adventure. An ironic sort of foot-note it happens to be. For one of the consequences of that last week of hers, of the pulling down of the pillars of her temple, conspicuously—maliciously, I might almost say—falsified her expectations. The Corbett family, those upholstered complacent Corbetts, put in the pillory for once, wincing at sneers to which no answers could be made, trying with a sort of ludicrous futility to wipe off the stain of an indelible disgrace; that expectation, which must have been in the back of her mind from the beginning to the end of her episode with Gilrain, was never realized.

There was indeed the space of an hour or two when they confronted it. Constance and Frank Crawford, that is to say, and shrewd old Doctor Darby, a Mr. Worldly-Wise Man, if ever one there was, and Rodney Aldrich, all summoned in the first five minutes Greg worked at the telephone. Five unusually acute intelligences, these were; but it was, after all, due to no resourcefulness of theirs that the almost unendurable course of events they foresaw was evaded. It was partly plain good luck, and partly a shrewd guess by a member of that tribe whose activities they dreaded the worst, a reporter.

The good luck was this: when Gregory, summoning all the resolution he possessed, informed the police at the Chicago Avenue Station that his brother's wife had been found murdered in her boudoir, and that the family had reason to suspect that a man calling himself Frank Gilrain was the murderer, he was cut short in the middle of his statement as to how the man looked, and where he had last been seen, by the amazing information that Gilrain was then already locked in a cell, booked under the charge of carrying concealed weapons; and that a search had revealed the fact that he had on his person a sum of thirty-two hundred dollars, in bills of large denomination.

The theory of robbery was too easy and obvious for the police not to jump at. Greg and Rodney knew, of course, that this theory could not hold water for more than an hour or two; but it did give them time to breathe, and Gregory managed a non-committal answer to the question whether or not that sum of money had been taken from Hugh's house, promised an immediate investigation, and hung up.

"I never kept any money about," Hugh said, when they questioned him, "but I don't know about Helena. She does all the banking and bookkeeping. She is very good at that—was, I mean. You will find everything in good order, I imagine, right in her desk there."

With this permission it didn't take them a minute to find the counter-foil of the check, the last she ever drew, for thirty-two hundred dollars, made out to currency. It crossed their minds at once that she had drawn it for Gilrain, and the question under what influence, what compulsion, she had done it asked itself instantly. But when Hugh got the drift of their thoughts, he discouraged the notion that they had found the clew.

"Blackmail?" he said, with a smile. "You will draw blank in that cover. She never would have tried to buy silence from anybody."

He added quietly to Constance, "There are a lot of things she wasn't that she might have been; things that plenty of us are."

He proved to be right about that. The search they made through her letters and papers revealed no hint that she had felt herself in anybody's power, let alone in Gilrain's. They were still completely at a loss, therefore, when Rodney and Greg went down into the drawing-room about ten o'clock to receive the reporters.

They were much too wise, of course, to attempt to take the line that this was a private matter, none of the public's business. Greg told, with an admirable appearance of complete candor, the story of his return to the house with Hugh from the laboratory where they had been discussing a matter of important business. He told how they found the body; made a note on the absence of the servants, and the servants' explanation of how it came about. He described the loaded but undischarged revolver, which lay by Helena's hand, and admitted that the nature of the wound precluded the theory of suicide. When he got to the end of the story, he answered their questions about the facts freely.

But when the questioners asked for theories, speculations, he turned them over to Rodney, and Rodney, while he made no bones of admitting that they had a theory which accounted for the crime, was adamant when it came to revealing it. Publication at this stage would be fatally premature, and the issue was so grave that he didn't even feel justified in taking them into his confidence, though he knew how high a standard the newspapers, in the main, lived up to in the matter of respecting such confidence.

This was pure bluff. He and Frank and Gregory were casting about desperately for a theory other than the amorous one which was staring them in the face. But the admission that they had no theory would have fired the imagination of every one of those reporters, and by one o'clock, when the papers went to press, there would have been half a dozen which their respective authors would have been ready to fight for to the last gasp.

One of the group, who went away with a good grace enough when Rodney dismissed them, was a man both he and Gregory had encountered professionally before. In the presence of the others he had made no parade of this fact, had kept in the background, rather, and asked only a few perfunctory questions. But half an hour after the others had gone, he came back, and asked for a private interview. He was the sort of reporter, in these days of cooperative press bureaus and rewrite men, oftener encountered in fiction than in fact—a veteran of the old tradition.

"I haven't come to ask for anything to publish," he assured Rodney, who received him. "I have an idea I know what your theory of the crime is. At least, I have one of my own, and I suspect yours squares with it. I am not going to ask you to confirm it, either, unless you like." He paused there for a moment, then deliberately shot his question in. "Has Mr. Hugh Corbett's work in his laboratory lately had anything to do with the war?"

Rodney is still proud and amazed over the feat of self-control he then and there performed, in not embracing that reporter with a gasp of joy. He held his breath for ten seconds, before he trusted himself to speak; but when he did it was in his coldest professional tone. "I can't feel warranted in answering that question without consulting Corbett," he said.

"I'll give you a little more to go on before you do that," the reporter went on. "That is not just a snap guess of mine. I have been working on these German spy cases for months. Their main industry, just now, is blowing up munitions plants, of course, and I have no doubt they have laid some sort of plans for the Corbett works at Riverdale; but it strikes me that there may be an even closer connection through the laboratory. I suppose they think they already know all there is to know about metallurgy. Still they would hardly leave a man as famous in that line as Hugh Corbett without paying him some attention.

"Well, here's where it joins on. They're doing most of their work through the I. W. W., and other radicals and pacifists and, of course, Mrs. Corbett's connections with those circles are well known. It strikes me as natural that they should approach her, and that there might have been some conflict in her mind between what she took to be her duty under her principles and her loyalty to her husband. Or, for that matter, she may simply have been leading them on all the while with the idea of finding out what they meant to do, not realizing perhaps how desperate they were, or what a serious business it was. Well, there's my theory, and you can see for yourself how my question fits into it."

"I think Corbett will be willing to answer your question, but I'll go and ask him," Rodney said, and managed not to burst until he got out of the room. They gave that reporter the answer he wanted, told him that the work Hugh was doing in his laboratory had indeed something to with the war. If they had dared, they would have given him a thousand dollars as an unworthy token of their gratitude. He had shown them the way out—the only possible way out.

They found in Helena's bank-book the deposit of that last three thousand dollars. They asked Hugh about this and found that it was nothing he knew about. Frank Crawford was a director in that bank, so they assigned him the job of discovering where the check came from; and about one o'clock that night a shivering receiving teller, answering the phone in his pajamas, confidently told him. Yes, it was a thing he would be willing to swear to. They had been watching Bertsch's checks for weeks, under instructions to report anything that looked at all suspicious. Hugh's denial that he had ever done any business with Bertsch, on top of this, gave them something more than conjecture to go on.

With that, Rodney went to the state's attorney, next morning at breakfast time, and contrived to convince him—without presenting the situation directly in that light, that there was more *kudos* for him in the political aspect of the crime than in the personal. He took Rodney to his office with him, and sent for Gilrain.

By ten o'clock Gilrain had made a confession—in the main true. Helena, he said, had agreed to rescue him from the presumably treacherous doctor whom Bertsch had consigned him to, to shelter him for a week, and to serve as intermediary between Bertsch and himself, for the transfer of the three thousand dollars necessary to carry out their plans. But at the last moment, he said, she had welshed, and upon his demanding the three thousand dollars which she had brought home that day, had threatened him with a revolver instead. He had shot her, under the belief that she had been upon the point of killing him. He was willing, he said, to tell all he knew about Bertsch and the other members of the conspiracy—he conveyed the impression that he knew an appalling lot—in consideration of leniency being exercised in his behalf. He did not ask complete immunity. Indeed, in his shattered condition, that morning, incarceration—safe incarceration—for the duration of the war, looked better to him than a precarious liberty.

It was Rodney's suggestion that he be permitted to plead guilty to an indictment for manslaughter, and the state's attorney, sighing over the lost opportunities offered by a high society murder trial, finally consented.

Thus it came about that by the day set for the funeral, all danger of the outbreak of the uglier scandal—the really indelible disgrace which had seemed inevitable for an hour or two that Friday night—was definitely passed.

There was, of course, a lot of excitement; there were newspaper head-lines that bruised like blows. There was a high-voltage crackle of speculation. Constance and Eileen were often aware, when they came into a company of their friends, that the current of conversation had been abruptly switched to another circuit. But all this, compared to what might have been, seemed like the result of a heavenly intervention in their favor. Indeed, it was known in the family that Eileen seriously regarded it like that.

Discussion simmered down to two alternatives: one that Helena, in a fanatical devotion to her pacifist and anti-nationalist principles had been prepared to betray the secrets of her husband's laboratory (or to connive at the destruction of the plant at Riverdale) but had experienced at the last moment a change of heart which had cost her her life; the other that she had never meant anything of the sort, but had merely led the plotters on in order to learn—and the better frustrate—their plans.

It was this latter—the sentimental-heroic version—that finally gained almost universal acceptance. An ironic footnote it makes to Helena's stormy life. One hates to imagine her poor ineffectual ghost becoming aware of that gossip—learning how that last week of hers on earth had come to be regarded.

XXXIII

You know the Corbett family well enough by this time, I think, to understand how this unexpected denouement of the tragedy affected them. They would have faced disgrace for Hugh, would have fought for and beside him back to the last ditch. They would have sympathized with him in his misfortunes, in any misfortunes, that is to say, that they could interpret even dimly in that light.

But they were a realistic lot, and they enveloped Helena's death in no romantic or sentimental atmosphere whatever. None of them had ever liked her. The nearest thing to it in the family had been Robert, Senior's, touch of gallant admiration. They regarded it as an unqualified misfortune to Hugh that he had ever seen her, and her taking off, by that same token, as a piece of plain good luck for her husband. What was more, they felt pretty sure that Hugh himself hadn't cared much for her after he was fairly over his first infatuation, and that he had, in words of one syllable, been making the best of a bad job.

Even their heavy-handedness would hardly have gone the length of open congratulation, nor would they have expected him to avow the sentiment which, as a matter of plain common sense, they felt he ought to feel. There were certain minimum decencies even among their outspoken selves, which they expected to maintain. But Hugh's conduct, during the fortnight that followed the funeral, became, as the days went by, an irritating enigma, a thing they observed with what patience they could command, incredulously. This state of mind was most marked in his mother; just as it was least so, or absent altogether, in Constance. Consequently, it was over Constance's head that Mrs. Corbett's slowly accumulated high tensity of exasperation finally burst.

When one considers the facts, it isn't very hard to understand how she felt. Gregory's telegram, containing little more than the bare announcement that Helena had been murdered, had reached her and her husband in San Francisco before they had fairly got the alkali dust from their journey west out of their lungs. Its guarded phraseology made it horribly alarming.

She lived through three absolutely ghastly days on the way back with her husband, and from Cheyenne on, with Bob, who deepened the gloom rather than lightened it by treating their unspeakable surmise with a gloomy certainty. Of course, Hugh had killed his wife. Bob had felt quite sure all along it would only be a question of time before he did.

It was, of course, in the highest degree exasperating—in her relief from three days like that—to find Hugh as gloomy as he might have been expected to be, if everything had turned out as badly as possible, instead of incredibly well. She stayed bottled up for three or four days after the funeral, and then one morning she burst, as I said, all over Constance. It was a morning, too, that Constance had laboriously swept clear for dealing with large arrears in the way of letters.

Mrs. Corbett came in, very warm and rumpled and out of breath, stared with marked disapprobation at the bright little wood fire Connie had been luxuriating in, slammed open a window, muttered "You'd have suffocated in another ten minutes!" as a sort of defiant apology when the early March wind swept a handful of papers off her daughter's desk, and dropped panting in the chintz-covered wing chair.

"Of course, you get warm when you hurry like that," Constance said. "Mother, I'll have to put it down. It's blowing all the smoke out of the chimney. Let me get you a drink of water."

"Gin and water," growled Mrs. Corbett. "Raw gin. That's what I'd like. No, of course, I don't want any. I've been talking to that brother of yours. Another ten minutes, and I'd have tried to shake him. That's what he needs."

There were three of Constance's brothers she might have been talking to that morning, but Constance had no need of asking her which one she meant.

"I should think he had been shaken enough in the last two weeks," she observed, which for a while reduced Mrs. Corbett to inarticulate mutterings.

"I've been trying," she said at last, "to get a little bit of common sense into him. I wanted him to leave that horrible house of his and come back to us, his old room, things as they were. Bob's going to say around for a while, and Anne talks of coming. We'd be a family again, like old times. The best thing in the world for him. Only he wouldn't hear of it.

"It was on my tongue to tell him," she went on finally, "that if he meant to go on like this, I didn't want him to come. I can't bear the sight of a sick cat, and that's what he's acting like. Oh, I didn't say that,"—this was in acknowledgment of Constance's look of horror. "I held my breath instead. I don't like to cry even when there is something to cry about. My nose gets red, and I feel like a fool. I didn't on the train, not a drop, all those three days while I had to watch your father turning old under my eyes, thinking what those idiotic telegrams of Greg's made us think. And then we got home to find that what had really happened was the best piece of luck Hugh's had since the day he first saw the woman! You can't deny that's true, and neither can he. It is all infernal nonsense. But he has got a look about him. . ." The tears came again just at the memory of it. She squeezed them bruskly out of her eyes and surrendered.

"What *is* the matter with him, Connie?" she demanded. "He's like a man hagridden. Is the woman haunting him?" She turned suddenly and stared at her daughter. "I have thought, off and on, that you knew something the rest of us don't. I believe you do. There has been a sort of look about you, too, now I think of it."

Constance was a little disconcerted with the suddenness of this attack; but she quickly pulled herself together.

"I don't think I've got any special look," she protested, turning to her dressing-table mirror, as if for confirmation. "Of course, I've been through it all with him from the beginning. I don't think you would find it so hard to understand how he is taking it, if you'd done that. He was all worn out, of course, when it happened. He hadn't had any regular sleep or meals for a week. He had been working so crazily hard."

"Work!" sniffed his mother. "Work never hurts a Corbett." She turned, once more, a penetrating thoughtful look upon her daughter.

Constance hurried on, "And what I think makes it harder for him is that he knows it's good luck, and he can't be sorry. That would be positively ghastly, I think, to have people sympathizing with you over something you feel like a criminal for being glad about. And not have a soul anywhere that you could tell the truth to."

Mrs. Corbett scouted this theory as fine-spun nonsense. "Why can't he tell the truth to us? We know it already, don't we?"

In the next breath she answered her own question. "No, we don't. That's exactly the point I am getting at."

Another momentary silence, and then before Constance could summon her breath to protest, she pounced. "Tell me exactly what Jean's got to do with this."

At that Constance slumped. "If you know she has got anything to do with it, you must know pretty near as much as I do," she said. She paused there a moment in the hope that her mother would go on to reveal the sources and the extent of her own information. But

Mrs. Corbett merely waited grimly, and with a sigh Constance began the tale.

"I can tell you all I had anything to do with," she said. "I had talked with Jean just that afternoon, after the concert, so I knew a little and guessed a good deal of how things were between them. When Greg telephoned for Frank and me to come right over to Hugh's house because they'd just found Helena there dead, I waited long enough to call up Jean and tell her. I couldn't bear the thought of her seeing the morning papers, unprepared. And, of course, we didn't know then what the papers would say. What they *mightn't* say. As soon as I got a good chance with Hugh I told him I had done it. He seemed relieved then. But by the middle of the next morning, when he hadn't heard anything from her, he was terribly restless—frantic nearly.

"So I offered to go and see her. And I did. Drove straight over about ten o'clock. It was a shock to me to see how she had taken it. I had been with her just the day before, you see, and had been, well, fairly carried off my feet by her courage. She is the bravest little thing, always. And that day there was a perfectly terrifying prospect ahead of her; not knowing what despicable thing Helena might have planned to do. Or might already have done. She never even wavered. She was ready for anything. Ready to see anything through. Ready to go through fire or over hot ploughshares. It simply took my breath. I didn't know whether it was right or wrong; but for the time, I didn't care. It was so splendidly beautiful.

"But that next morning, when I saw her, she had completely gone to pieces. It was just a panic. I couldn't understand it at all then. I don't very clearly now, because, of course, as far as practical results are concerned, Helena's death makes everything come right. But at the time, it seemed just to have annihilated her.

"The thing she seemed most terrified about was that Hugh might come to see her. It seems she had made him promise he would, the night before, over the telephone. He had called her up from the laboratory, just after she left me. She wanted me to make him promise *not* to come. I tried to quiet her. I thought perhaps she had a wild idea that Hugh had killed Helena himself. But it wasn't that. And there didn't seem to he anything else to say.

"She did manage to pull herself together, a little, just as I was going, and gave me a message for him. I was to tell him that she wouldn't go away, if he wanted her not to.

"Well, that was what I had to go back with to Hugh. I tried to soften it down, of course; made as little as I could of her not wanting to see him, and as much of her being willing to stay, in case he didn't want her to go south with Ethel and Mother Crawford. But it didn't do any good.

"He saw it all just as if he had been there. He wasn't angry, or hurt, or even surprised. I was all three, of course; angry a little and surprised a lot. And he explained it to me with that same look on his face that he has had ever since. She came to the funeral but didn't see him. It was the next day, of course, that they started for San Antonio. I'm not sure she didn't send him some sort of word; but I don't believe she did."

Down in her heart, Mrs. Corbett was as fond of Jean as any of them—had been ever since the days of Anne's wedding. Against the mere breath of hostile criticism she would have defended the girl as hotly as Constance herself; but the rather doting affection that all the rest of her family lavished on Jean made the expression of her own seem superfluous, and her favorite attitude had always been a grumbling humorous dissent from the extravagances of the others. Now, in a moment of genuine indignation, the knowledge that anything she said about the girl would be subject to a heavy discount, drove her farther than she would otherwise have gone.

"I have been a fool," she burst out. "We've all been fools not to see that there was something behind those innocent ways of hers. She has been making love to him, I suppose, ever since she came back from England. But this that you have just told me, is the first I have known of it. Hugh hasn't said anything to me. That was just a guess of mine. I thought there might be something like that. She ought to be whipped! Oh, the way she's taking on now doesn't need any explaining! I can understand it well enough. Very romantic it was, of course, as long as it was only a question of notes and kisses,—understanding him so much better than his wife did, and all that! But now that it has come down to the question of common every-day marriage, it isn't so nice. Though 'she won't run away, if he wants her not to'! Bah!"

It was not often that any one attempted to check this formidable lady in full career. About the only person who had ever tried it was Hugh. But Constance, though she trembled, did it now.

"Mother," she said, "you shan't talk about Jean like that! Not to me!"

"What!" boomed the old woman. "I'll talk about her as I please. To anybody."

"You won't," said Constance, "because you know it's not fair."

A realization on Mrs. Corbett's part that this charge was entirely true added itself to her astonishment over her daughter's defiance. She subsided, muttering, and gave Constance a chance to go on.

"I think," Constance said, a word at a time, "that Jean is about the finest, bravest, straightest person I know. Most of us are cowards beside her. I am, anyway. She's always loved Hugh, of course; and she's been the only one of all of us, lately, who *has* loved him—in a way that did *him* any good, I mean. The rest of us have sat around talking about poor old Hugh and saying what a pity it was that his life should have been spoiled by that dreadful marriage of his. But she loved him well enough to like Helena, too, as long as she thought he did. And she helped him. Made him happier than he's been before—ever, I guess. And she'd have done anything, I believe, that she thought would make him happier. Even then; though she didn't know they were—lovers.

"She didn't find that out until a little while ago—on Philip's birthday, that was; up at our house at Lake Forest. I don't know how it happened. It just—flamed up, I suppose. She came back from there the next day ready, I'm sure, to do anything he wanted her to. Oh, she didn't tell me much, but I knew before she'd told me anything. It was just there in her face, for anybody to see that wanted to look. Rose Aldrich did see it; spoke to me about it."

Mrs. Corbett had listened to this protest with no more interruptions than an occasional incredulous snort or two; but at this point she propounded a question.

"All right; be as sentimental about it as you like. But how do you account for the way she has acted since? How does Hugh account for it?" She sat back more comfortably in her big chair, crossed her legs comprehensively, lighted one of her abominable cigarettes—good signs of her recovery of her normal frame of mind, these were—and settled back to listen.

"It isn't easy to make it sound sensible," Constance admitted. "But I think I can see how she felt. It was wrong—I mean it was what everybody would call wrong—for her and Hugh to love each other. But she was ready to make any sacrifice that it cost; ready to go through and pay the price of it, if Hugh wanted her to. And then all at once what would have been such a desperate thing for them to do, such a hideously costly thing, was made perfectly safe and respectable because Helena, with a horrible sort of difference, did it first. Helena had a lover just as Jean did. But Helena's lover killed her, and that was what made

Jean safe with hers. And it made her love for Hugh seem as horrible as Helena's. As if it might, except for luck, have happened the other way. Oh, you can't talk about it. If you don't see it, you don't. But Jean did, and Hugh did, too. And he made me see it, partly anyhow."

Mrs. Corbett, after a profane and purely rhetorical demand to be told what the world was coming to, subsided into a thoughtful silence. Constance, her eyes bright with tears, which she didn't brush away, sat staring at the blaze in the open grate.

"I wish I knew," she said at last, "whether I have got or ever did have courage enough to throw away all the small things for the one big one. Whether I'd ever have married Frank no matter how much I loved him, if it hadn't happened to be a perfectly sensible, correct thing to do."

"You can thank your stars you don't," her mother said gruffly, with the long exhalation of pungent smoke. "The girl's mother knows. What she had to do didn't involve anything disreputable, to be sure. But it cost her almost as much. And look at her now. Worn away to a wisp! You wouldn't change places with her?"

"No," Constance admitted with a sigh. "I suppose not."

"Well, there we are," said Mrs. Corbett. "If you're right about Hugh, and if all that ails him is that Jean has gone away without saying good-by to him, why it will all come right in time, I suppose. She'll get over her flutters, he'll get over his mopes, and they'll patch it up and think they're the happiest pair in the world. But, Connie, I don't believe you're right about it. I believe there is something else. I don't believe a man over thirty could look like that over anything a snip of a girl might have done to him. That explanation will comfort your father, though, and he needs comfort badly enough, God knows. And it may satisfy Greg."

She had begun to move, ponderously, toward getting to her feet, but with this mention of her eldest son she sank back into her chair again. "Greg's worse than I am, you know," she said. "He's simply got Hugh on the brain. Calls me up from the office two or three times a day. He wants your father and me to take him somewhere; which we'd do in a minute, of course, if he'd go. But he won't. But Greg thinks that anything may happen if we let him go on like this; thinks he may go clean off his head. Or do something—desperate."

"Do you suppose Greg knows anything that we don't?" Constance asked.

"Oh, he had a talk with Hugh; a 'sensible' talk. The day before the funeral. He's told me all about it. It seems Hugh's made some sort of discovery out there at his laboratory. . ."

"'Corbettite,'" said Constance. "I know about that. That's what he was working on, that last week. Doesn't Greg believe it is a discovery?"

"Why, as a scientific thing—yes," Mrs. Corbett said. "Greg thinks it may make him famous, fifty years from now; among scientific men, anyway. But Hugh has an idea it can be used now. In the war. For airplane engines. He wanted to turn it over to Greg, for him to make an enormous lot of, out at Riverdale, and he took it hard when Greg refused to consider it."

"Why did he refuse?" Constance demanded, aroused at once, as always she so easily was, on Hugh's behalf.

Her mother nodded. "I took it that way, too; abused Greg like a pick-pocket for ten minutes without waiting to hear any more. I wouldn't like to be a Prodigal Son's elder brother, for a fact. He took it so patiently he made me ashamed of myself. He was all broken up over the way Hugh had felt about it. But he assured me, seriously, that as a manufacturing proposition, a scheme for bottling lightning-bugs would have been just as practicable. Hugh's never made more than a pound or two of the stuff at a time, he says. Doesn't even know that it can be made in quantities. Hasn't any idea how much it would cost, if he could. He admits that he could have bought gold cheaper, pound for pound, than the samples he has made have cost him.

"Oh, that doesn't mean anything!" she exclaimed when Constance looked aghast at that. "Only that experiments of that sort always cost like the devil. But that's another thing, of course. Corbett & Company are going to be hard up for a while, Greg says. Until he knows how this tractor business is coming out. He's making a great big investment in that and doesn't feel at all sure that he'll get any of it back. He talks about passing the next dividend just as a matter of precaution.

"And then, on top of that, comes Hugh with a thing Greg says you might easily spend half a million dollars on before you knew for sure that you really had something valuable, and another half million after that, making people believe that you had."

Constance's eyes filled up again, at that. "Poor old Hugh," she said.

"You can't deny it was sensible," Mrs. Corbett remarked, as she lighted a match for a fresh cigarette, but she paused in the act of applying it, to add in a ferocious whisper, "Too damned sensible!" and let the flame reach her fingers unheeded.

"What worried Greg most," she went on, after this error had been duly recognized and corrected, "was that Hugh was so meek about it. Made no row at all; didn't even argue. Just said, after a while, that he saw Greg was right about it, and went out.—Well, he was," she concluded furiously, "and I told him so."

She had announced her intention of going home and she allowed herself to be helped into her coat, when she turned on her daughter with another question.

"Connie, can you pray? Really, I mean. With a belief that your prayers were going anywhere? I haven't—like that—in years. But I'll have to, pretty soon, unless this Verdun thing stops. And something happens to Hugh. He's one and they're millions. Great God, what a world!"

XXXIV

S omething did happen—not precisely to Hugh though the effect of it got round to him in time—within a week of the talk between Mrs. Corbett and Constance.

It was an episode which will come to be regarded, I venture to guess, as one of the curiosities of history, when Time has given us a perspective upon it and its results; so mad it was in its inception yet so successful, so trivial yet, considering the detonation it produced, so capitally important—namely, the bandit Villa's projected conquest of the United States, his invasion of the State of New Mexico, his sack of the town of Columbus, his unhampered retreat, his immunity from retribution.

Looked back upon from a day a little more than two years later when I write these lines; from a day when we are buying each fresh edition of papers to learn whether the thin line of English in Flanders still holds or whether the German torrent is breaking through upon the Channel ports, from a day when our ships, their decks packed with troops so that they look like a covering of khaki-colored moss, are putting out to sea in a frantic urgency of haste lest our tardy reenforcements arrive, after all, too late; looked back upon from today, that raid of Pancho Villa's seems as remote, as completely the affair of another epoch, as Dewey's battle in Manila Bay.

Yet it is my belief that History—if there are to be any more histories—will attribute to it a greater causative importance than the sinking of the *Lusitania.* This was too much, we said. Our patience had been tried too far. Let this murderous bully be caught and punished, without more ado. And then, blankly, we began to realize that even this petty piece of retributive justice was beyond our immediate military resources to accomplish. Days passed and more days and still the punitive expedition did not start. The army had no supply trains, no airplanes that would fly, no machine guns worth mentioning. There were a thousand deficiencies of *matériel,* but greater than these was the deficiency in men. It was only by stripping the border, already too lightly guarded, that a mobile force of the few thousands needed could be scraped together. And when, finally, it was possible for them to move, they were obliged to move not so much in pursuit of Villa, as, with infinite circumspection, where and how they could without giving offense to Carranza, who had proscribed the use of railways and the passage through towns or cities. The thing was an appalling farce, yet it was deadly serious. If we offended Carranza, Mexico would make war on us. And Mexico, bankrupt, comic-opera Mexico, if one reckoned by immediate resources in men and guns, was more than a match for us!

It became apparent almost at once that the National Guard would have to be called out in order to turn the trick at all, and it was at this point that the thing came home personally to the Corbett family.

Frank Crawford was a graduate of West Point. It had been with real reluctance that he left the army to take charge of his mother's affairs and after he had fairly settled himself in business harness, he went into a cavalry regiment in the National Guard. It had become a hobby with him; a sad sort of hobby, Constance used to say regretfully, for he gave his precious time ungrudgingly, yet never with any very confident hope that it was well spent. As a real soldier he had kept abreast, as well as he could, of military science, and he was under no roseate illusions about the Guard. His colonel detested him for a killjoy.

This colonel, it may be noted, was a genial soul, proprietor of a widely ramified coal business, and a republican committeeman; a genuine patriot according to his lights, an excellent man to put down for a speech when there was nothing particular to be said. He possessed, in short, all the qualifications for colonel of a regiment except that of being a soldier. He honestly believed, with his whole soul—I say nothing about his mind—that his regiment was one of the finest and most formidable military organizations, for its size, in the world. Frank Crawford's perpetual faultfinding struck him as not quite treasonable perhaps but a bad thing for *morale.* (This was a word he had picked up in the last year or two, and used indiscriminately.) A knowledge that he couldn't get on without the only trained officer in his organization, combined with a natural but unadmitted awe for Frank's social and financial importance, was all that kept his irritation within any sort of bounds.

"We're going to be called out," Frank told Constance, after a glance at the head-lines of his newspaper one morning, three or four days after the raid. "That's as sure as God made little apples. Smedley telegraphed the adjutant-general yesterday, that we were ready to start on twenty-four hours' notice. We're only seventy-five percent. up to peace strength, of course, and nowhere near half equipped; but at that, we're better than most Guard organizations. It may be a few weeks or a month or two; but it will come, and Lord what a show we'll make of ourselves! However, it will be a good thing for us—a little real fighting."

His wife stared at him. "You mean *you* will go?" she asked incredulously, and with that he stared back at her.

"Of course," he said.

"Yes—of course," she acquiesced, rather limply, after a moment of silence. "Only it seems so impossible somehow—for you."

It took her two or three days to digest the idea at all. It seemed the stuff of nightmares rather than of logical daylight reality, that Frank should actually be contemplating leaving his bank, his office, his clubs, his prosperous safe affairs, his expeditions with the children, his daily intimate life with her, to go away in a uniform to fight, die perhaps, somewhere in Mexico. It couldn't—a prospect like that—it simply couldn't be true.

Since August, 1914, the great fact of war, the monstrous thing that was happening there in the fields of France had never been wholly out of her mind. The news of it, which she read daily in the papers, colored her days as it was bad or good. Activities connected with the relief of conditions it created had filled up what once had been her spare time. If any one had told her she didn't realize there was a war going on, she would have replied indignantly that she did. Her sister-in-law was an English woman whose husband and two sons were at the front, and she had now a brother there of her own. Her mother was watching the mails for Carter's first letter. And yet, it was the simple truth that what war really meant never came home to her until her husband, her very own Frank, the children's father, said across the breakfast table that of course he would go when the regiment did, and that the regiment's departure was, in his opinion, only a matter of weeks.

She was still feeling a little dazed over it one afternoon when her brother Bob dropped in ostensibly to see if Frank had a copy of the *Plattsburgh Manual* that he could borrow.

"I enlisted in the Battery last night," he told her, when she produced the volume. "I think that's as good a chance of getting in as there is. They say it's a sure thing they'll go."

The organization Bob referred to, was a battery in the state's only artillery regiment, whose alphabetical designation had the same sort of distinction, background, atmosphere that "Fifth" has among the ordinals which designate New York's avenues. The cavalry would have been Bob's more natural choice, perhaps; but that branch contained no such *corps d'elite* as this battery.

It was when she heard this announcement of Bob's that Constance got her first thrill of pride out of Frank's decision to go. She was glad not to have to explain why he was not going. She discovered she was proud of Bob too. She had always loved him, of course, in a sisterly way. Not as she loved Hugh, nor, not quite, as she loved Gregory and Carter. Love is not, perhaps, just the best word for that sense of an indissoluble bond, for it can exist quite apart from any affectionate companionship; but it generally goes, unscrutinized, by that name. Now, though, as she looked at him, a gush of unwonted warm affection came up for him in her heart. She dropped down on the arm of his chair, and took hold of one of his hands.

"I'm glad you're going," she said. "In a way I'm glad Frank is, only—. Well, I'm glad for you, and for her, that there isn't a girl you're leaving behind; that she doesn't exist, I mean. That's sort of an Irish bull, I suppose, but you know what I mean."

"She exists all right," Bob said. "That's what I came around to tell you. It's Olive Heaton. I thought perhaps you'd have guessed."

To the Bob she had always known, Constance might have observed that it would need a courageous guesser to attribute any significance to his light-hearted love making; but this, somehow, was a new Bob, and she didn't say it.

"I asked her yesterday afternoon," he went on, "before I enlisted. She says it's all right, and that she'll marry me before we go."

This announcement of Bob's was quite as much of a bomb for the rest of the family as for Constance, since she merely partook of the general skepticism concerning the chance of his falling seriously in love with any woman it was possible for him to marry. His choice of Olive Heaton was a weight off their minds, for she was, unmistakably "their sort" of person; a real person, too, though often cited by the more conservative of mothers as a horrible example of what we were coming to in these degenerate days. The fact was that Olive had never got on especially well with her mother and after that lady's second marriage she had taken an apartment and gone to live by herself, a course which her ample share of her father's fortune put beyond the reach of effectual resistance. It was what came, the critics said, of having allowed a headstrong girl her own way in everything since she was ten years old, the pursuit of her whims, from toe-dancing to the breeding of police dogs, the extension of her linguistic gifts to an absolutely immoral familiarly with French and Italian. Why the girl could flirt as easily with an opera tenor as with a college boy! And she was still a mere child, in years—twenty-three or so, and she didn't look that—when she told Bob she would marry him.

Mrs. Corbett had always been her strong partisan, having freely expressed the opinion, whenever the topic was broached in her presence, that the girl's mother was a fool and that Olive herself would have been one to stay a day longer than she did under the maternal—and step-paternal—roof. She was openly exultant over Bob's news and went to see her prospective daughter-in-law and tell her so the day she learned it.

"I haven't a good word for him," she observed candidly to Olive. "Not that that needs saying. All his good points are there for anybody to see. But the others are, too, I suppose. He's a handful but I've no doubt you know it. And you've got good hands. Your eyes are open, unless they're dazzled by this new uniform of his." She turned a thoughtful look on the girl, who met it candidly.

"It isn't that," she said. "At least, it would come to the same thing without it. I have always wanted to marry Bob."

Mrs. Corbett nodded approvingly. "Exactly what he needs," she said, "is a wife who knows what she wants.

"We're keeping very quiet, of course," she added, "on account of Hugh; but you'll come around to a family dinner, won't you, in a night or two? Dreadful things they are to be sure; but it's what comes with marrying into a big family."

Olive replied appropriately that she loved big families. Whereupon Mrs. Corbett sighed voluminously.

"Of course," she conceded, "I can't say I'm sorry I had six children, because then you could ask me which and how many of my six should never have been born. And when you come down to it that way why there aren't any. They don't go with a quiet life, though. Out of so many you'll always have one at least to worry about—little or big. I used to say that when the last of them was twenty-one, I'd wash my hands of them. Good lord, I've had more to worry about since they're grown, than ever their mumps and measles gave me."

"I hope you have good news from Carter," Olive said.

"A cable or two," Mrs. Corbett told her. "We shall be getting a letter any day now. Oh yes, Carter is the natural one to worry about. He will be at one of their schools now, learning to fly. But if he falls instead"—the grim lines in her face deepened; but her voice was steady—"if he is killed over there, he'll die happy, knowing he has done his thing. And so in a way, there is nothing for me to worry about. Because there is nothing for me to do. The worrying thing is when you feel there must be something that you could do if only you weren't too great a fool to see it. It's Hugh I'm worried about now."

"Bob's told you his idea, I suppose?" Olive ventured.

"Bob's idea!" his mother echoed astonished, "I didn't know he had any."

Olive laughed. This was going to be a mother-in-law after her own heart.

"Bob thinks," she said, "that the thing for Hugh is to enlist with him. He says the trouble with Hugh is that he has always had too many ideas, and that there's nothing like being a soldier, for getting over them."

"I'll apologize to Bob the next time I see him," Mrs. Corbett exclaimed. "That's the first sensible suggestion about Hugh that has been made by anybody. Why the devil didn't I think of it! Or Greg! Greg's supposed to have common sense." Then with a keen look at the girl, "I'd like to know, as a matter of fact, whether Bob said that to you, or you said it to Bob. Of course, I never shall. Well, you'll come to dinner? Thursday night? We'll all be there. The whole tribe of us. Except, possibly, Hugh. None of us have seen him for days, and I'm not sure if we can get hold of him."

Hugh didn't come to the dinner—not at least, until it was over, the fact being that during the excitement over Frank and Bob and the imminent prospect of a war with Mexico, he had quietly slid out of sight. But around nine o'clock, when the women had left the table, and the men, Robert, Senior, that is to say, Gregory, Frank and Bob were getting on with their cigars, he walked into the dining-room of the big house, nodded to the others, and with a thump on the back and an excruciating grip of the hand, congratulated Bob.

"I've been out of town," he said. "Didn't get back until eight. And then I found all your messages at the laboratory. It's great stuff. I'm delighted about it. Where's Olive? I want to wish her luck."

"She's somewhere around the place," Bob said. "Only, for heaven's sake don't shake hands with her the way you did with me, or you'll break her bones. You're looking pretty fit. Where've you been?"

It was a natural question to ask, for the change in his appearance was simply electrifying. That look about him, which his mother had described as hagridden, was gone. Indeed, to say that he was himself again hardly does justice to the change. He was himself only lit up somehow to a higher candle-power than usual.

They had been talking about him only a little while before he came in, and the great idea—Olive's idea was the official designation of it, though she persisted in her attribution of it to her fiancé—had been thoroughly canvassed in all its bearings. There was not a dissenting voice. They all agreed that here was a solution to Hugh's problem. So, when Gregory said around the table after a look at him, "He's gone and done it for himself," they all knew what he meant. And all agreed that he had probably hit upon the explanation of the change in Hugh's looks.

"Yes, I've done it for myself," Hugh said, pulling up a chair and reaching for a cigarette, "that is, I've done something. What is it that I've done?"

"Enlisted?" Frank prompted. "What in? The cavalry, I hope, though none of the ordinary runts we get for horses could carry you."

"Well, you're right, in a way," Hugh said. "I've decided not to enlist; but it comes to the same thing." He smiled thoughtfully at the blank look he saw go over their faces. "At least," he added, "it's up to Greg." Then he turned to his elder brother.

"If you'll take up that new bearing metal of mine, manufacture and market it, sell it for the purpose it is needed for, make people believe in it, put it across, then I'll enlist, like a shot. I can give you a bit more to go on, in the way of equipment, costs and so on, than I could when we talked two weeks ago. But I don't believe you'll do it."

Greg's face set. "You know perfectly well why I won't do it," he said, and turned to his father. "I haven't a word to say against this discovery of Hugh's as a scientific thing," he went on. "I don't pretend to understand it. If Hugh says he's got it, he has—as a scientific discovery. But as a commercial proposition it's moonshine. That's what I honestly think, and I can't say anything else. Of course, if he can convince you, and you two outvote me, I'll take your orders and I'll do my best."

Hugh read his father's troubled glance with a smile. "I'm not putting it that way," he said. "I haven't any vote in Corbett & Company. I gave that up three years ago. And I'm not asking you to go over Gregory's head, nor asking him to go against his judgment. I only put it up to him again, so that you'll understand what I'm going to do. I'm going to manufacture that stuff myself."

"Hugh, for heaven's sake, don't fly off the handle like that," Gregory expostulated. "You're not a manufacturer. You don't know a damn thing about business. You're not a salesman. And that stuff will be about the toughest selling proposition I ever heard of. It would take an ungodly lot of money to swing it, and you're going to be comparatively hard up for a year or two, if Corbett & Company is to begin passing dividends. The thing's driven you half crazy already. Drop it, man! For God's sake drop it, and go off with Bob."

"I've been dropping things all my life," Hugh reflected, and then his voice sharpened to an edge which made their nerves quiver. "But I'll give you my word I'm not going to drop this. I'm going to see this thing through. I don't know anything about business, and efficiency, and costs and all the rest of it, but I'll learn, and I'll make it work. I'll make myself a salesman; a missionary, if you like. I'll make this stuff, in the quantities they need, and I'll make them take it, if it costs every cent I've got, or ever expect to get. That's that! So you don't need to worry about me any more."

In that lazy lounging way of his, which always contrasted so oddly with his moments of intellectual excitement, he got to his feet and pushed his chair away. "I want to find Olive," he said. "Where are they? Up in the drawing-room?"

Up in the drawing-room he electrified them again. Olive was not the only one who gasped when he kissed her instead of shaking hands. A kiss is, of course, infinitely variable both in the degree and in the kind of feeling it can carry. It is equally above disguise and misunderstanding; a singularly precise language, in short—within its range. Hugh's kiss lacked, distinctly, the touch of ceremony which the occasion might be thought to call for, and it had rather more—steam behind it. Yet it was curiously impersonal, too. He took Olive in his stride, as it were, and went on by.

Then, becoming aware of the sensation he had created he pulled up and apologized. "Bob told me to," he said. "At least he told me not to shake hands with you and I took it that way."

The girl's color had flushed up to her forehead and she literally had to get her breath before she could speak. She hadn't supposed, wise young thing that she was, that she could possibly be so disconcerted by a mere unexpected kiss. She had met Hugh often enough, of course, but had never happened to get directly in his path before. He had broken over her like a wave.

"Oh, I'm glad you did," she said. "I liked it. Only I was surprised."

It occurred to Bob, standing by, that it was lucky for him that Olive hadn't seen Hugh first. She was looking up at him now with a distinctly more personal interest than a newly engaged girl might reasonably be expected to feel in any man but one. But Hugh, just at a point when he could so pleasantly have started something, made merely the little set speech he should have begun with, excused himself with a nod and a smile, and went over to his mother—whom he also kissed.

"I'm back," he told her, and a ring that there was in his voice put into the two words all the reassurance she wanted.

"So I see," she said, with a long keen look at him. "Back just to go away again?"

"I've not enlisted, if that's what you mean," he told her. "But it's just as good."

"I suppose you'll tell me what it's all about when you get ready," she said. "Here's a letter from Carter, that the rest have seen. You'll be glad to read it." She fished it up out of her corsage, and handed it to him as she spoke.

Constance, standing by and watching him eagerly, was puzzled—for Frank had given her a twenty-word summary of the talk down-stairs. She saw what his mother did not, a curious, just momentary, wince go across his face—a thing that looked like a twinge of pain.

He carried the letter off to one of the side lights to read it. And when he came back with it to his mother, Constance saw that his face was shining with excitement and pride, and that his eyes were bright with tears. He didn't put it back into the hand his mother had stretched out for it.

"I'd like to borrow it for over tomorrow, if I may," he said. And added, "I want to show it to Jean."

Of course, everybody within range of his voice cried out at that. And the others, having had it relayed to them, came crowding up with questions.

Jean? Where was he going to see Jean tomorrow? Were they all coming back with her? When did he get his news?

"Nobody is coming but Jean herself," Hugh said. "And she'll only be here for an hour or two, I think. They're going to California—Mrs. Crawford and Ethel. The raid has stirred everything up so in San Antonio that Mrs. Crawford can't stand it, and Gilbert's gone with Pershing. So there's nothing to stay for. Jean follows them; but she has an errand to do here, first."

"Hm!" said Mrs. Corbett. "So that's it, is it?"

She had said the thing which the others contented themselves with merely thinking. It was a reconciliation with Jean, then, that accounted for the change in Hugh. That was all there was to it, after all. They had been worrying themselves into the grave, here, for the past two or three weeks over a mere lovers' misunderstanding. It was all expressed with complete adequacy in the old lady's grunt.

But Constance, still watching her best loved brother's face, was not so sure, and when presently their eyes met, the look she saw in his confirmed her misgiving. Later, when she got a chance, she led him away into the billiard room.

"I want you to tell me a little more about Jean," she said. "I'm anxious about it. Do you mind?"

"Oh, no," he said, dropping down on the cushioned settee beside her. (It was between those two same cushions that Jean—little Jean then—had tucked her precious place-card, with the funny toast he had written for her on it, and forgotten it there, and come back for it in the dead of night, and captured her burglar.)

"It isn't what mother thinks," Hugh said, "—and all the rest of them. I suppose you guessed that. I mean it isn't that the thing between us is 'made up' or going to be. There isn't anything to make up, of course. I can only guess why she's coming. All she said in her wire was that it was necessary that she see me for only an hour, before she went to California. She asked me especially not to meet her at the train; said she'd come to the laboratory."

"I don't see," Constance said, after she'd thought it over for a while, "how you know that she isn't coming back to—well, you needn't call it making it up unless you like; but what that comes to?"

"Well, there's that word necessary. That's enough all by itself. She wouldn't have used it if that's what she meant. But what makes me sure is her asking me not to meet her at the station. You see I did meet her there once—the first time I ever saw her. She couldn't have found a gentler way of telling me, supposing I needed telling, or one more like her. No, it's a case of conscience. She feels she ran away and that she has to come back."

Then, as Constance reached for his hand and lifted it to her face, and he felt the warmth of her tears upon it, he straightened up a little bruskly. "Don't you worry about me," he said. "I've been through that and come out on the other side."

XXXV

This was no mere brotherly reassurance. He had come through his dark valley of self-questioning and indecision, had struggled out of the bog to firm land again. It had been a nightmare for a fact. One can not be a Protestant of as extreme a type as Hugh, standing alone before his God with no intermediary whatever, without even an intervening social atmosphere; one can not be his own chief justice, the pope of his own religion, without having to pay, in moments of crisis, for the glorious arrogance of that position. If one has said, consciously or unconsciously to himself, "I alone am responsible for myself; no rule has any validity regarding my conduct except as I apply it to myself," he must forego, in times of storm, the shelter of the rule, the sense of righteousness which obedience to the rule lends to the great majority of mankind.

What made it worse for Hugh was that this assertion had always been unconscious. He was no casuist. He had never devoted any of the powers of his mind or imagination to speculations concerning individual morality, until the discovery that he had fallen in love with Jean forced them upon him. And even then, after a few brief hours, Corbettite crowded them out again.

When Greg, out there at the laboratory, had interrupted his description of the great discovery to tell him that his wife had a lover, he was in much the same position as that of Archimedes, whom the Roman soldiers, engaged in the sack of Syracuse, found drawing his diagrams in the sand, unaware that the city had been besieged. Only, of course, Hugh was not an old philosopher, with all his life behind him, his great gifts given to the world, ready to die. He was young! Life and love were drumming in his veins, when this realization of irretrievable disaster was, that night, brought home to him.

There was no shelter for him under the rules, no comfort in the distinction that while his love affair with Jean was technically innocent, Helena's was guilty, and that at the price of her guilt his own innocence had been purchased. Not even his wife's death nor his own almost miraculously lucky escape from the horrifying consequences of it, changed the essence of that situation by one iota. There was no clear course that he could steer.

It was Gregory again who brought that home to him, when he cried out, over Helena's body there, "Good God, Hugh, isn't there anybody but yourself in the world?" The conviction that there never had been anybody but himself in the world, so far as his own calculations and decisions went—that intolerable conviction was the one that was rammed home to him during the succeeding days.

The task, whose moral necessity he had foreseen, when kneeling, he had looked down into his wife's beautiful dead face, a review of his life, the appraisal of it, the discovery of the secret of its failure, was one that he had settled to with dread, and continued to pursue only by dint of keeping his resolution screwed up to the highest pitch. He went back as far into his boyhood as he could remember, and tried to rebuild the whole thing, to reassemble the picture under his eyes.

The picture his mood had conjured up was, of course, a caricature, an absolute monster of egotism. He had moments of realizing that this was true, and he made an effort, at last, to dismiss the monster, which like Frankenstein, he had created, to dissolve him back into his elements. He had something more important to think about— Corbettite.

His talk with Gregory about it, the one Mrs. Corbett afterward reported to Constance, staggered him. Hugh was not the typical inventor, the sort of wild-eyed visionary who wanders about with his head in the clouds, disdainful of his feet, and just for that reason Gregory's arguments went home with a terrible cogency. The distinction he made between the scientific discovery—a laboratory affair—and a marketable commodity, was one that Hugh himself, in more normal circumstances, would not have needed to have pointed out to him. But the circumstances were not normal.

Mrs. Corbett might say what she liked about work never hurting a Corbett; but no man could have gone through what Hugh had gone through during that last week in the laboratory without an immense exhaustion of spirit, a weakening of all his vital reserves. He was in that state when the crash came—Helena's murder, Jean's flight.

Constance had come pretty close home here with the remark she made to her mother that it must be positively ghastly to have people sympathizing with you over something you felt like a criminal for being glad about. He didn't feel glad over Helena's death to be sure; but it was true, just as it had been in his former great emotional crisis with her, that the excruciating thing was the failure of his emotions to run true to form. He didn't feel the thing which logically he might have been expected to feel. Helena's death, which ought to have made everything right, somehow made everything wrong between him and Jean.

The imaginative bond which united these two was so close, so insufferably tight, that he felt the shock of the tragedy with her nerves as well as with his own and knew besides that she felt it with his. He hadn't needed Constance's vivid report to enable him to experience Jean's sick revulsion. The trouble between them was not a misunderstanding; but the opposite of that. There was nothing, then, for messages, letters, even a personal encounter to clear away. There was nothing to be said, nothing to be explained. The one real solvent to the situation, for there was one of course, neither of them thought of.

It was in this spiritual state that after his talk with Gregory he flogged himself back to the consideration of Corbettite, and what he was going to do about it. All his vision, his faith in the great discovery, even his consciousness of the desperate need of it, was gone, except as a matter of memory. He had believed in it once. He had seen the need of it once, and clinging to that memory he went to work at it again, trying to project it upon the new scale that Gregory had shown him the necessity of working upon. He spent his days over his work-table, completely incredulous of the possibility of ultimate success. He spent his nights, long hours of them when he could not sleep, trying to flee from that Frankenstein monster of himself, which he had created. I don't wonder that Mrs. Corbett, from the glimpse she got of him during those days, spoke of him as hagridden.

Most men, most imaginative men at any rate, climb, sometime in their lives, to a Gethsemane. Hugh's came one night, a little after Villa's raid, when the prospect of our going to war with Mexico became a clearly visible thing.

It offered him a way of escape from Corbettite. It offered, as an alternative to his tormented gropings, a single clear thing to do. One of these beautiful straight things that would not tangle itself up. For the mere writing down of his name upon an enlistment roll, the mere taking of an oath of obedience, he could get shelter under the rules, could enjoy the heavenly relief of taking orders from somebody not himself; he could work at something clearly serviceable. Work, at first perhaps, with his hands. And at the same time, he could be doing a thing that Jean would understand and, he believed, in her heart approve. This was the temptation he faced, agonized over, and finally conquered. What had enabled him to conquer it had been the realization that to turn away from Corbettite now and enlist in the army would be merely a repetition, another of those withdrawals responsible for the failure he had made so far of his life.

He had made an ignominious failure of it, a ludicrous failure—one that God, anyhow, might laugh at—pride going along before destruction, a spirit at its haughtiest, always, just before a fall. And what had he done when he fell in the bog? Got up and struggled on through? No, he had not once done that. He had contented himself with the fatuous assertion that the road should have been there, anyhow. When he had failed to persuade his father to adopt his method of solving their labor troubles he had resigned—with a gesture!—from Corbett & Company, and gone outside the fence. When the strikers had refused to follow his advice, and howled him down in the hall he had hired out at Riverdale, he had shrugged and acquiesced. Let them stew in their own juice! When Gregory had hurt his feelings by betraying a fear lest his share in authority under his grandfather's trust might prove embarrassing, he had, in all but legal formality, withdrawn from the trust. When his marriage had shown itself not to be the perfect alloy of his dreams, he had abandoned it to chance. "Anything for a quiet life!" was about what his compromise with Helena came to. Even his country he had, in effect, abandoned, when it failed to react in a way he considered appropriate to the tragedy of the European war. The America of the school books, he had told Jean, did not exist!

Now, here was Corbettite, a real thing, a necessary thing, all it should be, except a practicable thing; and, confronted by the difficulties of making it practical—real difficulties to be sure, and to Gregory's eyes insuperable—he contemplated withdrawing again. He was right, as he had been right before. But Gregory wouldn't believe it. The world wouldn't believe it. Well then, let it go.

No, by God! By his own God, with whom he had been wrestling lately as Jacob of old had wrestled, he wouldn't let it go. That door was shut. That way of escape cut off. If it took his fortune, his life, his happiness, even his reason, he would fight it out on that line. With this decision, he wiped the sweat off his forehead and straightened his back, and thereupon, like a miracle, the pack he had been staggering under dropped from his shoulders. He was his own man again.

The prime difficulty about making Corbettite in quantities was the immense amount of electric current that the process needed. He would have to go where he could get it in unlimited quantities, and cheap. He thought first of Niagara Falls, then remembered the great Mississippi dam, not five hours away, and nearer the lead supply. He packed his bag and took a train, and spent a week among the small factory towns the dam supplied with power, looking for a factory that could serve his purpose. It was from this journey that he returned to find the news of Bob's engagement, the invitation to the family dinner, and Jean's telegram.

It had been all very well to tell Constance that Jean's return didn't mean what their mother and the rest supposed it did. The reasons that he gave her, for his convictions on this point, were what he had honestly worked out and accepted for himself. And the serenity with which he had told Constance not to worry about him had been a genuine thing, too, to the extent at least of not being a conscious pose. Nevertheless, when he got back to his laboratory—he meant to spend the night there rather than at his house—it was natural that he should put off going to bed and trying to get to sleep as long as possible. He was not yet sleeping more than half as much or quarter as well as he ought to, and he had not altogether got rid of his nightmare. Unless he succeeded in working himself to the point of exhaustion first, that telegram had distressing possibilities for him—dreams, impossible dreams, unreasonable hopes, panicky fears over that interview that was going to take place sometime tomorrow between them. He simply must not get started thinking about it, that was all! If he did he was lost.

So when he had got into pajamas and dressing-gown and loaded a pipe, he went to work, with a leather-bound Kent at his elbow, figuring out necessary alterations in the building he had in mind, weights and supports for line shafts and machinery, an infinitely laborious sort of occupation for him, and one that under other circumstances he would have turned over to some one else. But the old grandiose days, when cost was the one consideration that never entered his head, were gone. He was cheese paring now, for he foresaw, plainly enough, that for the next twelve months, at least, he would need every cent he could lay his hands on.

But even this occupation, with all the power of self-discipline he could apply to the enforcement of it, did not avail to keep Jean out of his thoughts. Her telegram, which lay there on the desk, kept attracting his eye, and interrupted his calculations. He put it away in a drawer, but merely with the result that the drawer handle charged itself with the same sort of electricity. His hand strayed to it as his eye had strayed to the typewritten yellow sheet. At last he took it out again and crushed it up into a ball, and gripped it tight against the palm of his left hand.

Hour after hour he worked doggedly on in the paradoxical determination not to stop until he had stopped thinking about her. But what he did at last, with a little sound that was half groan, half laugh, was to push away his blue prints and his sheets of figures and press that limp ball of paper against his lips, bury his face in his hands, and let go; open the door and let the image of the girl come as she would into his thoughts. Strangely, instead of tormenting, her imagined presence quieted him, brought him comfort, relaxation. His elbows were on the desk. His head weighed heavier upon his supporting hands—and he fell asleep.

When he awakened, the gray light of a cloudy April morning was in the room. His watch, which lay on the desk before him, showed seven o'clock; but he felt as if he had slept a long time. A deeper slumber, it must have been than any he had had in long weeks. His arms and legs were bloodless and so stiff with cold and inaction that he could hardly command their movements.

He got up creakily and went into his little sleeping apartment to get himself ready to face the day—the day which was to contain, somewhere, that unforeseeable hour with Jean. He dreaded it now. Wished it would come soon. The hours he would have to wait for it seemed intolerable.

He had thought he was alone in the building, and was a little surprised to hear his man moving about down-stairs. He hadn't supposed he came as early as this. Just when he was half shaved, he heard another step coming up the stairs—not the step of Jean's faithful burglar, a step incredibly like her own.

And then, still more amazingly, a voice—hers beyond the possibility of a doubt—calling his name. But the really amazing thing, the revolutionary thing, was the fact it proclaimed. Not merely that she was there—that was surprising enough, of course, at this hour in the morning—but that she was Jean, his Jean, the Jean of his memories, the Jean he had been wont to ride with mornings; who put clean out of existence, in just that one syllable, the horrified, panic-struck, revolted Jean whom Constance had told him about.

His heart missed a beat. Then, literally leaped. And he heard his own voice saying, "I'm in here; but I'm only half shaved. How in the world did you come so early?"

"It can't be so very early," he heard her say. "It must be ten o'clock."

"Ten o'clock!" he exclaimed. "It was seven only about a quarter of an hour ago."

"Your watch says seven," she informed him, "but it's stopped. Shall I wind it up and set it for you?"

Good lord, what a sleep he'd had!

"Yes, I wish you would, if yours is right," he said. "I'll be out in five minutes."

"Was it that chair you went to sleep in?" she asked. "Over those blue prints?"

He admitted it was. "Try it yourself," he suggested. "It must be more comfortable than I supposed."

He told himself, as he wiped his razor and put it away, that this must be a dream. It couldn't be possible that it was real, or founded on reality, that sense he had got, just from the sound of her voice and the knowledge that she was there in the next room, that everything had suddenly come right once more; that unfathomable feeling of security. The approaching interview, as he had foreseen it yesterday, was fraught with infinite possibilities of pain for both of them. Nothing had happened since then. Nothing was changed. This must be a dream. And yet it seemed like an awakening from one, from a nightmare. Then his nerves grew taut again.

"Jean," he said, "there's a letter there on the desk—just about under your left hand it will be—that I want you to read. It's from Carter to his mother. I borrowed it for you last night."

"Yes," she answered, and her voice, too, changed its quality as she spoke. "Here it is."

There was a silence after that until, fully dressed, he came out into the library. He had come softly, and she did not hear him until he was fairly in the room. The letter she was still reading lay upon the topmost of the blue prints, and the crumpled handkerchief in her hand was being used intermittently to cope with tears.

When she saw him she would have risen. But he said, "No, finish it. I meant to have given you time." Obediently, she turned back to the letter.

He came around the desk, half seated himself on the end of it and watched. For a long time after she must have finished, she sat there gazing through a blur of now disregarded tears at the last page of the letter. He, with one knee pulled up, clenched in the vise-like grip of his two great hands, looked out the window over the roofs. He felt, presently, that she had looked up from her letter to his face, but it was a matter of interminable seconds before, looking down, he met her gaze.

"Oh, I know," she said. "But. . ."

There are no words for the language of looks. In Jean's face there was a sort of smile; a tenderness, compounded of pity, and love, and admiration for the boy over there in France. But all that was a mere riffle across the surface of it. For the deeper thing that spoke in it, was a reaffirmation of what it had said before—the last time their eyes had met. Weeks ago. There on the frozen beach at Lake Forest.

His whole body went rigid with tension that increased to an agony, then relaxed.

She drooped her head at last, and pressed her trembling hands to her face.

"Oh, my dear," he whispered, and gathered her up into his arms.

She managed to say, between gasps, "Wasn't it perfectly—ridiculous—our thinking anything could make a difference—to this."

THIS IS, OF COURSE, NO more the end of Hugh Corbett's history than the festivities connected with the wedding of his sister Anne were the beginning of it. The capture of Jean's burglar in the midst of those festivities seemed, to his biographer, to offer a good opportunity for picking up the thread. The event of this April day, nearly five years later, is an opportunity for laying it down.

Not so much because it is an end of something, as because it is a fresh beginning; the beginning of something not yet—as I write—ended, nor even far enough away to be seen in its true perspective.

That determination of his not to give up Corbettite because the practical world, typified by Gregory, the world that so immensely needed it, would not, in its ignorance, believe in it; his decision, under the agonizing temptation to do something else, to force that belief upon the world, his acceptance of a moral responsibility for the enforcement, marks another, and perhaps the most important, of his critical angles.

It was a change that could not, at his age, have been wrought in him under less fierce a heat than that generated in the white arc of passion and of tragedy those recent days had brought home to him. It had transmuted the metal of his soul as the arc in his laboratory transmuted lead into Corbettite.

I believe it really to be true, that the Hugh who emerged from that fiery furnace of pain and humiliation had been born again; that he had a new fiber; an accessibility to fresh conceptions. The chief of those conceptions, of course, was of the necessity, at last, of giving up, as a prime consideration, the maintenance of his intellectual integrity; of submitting himself to be digested into a bigger thing than himself. If that be religion, and I'm inclined to think it is, then Hugh had found it.

Neither he nor Jean called it by that name, but it was clear that they felt it that way.

There was a touch of gravity about their behavior that day which Mrs. Corbett characterized, broadly, as some more of Hugh's damned nonsense. Constance cried out at that, but Jean only smiled.

This was around six o'clock at the big house. Hugh was coming, when he had finished some work, for dinner. Constance had brought Jean, after a preliminary examination, to tell the news to her mother. Mrs. Corbett, feeling a good deal more emotional and relieved about it than she was willing to appear—than she *could* consistently appear, since she had said straight along that the difficulty about Jean amounted to nothing—was exhibiting a sort of ferocious good humor. She wanted to know why Jean was in such a hurry to go to California; what was to prevent her from making them a little visit, now she was here.

Jean admitted there was nothing, so far as her own affairs were concerned. "But Hugh's going to be so busy getting his factory started— every hour just now will mean a day, later, he says. And I know I'd be in his way."

"Of all cold-blooded. . . !" Mrs. Corbett exclaimed. "And even today, instead of taking you off holidaying, he listens to you just long enough to make sure that you really mean to marry him, and then tells you to run along and talk to the women!"

"I was hours at the laboratory," Jean protested. "I had lunch with him there. And he's called me up on the telephone twice since!"

"And he might as well have come along with you for all he'll have done since you left; instead of sitting there pretending he's a business man. A nice job he'll make of that!"

"He'll succeed at it," said Jean, rather crisply. "He'll succeed— wonderfully."

Mrs. Corbett grinned. "Of course he will, you little spitfire," she said. "Do you think you can tell his old mother anything about him?"

She went on to say, after a ruminative silence, "If he's really turned the corner—and you and I believe he has—he'll be turning up at Riverdale, the first thing Greg knows, and giving him the surprise of his life. And he won't do it by hiring a hall, either!"

That startled Jean a little. She thought herself the only person in the world who had divined that intention of her lover's—to go back to that old battle-field and win a victory. There was both wonder and affection in the look she stole at Hugh's mother. But the older woman only grinned back.

"I don't know why the notion of Greg getting a surprise always pleases me so much, but it does. Perhaps because I think surprises are good for him."

Hugh turned up on time for dinner, with his father and mother, Constance and Jean. Mrs. Corbett had horrified Constance with the suggestion that they make it a party for the open announcement—to the family—of the engagement. This was probably not serious on her part, but she did insist, with outrageous gusto, in refusing to speak of it with bated breath and decent euphemism.

For the five who sat down about the board, it made an hour that each of them remembers with a quite peculiar satisfaction, not from anything that was especially talked about, but from a sense of restoration and peace that there was about it. And then, a little after nine Hugh took Jean down to the station to see her off for California.

They had started a little earlier than necessary, and they stood for a while out in the concourse—under the bulletin board—waiting for the train to be announced.

"If you weren't so—ruthless," Hugh told her with a smile, "and had waited three days or such a matter, I could have gone part of the way with you. Across Illinois. Because by then I'll be ready to make another trip back to the factory."

"I'll wait if you want me to," she said. "I'll—do anything you want me to. Anything in the world."

"I don't quite know why I don't," he reflected. "I suppose it's because I'm still walking softly for fear of waking myself up. Not wanting to press my good fortune too far. Like asking one favor too many of a fairy godmother. And after all, you won't really go away, wherever you are."

"It's wonderful—how well we can get on—without each other," she assented. "There's the train. They'll let you through the gate, won't they?"

They had the better part of half an hour there in her section of the Pullman, before it was time for him to go, but all the time they talked only a little, mere punctuation of the silences, which after all told more.

The future they contemplated would have looked uncertain enough to most lovers. It had never been said between them, that Corbettite was to be made a serviceable thing before they married, but this understanding was implicit in all their references to it. And after Corbettite, in the minds of both of them, for Hugh there was—France; for Jean, too, perhaps. It was not possible to plan, of course, nor even vaguely to foresee.

When at last Hugh bent over her for a farewell caress, there was no attempt to fix the day when they should see each other again. Both had tears and tight throats, but there was a wonderful serenity in their hearts.

"We don't know much about anything," Jean said unevenly. "But this is safe. Nothing can possibly happen to it—to you and me."

There was no rhetoric about that. In a world of chaos that, underneath, was the everlasting arms.

THE END

A Note About the Author

Henry Kitchell Webster (1875–1932) was an American novelist and short story writer. Born in Evanston, Illinois, Webster graduated from Hamilton College in 1897 before taking a job as a teacher at Union College in Schenectady, New York. Alongside coauthor Samuel Merwin, Webster found early success with such novels as *The Short Line War* (1899) and *Calumet "K"* (1901), the latter a favorite of Ayn Rand's. Webster's stories, often set in Chicago, were frequently released as serials before appearing as bestselling novels, a formula perfected by the author throughout his hugely successful career. By the end of his life, Webster was known across the United States as a leading writer of mystery, science fiction, and realist novels and stories.

A Note from the Publisher

Spanning many genres, from non-fiction essays to literature classics to children's books and lyric poetry, Mint Edition books showcase the master works of our time in a modern new package. The text is freshly typeset, is clean and easy to read, and features a new note about the author in each volume. Many books also include exclusive new introductory material. Every book boasts a striking new cover, which makes it as appropriate for collecting as it is for gift giving. Mint Edition books are only printed when a reader orders them, so natural resources are not wasted. We're proud that our books are never manufactured in excess and exist only in the exact quantity they need to be read and enjoyed.

Discover more of your favorite classics with Bookfinity™.

- Track your reading with custom book lists.
- Get great book recommendations for your personalized Reader Type.
- Add reviews for your favorite books.
- AND MUCH MORE!

Visit **bookfinity.com** and take the fun Reader Type quiz to get started.

Enjoy our classic and modern companion pairings!

Printed in the USA
CPSIA information can be obtained
at www.ICGtesting.com
JSHW022204140824
68134JS00018B/858

9 781513 283524